Bitter Thaw

a novel

Jessica McCann

Perspective Books

This is a work of fiction. Characters, places, and incidents are products of the author's imagination. Locales and public names are sometimes used for atmospheric purposes. Any resemblance to actual people, living or dead, or to businesses, companies, events, institutions, or places is coincidental.

Copyright © 2023 by Jessica McCann
Second edition, January 2024

All rights reserved. No part of this publication may be reproduced, distributed, or transmitted in any form or by any means, without prior written permission.

Trade Paperback ISBN 978-0-9994602-7-6
Hardcover ISBN 978-0-9994602-8-3
E-book ISBN 978-0-9994602-6-9

Phoenix, Arizona
www.JessicaMcCann.com

Cover images by Yuliya Derbisheva and GC402 via istock.com

Recognition for Jessica McCann's Historical Novels and Nonfiction

All Different Kinds of Free

Freedom in Fiction Prize

Editor's Choice, *Historical Novels Review*

"Moving account of one woman's perseverance... amazing storytelling." – *RT Book Reviews*

Peculiar Savage Beauty

Arizona Book of the Year

International Rubery Award, shortlist

"Gripping, atmospheric... insightfully etched characters."
– *Publishers Weekly*

"McCann has crafted an unforgettable novel."
– *Booklist Online*

WORDS: Essays on Reading, Writing, and Life

"In an endless sea of books of essays on
writing, *WORDS* comes across fresher and more genuine than
the rest." – C. Hope Clark, award-winning mystery author and
editor of FundsforWriters.com

For mothers and fathers,
and daughters and sons.

For people who wish to forget,
and people who struggle to remember.

For those who must have life's answers,
and those who believe there are none.

For each of us.

Life in the 1950s

BITTER RAPIDS, Minn., Jan. 23, 1952

For Immediate Release

/National Newswire/ -- Last night's low temperature in Bitter Rapids, Minnesota plunged to -30 degrees, the area's second-coldest temperature since 1909, which was recorded at -55 degrees. The town with a population of 6,200 people sits along the Rainy River, near the border of Ontario, Canada. It is recognized as the coldest place in the continental United States and the fifth coldest on Earth.

(Source: National Weather Service)

May 1952

Bitter Rapids, Minnesota

Maakade (*mok´a-day*) drove his shovel into the springy brown carpet of spruce needles. The solid dirt beneath held strong. Reverberations from the impact of steel striking earth traveled up the handle, shocked his joints. Though the spring thaw was well underway, the rich soil deep within Koochiching State Forest was never entirely free from the bitter freeze. Maakade believed some foundations were impossible to fracture. Still, he lifted his shovel and attacked the earth again.

The men working beside him also struggled with the mandate to break the earth between the Rainy River and the old logging road, to reinforce a retaining wall built by Civilian Conservation Corps workmen during the Depression. Sweat darkened the underarms of their striped jumpsuits, despite the raw morning air. The government no longer funded the CCC to do such work. Why would they when inmates were in abundance to provide free labor? The men jabbed their tools toward the ground, jumped onto the shovel blades with their leather boots and hefty weight, endeavored to split the earth, perhaps an inch, if they were lucky.

Maakade paused to catch his breath. He watched the water churn and rush downstream, frigid and pure from fresh snowmelt. A chiffon mist drifted out over the smooth rocks of the riverbank. He inhaled crisp, pine-scented oxygen deep into his lungs.

Prison guards watched the work crew from up the bank. Distanced from the icy mist of the river. Close enough to crack a skull when necessary.

"Get your black ass back to work, boy," the foreman shouted. "Don't make me come down there and get my boots wet."

Maakade thrust the shovel back at the frozen ground without looking back toward the voice. No need to give Foreman Ogren a reason to get his boots wet or his baton bloody.

Most men still called him "boy," even though his raven hair was streaked with gray. They called his ass black. That, he did not mind. His mother had named him *Maakade*, the Anishinaabe word for black, out of love, so he would always remember the blood his father had given him. When his father died and his mother took Maakade to live with her family among the Ojibwe tribe, he learned he would never be permitted to forget the black half of his blood, for better or for worse.

Across the river, an enormous bird swooped down from the jagged treetops, sounding an alarm call. *Kyak-kyak-kyak.*

It was not only Maakade who paused at his work now. All the jumpsuit-clad men halted their shoveling to watch the massive creature – easily four feet from wing tip to wing tip – glide down to the river. Its snowy, ebony-flecked feathers and vast wingspan gave the bird an otherworldly air. It perched upon a fallen cedar and folded up its great wings. Even the guards were intrigued and eased their way down the embankment for a closer look. They rubbed their jaws, scratched their heads. None had seen such a bird, had ever even imagined one could exist.

None, except for Maakade. His eyes darted downstream and into the woods. His head jerked to look sideways and over his shoulder.

The other inmates noticed his agitation and a prickle of unease crept up their hairy arms. "What's the matter, Maak?"

"That is a gyrfalcon."

"So?"

Maakade could've said more. He could've said the mighty falcon comes down from the Arctic only in winter, never in spring. He could've said it flies and hunts by night, never by day. He knew the falcon was an omen, a warning sent to him by his Wolf Brother. He knew he could not say such things.

With a flourish, the great bird took flight again, winging low, its orange feet skimming the choppy water. The men watched until it disappeared into the mist upstream.

"All right," the guards said. "Show's over."

The work crew returned to the task of breaking the earth, but Maakade's attention remained upstream. Ogren strode toward him, smiling, baton poised, pleased with the excuse to release some pent-up frustration. Maakade sensed the guard's approach. He did not flinch. He merely extended his arm to point upstream.

Ogren slowed, despite himself. He glanced upstream, squinting into the sun that had finally broken over the trees and made the river sparkle. He saw what had captured Maakade's attention. A small canoe, careening downstream, pitching and bobbing over the torrents.

"Still too damn cold to be out on the river," he said.

Maakade nodded slowly, his gaze fixed on the tiny watercraft. In the distance, somewhere in the mist, the gyrfalcon sounded its warning cry again. Once more the group was captivated by the change from the mundane. They moved together in a huddle along the riverbank watching the canoe and its two small passengers approach the white water.

"Jesus, they're just kids," said one of the inmates.

"They'll never make it through those rapids," said another.

A pulse of energy surged through the group. Heavy boots shifted on the hard-packed riverbank. The men glanced back and forth, at one another, out to the river.

Voices mixed with the roar of the water in the distance – panic-stricken young voices – as the canoe angled down into the first tier of rapids. The craft disappeared in the foam. Maakade counted his heart beats. One, two, three, four. Finally, the canoe spurted up out of the river, nose first. It flipped end over end, catapulting the boys into the air. Time slowed. The boys seemed to hover midair before plunging into the frigid water, among the uneven rocks.

"I'll radio for help," shouted one of the guards, turning to scramble up the bank toward the bus.

No one else moved. They waited a lifetime, breathless, until the boys' heads finally broke the water's surface.

"Are you going in after them?" Maakade shouted to the remaining guards as the boys were whisked down the river toward them.

"I can't swim," Ogren said. The others shrugged their shoulders, pushed their palms upward in evasion.

Maakade crouched down to tear at his boot laces. He looked in the direction of his fellow inmates. "Get further downstream."

He stood and kicked off his boots, shed his jumpsuit and ran toward the river's edge in his undershirt and shorts. The glacial air stung his sweaty skin. He knew the water would be far worse. He pushed the fact from his mind. Little John – an inmate seven-feet-tall, if he was a foot – bounded along the riverbank like a giraffe. The foreman shouted after them both, telling them not to be getting any ideas about running off, thumping his baton against his palm.

Maakade's feet hit the icy water. For a fraction of a second, he hesitated. He took two more running strides and dove slanting into the rushing river. Every muscle in his body seized with the shock of cold. The current pulled him like a stone to the inky depths of the water. It squeezed the air from his lungs – giant bubbles of oxygen blasting from his nose and mouth, escaping to the surface. His body was yanked downstream, submerged, paralyzed.

He must not panic, he knew. *This is my river. The river of my people,* Maakade reminded himself. The Anishinaabe and the Rainy River had served one another since the dawn of time. He had swum and fished and washed in the river since he was strong enough to stand. *Omagakiins,* his mother had called him. Little Frog.

Maakade extended his body underwater, pushed his feet out in front of him, let the current carry him downstream and up until he felt the sun on his face again. He rolled to his stomach and swam perpendicular to the current until he reached a fallen trunk wedged in the rocks. With his arm looped around a thick branch, he scanned the water upstream.

The boys had managed to find one another in the foamy water and clung together as they tumbled through the rushing torrents. Maakade timed their approach and lunged back out toward the center of the river, crossing the current, just in time to grab hold of the boys.

"Hold on!" Maakade shouted, catching a mouthful of water. He spat and shouted again. "Lay flat!"

They clung to his body as he powered across the current toward the shore. The larger of the boys kicked his legs to help propel their tangle of bodies and limbs. Maakade spotted another fallen tree jutting from the shore and grasped for it as the current pulled them toward the next tier of rapids. The rough bark tore the skin of his palm, but the frigid water had numbed all pain. The boys scrambled along his lanky frame like climbing a rope-bridge, through the water and up onto the trunk. They collapsed, hugging the branches, holding each other, faces pressed against the jagged bark. They gasped for air. Their bodies shook violently in the cold.

Blood oozed from Maakade's palm, spiraled down his forearm into the river. The muscles in his shoulders began to tremble. His frozen fingers lost their grip on the branch. The current ripped his body from safety and propelled him toward the white water, where he disappeared into the mist and rocks.

Life in the 1990s

PHOENIX, June 26, 1990

FOR IMMEDIATE RELEASE

/National Newswire/ -- The temperature in Phoenix soared to a record-high 122 degrees today. Sky Harbor International Airport was forced to shut down for several hours, as a result. Aircraft manufacturers do not have performance data above 122 degrees, therefore all aircraft were grounded until the temperature dropped below that threshold. Phoenix ranks first among the hottest cities in the United States.

(Source: National Weather Service)

August 1990

Phoenix, Arizona

Apri tips the syrup bottle and drowns the blueberry toaster-waffles on her plate. When was the last time she had a free morning to eat breakfast at the kitchen table, sip coffee, read the newspaper? Her summer classes at the community college had concluded, and April miraculously had the day off work. No textbooks to study. No research papers to write. No patty melts and iced teas to serve up to fussy old people who tip a quarter and a dime.

She stuffs a drippy forkful of waffle into her mouth, unfolds the *USA Today,* and sighs.

Frank shatters her serenity. He lumbers into the kitchen, rubber flip-flops thumping along the linoleum. April rolls her eyes.

"You're not at work," he says.

"Nope," she says.

"How come?"

"And a lovely good morning to you, too, Daddy Dearest."

"Dial it down, April," Frank says. "I'm just surprised. You're never home."

She folds the newspaper backwards and in half, sets it down on the table to read.

Frank pours a cup of coffee. He looks out the kitchen window to the backyard. It's late August, eight in the morning, and the giant thermometer dial on the patio reads 97 degrees.

"Hot."

His daughter looks over at him. Does he mean the coffee or the weather? Does it matter? She returns to the article she had been reading about a 1955 cold case.

"Hey, Dad, where in Minnesota are you from again?"

"Why?"

"I'm reading this article about a body they found wrapped in a quilt along some river in Minnesota, like thirty-five years ago. That's about when you and Gram moved, right?"

Frank opens the freezer door. "Where's the waffles?"

"Just polished them off," she says.

He stares into the open freezer, lets the cold air pour out and chill his face. He touches the buildup of crusty ice on the interior walls.

"It says they never identified the body," April takes another stab at conversation. "Some gung-ho cop up there decided to take another look at the file after all this time. Probably hoping to solve a big case, get a promotion, and get his butt out of Podunkville."

She pauses a moment, reads another line or two.

"It's a little town called Bitter Rapids, near the Canadian border. Ever heard of it? Is it near where you lived?" she asks.

Frank slams the freezer door shut. "What am I supposed to eat?"

"Have some toast," his daughter suggests. "And fruit. That's healthier than syrup-coated waffles anyway."

"If it's so healthy, why didn't you eat that and save me the waffles?"

"Because I'm a strong young woman in the prime of her life, and you're an old chubby guy who should be watching what he eats."

Frank belts out a slow, fake laugh. He rummages through the pantry cupboard and finds the remains of a loaf of bread – two moldy heals in the bottom of the bag. He holds it up, shakes it in April's direction. He waits for her to turn and look, but she doesn't take the bait. She's transfixed by the newspaper. Frank tosses the bag across the kitchen toward the open trash can. It bounces off the edge and lands on the floor.

"They printed a color picture of the quilt in the paper," April says. "The police chief is hoping someone, somewhere will recognize it and be able to tell them who it belonged to. Isn't that wild?"

She holds the paper up to show him. Frank doesn't respond.

"Maybe it's my imagination, but the quilt kind of seems familiar." April studies the photo a little longer. She stands and carries the paper over to her father, holds it out for him again. "What do you think?"

He glances at it and turns back to the half-empty pantry shelves. "I think it's a quilt, April. All quilts look alike."

The telephone rings. Father and daughter stare each other down as the 1970s-era harvest-yellow phone on the wall ding-a-lings a second time, and a third.

"Why don't you make yourself useful and answer that, while I see if there's any food left in the house at all," Frank says.

April tosses the paper on the table with a huff and strides across the kitchen to answer the phone.

"Hello? Yes. She what? You've got to be kidding me," April rakes her fingers across her forehead. "Well, what do you want us to do? Fine. Whatever. We're on our way."

Frank is already dumping his coffee into the sink. "Let me guess. That was the nursing home."

"Does anybody else ever call us? Gram's freaking out about who-knows-what. Pulled the oxygen tube out of her nose and got out of bed. Fell down, then took a swing at the nurse who tried to get her back up."

They stand for a moment, surveying the kitchen, mourning the loss of yet another potentially carefree Saturday. Frank opens the dishwasher and places his empty cup on the top rack. April clears her dishes from the table and hands them to her dad.

"Go get dressed," she says. "I'll cut some fruit. You can eat while I drive."

Franks rubs the back of his neck. April closes the dishwasher door and opens the fridge. He turns and walks to his room without responding.

"Gee, thanks, April. You're such a good daughter," April mutters sardonically as she centers a cantaloupe on the cutting board. "Aw heck, don't thank me, Dad. I'm delighted to spend my first day off after summer school to drive your grumpy ass to the old folks' home."

She raises a chef's knife into the air and brings it down in a punishing blow. The ripe melon splits in two, its tender guts exposed.

* * * *

Frank and April hear the chatter of the nursing staff when the elevator doors open. As they turn the corner to the nursing station, a hush falls. All eyes are on them as they walk down the hall toward Evelyn Parson's room. The door is propped open.

"It would be different if you had dementia, Mrs. Parson. The nurses would understand outbursts like this." The doctor stands at the foot of her bed, arms folded across his chest. He shakes his head. "But under these circumstances, you're just being difficult and mean. I don't want to sedate you, but this behavior can't continue. You need to be respectful to the staff. You need to do as you're told."

Evelyn crosses her arms right back at him. "Bite me."

April erupts in laughter and leans against the door frame. Frank dashes in the room. "Mom! What the heck?"

The doctor asks to speak with Frank outside the room. Frank shoots his mother a hard look and follows the white coat into the hall. April sits down on the bed and adjusts the oxygen tube in Evelyn's nose, tucks the thin hose back behind her ears.

"So, what's got your panties in a wad today, Gram?" she asks.

Evelyn pulls the newspaper from the bedside table and drops it onto April's lap. She points a spotted finger at the front page.

Her long, tobacco-yellowed nail taps the photo. April's eyebrows shoot up, her mouth drops open.

"I knew it," she says, her gaze fixed on the colorful quilt. She looks up at her grandmother. "You guys know who this quilt belongs to. You know who the dead guy is."

Evelyn peers into her granddaughter's eyes. She draws in some oxygen through the tube in her nose. "I need to get home," she wheezes, "to Bitter Rapids."

The men re-enter the room. Evelyn repeats herself. "I need to get home, Frank."

"No, you don't, Mom."

"I need to get home to Minnesota." Evelyn addresses the doctor now.

Out of the question, he tells her. She can't take her oxygen tank on an airplane. I'll take the bus then, Evelyn says. No. Travel is too risky for someone with emphysema and chronic bronchitis, he says. Sitting in one position for extended periods of time would cut off circulation, make blood settle in the extremities, create clots, cause a stroke. He shakes his head at her, in a silent gesture that says you can't travel, and shame on you for smoking all your life.

"Then I'll drive myself," Evelyn says, swallowing down a few choice words she wants to add. She pushes back the blanket and slides her legs to the side of the bed. "I'll just take lots of breaks to walk and stretch."

"Cripes, Mom. You can barely go to the toilet on your own. You're not driving across the country."

April watches her grandmother pause and blink hard. She shoots her dad a dagger-filled glance. *Wow*, she mouths at him. The doctor drops his chin, stares at the floor. Frank exhales and rubs his temples. He eases toward the bed.

"Look, Mom, I'm sorry." He rubs her back for a moment. "Okay? I really am. But you can't fly and you can't drive."

Evelyn turns her head to look at her son. His eyes plead with her. *Let it go.* The pump on the oxygen tank expands and contracts rhythmically. *Hiss, click, shoop. Hiss, click, shoop.*

"There's nothing there for us," he lowers his voice to a whisper. "Isn't that what you've always told me? Nothing but pain, and memories best forgotten."

"I was wrong, Frankie," she says. "I need to go back. I need to face it, to set the record straight before I die."

"Come on now," Frank says, stepping away. "Don't talk like that."

April reaches for Evelyn's hand. It's icy cold.

Hiss, click, shoop. Hiss, click, shoop.

"I'll drive you, Gram."

Frank turns toward the window. He releases a frustrated sigh, puts his hands on his hips, shakes his head slowly.

The doctor looks from Frank to April to Evelyn. He moves toward the door, pauses a moment for one more look. "I'll have a nurse type up the discharge paperwork."

* * * *

Frank and April set up Gram and her oxygen tank in her old bedroom at the house, and for two weeks, they argue.

He tells his daughter it's dangerous for two women to travel alone – peeing at filthy truck stops, sleeping in cramped motels, driving for hundreds of middle-of-nowhere miles. She tells him she can take care of herself. Okay, but can she take care of a sick old lady? Frank wants to know. April is less sure of that part. Come with us, if you're so damn worried about it, she fires back at him. Going back to Bitter Rapids is a bad idea, he says, and storms out.

Father and daughter continue to bob and weave, and paw and parry, until finally, during breakfast, April decides to go for the body shot.

"You know who that quilt belongs to," she accuses. "You know the dead guy."

Frank pounds the table with his fists. He stands and goes to his room. April draws her finger around the syrup pooled on her empty plate, stuffs the sticky sweet digit in her mouth, sucks it clean. Frank returns a moment later and hands April a framed snapshot. She recognizes it. It has been on his bedroom dresser forever, though she'd never paid it much attention. Now, April sees it with fresh eyes. A black and white photo of her Gram as a young woman, kneeling on the ground with a picnic basket beside a four-door Oldsmobile. A little boy sits beside her. Spread beneath them is a quilt. *The* quilt.

April stares at the photo. The hands on the plastic wall-clock tick off the seconds. She touches the glass of the small frame with her index finger, traces the edge of the quilt.

After a moment, Frank tosses a triangular scrap of fabric onto the table. It's hemmed along two sides. The third side is jagged, frayed. April sets down the frame and picks up the fabric.

"Whoa," she says. The young woman turns the scrap over in her hands, rubs her thumb across embroidered words.

> *The best kind of sleep beneath heaven above,*
> *is under a quilt handmade with love.*
> *For Frank and Evelyn, married June 15, 1938*

"Gram told me to cut the corner off with my pocketknife," Frank says, "so no one would know who it belonged to."

"Holy shit," April says under her breath, laying the quilt fragment on the table and looking up at her dad. Her eyes flicker with new comprehension, and with a thousand questions. She glances down the hall, toward her grandmother's bedroom. She whispers, "Oh my God, Dad. Did Gram murder somebody?"

"No. Of course not. But," he says and pauses. He breathes in a slow, deliberate lungful of air and releases it. "Now you can see why she can't go back to Bitter Rapids."

April strokes the tattered fabric. "Now I see why she *has* to go."

September 1990

Phoenix, Arizona

Arrangements are made, excuses are given, and plans are drawn for the "Great Parson Road Trip of 1990." Frank will take a leave of absence from work. April will take off the fall semester from school. Upon their return to Phoenix, she'll work full-time until the spring semester to help offset the cost of their insane excursion.

Now, in mid-September, Frank and April stare at the assortment of suitcases, sleeping bags and folding lawn chairs piled in the driveway. Eight oxygen tanks stand in a row like soldiers. They decide April's ten-year-old Toyota Corolla hatchback has a better chance of making the cross-country haul than Frank's 1973 Pontiac station wagon. But now they question the feasibility of fitting in everything they need for the trip.

"We can put the tanks and the ice chest in the back," Frank suggests, "and tie the rest on the roof."

April laughs at the image that springs into her mind – a mountain of baggage teetering atop her small car. She shakes her head no, but says, "Let's do it."

They set about piling items and securing the heap with bungee cords, moving this here and that there, until they find the right combination. The overnight temperatures have finally dipped below ninety degrees, and the air almost feels cool when they begin. As they work, the heat radiates up from the cement. The sun glints off the car windows. Islands of sweat take shape in the underarms and down the back of Frank's Eagles T-shirt. It's faded, a little threadbare around the collar, a bit snug in his midriff. Evelyn says it's ratty. Frank says it's comfortable. It reminds him of a happy time in his life. He needs all the reminders he can get.

April pauses from their work to sweep her long, flaxen hair back and up into a ponytail. She twists the mass of strands into a bun high on her head and secures it with the elastic band she wears around her wrist. She thinks about the adventure ahead of them, about the first time she will cross the Arizona border into another state. The sweat at the nape of her neck begins to evaporate. The cool sensation makes her wonder if it will be cold when they get to Minnesota.

Frank's mind is stuck on how long the trip will take. He regrets the lie he told his boss – that he needed a leave of absence to drive his ailing mother to the Mayo Clinic in Minnesota. The man hadn't questioned why the new Mayo facility in nearby Scottsdale wasn't good enough, though Frank had a lie prepared for that, too. Just in case. He hopes he'll still have a job when he returns. *How many lies have I told in my lifetime? How many secrets have I kept?* Too many to count. Frank pushes on the baggage heap to test its stability. He unhooks one of the bungee cords, pulls it tighter and secures it further around the pile. He tests the stability again. He silently asks God not to let everything come crashing down on the highway, and promises not to tell any more lies if He brings them all safely home from the trip.

"I'm ready," Gram calls from the front door. She pulls an oxygen tank on its wheelie-cart beside her with one hand. She lugs a hefty wood box under her other arm.

April eyes the box and smacks her forehead with the palm of her hand.

"We should have put everything in the back seat and strapped your Gram on the roof, instead," Frank mutters under his breath. "Beverly Hillbillies-style."

But Evelyn isn't as old as she looks, and her hearing is just fine.

"There'd be less crap to stow if you hadn't insisted on coming along," Evelyn says. She glances in the back seat. "There's room for my box on the floor back there."

Frank tucks the box behind the passenger seat, and April climbs into the rear. He needs the driver's seat pushed all the way back. Without any leg room, April sits lengthwise across the bench-style seat, her head leaned back against the triangular side-window. Gram settles into the front, and Frank tucks in the oxygen tank beside her legs.

He double-checks to make sure the house is locked. Then he climbs into the Corolla and starts the engine.

"I'm hungry," Gram announces.

"We'll get something when we make our first stop in Camp Verde," Frank says.

"I want breakfast at Smitty's one last time."

"It's not going to be your last time, Gram," April says, reaching forward to squeeze her grandmother's shoulder.

Frank backs out of the driveway onto the street.

"Doesn't matter," he concedes. "I'm hungry, too. Might as well eat now."

They settle in a booth in the restaurant's smoking section. The waitress, Laura, greets them by name. April works with Laura at the restaurant, and Frank always requests her section when he brings Evelyn to the all-you-can-eat fish fry on Friday nights. Laura balances a Diet Coke and two cups of coffee in one hand. She has an ashtray in the other, sets it down in front of Evelyn.

"Steak and eggs all around?" she asks.

They all nod.

"And rye toast for you, right Frank?" she asks.

"Yes, thanks," he says. "I'm always amazed that you can remember all your customers' orders."

"Only my best customers." She smiles, tucks a wisp of hair behind her ear.

Frank takes a drink of his coffee as the woman walks away. April watches him, notices the hint of pink in his cheeks.

"You should ask her out, Dad, when we get back."

Frank shrugs his shoulders, shakes his head a little from side to side.

"She likes you," April continues. "I can tell. She talks to you differently than her other customers."

"Pft," Frank responds. "I'm old enough to be her dad."

"Maybe if you had her when you were ten," April laughs.

Evelyn taps a Lucky Strike from its pack.

"Leave the man alone, April," she says, the cigarette bobbing between her lips as she speaks. She holds a lighter to it and takes a drag. "Maybe he doesn't want the hassle of another woman in his life."

Frank is mute, takes another drink of coffee, scratches at a gouge in the Formica table with his thumbnail. April watches Evelyn exhale smoke out her nose, past the oxygen tube in her nostrils.

"With all due respect, Gram, just because you married your soulmate and never wanted to be with anyone else doesn't mean Dad feels that way. Maybe he doesn't want to be alone the rest of his life."

"Maybe the two of you should change the subject," Frank interjects.

Laura approaches the table with their food. She serves Evelyn and April first, then sets Frank's plate in front of him. She smiles, asks if he wants anything else. He coughs, says no thank you. She insists on at least freshening his coffee and returns quickly with a full pot. When Laura leaves them to their meals, Evelyn speaks up again.

"You know, April, sometimes it's better to be alone."

April shakes her head. She cuts her steak, stabs a piece with her fork, and dips it in her egg yolk.

"How can you say that, Gram, when you've never *not* been alone? You don't even know the alternative."

Evelyn hesitates a moment. She watches April chew a mouthful of food and take a long drink of soda through a bendy straw. She pushes the hash browns to the side of her plate with the butter knife. It's all going to come out when they get to Bitter

Rapids anyway, might as well start telling the girl now. There was so much to tell, after all. So very much.

"I do know the alternative," Evelyn says. "Because I had a second husband."

"What?" April sputters. The bubbly cola burns in her sinuses, makes her eyes water.

"Arthur Specht," Evelyn continues. "We married in 1946. That's what women did in those days, April. It's what we *had* to do. Your dad was only five years old when his daddy died in the war. And Denny was a baby. I needed a husband to provide for my sons, and Art was willing."

April sets her knife and fork on her plate. She has no words, no idea whatsoever how to respond to this bombshell. She glances at Frank, who continues eating his breakfast without so much as a flinch. Her dad has a brother. Her grandmother had a second husband. How is it even possible this never came up before? Because Frank and Evelyn made sure it never came up, April realizes.

Before they'd embarked on this trip, the young woman would have thought this was a colossal secret. Only now does she begin to realize it's just the tip of the iceberg. That's why her dad was so dead-set against this trip. The feeling of exhilaration April felt about driving cross-country evaporates. It's replaced by a stab of anxiety; she doesn't know her family at all.

LIFE IN THE 1950S

Every Woman's Standard Medical Guide

The Graystone Press, 1948

PREFACE

From childhood to old age, every phase of a woman's physical development has its "mysteries" and its complications. Each girl, each mother, and each matron are subject to diseases and discomforts peculiar to the particular epoch of her life. In all of these, it is the aim of *Every Woman's Standard Medical Guide* to provide the woman with sound and authoritative counsel and give her helpful information on the care and cultivation of a healthy body and the conduct of a happy life.

1952

Bitter Rapids, Minnesota

*E*velyn charged through the emergency room doors of the county hospital.

"Where are they? Where are my boys?"

The reception nurse rushed to the distraught woman, assured her that Frankie and Denny were okay. The women embraced. They'd known one another since they were schoolgirls. It was the way of small towns.

"Oh, thank God," Evelyn breathed. "I need to see them, Ruth."

Nurse Ruth ushered her down the hall toward the boys' room. Sheriff Carrigan stood watch outside the door of another room. He patted Evelyn's back as she passed by, and she nodded to him gratefully.

Little Denny lay in the hospital bed under a heap of blankets. Frankie sat in a chair, holding an icepack to his bruised knee. He wore borrowed scrubs too large for him, rolled up at the ankles. But they were dry. A blanket draped over his shoulders. Evelyn went to him first. She took his face in her hands, looked him over, kissed the top of his head.

"What on earth were you two doing on the river, Frankie?" She didn't expect an answer, and she didn't wait for one. She went to Denny, brushed a wisp of blonde hair away from his closed eyes.

"He's just sleeping, Evie," Ruth anticipated her question. "He's had a hard day."

"But he's all right?" Evelyn asked, keeping her eyes on her younger son.

Ruth nodded, yes. She explained both boys came in with hypothermia. The nurses changed them into dry clothes, warmed them with heated blankets. They both had some bumps and scrapes here and there, but they should be just fine. No broken bones.

"The doctor will come talk with you in a little bit," Ruth added and then left the mother to be alone with her sons.

Evelyn gazed at Denny, creases of worry etched in her face. She combed her fingers through his fine curls.

"What happened, Frankie?" she asked without looking at him. He knew she expected an answer this time.

"We just wanted to take the canoe out," he said, staring down at the floor. "I guess we put in too far up river. I don't know. The rapids were too much, and we capsized."

He paused for a moment. Evelyn was silent. He knew she wanted more detail, that she'd remain silent until he provided it. He held out for another minute, but Mom always won this game.

"We were under water, and then we got pulled away by the current," he continued. "I grabbed hold of Denny and held tight, but I couldn't get us to the bank. I tried as hard as I could, Mom, honest I did."

Evelyn nodded. She believed him. "It was an accident."

"A Colored man swam out and grabbed hold of us," Frankie said. "He got us to a tree along the shore. But then he got pulled away. I don't know what happened to him. Some other big Colored in a prison jumpsuit carried us up the bank, and Sheriff Carrigan brought us here."

Evelyn pulled Frankie in for a hug, planted a second kiss on his head.

"I'm just glad you're both safe," she said into his tangled mop of hair. "You rest now. I'm going to go find the doctor and ask when we can go home."

Out in the hall, the doctor stood with Sheriff Carrigan and talked in a hushed voice. Evelyn approached them, grasping their hands one at a time and thanking for them taking care of her sons.

The doctor said she could take the boys home as soon as she was ready, but he explained that hypothermia was still a concern. She should be on the lookout for warning signs – shivering, mumbling, confusion, low energy. Keep them warm, he said, and let them drink all the hot cocoa they wanted. It'd be normal for the boys to be tired, after the day they'd had. But if they seemed overly drowsy or if Evelyn had trouble waking them, she was to call the hospital right away. Evelyn placed her fingertips to her mouth, making mental notes of everything the doctor told her.

"Is Art on the road?" the sheriff asked.

"Yes," Evelyn said. "He's due back tomorrow."

Evelyn's second husband sold neon signage, and his work took him all over Minnesota and Wisconsin.

"Frankie said the man who rescued them was swept down river," Evelyn said. "What became of him?"

"They got him fished out. Cold and wet, but he's just fine," Carrigan said, tilting his head toward the closed hospital-room door behind him.

Evelyn placed her hand over heart. Relief washed over her.

"May I speak to him?" she asked. "I'd like to thank him."

The men exchanged glances. Carrigan rubbed at his chin and wrinkled up his face.

"I don't think that'd be best," he said.

She leaned to the side, craned her neck to see through the small window in the door. The doctor took hold of Evelyn's arm and steered her away from the room. He'd pass along her thanks, he assured. Her focus should be on the boys.

"I'd prefer to thank him myself," she said. "I'll only be a minute."

"He's a scoundrel, don't-cha know," Carrigan said. "Not the sort a lady should be in the same room with, Mrs. Specht."

"But he saved their lives," Evelyn asserted. "He can't be all that bad."

"That was a fluke." Carrigan's tone took on the timbre of a lawman. "The guards say he only did it hoping he could run off once he got down river. He's going back under lock and key once the doctor discharges him."

Evelyn tried to shake loose the discrepancy in her mind. She thought back to what Frankie had told her, compared it to what the sheriff said. The stories didn't reconcile. She wanted to see this man herself. But the doctor had already led her back to her sons, said they could go home. Denny sat at the edge of the bed, disheveled and droopy-eyed.

"I wanna go home, Mommy."

The doctor was right, she conceded. Her focus should be on the boys.

* * * *

Evelyn heated a can of tomato soup and made grilled cheese sandwiches for dinner. She warmed hot cocoa on the stove, brought it to the boys' beds where she had tucked them in snug and warm. Then Evelyn sat and read aloud from *The Twenty-One Balloons* by William Pène du Bois.

"Half of this story is true and the other half might very well have happened," she read from the book about a professor who flew across the Pacific Ocean in a tiny wicker house carried by hot-air balloon. Denny drifted off to sleep quickly. Frankie was rapt by the story of invention and exploration.

"It seems strange to me that mechanical progress always seems to leave the slower demands of elegance far behind," Professor Sherman lamented in the story.

When Frankie finally succumbed to exhaustion, Evelyn clicked off the lamp and eased from the bed. She retrieved a chair from the kitchen and sat in the boys' room as they slept. She knitted by the dim light from the hall to stay awake. She worked the soft pink yarn expertly, row by row. It would be a blanket when she finished, for the little girl she hoped yet to have.

Every so often Evelyn dozed off, then woke with a start and rushed to the boys' bedsides. She pulled up their blankets, pressed her lips gently to their foreheads to make sure they were not cold or shivering. Then she took up her vigil again, knitting in hand.

She roused, late in the morning, with warm sun pouring through window glass and across her face. The click of the side door made her jump.

"Hi, Frankie. Where's your mom?" She heard Art's voice in the kitchen and saw that Frankie's bed was empty. Evelyn stood and tiptoed out of the bedroom.

"Oh, Art, I'm so glad you're home." The man of the house was removing his overcoat and placing his fedora on the hat rack. He leaned sideways a bit, so Evelyn could place a kiss on his cheek. Then he caught sight of her.

"You look like something the cat dragged in," he said. He noticed the untidy kitchen, and his voice rose in panic. "What's wrong? Is Denny sick?"

"Denny's okay," she responded. "Both boys are. But there was an accident, down at the river."

Evelyn gave her husband an abridged version of the events that had transpired in the past twenty-four hours or so. Art paced the kitchen, rubbed the back of his neck. Then he looked Evelyn square in the face.

"You have one job while I'm gone, Evelyn, and that's to keep the children safe. Jesus H. Christ. One job."

"It's not her fault," Frankie spoke up. "She told us we could play outside, but to stay close to home."

Art looked down at the twelve-year-old boy, who was still swimming in his oversized hospital scrubs.

"Dammit, Frankie, you're too old to be goofing off and disobeying your mom," he said. "And to make it worse, you put your brother in danger. What did you think you were doing?"

Frankie shrugged his shoulders.

"You didn't think," Art said. "You never think."

"Art," Evelyn placed her hand on the man's arm. "He's just a boy. It was an accident."

Art shook his arm loose and stormed down the hall into Denny's room.

"Holy God!"

The shriek of terror shot through to Evelyn's very core. In a half-second, she and Frankie stood beside Art in the bedroom, watching Denny writhe and convulse beneath the covers. The boy had vomited, and he was drenched in sweat. Art threw back the covers and swept Denny up in his arms. Evelyn was already back in the kitchen, her purse and car keys in hand.

Art placed Denny in the back seat and climbed in beside him. Evelyn struggled to get the key into the ignition. She fumbled and dropped the keys to the floor. Frankie quickly scooped them up, handing them over. She enveloped the keys and his small hands in hers for a split-second, then started the car and sped to the hospital.

* * * *

The staff whisked Denny through the double doors into the nerve center of the emergency room. Nurse Ruth held the parents back when they tried to follow. All they could do was wait.

Evelyn sat slumped forward with her elbows on her knees, her forehead propped up by her fingertips. Frankie stood beside her and rubbed her back. Art paced – from the reception desk to the row of vending machines, from the double-doors to the grouping of vinyl-covered chairs. After an hour had passed, Art strode to the desk and demanded to know what was happening. Ruth explained they were running tests. These things take time, she said. The doctor will be out with an update as soon as he has information, she said. Art threw his hands up in frustration, resumed pacing.

Finally, the doctor emerged from the double doors. He approached the family, as they sprung forward to meet him.

"I'm afraid I don't have good news," he said. This was the worst part of his job. The man removed his glasses, folded them carefully and tucked them into the pocket of his white overcoat. Delaying only made it harder for the parents. He knew this. Still, he paused. Evelyn seized his hand. The doctor saw the desperation etched in her face and patted her hand.

Art put his arm around Evelyn's shoulders.

"Denny is resting comfortably," the doctor began. "An x-ray revealed intracranial pressure. He likely struck his head in the river yesterday, which caused swelling of the brain as well as hydrocephalus, or fluid build-up. There's only a small amount of room for the brain inside the skull. Excessive swelling and fluid causes pressure, which can lead to brain damage. So we drilled a hole in Denny's skull, to release the fluid and help reduce some of that pressure."

Evelyn felt her throat constrict as she fought to take air into her lungs. A vision flashed through her mind of her little boy, lying motionless on a cold hospital table, doctors in white masks drilling into his precious little head. She pulled away from Art and stepped toward the doors.

"I need to see him."

"You'll get to see him soon, Mrs. Specht," the doctor assured. "But first I must finish telling you what we know."

Frankie's eyes began to burn. *There's more?* he thought. *More than drilling a hole in Denny's head?* He shrank back toward the waiting room chairs, tried to swallow the lump forming in his throat.

"Denny wasn't breathing when he arrived," the doctor continued. "We intubated him, that is, we inserted a tube into his airway and placed him on a ventilator for breathing."

The doctor paused again.

Evelyn pressed her hands together near her heart. She entwined her icy fingers, held her breath, waited for the doctor to continue.

"Once we had Denny stabilized, we ran an EEG, which is a test that measures brain activity. Unfortunately, we found almost no measurable activity."

Evelyn squeezed her eyes shut tight.

"What does that mean, exactly?" Art asked.

"Denny is brain dead, Mr. Specht. If we remove him from the ventilator, he will die. I'm very sorry."

"So, we'll just keep him on the ventilator," Evelyn said, staring at the doctor's chest, drilling through to his heart, just like the man had drilled into her son. "Until he wakes up and starts breathing on his own."

The doctor lowered his chin, looked at the floor. That was often the first response from a loved one. Denial. Desperation. The doctor shook his head, no. "Denny will never regain consciousness."

Frankie couldn't quite understand the rest of what the doctor said. It sounded as though the man was talking from under water.

Denny's condition would never improve.

There was nothing more that could be done.

The most humane course of action would be to remove him from the ventilator.

Allow him to pass peacefully.

The light dimmed.

Frankie's knees buckled.

The world turned black.

1990

Page, Arizona

"Heck of a long day," Frank says.

It's nearly midnight. Father and daughter sit on aluminum lawn-chairs outside their motel room. Evelyn is deep asleep inside.

The trio had driven north for 270 miles their first day on the road. It took ten ridiculously-long hours. They stopped in Camp Verde and in Flagstaff, at three rest areas and a handful of pull-offs. It was vital, both the pulmonologist and cardiologist had stressed, that Evelyn stand and walk every hour to prevent blood clots.

April dutifully walked with her grandmother at each stop. At first, Gram tried to generate small talk. April didn't play along. Frank drove the entire day in silence. Gram stared out the window. April slouched in the back seat, listening to music through the headphones of her cassette-tape player. Metallica. Guns N' Roses. Mötley Crüe. Repeat.

They ate a late dinner in Page, before checking into the motel. It was during dinner when Evelyn finally told April about that fateful day at the river and how she'd lost a son. April was spellbound. She was still angry at Gram for harboring such a secret, yet she was moved by the woman's palpable grief, still fresh after so many years. How are you supposed to respond to a story like that? April had no clue.

Frank listened to his mother's story with nearly the same rapt attention as his daughter. He already knew what had happened, of course, but he'd never heard the story from Evelyn's perspective. They'd never talked about it. He had only ever experienced those moments through the lenses of his twelve-year-old eyes.

"I'm sorry about your brother," April says now. She looks at her dad. He keeps his attention trained on the distant, invisible landscape in the pitch-black night, but he acknowledges her with a nod. She turns her head, stares out into the same darkness.

The city of Page sits on a postage stamp atop Manson Mesa, in the high desert of Arizona, about twenty miles from the Utah border. Thousands of feet above sea level and 600 feet above Lake Powell, the air is crisp, fresh. Without the glare of big-city lights, the sky is awash with stars. The sweet, earthy scent of creosote hangs in the air, a remnant from the touch of fall rain earlier in the day.

April has never experienced such tranquil darkness, such absolute quiet. She closes her eyes for a moment. There's no drone of traffic, no hum of roof-top air conditioners. A gentle breeze wafts across the vast terrain. April rubs the goose bumps on her forearms, then folds her arms, gives herself a hug.

"It's weird how Gram talks about things from back then." April fills the stillness she both loves and hates. "She makes it sound like she was the perfect little fifties woman, doing whatever her husband and the doctors told her to do. I have a hard time believing she really acted that way."

"It was a long time ago," Frank says. "The years change us, for better or for worse."

"Whoa," April says. "That has to be the most philosophical thing I've ever heard you say."

Frank chuckles. "I have my moments."

They sit in silence again. An owl hoots from somewhere nearby. April looks around, squints into the dark night. She feels the nocturnal creature's presence, but she can't see it. She waits for it to speak to them again.

"Since we're on the subject of moms," Frank disrupts the magic, "did you call yours before we left town?"

"Why would I?" April asks.

"We're going to be on the road a long time, April. She'll be worried if she calls home and can't get ahold of you."

The young woman scoffs. April's birthday was four months ago, so she doesn't expect another call from her mom until Christmas. It stings, when she thinks about it. She swats the pesky thought away, like a mosquito, but the painful bite remains.

"I don't care if she worries."

"Don't be cruel, April."

"It was cruel of *her* to walk out on us," April says, her voice flat.

Frank takes a moment. He knows how hard it has been on April since her mom left them. It has been hard on him, too. But he'd had to set aside his own pain, to become two-parents-in-one. What did he know about braiding hair and having tea parties? About training bras and feminine hygiene products? He had learned, though. And April's mom had mailed him a check every month, for clothes and schoolbooks and whatever else their daughter needed. Somehow, they made it work.

"She wasn't cruel on purpose," he says.

The young woman blows a gust of air through her teeth and rolls her eyes. April looks so much like her mother, Frank notices. The arched brows and slender nose. Heart-shaped face and exasperated expression.

He adds, "Some people just aren't cut out to be parents."

His ex-wife excels in her career as an interior designer. Yet, when it comes to motherhood, she flounders. Frank lost count of the times he had come home from work or woken in the middle of the night and found his wife sitting on the bathroom floor, her face swollen from crying.

"I don't know how to do this," she'd whispered between hiccuppy breaths.

A person can only live with that kind of self-doubt and anxiety for so long. Early one morning, when April was just eight years old, Frank's wife told him she was moving to California.

"She only left because she thought you'd be better off without her."

April cackles at the irony. "Well, there's one thing she and I agree on."

Conversations about April's mom never go well. Frank is running out of things to say, of ways to explain something he still struggles to understand himself. He rises from his chair and pats her shoulder. "Time for bed, kiddo."

* * * *

They hit the road in the morning, later than planned. Evelyn had slept until nine o'clock. Frank and April worried about waking her after the long day they'd had. April notices the heaviness in Frank's eyes and offers to drive. He doesn't argue. Ten minutes outside of Page, he's snoring in the back seat. Gram tears open a package of granola bars and hands one to April. The women crunch their breakfast as they make their way north into Utah, past Glen Canyon, through Vermilion Cliffs.

"God, it's beautiful here," April says. "The pictures you see are pretty, but they don't do it justice."

The bitterness she felt the day before has dissipated. Those feelings seem small in the context of this new panorama. She drinks in the vast stretch of red earth, the towering sandstone canyons sculpted over millions of years by the Colorado River.

What mysteries hide inside those cracks and fissures? April wonders.

"We came through here on our way to Phoenix back in '55," Gram says. "There was a different road then, further east, through Monument Valley and the Navajo reservation. It was back before they built the dam we passed a little bit ago."

April nods, and Gram continues.

"That town we just stayed in wasn't even there yet. Just the Navajo people and their little mud *hohrahns,* and their sheep. It seemed like such a lovely, down-to-earth way of life. I always said I would come back here to live after your dad grew up."

"Why didn't you?" April asks.

"That's just not what women of my generation did," Gram says. "We couldn't chase our dreams in the same way you girls can today."

A massive hawk glides high over the roadway. April cranes her neck to watch when it suddenly dips and disappears beneath an arch in the rock face. *Speaking of chasing dreams*, she thinks. The crimson-striped canyons and cliffs beckon her to discover their secrets. If only the travel schedule wasn't so damn tight.

"We got a little taste of freedom during World War II, when all the men were off fighting," Gram continues. "They put women to work in factories and other places. We even got our own professional baseball league. I took your dad to see the Millerettes play in '44, one of their first games. I was pregnant out-to-here with Denny, and we made the long trip to Minneapolis by bus."

Gram pauses to chuckle, remembering what a sight she must have been maneuvering the narrow bus aisle with a giant stomach and tiny boy.

"They weren't too good though," she continues. "Couldn't get more than a few dozen people out to the stands. Didn't even last the season. We listened to the Kenosha Comets games on the radio after that."

April smiles. Gram had always followed the Twins, listened to their games on the little radio in her bedroom. This was the first time April had heard anything about women's baseball.

"I was never terribly sporty, but oh, how I envied those girls. Traveling from town to town to play ball," Gram reminisces. "But I'm getting off track."

After the war, she explains, when all the men came home, the women were fired so the men could have their jobs back. Many soldiers went to college, so they could get better jobs. There wasn't enough room in the workplace or the colleges for young women to do much more than become secretaries or get home economics degrees. Oh, a few worked as schoolteachers or nurses, until they started families.

"We married what we wished for ourselves," Gram says. "If a woman dreamed of being a doctor or an engineer, that's who she married, just to be close to that life in some small way. I suppose that's what attracted me to Art. He owned a small neon shop. Half his time was spent on the road, traveling to towns near and far with his sample case of colorful tubes, selling people on the glamour of big bright signs like the ones they have in Times Square and Las Vegas. People respected him. The first few years we were married, I couldn't wait to hear all about his trips when he got home. Lord, how I wished I could trade places with him, could have that kind of value, feel that kind of freedom."

April emits a puff of air from her lips, rolls her eyes. "Man, I can't decide if you're freaking me out or pissing me off."

The young woman rattles her head to somehow make sense of what she's hearing.

"This doesn't sound like you at all, Gram. I was thinking that yesterday, when you said the sheriff wouldn't let you talk to the man who rescued dad in the river. The woman I've always known does what she wants and doesn't take no for an answer. Times must have been a *lot* different back then."

"They *were*," Gram says, and then flashes April a familiar, sly smile. "But, just because I didn't talk to the man at the hospital that day doesn't mean I took no for an answer."

Evelyn

Oh, April, nothing was the same after Denny died.

At first, we were all just numb.

Our small town had attended more than its fair share of funerals by then, because of the war. We'd shed tears and said our good-byes to plenty of young men cut down in their prime. Fathers, sons, brothers, and friends. Husbands. But Denny, that was different. He hadn't gone off to fight evil and protect freedom. I'd never even considered the possibility of losing him. Even after that awful day at the hospital, it didn't seem possible that he was really gone.

Then we had the funeral. I'll never forget walking into the church and seeing his tiny coffin.

 A child's funeral is wretched, April. I hope you never have to attend one. The anguish creeps up on you like a mountain lion. It pounces on you and rips open your throat. There's nothing you can do but sit there, completely helpless, and feel the life drain from your body. Afterward, and forever, you watch from outside of yourself as the loss eats away at your insides, like that lion is feasting on what little is left of you.

No one knew what to say to me or how to act around me after that. Our refrigerator and freezer was jam-packed with hot dishes from the neighborhood. Everything else in my life was empty.

My mother was no help. She'd been angry when Frank and I married right out of high school. She never really got over that. Mother had wanted me to go to Bemidji State Teachers College, so I could meet a man with better prospects than my high school sweetheart. Frank was a mason's apprentice. Mother always said I should marry a man with a job that required him to wash up before the workday, not after.

She was always distant with her grandsons because of that, even after Frank was killed. Why she took out her resentment on them has always been a mystery to me. My marriage to Art warmed her up a little. But too much time had passed, I think, for her to know how to comfort me. In her defense, no one really knows how to comfort someone who has lost a child.

Art wasn't the consoling type either. His way of dealing with loss was to keep moving, to outrun it. He dove back into his work with vigor, and he expected me to do the same. So that's what I did. I went to the butcher shop on Mondays, the grocer's on Tuesdays. Wednesday, I did the baking. Thursday mornings, I volunteered at the Salvation Army. Laundry was washed and starched and ironed on Fridays. Dinner was on the table each night at six o'clock. Life continued just as it had before. At least, that's how I made it appear from the outside.

I often wondered, during those first weeks, how long I could keep up the façade. When would I crack? I knew it was inevitable. More than anything, I wanted to talk about Denny. But that always led to tears, and tears made people uncomfortable. So, I mostly kept quiet, kept to myself.

One morning, I was rolling pie crust and looking out the window at Frankie in the yard. He was throwing a baseball high into the air and catching it in his mitt. It was the first time in weeks that he had gone outdoors. He spotted me watching him and smiled at me. It filled my heart with joy, seeing that precious smile, seeing him so full of life again. I had to look away quickly. I didn't want him to see me cry.

In that moment, I realized how lucky I was to still have Frankie. That river could have taken both my sons. It was past time I thanked the man who'd risked his life to save them. I wanted to tell him how grateful I was for that. I wanted to tell him Frankie was doing okay. I wanted to tell him about Denny.

I'd never been inside a prison. I had no idea what to do, or say, or even wear. April, I was terrified. It's silly when I think back on it now, all that time I spent in my stockings and slip staring in the closet, deliberating on an outfit. Did it really matter whether I wore a sheath dress or A-line, whether I paired it with t-strap heels or Mary Jane flats? I can still remember what I settled on, though. A cream-colored linen sheath with matching navy heels, clutch purse, and pillbox hat. I was built like Marilyn Monroe back then, if you can believe it. And I planned to use that to my advantage, if the warden tried to send me away.

Visits were allowed on Sundays and Mondays, from nine o'clock until three. I'd called ahead to figure that part out. I'd also gone to the library and went through the newspaper files. There had been an article published about the river rescue, which I couldn't bring myself to read before then. I read it that day in the library, over and over again. My hands were shaking. I ran my finger along the sentences. The man's name was Maakade Carpenter, and he was serving a twenty-five-year sentence for murder. I looked around to make sure no one was watching, then tore out the article and stuffed it in my purse.

My fingers were filthy from the newspaper ink. I had to go into the ladies' room and wash up before I left. I can still see the river of black water and suds circling down into the drain, as I recounted the article in my mind. Murder. This man who'd saved my sons was a murderer.

You probably won't believe me, knowing what you know now, but I used to have a hard time keeping a secret. My family always guessed their Christmas and birthday gifts. My heart was always out there on my sleeve. Father would laugh and warn me to never play poker.

So, I waited until Art was back on the road for work before I went to the prison, to give myself a few days to wash the deception from my face before he came back home. Art had been of the same mind as

Sheriff Carrigan about me talking to Maak. I knew he'd be furious if he found out.

Art loaded the car for his business trip — his briefcase and colorful neon-tube sample kit, enough clothes and sundries for several days — and was on the road by eight o'clock Monday morning. Frankie took off on his bike somewhere to enjoy summertime. I walked to the sidewalk bench down the street from our house and waited for the bus that would take me to the Colored prison near Ely. That's the word we used back then. Colored.

*** * * ***

As I'd expected, the prison officer at the visitor's desk hesitated when I signed the ledger and asked to see Maak. He asked how I knew the man. I couldn't possibly have been his wife or blood relative. When I explained the reason for my visit, he wobbled his head and jibber-jabbered about why it wasn't a good idea. He said he'd pass my thanks along. I struck my best demure Marilyn-pose and thanked him for his concern and diligence in protecting the community and blah, blah, blah. Then I tilted my head a bit and touched his arm where it rested on the tall desk.

"It would mean so much to me if I could speak to him myself," I said, working my eyelashes. "I promise I won't be long."

He relented and led me to a room with several groupings of tables and chairs. He went over the rules for the visit — I was to stay seated on my side of the table at all times, I was not to touch the man or give him anything, and so on. He pulled out a chair for me, and I sat with my ankles crossed and purse in my lap, and he left me there alone. It felt like hours before the opposite door finally opened and a different guard escorted Maak into the room.

Soon as I laid eyes on him, I wished to God I had a poker face. Maak was an imposing man. Not overly large, but he walked tall, proud, even though his hands and feet were shackled together. His dark skin was especially striking against the stripes of his jumpsuit.

The guard led Maak by the elbow to the seat across from me. Small beads of perspiration dotted the guard's upper lip. The fellow couldn't have been a day over twenty. After Maak had settled in the chair, the guard stepped back and stood at attention near the door. His right hand rested on the club hanging from his belt. If Maak was at all nervous, it didn't show. There was no questioning which of the two men held the power in the room.

"Thank you for seeing me, Mr. Carpenter," I said. My mouth was so dry, I'm sure it came out a whisper.

"Yes, ma'am," he said.

I'd rehearsed a thousand times what I wanted to say, but in that moment, my mind was blank. I uncrossed my ankles and crossed them again the other way. Maak sat ramrod straight in his chair, unmoving. You could have heard a pin drop on the floor.

"My name is Evelyn Specht," I spoke up after an eternity. "My boys were in the river, that day. Frankie and Denny. I came to tell you how grateful I am to you, for what you did."

"Yes, ma'am," he said again.

I struggled with what to say next. While I had planned to tell him about the boys, all I could think about in that moment was that I sat face-to-face with a murderer. The relaxed, stoic demeanor of this man just didn't reconcile with the image I'd had in my mind's eye of what a murderer would look like.

"Why did you do it?" I blurted out, surprising myself.

"Do what?" he asked.

"Save my sons," I said. "You could have easily died yourself. Why would you take such a risk?"

Then he said, "What you mean to say is, why would a criminal take such a risk."

There was no question in what he said. There was no malice either. It was only a statement.

"You would not have asked any other man that question."

He was right, of course. I didn't try to take it back or pretend I had been thinking otherwise. The guard took a step toward him and said something about how he ought to show proper respect. I raised my hand to quiet the guard. Shocked as I was, I still wanted to hear what Maak had to say. Then I tucked my hands back in my lap, so the men wouldn't see them trembling.

"I have made many mistakes, and I have done terrible things," he said. "But I am not an evil man, Mrs. Specht. I could not stand by and watch a child drown."

A wave of shame came over me. I could feel my face turn hot and flushed. *Say something, Evelyn*, I shouted in my head. Nothing came to me. I just sat there, looking and feeling like a damn fool.

"How are they?" he asked. I must have looked at him quizzically, because he clarified, "How are the boys?"

His question made my eyes sting, and then it made me smile. Frankie, my oldest, was doing just fine, I told him. But Denny. Tears started rolling down my cheeks and I fished in my purse for a hankie. Denny hurt his head in the river, I continued, holding my breath to fight back the sobs pushing up hard from my gut. He died the day after, I somehow managed to say.

That was the first time I had said it out loud. Denny had died.

"He is in the *Land of Souls*," Maak said.

The Land of Souls. It was such a strange thing to say. I assumed he meant Heaven. Picturing my little boy in Heaven was more than I could take. I finally cracked. I must have blubbered for five minutes. Neither man moved or said a word. The guard averted his eyes to the ceiling. But not Maak. He looked me square in the face and watched me cry. It couldn't have been pretty, I'll tell you that, as I gasped and sobbed and blew snot bubbles.

It should have felt awkward, I suppose, the way his eyes held me and took in my pain. But it felt… wonderful. It made me feel loved for the first time since Denny's heart had stopped beating.

Once I had composed myself, I apologized for crying so.

"A mother weeps when her child leaves the *Land of Living*," he said. "Do not apologize. It is right. It washes away your grief."

The way he looked at me, the way he spoke, he was unlike anyone I had ever met. It was oddly empowering. I told him, "I've never heard anyone talk the way you do."

"My mother is Ojibwe," he said.

That's the Native American tribe in northern Minnesota. Frankie had said a colored man rescued him, but I could see then that Maak was only part black. I nodded to acknowledge the new information. I started to feel unsure of myself again and didn't know what to say next. Maak was still remarkably at ease.

"What kind of boy was Denny?" he asked.

Maybe it was obvious to him how badly I needed talk about Denny. Maybe he just appreciated having company. It didn't matter, really. All I needed was an invitation. I told him story after story, and he nodded politely, even smiled once or twice. I don't know for sure how long I prattled on, but the guard finally cleared his throat and said time was up.

I thanked Maak again, for the river and for allowing me to visit with him.

"Yes, ma'am," he said, as the guard ushered him back behind the metal door.

When I had walked into that prison, I told myself I only wanted to meet the man who saved my sons to thank him. But when I walked out, I knew I wanted more than that. I wanted to get to know this unusual man. I needed to figure out whatever it was he seemed to have figured out – the thing that enabled him to be so at ease, so sure of himself, even locked behind bars. And I needed to figure out a legitimate reason to visit him again.

LIFE IN THE 1990s

RALEIGH, N.C., Feb. 10, 1990

FOR IMMEDIATE RELEASE

/National Newswire/ -- Carl Sagan, noted astronomer, scientist and author, delivered the keynote address at the 5th annual Emerging Issues Forum of North Carolina State University. This year's forum theme was "Global Changes in the Environment: Our Common Future."

Sagan has been most focused on the issue of life elsewhere in the universe. He stressed that mankind has examined many dozens of other worlds, with instruments of enormous capacity. A massive amount of important and interesting information has been acquired.

"In these dozens of worlds, there is nothing, not the least hint of anything alive. Not a mouse, not a footprint, not a microbe, not even an organic molecule," he said.

"Life is something precious and rare. There is something extraordinary about the planet that we are privileged to live on. Life is rare."

(Source: North Carolina State University)

1990

Salina, Utah

The trio continues their journey north along Highway 89. Frank takes over driving at their first stop of the day. He prefers it. Focusing on the road makes it easier to pretend he's not listening to Evelyn, who has begun regaling them with stories about life in Bitter Rapids. Life there seemed the polar opposite of life in Phoenix. It was a place where snow fell seven months out of the year, and the hottest day in summer might hit seventy-eight degrees. Ice-skating on Rainy Lake from November to April. Gathering for fireworks shows in the town square on the Fourth of July. The peculiar sensation of knowing the name of nearly every single person within a twenty-mile radius of your home.

These are memories – not necessarily bad ones – that Frank had worked hard to lock away. *Never talk about our lives before Phoenix.* That was the rule. And he'd followed it.

Then that damned newspaper article rose up and breached the levee without warning. Now history was rushing at him with the indifference of a desert monsoon, a flash flood impossible to outrun. Frank scrambles to higher ground in his mind, as the events of that terrible morning surge toward him.

Denny found Frank filling his Boy Scout pack with food and clothes, baseball and glove, compass and canteen.

"Whatcha doin', Frankie?" his little brother asked, eyes wide with wonder. "Going camping?"

Frankie shook his head no. He tucked his jackknife into his back pocket.

"Are you running away from home?" Denny's voice raised an octave.

"I'm moving to Canada. I'll write you when I get settled somewhere."

Denny grabbed hold of his big brother's arm, his eyes brimming with questions.

"I can't live here anymore," Frankie said. "Art hates me."

"Art ain't so bad," Denny whispered and stuffed his hands in his pants pockets.

Frankie sighed, ruffled Denny's hair. With all his twelve-year-old wisdom, he said, "Art loves you and Mom a lot, and you guys love him. This'll be better for everybody."

Denny's eyes filled with tears. He balled up his fists and rubbed the droplets away. He declared that he was moving to Canada, too. The brothers stood silently for a minute or so.

"You can't go," Frankie finally said. "You're a little kid. You're not tough enough to make it on your own."

The small boy reared his arm back and punched his big brother in the gut. He declared, once again and with conviction, he was going to Canada, too. Frankie laughed and rubbed the spot where Denny had slugged him.

"Okay, Denny, maybe you are tough enough. Go, hurry and pack a bag. We need to leave before Mom gets home from the store."

Frank can still see little Denny beaming with pride, hiking alongside him down to the river, like it was yesterday. He watches the boy stow the packs under a seat of the canoe and climb into the vessel. Denny's toothy grin extends from ear to ear.

"I love all these pine trees," April breaks the silence in the car, rescues Frank from his memories. She peers out the small side window in the back seat. "Is this like the forest near where you grew up, Dad?"

"Huh?" Frank clears his throat, wobbles his head from side to side to cast out the memories. "Maybe, a little. I dunno."

They ride in silence for a bit. Then Evelyn speaks up. "The trees in Bitter Rapids are bigger. Ten times bigger. Greener, too."

Evelyn looks back at her granddaughter. April is smiling. Evelyn sees the delight dancing in the young woman's eyes. This adventure has made them both happy, despite everything else.

For so many years, Evelyn felt zero need to dredge up the past. What's done is done. She'd been content keeping it wrapped up and hidden in the underbrush along the remote riverbank. Still, keeping secrets from April had given her pangs of guilt every now and then. Lord knows the girl kept none from her.

April had needed a woman's understanding, growing up without a mother at home. Gram was there for April's first crush, and first heartbreak. Gram told her what to expect when that-time-of-the-month came along. And, when April needed a birth control prescription, Gram was the one to arrange the doctor appointment.

No more secrets, Evelyn tells herself, turning back to watch the road ahead of them. She cracks the window to let in some fresh pine air. She inhales the sharp, sweet scent. The tightness in her chest eases a bit. *Is it the medicinal energy of trees,* she wonders, *or the redemption of truth?*

Evelyn parts her lips, prepares to reveal another piece of her past. A short siren blast shatters the moment. Frank glances at the flash of red and blue lights in the rearview mirror and grumbles.

"Oh man," April says, turning to look back. "Were you speeding?"

"No," Frank snaps. He turns on his right blinker and drives onto the highway shoulder.

"You must have been speeding," she prods.

"Just be quiet, April."

The highway patrolman approaches the car with long, slow strides.

Frank turns the crank to lower the window. "Good morning, officer."

The officer tilts his head to look inside the car. He glances at Evelyn, then at April in the back seat. They smile and say hello.

"You have an awful lot of cargo strapped up top," the officer says, taking a step back to survey the vehicle. He reaches up and tugs at a bungee cord, pushes on the heap beneath the tarp.

"Yes, sir. Got my mother and my daughter with me, heading to Minnesota. These ladies don't travel light." Frank chuckles, tries to keep his voice breezy.

The officer walks the perimeter of the car, peeks through the hatchback window.

"What's with all the canisters in the back?" he asks.

"Oxygen tanks," Frank says, shifting in his seat, "for my mother. She's not well."

A lull hangs in the air. The officer reaches for the ticket pad at his belt.

"I'm going to have to cite you."

"For the tanks?" Frank asks.

They all blink at the officer. The man takes his time responding.

"Utah SB 41-6-186 requires all passengers ages eight years and older to wear seat belts," the officer says and turns his pad to a fresh page. "You're not wearing seat belts. That's a twenty-dollar fine for each of you."

"That's bullshit," April mutters from the back seat.

"Gosh, officer, we had no idea," Frank says. "We don't have that law in Arizona. But we'll buckle up right now."

"Yes, you will," the officer says, thumps his pen on the ticket pad. "But ignorance of the law is no excuse. With a cargo load like this, you're at an especially high risk of accident and injury."

Evelyn hoots and flips a hand up in the air. "If we get into an accident with all these oxygen tanks, we'll be blown to Timbuktu. Seat belts wouldn't do us a darn bit of good."

"Mom! Please. Just — ," Frank hold ups his hand. *Stop.*

April stifles a laugh and quickly looks down at her lap. The officer looks down, too, at his ticket pad. But Evelyn sees one corner of his mouth twitch ever so slightly.

"Well, you do what you must, officer," Evelyn says. "But if we're going to be stopped here while you dawdle over your paperwork, I need to get off my butt and move my limbs. Doctor's orders."

She opens her door and fumbles with the oxygen tank at her feet. Frank looks straight ahead, his hands planted firmly at ten-and-two on the steering wheel.

Evelyn shoots a stern look at the officer, and he quickly stows his pad, hustles to the passenger side of the car. He removes the tank and sets it on the ground. Then he extends a hand to the old woman.

"You're a fine young man." Evelyn smiles and hoists herself out of the bucket seat.

He can't help but smile back or notice how fragile her lean hand feels in his.

"Come help your mother," he barks, and Frank leaps from the car.

April flips forward the driver seatback and hustles out, too. "Come on, Gram, let's walk."

Evelyn pats the officer's hand, and then moves slowly down the shoulder with her granddaughter. The officer tells Frank he's going to let them off with a warning. Advises him to drive safely and make sure they all buckle up.

"Yes, sir. I sure will," Frank babbles. "Yes, sir. Thank you, sir."

The officer strides to his car and takes his time getting situated. He makes a grand gesture of fastening his seat belt with his eyes trained on Frank, who smiles earnestly and gives a thumbs-up. Finally, the patrol car eases off the shoulder and rockets up the highway.

April and Evelyn wait for the car to disappear around the bend before they double over with laughter. Frank shakes his head and joins them. "You're a fine young man," he says in a high-pitched syrup voice.

"Go ahead and mock me," his mother says. "But I just saved you sixty bucks, kid."

"You saved me twenty bucks, Mom. You and April would have paid your own dang fines."

* * * *

They decide to call it a day when they pull into Salina and spot a diner next to a Days Inn. After an early dinner of greasy patty melts, they split off. Franks tears a hotel coupon from the back page of the giant road atlas they keep in the car and heads off to get them a room for the night. The women set out for another walk.

Along the paved path to a "scenic overlook," Gram pauses to light a cigarette. April pulls the oxygen wheelie between them.

"You know those cigarettes are probably what caused all your problems in the first place," April says. "Why don't you just quit?"

Gram shakes her head, says without words, *it's too late now.* April understands. Gram is dying. Giving up cigarettes would only make her crankier in the time she has left.

When they reach the overlook, April pauses to read the national forest sign aloud.

"What is now high desert in Salina Canyon was once a humid coastal plain teeming with life. Sixty-five million years ago, the end of the Cretaceous period, dinosaurs thundered through swampy islands of vegetation and sandbars at this very site."

The women look out into the vast canyon. Its imposing scarlet walls rise in vertical layers from the base. Midway up, its angles shift to horizontal layers of whitish stone and streaks of black. Tufts of golden grass line the creek below alongside tall stands of scraggly green juniper. Petite leafy shrubs polka dot the rocky ledges.

"Keep reading," Gram says.

April steps back toward the sign.

"As the sea level fluctuated over millions of centuries, the beaches advanced and retreated, creating layers of sediment that formed the canyon walls. The reddish rock beds consist mainly of siltstone and shale. The whitish beds consist of sandstone and halite salt casts. Thick black coal seams are evidence of the abundant organic material that existed here millions of years ago."

They stand beside each other now, admiring the grandiose setting. A soft breeze whispers through the tree limbs, releasing a sweet fragrance of dust and rain. The creek flows silently five-thousand feet below them. High above in the cloudless cerulean sky, a hawk glides in circles on the air current.

"It makes you realize how insignificant we are, doesn't it?" Gram whispers.

"Insignificant?" April asks.

Gram is mute for a moment. April watches her, waits for more.

"All the centuries that humans have been on Earth, and it's only a miniscule fraction of the millions of years our planet has been around. And then there's us, our lives. Just a tiny speck of existence in all of mankind."

April makes a funny face at her grandmother and rolls her eyes. She looks back out to the canyon.

"I have to say, Gram, I've never thought of myself as just a tiny speck."

The old woman takes one last draw on her cigarette and stubs it out on the rock wall barrier to the overlook. She turns her oxygen wheelie around and starts back down the path.

"Give it twenty or thirty years," Gram says over her shoulder, "and you will."

April retrieves the errant cigarette butt, shaking her head at her grandmother's careless act of littering as well as at the woman's cynical words. She takes another moment to soak in the colors of the canyon. She looks down the crevasse, squints at the burbling creek far below as it glints and glitters in the late-day sun. *Poor Gram*, she thinks. *How can all this make you feel insignificant?* If anything, looking out over this natural wonder makes April feel important. Part of something grand and eternal. Alive. Strong. Connected.

*** * * ***

Back at the hotel, Evelyn tells Frank to take a hike so she can have a shower in privacy. Frank hesitates, thinking about his wheezing, unsteady mother standing alone in a slippery hotel tub.

"Won't you need help?" he asks.

"Not from you!" Evelyn takes her granddaughter's hand in hers, gives it a little squeeze.

A bolt of terror flashes inside April's mind. She looks at her dad. The alarm in her eyes couldn't ring any louder if she opened her mouth and howled. Frank grimaces, shrugs his shoulder ever so slightly, then turns and hustles out of the room in a flourish of relief. *That's what you get for saying you'd take her to Minnesota.* That is what April hears in the whoosh of his hasty escape. She forces herself to smile after the door slams shut.

"I'll get the water warmed up for you, Gram."

April lays the bathmat on the floor and turns on the water. She tests the temperature, making sure it isn't too hot. She hears Gram enter the bathroom and turns to see the woman standing in the open doorway, naked as a mole rat. April coughs and turns back toward the tub – to check the water again, to tamp down her nerves.

"Water's ready," she says.

Gram places her hand on April's shoulder and steps gingerly into the tub.

"Hold on to the safety rail," April tells her and pulls the stopper on the shower head.

Gram sighs as the warm water flows over her scalp and down her body. After a moment, she holds out a hand and asks April to give her some shampoo. The young woman opens the small bottle of hotel shampoo and pours the pearly-pink liquid into her palm. Gram rubs at her hair awkwardly, trying to generate a lather with one hand, to reach over and around to the opposite side of her head. Most of the shampoo washes from her hand, sliding down her back in a pink glob, into the tub and down the drain.

"Gosh darn it," she mutters, looking at her empty hand.

"Here, let me," April says, pouring more shampoo into her own palm.

April works up a lather and massages Gram's scalp. She focuses on the thin white curls. She tries to avert her eyes from her grandmother's sagging breasts and buttocks, loose-skinned elbows and knees, bony shoulders and hips. Gram uses the shampoo suds to wash her own stubbly armpits and private parts. April pretends to adjust the shower curtain while the old woman finishes cleaning and rinsing. Then she wraps Gram in a towel, directs the hazardous crossing from the tub to the bathmat.

"Easy peasy," April says.

But Evelyn can see that it makes the girl uncomfortable – an old lady's nakedness, all wrinkled and worn down.

"If I had a nickel for every person who's seen me naked or wiped my butt, I'd be leaving you and your dad quite an inheritance," Evelyn says and laughs.

April gives an obligatory chuckle. *Sure, right. Easy-peasy.*

＊ ＊ ＊ ＊

After getting Gram settled into bed for the night, April wanders the hotel to look for her dad. She finds him sitting in a plastic chair beside the outdoor pool. She flips the high latch on the metal gate and joins him inside the pool fence, slumping down into the chair beside him.

"Looks like you survived," Frank says and gives her a tight-lipped grin.

April guffaws and then lets go of a heavy sigh. She tips her head forward and rubs the back of her neck. They've only been on the road two days. Two. She keeps her hands on her shoulders, closes her eyes and eases her head back, breathes. Frank looks at her. The dusky tangerine sky gives her upturned face a ginger glow, highlights the spray of sun-freckles across her nose.

"We'll find a medical supply store in Grand Junction to get Gram's oxygen tanks refilled," Frank says.

His daughter stands again, clasps her hands and raises them high above her head. She stretches her lean body slowly from one side to the other to release the muscles along her waist and rib cage. She straightens her back and arches backward, lifting her chest to the sky.

"Maybe we should spend a day there," Frank continues. "It'll give us all a chance to recharge a little. Give us a break from driving."

April climbs back in the chair, pulling her legs into the seat with her. *Crisscross applesauce*, the kid inside her still says to herself.

"That would be nice," April responds. "It already feels like we've been on the road for a month."

They sit quietly for a bit, each reflecting on the trip so far. The endless sky deepens to a plummy cabernet. After a few minutes, April twists in her seat to face Frank.

"Did you ever meet Maakade after that day he rescued you in the river?" she asks.

Frank's hands tighten on the armrests. He blinks rapidly. "Gram told you about Maak?"

"Not much," she says. "Only that she visited him at the prison after Denny died."

Frank shifts his weight abruptly from April, as though she had struck him. He brings his thumbnail to his mouth, bites at his cuticle.

For the first time, it dawns on April that Frank and Evelyn not only kept secrets from her, but also from each other. The realization creates a fresh tremor in her already unbalanced emotional state. April silently scolds herself. *That wasn't my secret to share.*

Of course, she has no idea how many secrets are buried, and which ones are hidden from whom. How is she supposed to know what's fair territory to discuss? How could they expect her to know? Besides, she concludes, that's a bell she has already rung.

"Gram also sort of implied, um," April presses on, "well, I think she might have visited him more than once."

Frank nods his head slowly, as the revelation washes over him. The distant mountains evaporate in the darkness as night takes hold. The parking lot and landscape lighting pops and buzzes to life. Frank and April flinch at the sudden glare of light. Then they chuckle, appreciate the disruption of tension. Under the intensity of the spotlights, Frank feels a sudden urge to confess, to tell April his piece of the story.

"I'm not really surprised she never told me that," he says.

He feels the tide of new information wash back out to sea, pictures a shore scattered with the remnants it leaves behind. Jagged traces of shells and debris. Serrated fragments of truth and lies.

"Those years in Bitter Rapids," Frank pauses. "After my brother, you know."

He searches for his thoughts like bits of buried sea glass. "It was rough. I know she blamed me for Denny's death."

April looks away, focuses on the invisible mountains, her teeth clenched. She swallows hard, hoping he will continue, yet questioning whether she truly wants to know more.

"I know she still blames me for a lot of things," he says.

Frank

To be honest, April, I really don't remember much from the weeks after Denny died. It was summer, and normally I would have been riding my bike down to the river to fish or to meet up with the guys to play baseball. Of course, I should have been doing those things with Denny. He tagged along wherever I went.

It's almost like those days and weeks and months never happened. They're just a big black blotch in my memory.

But there's one day I remember perfectly. I went outside with my baseball glove and ball. It was midmorning and there was still dew on the grass. I recall looking down at the toes of my sneakers as they soaked up the dew and turned dark. It made my feet cold. There was still a bite in the air. Mornings are always chilly in northern Minnesota, even in the summer.

I stood in the middle of the yard, just spinning the ball in my palm. The horsehide and stitches felt good against my skin. I plunked the ball into my glove a couple of times. There are few things as satisfying as the sound and feel of a baseball thumping into the palm of your glove. Solid. You know? Leather on leather.

Pretty soon, I was tossing the ball up and catching it behind my back. I was cold. I had to start moving around or go back inside. So, I began throwing the ball higher into the air. I'd watch it rise and crest in the clear blue sky, track it as it came back down and run to catch it.

Everybody thinks Minnesota is only about hockey, but we love our baseball, too. At least we did back in those days. You know, Ted Williams played minor league ball for the Minneapolis Millers back in the '30s, before he went on to the Red Sox. Quite a few Hall of

Famers came up from the Twin Cities farm teams. We even had a girls' team for about a year, during World War II.

Anyway, I was out tossing the ball around in the yard, picturing myself in the outfield at Nicollet Park. After a little bit, I don't know how long, I glanced around and saw my reflection in the kitchen window. I was smiling.

Then I noticed your Gram in the house, watching me from that same window. My God. She looked so wounded. It paralyzed me. When she saw I was looking back at her, she turned away. Her shoulders were shaking. I knew she was crying. I knew she was thinking that Denny should be out there playing catch, too. And he would have, if it wasn't for me.

I went to my room and stuffed my baseball gear under the bed. Never tossed a ball around again.

LIFE IN THE 1940s

HOLLYWOOD, Calif., Nov. 1, 1947

FOR IMMEDIATE RELEASE

/National Newswire/ -- Now showing in theaters across the country, *The Return of Rin Tin Tin*. The most heart-warming picture of them all, with the greatest animal star of all time!

A young war orphan, Paul, distrustful and tormented by nightmares, is placed in the care of a priest at a remote California mission. When a spirited German shepherd named Rin Tin Tin escapes from a cruel owner and finds his way to the mission, the boy and the dog form an instant bond. Paul is crushed when the kennel owner shows up to take the dog away. Later, when a pack of ravenous coyotes attack the man, Rin Tin Tin has a chance to restore the boy's faith in all that is good.

(Source: Eagle-Lion Films)

1952

Bitter Rapids, Minnesota

William R. Marshall Junior High School, being situated in a small town, was a small school. About forty students attended Marshall Junior, in grades seventh through ninth – arguably, the three most awkward, excruciating, and tumultuous of all the grades.

Forty small-town kids. Frankie knew them all. They all knew him, and they all knew little Denny had died after the river accident. Frankie carried the weight of that knowledge like Atlas himself. He lumbered through the school halls, hunched from the burden, eyes cast downward. He ate lunch alone. He pretended not to hear the whispers behind his back.

Denny couldn't swim. Frankie wanted him to die.

I heard Frankie went insane after the accident. His folks only let him out of the house for school.

If you go down to the river at sunset, you can see Denny's decomposing ghost standing on the banks.

Teachers added to the weight, too, in their well-meaning ways.

"I understand what you're going through," the gym coach said when Frankie wandered in after the bell. "But you can't go around feeling sorry for yourself forever. Give me five laps, and pull yourself together, son."

And when Frankie stared out the classroom window during arithmetic, his ancient teacher threw a piece of chalk at his head, scolded him. "I know you had a tough summer, but it's time to quit moping around, and focus on your school work."

The only bright spot was Miss Wallace. She was new to Bitter Rapids, fresh out of Mankato State Teachers College in southern Minnesota, and taught history and English in all three grades. Miss Wallace was smart and idealistic, modern and lovely. The girls at Marshall wanted to be her. The boys wanted to marry her. Like the others, Frankie was fascinated with the young woman's form-fitting pencil skirts and cropped cardigan sweaters, her carnation-pink lipstick and black kitten heels, her hourglass figure and polished fingernails.

He also admired her wide-ranging scope of knowledge, her avant-garde way of teaching. In history class, Miss Wallace's students wrote poems about the Revolutionary War, rather than research papers. She ignored the assigned-reading curriculum in English class and allowed her students to make their own book report selections. While other classes were reading conventional novels like *The Adventures of Huckleberry Finn* and *Little Women*, Miss Wallace's students were testing their boundaries with *Catcher in the Rye* and *The Heart is a Lonely Hunter*. Frankie read Edgar Rice Burroughs' exotic pulp fiction *Tarzan of the Apes*, savoring all the wildness, romance, and adventure typically denied a teenager in the 1950s.

Yet, the thing Frankie liked most about Miss Wallace was her *newness* – a rare and precious small-town gem. To Miss Wallace, he was a clean slate, at least in Frankie's mind. And a fresh start as a whole new person was what Frankie longed for most.

****

"Do you want to tell me what this is?" Art tossed Frankie's first-quarter report card onto the kitchen table.

Frankie didn't bother picking it up. He knew his grades were abysmal. He looked up at his stepfather from his seat at the table.

"It's my report card," he said.

Art shoved the table toward Frankie, pushing him backward in his chair. Frankie's arms flailed as he fought to stay seated and keep the chair from tipping over. Then he set his balled-up fists on his knees.

"Don't wisecrack me, son." Art's tone was measured. It made the hairs on the back of the boy's neck prickle. *I'm not your son,* Frankie thought. Evelyn, standing silently by, reached out and touched Art's forearm for a heartbeat. Art shot her "the look," that one that said it wasn't her place to moderate him, and she removed her hand.

"Tell us why your grades are slipping, sweetheart," Evelyn said.

Frankie kept his eyes cast down. *Maybe because it's impossible to sleep at night next to Denny's empty bed. Maybe because it's impossible to stay awake in class. Maybe because when I close my eyes, even for a minute, I see Denny's little body whirling under icy water, over jagged rocks, into a million tiny bubbles of darkness. Maybe because nothing matters anymore.*

"I don't know," Frankie mumbled.

"You don't know," Art repeated the boy's words in a slow, flat tone. He crossed his arms and glared. "Well, I know. It's because you're not applying yourself, and that changes right now. You're to come straight home after school every day to do your homework and study until dinner. You'll wash the dinner dishes every night, and then go back to studying until bedtime."

Evelyn twisted her apron in her hands, waited for Art to say more. There was always more.

"And you'll be shoveling the drive every day, or mowing the yard every week, depending on how long it takes you to get your act together," Art continued. "If we don't see some improvement soon, in your grades *and* your attitude, there'll be more consequences. Understood?"

"Yes, sir," Frankie said.

Evelyn spoke up. "Go to your room now, and get started on your homework."

Frankie stood, pushed in his chair, and walked to his room in the hunched posture he'd perfected over the years.

"You always take his side," Frankie muttered at his mother, once he was safely out of earshot of the adults.

"I suppose you think I'm being too hard on him," Art said, directing his attention to his wife. "But you were too soft on him, Evelyn, while Frank was off fighting the war. You spoiled that boy."

Art stepped closer and placed his hands on her shoulders. She forced herself to look up at him, to look him in the eyes.

"It's not your fault," he continued. "A woman can't be expected to raise a boy on her own. And it's not too late to fix him. It just requires discipline. The kind of discipline only a man knows how to deliver. You understand that."

Evelyn acknowledged him with a nod. She wanted to thrust her knee into his groin, and tell him he'd be wise to stop underestimating her as a mother, as a woman. Or, she wanted to lean into him, to weep into his chest, to feel his arms around her. She did neither. Instead, she reached up to straighten his necktie.

"Thank you, Art. I don't know where we'd be without you."

She stood on her tiptoes to give him a kiss. Art leaned forward a bit and turned his head to the side. Evelyn slipped her hand behind his neck and let her moist lips linger on his cheek. She wondered if, maybe this time, her acquiescence might coax him into an embrace.

Art stepped back. He removed her hand from his neck and patted it.

"That's my girl," he said.

Art retreated to the dining room and fixed himself a Black Russian – a handful of ice cubes, three glugs of vodka, a dribble of coffee liqueur. Precisely the same, every night. Evelyn remained in the kitchen and checked on dinner in the oven – test the potatoes for tenderness, ladle drippings over the meat, add a sprinkle of pepper. The same, every night.

LIFE IN THE 1990S

GRAND JUNCTION, Colo., Aug. 5, 1990

FOR IMMEDIATE RELEASE

/National Newswire/ -- Grand Junction Community College (GJCC) has added an Environmental Restoration Degree. The new program centers on strategies for environmental damage remediation and improved natural resources management.

In 1943, the U.S. War Department purchased land in Grand Junction, Colorado, for a uranium oxide refinery to the Manhattan Project, an endeavor during World War II that produced the first nuclear weapons. Activities continued there until 1971, during which time radioactive materials were stored or disposed of on-site.

The primary goal of the new GJCC degree program is to offset a substantial shortage of scientists and engineers needed for environmental restoration at these sites.

(Source: International Nuclear Information System)

September 1990

Interstate-70, Central Colorado

Tuning the car radio is impossible in the mountain ranges of central Colorado. Frank turns off the static. The grim scars of mining operations past and present add to the void. Decapitated peaks. Stained plateaus. Sterile valleys. Frank is desperate to fill the ugly emptiness with something other than his buried memories and his mother's maudlin stories. He snaps his fingers a few times and reaches toward the back where April is tucked in cross-legged.

"Hand me a tape," he says. "Something from Cream. Or Yardbirds."

April makes a gagging sound. She opens the flap on the faux-leather box that holds their music. She runs her finger across the spines of the plastic cassette cases.

"Sorry, but I cannot stomach any of your old dude music right now," she says. "Here, pop this in."

April hands a tape forward, and Gram intercepts it.

"You want an old woman on her last breath to listen to something called Megadeth?" she says and thrusts the cassette back at her granddaughter. "I don't think so."

"Fine," April says.

"Can't we just talk for a while?" Gram asks.

Now it's Frank's turn to make a gagging sound. "I need music. For the love of God, April, give me a tape."

April looks back at the line-up of cassettes. "Ozzy?"

"A man who bites the heads off birds," Gram grimaces. "Do you have any Carpenters?"

"The point of music is to keep me awake while I'm driving," Frank says.

"Madonna?" April asks.

Gram says that sounds wholesome.

"I'll give you a hundred dollars right now if you even *have* Madonna in that case," Frank belts out.

Father and daughter are laughing now.

Gram folds her arms across her chest and harrumphs. Listen to whatever you want, she mutters.

"Sorry. Sorry," April says. She clears her throat to stifle her laughter. She runs the tips of her ring-fingers below her eyelashes, to whisk away the gathering tears and keep her thick black liner from running down her cheeks. Then she passes forward another option.

"Billy Joel's greatest hits?" Frank angles the case in Gram's direction. She takes it from him, removes the cassette and slips it into the dashboard tape-player.

Frank fingers the opening notes of "Piano Man" on the steering wheel. April joins in from the back seat with her best harmonica pantomime. When Joel croons, "It's nine o'clock on a Saturday," he's joined by the Parson family. And then – all the way through "Captain Jack" and "New York State of Mind," and "The Stranger" and "Only the Good Die Young" – three generations sing and drum and boogie in their seats, and forget all about the purpose of their road trip for fifty-three of Billy Joel's greatest minutes.

＊＊＊＊

Frank and April sit outside the hotel now that Gram is asleep. It beats being cooped up in the car, or in a tiny room.

"So, I guess this is becoming our thing, huh?" April says.

"Guess so," Frank replies.

April pulls the hood of her navy-colored sweatshirt over her head. BRONCOS is emblazoned in orange across its chest.

She bought the sweatshirt at the Longs Drug across from the hotel where they are staying in Denver. It was drizzling when they arrived just after dinner time. The temperature on the digital bank building sign read sixty degrees. She knew the temperature in Phoenix at that moment was probably thirty degrees warmer. She also knew that by morning, the Denver temperature would likely be in the forties.

"I can't believe how cold it is right now," she says and pulls her feet up onto the chair seat. She tucks her knees up into the sweatshirt, stuffs her hands in the front pouch. Only her face and tennis shoes peek out from the blue blob into which she has morphed.

Her dad laughs, tells her, "Just wait."

"You know that Mark Twain quote?" Frank continues. "He said something like, 'The coldest winter I ever spent was a summer in San Francisco.' Well, I guarantee you that means he never spent time in northern Minnesota."

He laughs again.

"That's a pretty maniacal laugh," April remarks. She makes a mental note to go shopping tomorrow. She packed all wrong for their trip, she realizes. *I need sweatpants*, she thinks. *And socks. Thick socks.*

Frank breathes in the crisp air, becomes aware of the brisk wind ruffling his hair. It surprises him to realize he's actually enjoying the chill, that he's almost looking forward to feeling the burn of frigid Minnesota oxygen in his lungs again.

"I think this trip was a good idea," April says after a little time has passed. "Even though I have no idea what to expect when we get to Minnesota, and that scares the crap out of me, this is kind of nice, spending time with you guys, sort of like a vacation."

Frank raises his eyebrows and bobbles his head.

"Not that either one of us would know what a vacation is," she adds. There's no inflection in her voice.

Frank looks at his daughter. Her poker-face is trained on the city lights. He'd always meant to take her places when she was growing up. He'd imagined her in water wings, dipping her tiny toes into the ocean. And, wouldn't her face have lit up walking down Main Street in Disneyland, while an old-timey barbershop quartet serenaded her with "Let Me Call You Sweetheart." But they'd never even made it to the Grand Canyon, only a half-day's drive from home.

"It's hard to take vacations when you're raising a kid alone," he says, more to himself than to her, and looks back up to the sky.

The young woman looks over at her dad. The wind lifts his hair, and she sees graying at his temples. *When did Dad's hair start turning gray?* She can't even fathom how hard it must have been for him raising a daughter by himself. It's a wonder his whole head of hair wasn't stone white by now. Still, she isn't able to entirely let him off the hook for his parenting lapses.

"I don't really care that we never took vacations, Dad. But I *am* still pissed that you kept so many secrets from me."

Frank drums his fingers on the chair's arm.

"Are you still a virgin?" he asks without looking at her.

"What, what?" April sputters, part hysterical and part horrified.

"You don't have to answer that," he says quickly. "I don't *want* you to answer that."

The young woman shakes her head, while she continues to scoff and sputter. "What the hell, Dad."

He lets the rhetorical question hang in the air for a moment.

"Look, I only said that to make a point," he finally says. "Everyone has secrets, April. Even people who love and care about each other don't always tell each other everything. There are a million things that don't necessarily come up in normal conversation between a father and daughter."

April breathes deeply to settle the marching band playing in her stomach and rib cage.

"Yeah, I get that," she says. "And when it comes to our sex lives, I totally get that."

They each grimace and avert their eyes as if to codify an agreement, on this point if nothing else.

"But when it comes to you telling me you had a little brother who died when you were young? Or that you used to love to play baseball?" She looks at him in earnest, reaches over and gently grips his forearm. "Those are things a father should share with his kid."

Frank sighs, continues to look away. He reaches across his midriff and pats her slender hand, once, twice. He breathes in a stuttered breath, exhales noisily.

"Ask me something," he says after another wordless moment passes between them. He wonders if his terror is obvious, if April can hear it in his voice. "About my childhood. Or, whatever."

April pulls her head back with a little jerk of surprise and smiles sweetly. Her mind is awash with questions she's been dying to ask for weeks. *Did you ever meet Maak?* He still hadn't answered that question, after all. *And who the hell is the dead guy, for heaven's sake?* She slips her hand away from his arm and strokes her chin with her forefinger and thumb.

"Hmm," she teases, trying to ease the mood, trying to buy a little time to think of the right question. She knows better than to launch into one of those heavy subjects just yet. But what might get him to really open up?

Frank squirms in the plastic lawn chair. "The timer on this offer is about to expire, little girl."

"Okay, okay, sorry!" She makes a frog-face, the one she always makes, with her tongue sticking out, when she's flustered. Frank laughs.

"I've got it." She clasps her hands together in front of her heart, then releases them and stretches out her arms, wiggles her fingers like she's drying her nail polish. "Did you have a best friend growing up?"

Frank's jaw tightens and his chin drops. A best friend? Memories come to mind of April and her tight little circle of friends – the roller skating and sleepovers, the long days at the mall and double-dates. Frank never had any of that. His little brother had been his best friend. After Denny died, Frank was mostly alone. Then the second accident at the river happened, and they had to flee Bitter Rapids. How does a kid make friends after that?

As much as Frank wants to share all that with his daughter now, he just can't bring himself to say it out loud. He silently curses himself. *Damned coward.*

He reflects a moment longer, and a brightness returns to his eyes. Then a smile. "Yes, I had a best friend. His name was Scout."

Frank

We got Scout about a year after Denny died. He was the most handsome German shepherd you'd ever see, April. *The Adventures of Rin Tin Tin* was all the rage on TV, and I guess people everywhere were snapping up German shepherd pups. But I'd loved German shepherds ever since mom took us to see *The Return of Rin Tin Tin* at the theater. That was maybe a year or two after my dad was killed in the war, and I suppose I could relate to the kid in the movie and the bond he had with Rinty. That's what we kids called him. Rinty.

Man, Scout was special. He was my best friend for eleven years. Hell, probably even still.

I remember coming home from school one day with my report card. It had been a rough year all around, and my grades were terrible. I'd been failing most of my classes, and Art was beside himself, really cracking down on me. By spring, I had gotten the grades up to mostly Cs, maybe an A in gym, and I hoped that would be improvement enough to get him off my back.

He looked at the report card and showed it to my mom. Then he set it down on the kitchen table. Neither one of them said a word. I couldn't read their faces. Then Art told me to go out to the garage with him, and I nearly vomited.

The garage was where Art "taught me the importance of discipline," which meant that's where he beat my butt. Even now, just thinking about him removing his belt and telling me to drop my pants makes me break out in a cold sweat.

That's why I never raised a hand to you, April.

Hitting a kid like that doesn't teach him a darn thing except fear, and maybe deceit. I spent a lot of my youth plotting and making up lies to avoid a strapping from that man. And I never wanted you to feel that way, to become that kind of person. I never wanted you to be afraid of me…

Anyway.

That day, Art led the way to the garage, and Mom came with us, which was strange. She always stayed in the house when he was handing out discipline. But I knew she was pretty disappointed in my grades. So, I figured, well, I don't know what I figured.

I opened the side door to the garage, and that's when I saw Scout. When he saw us, that pup ran right to me, like he knew I was his and he was mine, even before I knew. I got down on the ground and he jumped all over me. He was all ears and feet!

Mom said it was Art's idea. That having a dog to take care of would teach me responsibility. She said I could name him, and I immediately said Scout. I'm not sure how the name came to me. It just seemed to fit.

He was mine to raise and train and protect. He taught me a lot, too, when I think back on it. About courage and loyalty, and about what it means to be a good person.

Scout was never on a leash. He knew to stay by my side when we went out, and he always came when I called him. Even if he took off after a raccoon or something, all I had to do was call him. He would freeze in his tracks, turn and run full speed back to me.

Boy, was he smart. And strong. He weighed probably eighty-five pounds by the time he was full grown, all muscle. He could climb a tree! He'd run at it full speed, low and fast like a Ferrari, scuttle up the trunk to a big, low branch. He'd stand watch for me coming up the road after school. Soon as I'd round the corner, he'd barrel back down and sprint the half-mile to meet me. His tongue would hang out the side of his mouth as he pranced along beside me, looking up at me with his big brown eyes.

He was the happiest darn dog. Happy just to *be* with me. When I think back on it, I wonder if he could sense how much I really needed that. You know? That sort of unconditional devotion only an animal can give you. It's like he gave me permission to be a kid again, to be happy again.

Scout saved my life, in more ways than one.

1990

Denver, Colorado

Navigating morning traffic is nothing new to Frank, and rush hour in the Mile High City isn't as heavy as in Phoenix. Still, he doesn't know the streets and highways here. He isn't accustomed to Denver's brand of roadway etiquette. While April, as navigator, fumbles with the atlas, Frank white-knuckles through lane changes and merging commuters.

"You need to get onto I-25 north in a couple miles," April says. "Then stay to the right, and take exit 216-A/B to merge onto I-76 east."

They'd taken an extra day to rest in Grand Junction, and then another in Denver. They'd all needed it. Now they felt recharged, relieved to be back on the road, anxious to get the trip back underway.

"The 25 to 216 to the 76," says Frank. "Got it."

April closes the giant book of maps, keeping a finger tucked between the Colorado pages, just in case.

They silently continue on, while traffic hums around them – mostly boxy Jeep Cherokees and Dodge minivans, along with all makes and models of pick-up trucks. Billowy pewter clouds overhead cast shifting shadows onto the highway pavement and grass-covered berms. Jagged mountains loom in the distance, the color of lavender and lapis, capped with snow.

April points toward the exit when she sees it coming up. Frank navigates to the right lane, merges onto Interstate 76 going east. Most of the traffic now is heading west, toward Denver. It occurs to Frank that, throughout their trip so far, they almost always seem to be going the opposite direction as the rest of the world. He worries about what that means.

The scenery whooshing by shifts to sprawling grassland, as the Corolla makes a gradual descent in elevation toward Nebraska. They have the road to themselves. Gram's head bobs as the long road hypnotizes her.

April cracks her window an inch or so, letting a gust of earthy, dry-grass perfume into the car. In her peripheral view, she notices Frank inhaling deeply, imbibing the heady fragrance. She rolls the window down all the way and stretches her neck to feel the wind on her face, like a dog that's been pent up too long. She lets her mind float with the powerful scent to a long-buried memory.

It's December 1, 1979, and she's sitting on the back patio with Dad after school. She's eight years old. It had rained all morning, and now the sky is clear and the Phoenix sun is warming the dormant Bermuda in the yard. Steam rises from the fawn-colored grass, only about an inch high, maybe two. But April thinks about the tiny red ants that live in the dirt beneath the Oleander bushes along the chain-link fence. To them, it must look as if the entire world is blanketed in thick, ominous fog. To them, it must look as if the world is coming to an end.

That's when April hears Dad say, *Mom is going away for a while.* She got a job offer in California, a once-in-a-lifetime opportunity. It'll be great for her. *How long will she be gone?* April asks. Dad doesn't know. *But we'll get along fine, just the two of us, until she comes back.*

But they don't get along fine, just the two of them. Dad doesn't sleep. April cries when she wakes up in the morning, and Mom is still gone. After a few months, Gram moves in, sleeps in the third bedroom, the one Mom and Dad said would be the baby's room, when April would become a big sister some day.

They do get along, after a while, the three of them. But they're never fine. April never becomes a big sister. Mom never comes home.

April watches the Nebraska prairie swish by as their car speeds down the interstate. She spots a mule deer far in the distance, standing amidst the vast expanse of shortgrass and sagebrush. The animal holds its head high, alert, searching perhaps. It's alone. April's chest constricts. The sharp air attacks her hair, making it whip and coil about her head like Medusa's snakes. She pulls herself from the open window, turns the crank to close it up tight. She sweeps her hair from her face and into a ponytail, trying to sweep the memories away with it.

She glances toward the back seat and sees that Gram is now awake.

"So, what's the story on the quilt?" April asks.

"Oh, for cripes' sake," Frank mutters.

Gram shifts in her seat, scoots her butt forward to get closer to April, looks out the windshield at the road ahead. She places her hands on the seat-backs to steady herself. She's smiling.

"My mother-in-law made it as a wedding gift," Gram says. "It was exquisite. We put it on our bed, of course, and there it stayed through our whole marriage, through Frank's service overseas, and after he died. She was a talented quilter. A lovely woman."

Gram pauses to reflect. Mother Parson had been the antithesis of Evelyn's biological mother. From the way she doted on her grandbabies to how she'd magically appear on the doorstep with a hot dish in hand when Evelyn needed it most. *How different life could have been.*

"She died in her sleep. The doctors said it was an aneurysm," Gram continues. "Frank was fighting somewhere in France at the time. I had to tell him in a letter."

April clicks her tongue and draws up her face in dismay. She shifts a little to see her grandmother, puts her hand on top of Gram's and strokes the soft, spotted skin with her thumb.

"After I married Art, he wanted me to get rid of the quilt," Gram says. "I understood why he wouldn't want it on my bed, of course. But he wouldn't even let me pack it away in the cedar chest. It made no sense. It was a family heirloom, after all, something I had hoped to pass on to my boys one day."

Gram pauses again. April glances at her dad. His eyes are trained on the road, his hands set on the wheel. She notices the little knot in his cheek that bulges when he clenches his jaw.

April casts her eyes down, studies the letters on the gear shift, waits for Gram to collect her thoughts.

"I convinced him it would be wasteful to discard a quilt in such good condition," Gram continues. "He finally agreed we could keep it in the trunk of the car, for emergencies."

"Oh, the irony," Frank chimes in under his breath.

Gram ignores him, presses on.

"When Art worked at his office in town, he'd sometimes leave the car with me so I could do the shopping and run errands," she directs her story to April. "What he didn't know is that I used to take the boys out for picnics by the river in Superior. That's the national forest outside of Bitter Rapids.

"I'd pack cold fried chicken and milk and cookies, and I'd find a nice spot in the sun. Then we'd spread out the quilt and eat and then lie back and watch the clouds drift overhead. Your dad would tell me what the clouds looked like to him - dragons, castles, marching armies - and make up silly little stories to go along with them. Remember, Frankie? Remember those picnics?"

Frank smiles a little, biting his lip and blinking rapidly. He whispers, "Yeah, Mom. I remember."

"Lord, how I wish I still had that quilt," Gram says.

The forlorn statement makes Gram sound a hundred years old to April, instead of seventy. It causes a sudden tightness in the young woman's chest. She begins to wonder if her dad was right after all, about taking this trip and dredging up "ancient history." Is confronting the past worth the pain it brings? Or is it better to leave the past behind you and never look back?

The Pawnee Buttes emerge in the distance, as if in answer to her question, beyond gently rolling hills and windswept grassland.

The ancient sandstone mesas rise from the flat clearing like stacks of multicolored building blocks, constructed by God himself. A gathering of pronghorn antelope meander near a stand of cottonwood and elms. Windmills dot the landscape. Some are sleek, modern structures with electric generators. Others are old-timey, weather-worn contraptions that have pumped water for countless generations of cattle. Man's past and present co-existing with buttes carved out eons ago.

A sign along the highway tells of a public camping area and the Pawnee Pioneer Trail up ahead.

"This looks like a nice place to take a break and explore," April says, pointing, and Frank navigates the car toward the next exit.

LIFE IN THE 1950S

Every Woman's Standard Medical Guide

The Graystone Press, 1948

CHAPTER 10 – MARRIED LOVE, BY GLADYS HOAGLAND GROVES, A.B.

Every wife should expect and value criticism from her husband. If he is to feel that she cannot stand being criticized, they will never be able to be quite free with one another. If he has to keep bottled up within himself the things he wants to say to her, for fear she will have her feelings hurt too badly, they cannot be on a genuinely frank footing together. It also denies the one who needs criticism the opportunity for improvement.

1953

Bitter Rapids, Minnesota

Scout couldn't resist the sound of laughter coming from the kitchen. The dog trotted in from the living room and greeted each of the women gathered around the table with a tail wag and an arm nudge.

It was Evelyn's turn to host what Art called the "weekly fishwives convention." She told him the women met to discuss and coordinate their various volunteer activities – knitting hats and scarves for soldiers fighting in Korea, making cookies for the school bake sale, and the like. Sure, there was also a fair dose of gossip and catty talk, but he didn't need to know that.

Ginny, Fran, Mary, and Dottie sat around the kitchen table smoking cigarettes and drinking coffee. They shared an ashtray in the center of the table. Evelyn stood by the sink peeling potatoes and carrots to go with the evening's chuck roast. A cigarette dangled from her lips as she worked.

"Remember to bring all your knitting to my house next week, girls," Dottie said. "I'll pack them up and drop the box at the post office."

Mary cocked her head to the side and raised an eyebrow. She stared unblinking at the ash growing on the tip of her slim cigarette. "Seems like yesterday we were knitting for our boys fighting the Nazis."

The women had been friends since grade school. This was their second war together.

"Seems like yesterday we were in home economics class learning *how* to knit," Ginny said.

After making his rounds, Scout stopped at Fran's spot and laid his head in her lap. His tail fanned the air with helicopter swirls. She stroked his head, flattening his ears with each stroke.

"Isn't he the sweetest," Fran said, her expression soft from the adoration of Scout's amber eyes. "It's as if he knows."

Evelyn glanced back over her shoulder at them for a moment, then turned back to her potatoes. "Knows what?"

Dottie shot Fran a stern look. Silence clung to the cloud of smoke in the air. Evelyn set down the potato she was peeling and wiped her hands on her apron. She walked to the kitchen table and tapped her cigarette into the ashtray.

"Knows what, Frannie?"

Fran was overcome with an elated grin. "I'm expecting."

"We weren't sure if we should talk about it with you, because," Mary spoke fast, but then her voice trailed off and the group was silent again.

"I've told you girls, I'm holding up fine," Evelyn said. "News of a baby is a blessed thing. Don't hold back talking about it because of what happened to Denny."

Ginny took a final drag and stumped her cigarette out in the ashtray. "That's not why we were afraid to talk about it, Evie."

Now it was Ginny's turn to receive a stern look from Dottie.

"What's on your mind, girls?" Evelyn asked. "Spill it."

"It's just that," Dottie said, then paused. She ventured into the explanation like she was stepping onto lake ice in early spring, pretty sure it wasn't a smart idea. "You used to talk about wanting another baby, but you haven't had any news. We thought maybe there was a problem. So, we didn't want to talk about it, in case you aren't, well, if you can't."

"Ah," Evelyn said. She smiled and made her way around the table to give each friend a hug. "You're all so dear. Let me put your minds at ease. There's no problem. Art and I just decided not to have children."

Art and Evelyn had decided nothing. They'd never talked about more children, one way or the other. But it was damn hard making a baby without making love. They'd consummated the marriage on their wedding night, a requisite legality, and Art had hardly touched her since.

Dottie took a slow drink of her coffee, eyes narrowed, and studied her friend. The others seemed satisfied with Evelyn's answer. Talk of babies was no longer taboo, and they returned to it with gusto. Mary asked Fran if she'd been having morning sickness. Ginny offered up remedies that had helped her through those times. The conversation was cheerful. Laughter once again filled the kitchen.

Evelyn went back to the sink and her meal preparations. Her mind was still on Art. She thought about the life they shared, which was not the life she'd wanted or expected to have. Their marriage had been a business agreement, more than anything else.

Art hadn't gone off to war like Frank and so many others from the small town, because childhood polio had left him with permanent muscle atrophy and a slight limp. Bachelor life suited him well enough, but people had started to gossip. It began hurting the business. Marrying the young war widow gave him an instant family, his own way to serve his country. People respected him for it.

She told herself not to judge him. Lord knows, she'd needed a husband and a provider. And he did care about her. She believed that. She cared about him, too. They were friends.

Evelyn placed the peeled and chopped vegetables in a pot of water to set until dinner. Outside the kitchen window, afternoon sunlight made the snow drifts sparkle. She thought about the first time Frank had walked her home from school, how he'd dropped to the ground and made her a snow angel. He had always made grand, whimsical gestures like that. Remembering it made her heart skip and her stomach flutter, just like they had back then.

You're not a kid anymore, she scolded herself. What good were skips and flutters to her now? Frank was dead. She should be grateful to have someone who kept food on the table and a roof over her head. Passion was a luxury few could afford. These were the things she told herself, again and again.

"Time to go potty." Mary had twin boys and a girl, all younger than five years old. Her conversation often reverted to child-talk regardless of the company. She walked through the living room on her way to the bathroom and shrieked. "Evie, you better get in here! There's been a massacre."

"What on earth?" Evelyn said.

The women darted into the living room and witnessed the carnage – fluff and fabric shreds littered the floor. Art's favorite slippers had been murdered.

"Scout!" Evelyn bellowed. She dropped to her knees to collect the debris. The dog slinked into the room, head low, ears back, tail tucked between his legs. She shook a fistful of fluff at him. "Did you do this? Did you?"

Ginny placed her hand over her mouth to stifle a laugh.

"Who else would have done it?" Mary asked, snickering. "How many does that make anyhow?"

"Four pair," Evelyn answered, her lips pinched together. "Not to mention a fedora, a pair of leather work shoes and who-knows-how-many socks."

The women couldn't hold back any longer. They exploded with laughter, and Dottie gave Scout a stealth scratch behind the ears. Evelyn told them it wasn't funny and threw the fluff back onto the rug.

"It makes no sense," she said, and crossed her arms over her chest. "He's such a smart dog. Frankie's taught him so many tricks. He comes when I call, and he chases off the raccoons. But he destroys Art's things when we're not looking. Always Art's things. I can't seem to break him of it."

Mary helped Evelyn to her feet and offered to drive her to the store to buy another pair of slippers before Art got home. Fran and Ginny scrambled about the floor to recover and dispose of the evidence.

Dottie just watched. She took a drag of her cigarette and exhaled slowly. Then she mumbled under her breath, "You said it yourself, Evie. He's a smart dog."

★ ★ ★ ★

Maak lay on his back, his hands folded behind his head, his eyes trained on the small rectangle of graphite sky visible in his prison cell window. Thanks to the freshly-baked chocolate chips cookies Evelyn had brought during her last visit, Maak had been able to trade with his cellmate for the top bunk and their only view of the outside world – a sheet of dirty glass the size of a breadbox near the ceiling, above the piss-covered commode and rust-stained sink.

He watched the sleet fall diagonally past the window and tried to remember the feel of ice-cold air in his lungs, the smell of white pine smoldering in his campfire. The hardest part of his confinement was not the lack of freedom or the brutality of the men around him. It was the separation from *Kitche Manitou's* creation – sun, stars, moon, earth. The old men and old women of his Ojibwe people had told him the stories when he was a boy, the stories of the Great Spirit.

Kitche Manitou beheld a vision and knew in His great wisdom it was a vision to be fulfilled, they said. *Out of nothing, He created rock, water, fire, and wind. And into each one He breathed life, a different power and essence, its own soul-spirit. From these He created the physical world of sun, stars, moon, earth.*

Maak had heard the stories told many times, in many voices. The stories that had been told for generations. In his life, there had been no one to whom he could pass on the stories. No young siblings. No children. Still, he had been connected to the Creation.

And then, a fight, a flash of rage, a choice. And then, an arrest, a dispersal of judgment, a cell.

The men had twenty-minute calisthenics in the prison yard twice a week during the bitter cold. They were sent out to work in the warmer months. Old forest roads. Nearby farms. Quarries. It wasn't enough to sustain the connection. Maak was seventeen years into a twenty-five-year sentence. He was a bear forced into extended hibernation, while ripe blueberries fell to the ground just out of his reach.

Until that day at the river, the boys in the canoe, the woman in the smooth-linen dress and blueberry-colored hat. After several visits, after small talk was exhausted, Maak had told Evelyn about the Creation in the same way his elders had told him.

To the sun, Kitche Manitou gave the powers of light and heat.
To the earth, He gave growth and healing.
To the waters, purity and renewal.
To the wind, music and the breath of life itself.

The guard had laughed. Evelyn gave him a stern look, told him their discussion was none of his concern.

Maak had continued, emboldened. He told Evelyn how he missed them – the sun, the earth, the waters, the wind – in the way she missed Denny. He told her their absence created a fissure in his heart. Evelyn listened, and tears cascaded down her cheeks. Maak wondered if the tears were for his loss or for hers, but he did not ask. He could not remember a time when someone had wept for him in that way. He wanted to believe she was the first.

The sleet blowing outside the window reminded Maak of that day. He closed his eyes and saw her tears. *Purity and renewal.*

Tucked between his bunk and the wall was the copy of *Walden* that Evelyn gave him months before. Borrowed books from the library had become part of her regular visits. This book was different. She had bought it with savings from her weekly grocery allowance.

It's for you to keep, she had told Maak, *to read whenever you need balm.* It was a flourishing blueberry bush, planted between his bunk and the wall. It was his connection to the Creation. Evelyn understood. He believed she was the first.

1990

Gothenburg, Nebraska

A highway sign declares the town of Gothenburg is the last stop for services for fifty miles. The group takes the next exit and takes in the sights. In addition to "services," the small town is apparently home to both the Sod House Museum and the Pony Express Station and Museum.

"O-fer cute," Gram exclaims, while they navigate the tranquil tree-lined streets.

Frank smiles. His mother never did completely lose her Minnesotan accent or unusual expressions. He notices it even more now that they've embarked on this trip.

April marvels at the expansive shamrock lawns stretching from the road to quaint two-story farmhouses painted yellow and white and blue, with redbrick porches and jutting dormers, colorful shutters and neat trim. It *is* cute, she thinks. Such a stark contrast to her familiar Phoenix neighborhoods, with their gravelly yards and block-wall fences, the boxy ranch-style homes with flat roofs, painted a dozen shades of tan.

Frank pulls into a dirt lot adjacent to Ehmen City Park, where they spot the weathered log-cabin structure of the Pony Express station. They exit the car and perform their now-familiar drill of back stretching, knee popping, and bathroom searching. Gram declares it's too windy and heads for the museum entrance.

"I love the wind," April says, turning her face into it, her long hair whirling and fluttering behind her.

Father and daughter decide to take advantage of the fresh air. They meander along the crisscross sidewalks of the square-block park, heading toward the circular stone fountain that anchors the center. A chilly breeze sweeps across the grass and through the trees, sending autumn leaves fluttering onto the ground and into the fountain. They pause to watch the crimson and gold leaves bob on the surface of the glittering water.

"Do you ever feel *insignificant?*" April speaks up after a little while. She twists her hair into a bun and pulls the sweatshirt hood up over her head.

"Insignificant?" Frank asks. He turns to look at his daughter.

"Yeah, like, in the grand scheme of things."

Frank raises his eyebrows, thinks for a moment.

"No. I did when I was a kid, I guess, but not anymore," he says. "Not since *you* were born."

April places her hand over her heart and faces him. "Aw, Dad. That's really sweet. And a little corny. But mostly sweet."

Frank chuckles. "Well, either way, it's the truth."

They return to reflection as they move through the park. After a bit, Frank's eyebrows draw together. "Do *you* feel insignificant?"

"Nope," April says, drawing her lips together into a pucker, shaking her head. "Not in the least."

Frank tilts his head back and laughs out loud.

"I didn't think so," he says. "You've always been the biggest presence in any room, kiddo, even when you were a baby."

April chuckles. She can't disagree.

"So, what made you ask me that?" Frank prods.

"Gram," April says. "We were admiring all the huge canyons back in Utah, and she said it reminded her how insignificant she feels, like a 'tiny speck' in the world."

Frank exhales loudly. "That's a shame."

"And then she said I'd feel the same way, too, someday," April adds.

Her father clicks his tongue against the backside of his teeth. He wishes his mother's cynical declaration surprised him.

"All I can say to that is, well, your Gram isn't the best person to take life advice from," Frank says.

"No?"

"No," he confirms. "Look, I love my mom. She's worked hard her whole life, always tried to do right by me. I never had to worry if I'd have a roof over my head or food on the table. But...."

Frank pauses, struggles to find the right words. Honest words. Fair words.

"Remember when we talked about your mom the other day, and I said some people just aren't cut out for parenthood? Well, your Gram is one of those people, too," he continues. He pauses again, and then scoffs. "Guess that makes me a walking cliché. I married my mother, and I just now realized it. For cripes' sake. How pathetic is that?"

A familiar sting comes to April's eyes. How many times has she lamented that her mom was not there for her? All the times April needed to talk. All the times April needed to cry. All the times April needed to feel her mother's approval, her mother's understanding.

And now, she learns her dad has felt the same way about Gram? It had never occurred to her that a mother could be physically present in your life, and yet still not *be there,* still not give you what you most need. April swallows hard and blinks. She turns her face away, so Frank won't see the tear rolling down her cheek.

"Anyway, I digress," Frank clears his throat. "I guess the point I'm trying to make is, you get to choose."

She tilts her head to dry her cheek on the shoulder of her sweatshirt, then asks him, "Choose what?"

"Whether you feel insignificant or not. It's not a foregone conclusion that you grow old and have regrets and feel like your life doesn't matter," Frank says. "Over time, you can learn that, well, even though you can't control what other people do or what happens in life, you *can* control how you respond."

April mulls over her dad's words. *When did he get so smart and philosophical?* she wonders.

A tree swallow bobs on the wind currents and glides to landing in a nearby maple. Its iridescent blue feathers and white breast remind April of the happy cartoon birds in the old Disney *Snow White* movie. She watches it hop along the branches among the bright yellow leaves. In that moment, she chooses happiness.

April points, and says "O-fer cute!" in her best Minnesotan accent.

"For sure!" Frank says, and laughs.

* * * *

They pile back into the Corolla, as Evelyn chatters about the Pony Express and the Old West. The museum was interesting, she says, but she didn't care for the way they portrayed the Native Americans.

"I realize there was a lot of animosity in those days," Gram says. "Sure, it was dangerous for the pony riders, always a risk of getting attacked by Indians. But still..."

She shakes her head and scrunches her face in frustration. She waves her hand in the air, motioning back toward the museum. "That place made it seem like the Native people were all blood-thirsty savages. It makes me so mad."

April shrugs. Despite growing up in Arizona, she couldn't recall any of her school teachers going into any great detail about the Native Americans. She remembered that Christopher Columbus called them Indians because he mistakenly believed he'd landed in India. She knew a little about the Indian boarding schools and the forced assimilation to Euro-American culture. Other than that, April's only education about Native American life was the Old Western movies that played on the television Saturday mornings, the ones with Asian actors dressed as Indians in fringed vests who shot arrows at cowboys on horseback.

"What about the Indians who helped the pilgrims survive their first winters in the New World?" Gram asks. "And the first Thanksgiving?"

Aprils shakes her head and laughs. "I don't know, Gram. I think somebody just made all that up to create another holiday."

Frank chuckles.

"Don't laugh, Frankie. You know better," Gram says. "Don't you remember that poem you wrote for history class about the first Thanksgiving? It was for that teacher you liked so much in junior high. What was her name?"

"A poem? That I wrote in junior high?" A flush creeps across Frank's cheeks and lights up his ears. "Of all the things seared in my memory from back then, and you're asking me about a stupid poem. No, Mom, I don't remember."

April glances at Gram through the rearview mirror. The old woman looks as though she's been struck. She pinches her lips together and lifts her chin. April notices droplets glistening in Gram's pale eyelashes.

"Well, I thought it was good," Gram retorts. "I had all my friends read it."

Frank's nostrils flare, and he breathes noisily in and out.

"Can't we just drive and take in the scenery?" His tone is an octave lower. "Do we have to reminisce every darn minute?"

April draws her eyes from Evelyn's face and scans the landscape of flat, expansive grassland. She glances at her wristwatch. It'll be at least an hour until the next pit stop. An eternity.

"I spy, with my little eye, something orange," April says.

"No," Frank says. He shakes his head vigorously. "Not 'I Spy.'"

April slouches in her seat a little. The car hurtles down the highway; the wind whistles through its loose joints and sun-rotted weather stripping. From the back seat, Gram rears back her arm, punches Frank in the shoulder, and shouts, "Slug bug!"

"Hey!" he shouts back, and April explodes with laughter, as they zoom past a Volkswagen on the highway pull-off.

Frank grumbles under his breath. He adjusts his hands on the steering wheel, wiggles his fingers. April sniggers inaudibly, her shoulders shaking up and down. In the distance, far ahead, Frank spots another Volkswagen, bright yellow, heading their way. His shoulder still tingles from Mom's light punch. He knows April carries a more powerful wallop.

"I spy something green," he says flatly, eyeing a highway sign in the distance, deciding it's a reasonable concession. April and Gram take turns guessing, and the mile-markers flash past their windows.

Finally, they spot the much-anticipated truck stop, halfway between Gothenburg and Kearney. Frank pulls into the lot and up to one of the pumps.

"I'm gonna check the tires and oil while we're stopped," Frank says.

"'Kay," April says. "We'll go inside and check out the bathroom. I'll get us some snacks, too."

After using the facilities, Gram begins walking laps around the interior of the convenience mart. She zigzags the aisles, past the candy bars and beer, around to the beef jerky and cigarettes, and back again. The new habit of frequent movement during the trip has already given her new energy and stability, she realizes.

April does some browsing to kill time. She gravitates to a display of various doodads with inspirational quotes. She peruses refrigerator magnets and paperweights. She reads quotes about perspective and leadership, opportunity and teamwork. She spins a rack of key chains. One in particular catches her eye, makes her smile.

Key chain in hand, April grabs a bag of corn chips and extracts three bottles of soda from the cold case. Frank's paying for the gas at the register, so she sidles up beside him and sets her items on the counter.

"All this, too," Frank tells the cashier, motioning to the items. Then to April, "What have you got here?"

He picks up the key chain, reads the quote. It makes him smile, too.

"No one can make you feel inferior without your consent." ~ *Eleanor Roosevelt*

The group returns to the car, and Frank cleans the bugs off the windshield before they get back on the road. April leans against the car door and twists the new embellishment onto her ring of keys.

"What have you got there?" Gram asks, and April hands over the keys to show her.

"Huh," Gram shrugs one shoulder, while handing it back. "What prompted you to buy that?"

"Oh, I don't know," April lies, staring down at the shiny plastic bauble. "I guess it just spoke to me somehow."

There's no point in telling Gram about the conversation she'd had with her dad. It was a long story, April reasons with herself, and one that would probably hurt Gram's feelings. It's not really a lie, just an omission. Still, it gnaws at her. She thinks about all the grief she has given Gram and her dad lately about keeping secrets. *Am I a hypocrite?* April wonders if she should go ahead and tell Gram why the quote grabbed her.

Frank helps Gram climb into the back seat where she can sit sideways with her feet up.

The opportunity for speaking up expires so quickly. April marvels at how easy it is to just let the moment go, so much easier than confessing. As the minutes pass – after they pull out of the truck stop and turn onto the interstate – the moment just gets smaller and smaller, and further and further away, like the truck stop sign in the rearview mirror. April runs her thumb over the smooth plastic key chain, falls deeper into thought. What would be the point of bringing it up again, of telling Gram now? Or tomorrow? Or ever?

Perhaps the discomfort of a secret is easier to bear than the pain of speaking the truth.

Perhaps someone ought to put that on a key chain.

Life in the 1940s

HOLLYWOOD, Calif., March 16, 1945

For Immediate Release

/National Newswire/ -- Margaret O'Brien won an Oscar as "Outstanding Child Actress" for her unforgettable performance as Tootie in Vincente Minnelli's "Meet Me in St. Louis." She received the award last night at Grauman's Chinese Theatre in Hollywood at the 17th Annual Academy Awards.

"Meet Me in St. Louis" is a Christmas musical film about an affluent American family. It portrays a year in the life of the Smiths leading up to the opening of the 1904 World's Fair. In addition to O'Brien, the film stars Judy Garland, Mary Astor, and Tom Drake.

The film also received Oscar nominations for cinematography, screenplay and musical score, including Ralph Blane's and Hugh Martin's wildly popular "The Trolley Song."

(Source: Metro-Goldwyn-Mayer Studios)

1945

Bitter Rapids, Minnesota

*F*rankie sat at the kitchen table, his feet swinging back and forth in the grown-up chair. He painstakingly traced the alphabet letters in a composition notebook his kindergarten teacher provided for summer practice. Evelyn peered over his shoulder to inspect the work, drying her hands on the apron tied at her waist.

"You're doing a wonderful job, darling," she whispered and patted his back.

Denny napped in the bassinet beside the davenport. At night, Evelyn opened the sleeper sofa in which both her boys had been conceived. She made a bed of the cushions on the floor for little Frankie. In the morning, everything was set back in place.

The small apartment had been all the newlyweds needed, even after they brought Frankie home from the hospital. When Evelyn became pregnant a second time, the couple began to talk about buying a house. Then the draft notice arrived in the post. Frank left for basic training and, six weeks after, he boarded an army carrier bound for the Asian Pacific. Evelyn's stomach swelled. Little Frankie started Kindergarten in the fall. All the while, Evelyn refused to consider that the baby might arrive before Frank returned home.

Then, late one winter night, her water broke.

Evelyn had carried her suitcase to the car, returned to the apartment for her sleeping son, paused to breathe through a contraction before carrying him out. She braved the dark night, alone on the road, headlights illuminating her way, snow crunching beneath the tires, squeezing the steering wheel tighter and tighter as the contractions grew stronger and stronger. After arriving at the hospital, Frankie was tucked in an empty bed by one of the night nurses and Evelyn was whisked away by another to get an enema and have her privates shaved. The doctor was called right away, though he rose slowly from his slumber, and he took time for coffee and a roll before driving to the hospital. By the time he appeared, the sun had risen and the baby had been delivered into the nurses' capable hands.

The months that followed were bleak. The view from their tiny apartment was dark and cold, even after the cheerful smile of spring Calla lilies filled the window box.

Evelyn first felt the sunny warmth of hope on May 8, when news broke that Germany had surrendered.

"The flags of freedom fly over all Europe," President Truman said that day in a brief radio address. "Our rejoicing is sobered and subdued by a supreme consciousness of the terrible price we have paid to rid the world of Hitler and his evil band. Let us not forget, my fellow Americans, the sorrow and the heartache which today abide in the homes of so many of our neighbors—neighbors whose most priceless possession has been rendered as a sacrifice to redeem our liberty."

It was true. So many had made the ultimate sacrifice, and the war was only half-won. Still, Evelyn's heart once again beat with the conviction her husband would soon walk through their front door. Her faith grew a little stronger with each passing day.

Denny rustled in the bassinet, and Frankie cheered that his brother was awake. Keeping quiet while the baby slept was a difficult task for a five-year-old boy. It always ended with a giddy release of celebration when Denny awoke. Evelyn moved to retrieve a fresh diaper before the baby began to wail. Big brother turned on the radio, just in time for his favorite sing-along with Judy Garland about her jolly afternoon on the trolley.

"Clang, clang, clang," Frankie sang and hopped around the small kitchen.

Evelyn sashayed over with Denny on her hip and took Frankie's hand in hers.

"Zing, zing, zing," they harmonized.

Frankie spun away, clapping in rhythm to the upbeat tune.

Evelyn picked up the framed photo of Frank in his dress uniform, held it to her chest as she danced.

"I want to dance with Daddy," Frankie said.

"Okay," his mother laughed. "Make sure you hold it tight, so it doesn't drop and break."

She handed over the frame. The baby wriggled in her arms, so she set him down on his tummy. From the soft carpet, Denny pushed up on his elbows and cooed.

"Chug, chug, chug," Frankie sang and hopped, his stubby fingers pinched tightly on the silver frame.

Summer wafted through the open window. The Calla lilies danced with them, the sinuous white and pink blossoms swaying like ball gowns. Perfume and warmth filled the room.

The doorbell rang.

Evelyn dabbed the perspiration from her cheeks, while she approached the door.

"Careful not to step on your brother," she said with a lightness she hadn't felt in months.

She glanced over her shoulder, laughing, while she reached for the doorknob.

All oxygen seemed to be sucked from the room when she opened the apartment door. The Western Union Telegram man stood in the hall, his hat in hand.

1982

Superstition Mountains, Arizona

"Maybe we'll find the Lost Dutchman's Gold Mine this year," April said.

Her eyes flickered with the flame of their miniature camping stove. She and Frank sat on their sleeping bags, waiting for water to boil.

"Anything's possible," Frank said.

He soaked up his young daughter's optimism for a moment, then added, "It's not likely, though."

Frank marveled at the unlimited energy of an eleven-year-old, and felt a great deal older than his own forty-two years after sleeping on the hard-packed desert ground. The father-daughter backpacking trip into the Superstition Mountains outside of Phoenix had become an annual tradition since Deborah moved to California. It was the one thing Frank felt he got right as a single dad.

The sun was only a sliver on the horizon. A soft crimson glow began to illuminate the craggy landscape, creating deep shadows in the crevices of the state park's rugged mountain peaks and mesas. They'd hiked to Weaver's Needle this year. The imposing spire of weathered lava was the fabled location of the Dutchman's lost gold sought by treasure-seekers since the late 1800s.

"What would you do with all that gold if we found it?" Frank asked.

April closed her eyes for a moment and breathed in the dusty-creosote perfume of the desert. "I don't know."

"How can you not know?" he chuckled. "You talk about it every time we come here."

The girl shrugged her shoulders and took a bite of her granola-bar breakfast.

"I just want to find it," she said. "Then we could go back to it every year, and we wouldn't tell anyone where it is. It would be our secret."

Frank poured hot water into two aluminum cups. He wanted to tell her that keeping a secret isn't as fun and exciting as it seems. He tore open a packet of powdered hot chocolate with tiny marshmallows, poured half into each cup. *Having a secret isolates you.* He stirred the water, watched the powder dissolve.

"Nah," he said, handing April a cup. "We'd mine all that gold, and buy a private jet to fly around the world."

April giggled, conceded that would be fun, too.

They fell into a comfortable quietness. They ate breakfast and listened to the ringing song of desert quail in the distance. *pu-kwaaw'-cah, pu-kwaaw'-cah*

Ten or twelve of the pear-shaped birds emerged from beneath a thorny thicket of mesquite trees. The gray-brown plumage of the females and their youngsters blended with the surrounding rock and brush. Only the male in the group sported brilliant copper feathers on its head and wing tips, and vivid white stripes on its black face. He stood guard along the perimeter, while the covey clucked and crowed in nasal tones. They foraged among the geometric shadows of prickly pear and jumping cholla, their top knot plumes bobbing to-and-fro. A sentry male perched atop the arm of a nearby saguaro sounded a high warning call, and the covey scurried for cover in the brush.

A slight rustle about fifty feet from the camp clearing revealed the cause of the warning. Poised in the shadows was a slender coyote the color of honey. April took in a sharp breath – part fear, part thrill.

"She's not interested in us," Frank whispered.

The coyote was no larger than their neighbor's border collie.

"Is it a baby?" April asked in a hushed voice.

"No, she's full grown," Frank explained. He noticed the canine's loose skin and sagging teats. "Looks like a new mama."

"She's so pretty," April said, admiring the coyote's keen ears and narrow pointed face, its bushy black-tipped tail.

Frank nodded, almost imperceptibly, in agreement.

The coyote slinked toward the brush, ears flat, chest low to the ground.

A second warning call came from the sentry quail. In a flurry, the adult male of the covey charged from the prickly scrub. It ran headlong at the coyote – crowing loud, head high, feathers ruffled – in what could only be a suicide mission. The coyote leapt forward, taking the quail by the neck and killing it swiftly with a brisk shake of her head.

April's hand flew to her mouth.

The girl watched in stunned horror as the coyote turned, the quail swinging lifeless in its mouth. A stain of bright red drops marked the trail as the animal trotted off and disappeared in the shadow of Weaver's Needle.

A single tear ran down April's cheek. A hard knot formed in her throat.

"Why?" she asked, still speaking in a whisper. "Why did the quail do that?"

Frank patted April's back in the same way he'd tried to comfort her as a colicky infant.

"He sacrificed himself to save his family."

April punched the tear from her cheek with the heel of her hand. "I hate coyotes."

"Aw, honey, no," Frank said. He tucked a lock of April's unbrushed hair behind her ear.

"That mama coyote only did what she had to do, to provide for her pups. And the papa quail did what he had to do," Frank explained. "That's how life goes. Parents make sacrifices, they'll give their life or even take a life if they have to. They do whatever it takes to make sure their kids survive. Good parents, anyway."

Good parents. The phrase turned over in April's mind. She thought back to when her mom had moved out. The loss was like nothing April had ever felt. She remembered how her dad had hugged her tight while she sobbed and sobbed in the days and weeks that followed. "I'd do anything to make your pain go away." That's what he'd said to her. Now, she wondered what he had sacrificed for her in the days and weeks since to keep that promise. She wondered just how far he would go.

April turned to Frank wide-eyed and gripped his arm.

"Tell me you won't ever do that," she demanded. "Tell me you won't make that kind of sacrifice for me. I can take care of myself."

Frank pulled her into an embrace, kissed the top of her head, silently cursed himself for saying what he did.

"You don't have to worry about anything like that, kiddo."

He told her she was right; she could take care of herself. He told her she was smart and strong and brave; she could do anything she set her mind to do.

He told himself to keep his mouth shut and to do whatever it takes to protect her. Always.

Life in the 1890s

SPECIAL TO *THE NATIONAL TIMES*

Boarding School Deemed Best Method for Indian Assimilation

WASHINGTON, D.C. — The U.S. Congress approved a resolution to make attendance at federal boarding school compulsory for Indian children. According to a Congressional spokesman, the new law is intended to better assimilate the Indians as individuals in Western civilization.

Schools will be modeled after the success of the Carlisle Indian Industrial School in Pennsylvania, established in 1879 by Civil War veteran Capt. Richard Pratt. His approach to "kill the Indian, save the man," utilizes military-training principles and techniques to eradicate savage customs and practices in the children, while teaching them the English language and Christian values.

The Federal Bureau of Indian Affairs, tasked with executing tribal treaties, has been authorized to withhold food and other goods from any Indians who refuse to send their children to the schools. Federal agents will be dispatched to remove children from reservations and facilitate assimilation.

1943

Bitter Rapids, Minnesota

The work crew lumbered into the idling prison bus just before dawn, boots thundering down the aisle. Two guards sprawled across the back benches, rifles propped beside them. Two more sat in front, behind the driver. The door slammed shut with a swoosh, and the bus rumbled through the open gate onto the main road.

Neither the destination nor the day's project were divulged in advance. Some days, the ride out and back was more than an hour. Others, only ten minutes. Maakade tucked his hands up under his armpits to keep warm and hoped for a long commute. The longer the drive, the deeper into the wild they would go.

A few inmates grumbled about forced labor. The air became stale and moist from their expelled breath. The windows fogged.

"Shut your traps," Foreman Ogren snapped.

He stood beside the bus driver, swiped the inside of the windshield with his jacket sleeve. He slid open a side window, just a crack. Crisp morning air flooded in, keeping the fog at bay, halting the bellyaching.

Maakade never complained. He'd rather toil in the open air than wither behind locked doors. The first six years of his sentence had been spent suffocating within the prison's walls. Work was in short supply during the Depression. It wasn't to be wasted on criminals, degenerates, ne'er-do-wells. Then the Japanese bombed Pearl Harbor. President Roosevelt declared war. And the strong backs of men were once again in short supply.

His captivity had begun long before prison, of course. The rumbling bus always brought memories of boarding school along for the ride.

Every summer the noisy white bus had pulled onto the reservation, emblazoned with hard black letters: U.S. Bureau of Indian Affairs. The agents snatched the children, some as young as four years, from their families and homes. "Kill the Indian, save the man." That was the motto for assimilation, the justification for kidnapping children and boarding them in government-run schools where their native language and ancient teachings were starved and beaten out of them.

When the bus could be heard rumbling in the distance, Maakade's mother would shove him toward the reeds. *"Giimii, Omagakiins. Akandoo."* Run, Little Frog. Hide.

The boy had always obeyed his elders. Year after year, he was invisible, one with the water and the earth. Crouched amid the slender wheatgrass behind the beaver's mud-packed dam. Submerged beneath the marsh, sucking oxygen from a hollowed reed, beside the loon's nesting barge.

One day, when Maakade was ten years old, his mother's sister had pulled him aside, told him he must go with the white men the next time the bus came. We are suffering because of you, *Ninoshenh* told him. The Indian Bureau withheld rations, clothing, and other necessities from families who kept their children from school. His family would not survive another turn of the season.

"You are only half Indian," his aunt had hissed. "There is less of you to be lost."

Again, the boy obeyed his elder. His mother had wailed when the bus drove away with her Little Frog trapped inside.

"On your feet, then," Ogren said to the work crew.

The bus stopped at the quarry. Maakade was grateful to be pulled from the memory of his heartbroken mother. The vision haunted him often enough.

Into the quarry the prisoners marched like carpenter ants. Guards perched above, rifles in hand should the workers get malicious ideas about the shovels, sledgehammers, and pickaxes they would take up for the day's work.

By midmorning, their skin and jumpsuits were dusted gray and chalky. Soft silt from pulverized limestone caked gummy in the corners of their mouths and eyes, and where follicles of oily hair met sweaty scalp. The men cut at layers of bedrock – steel against stone – and dismantled segments of the earth formed eons ago. From the gashes, they hauled hundred-pound blocks and slabs up and out to the trucks. They moved like ghosts, ashen and invisible against the scarred quarry backdrop.

Maakade's life in prison wasn't fundamentally different than it had been during his time at Cross Lake Indian School.

When the big white bus had arrived with its latest batch of savages, the nuns herded the boys and girls off to separate halls to be sanitized. Maakade and the other boys were told to undress. They stood in a line, naked and shivering, as women in black robes wielded metal shears to prune their long hair. Fistfuls of raven locks drifted to the cement floor like dying leaves in autumn. The boys were ushered to basins of cold water, their arms, legs, faces, backsides and privates scrubbed by fair-skinned women wielding boar's hair brushes and lye soap.

Uniforms were issued. Stiff underpants and wool socks. Rigid trousers and button-up shirts. Like fabric made of fire ants against Maakade's raw skin. The clothes they'd arrived in, the piles of their shorn hair, remnants of their former lives and heritage, were collected into steel barrels, doused with gasoline, set ablaze. The caustic odor lingered in his nostrils even now.

At the top of the quarry, beside the trucks, Maakade swept up a fistful of moist pine needles and black dirt from the service road, breathed in the musky perfume of the earth to cover the stench of his past.

Perhaps the faces of the nuns had appeared softer than those of the prison guards today. But their rule of law and discipline were no less fierce. Maakade and the other children became ghosts of their former selves, ashen and invisible against the scarred backdrop of a world formed eons ago.

September 1945

Bitter Rapids, Minnesota

Evelyn first saw the potential of Arthur Specht at the annual Labor Day picnic, just after the war.

He was the type of man one might call solid, steady. He was hardworking, a successful businessman, focused on his goals. He needed a wife and a family, though he had neither the time nor inclination to do the work necessary to procure them.

The town was gathered in Central Square. They were sprawled on blankets in the grass. Men grilled frankfurters over charcoal briquettes in cast-iron hibachis. Women chased toddlers across the lawn. Children ran up and down the City Hall steps, lit sparklers crackling in their fists.

Evelyn strolled through the scene, Denny in one arm, perched on her hip, Frankie holding her hand. She saw Arthur standing among a cluster of men from the Chamber of Commerce - Mr. Logdahl who owned the grocery store, Walter Bursack of Wally's Tavern, Mayor Ettestad. They stood in a loose circle, amber beer bottles in hand, sports coats slung over their shoulders, fedoras angled smartly atop their heads. Arthur was the thinnest among them, the sole bachelor of the group.

Frankie pulled Evelyn toward the cotton candy machine. The Japanese had just surrendered. The war was finally over, and rationing already had eased. Sugar was available for things as ordinary and cheerful as cotton candy.

The boy pressed his palms against the glass box set upon the bright red metal stand. He watched the pink wisps float and spin inside while Mrs. Miller caught them with a paper cone. Denny was more interested in Evelyn's pearl necklace. The baby grabbed the string of white orbs and stuffed them into his gummy mouth.

Evelyn wrangled the pearls from Denny's tiny fist. He persisted and grabbed hold with the other hand.

"You look like you could use a couple extra hands," Arthur said. He'd wandered away from the group and was standing beside her with outstretched arms.

"That's kind of you, Mr. Specht. But he doesn't take well to men, I'm afraid."

"Please, call me Art."

He had a mild countenance as he looked from the young woman to her small sons. His faint smile and soft crinkles around his eyes spoke of something Evelyn couldn't quite place. Was it kindness or concern? Sadness or trepidation? Pity, maybe.

"I was sure sorry to hear about Frank," Art said. "He was a fine young man."

So, it was pity then. Evelyn averted her eyes. It had been three months since the telegram arrived, and she still had trouble finding the right words for the daily condolences. Art eased Denny from her, cradled the pudgy infant like an over-sized football.

"Hey there, sport," he said and bopped the baby's nose with his index finger. "What do you say you give your mother a little break."

Denny cooed and giggled. He reached out and grasped the man's finger. Art laughed.

"I'll be darned," Evelyn said. "He's never let anyone else hold him without wailing like a banshee. You must have the touch."

Art's eyes grew wider, and he shook his head. "I can't imagine how. This is the first time I've ever even held a baby."

Evelyn scoffed in disbelief. He was teasing, surely. Art glanced up and the glint in his eyes said, *it's true.* In the waning light of the late summer evening, she studied his face and tried to make sense of what she was seeing, what she was feeling. Evelyn had known him all her life. Mr. Specht was a pillar of the community, fifteen years her senior. She'd always thought of him as "a grown-up," just like her schoolteachers or Mr. Logdahl at the market. *How is it a grown man can live a life of such solitude that he's never even held a baby?*

"Mama, look!"

Frankie wormed his way between them, a tall cone of cotton candy in one hand and a wad of sticky fluff in the other. His lips, teeth, and cheeks were bubble gum pink.

"Oh, for heaven's sake!" In one fluid movement, Evelyn plucked the cone from Frankie and a handkerchief from her handbag. She licked the hankie and dabbed at the boy's sticky face. "You're a mess."

The boy thrashed his head from side to side and stepped back out of reach. He tilted his head and raised his shoulder to wipe his cheek on his shirt sleeve.

"Let the boy be a mess, Evelyn. He'll have to clean up and fly right soon enough."

Evelyn chuckled, handed the sticky treat back to her son. She told him to run along, go find his friends, and share his cotton candy with them. Frankie saluted her, the way his daddy had taught him before going off to war. Then he turned and darted across the lawn.

"So, when did it happen for you?" she asked.

"What's that?" Art returned.

"When *you* had to clean up and fly right?"

Their eyes connected for a moment. He smiled sadly and looked away.

"Can't remember a time when I didn't," Art said. "My father had, troubles, I guess you could call it. Never was around much. Finally ran off for good when I was fourteen."

She put a hand on his arm. "I'm sorry."

Denny wriggled and fussed. He stretched his arms toward Evelyn, opened and closed his tiny fists. She hoisted him back to her bosom.

"No boy should be without a father," Art said.

Evelyn closed her eyes for a moment. She breathed in the baby's clean scent. Ivory soap and Johnson's powder. She felt something tumble in her chest, a piece of her heart cracking and sinking into a dark abyss like the calving of a glacier. Then it struck her. Perhaps it was her youth she felt falling away. Evelyn looked into her baby's eyes. *I'm a grown woman. A widow. A mother to two fatherless sons.*

"Did your mother ever remarry?" she asked Art, barely above a whisper.

Her question made his posture shrink. He stuffed his hands in his trouser pockets and shook his head. "She passed the year I graduated high school."

Evelyn felt her throat constrict, choking off the thought she very nearly voiced. *You're all alone, too.*

September 1946

Bitter Rapids, Minnesota

"Tell me about your trip," Evelyn said to Art as they scouted the Central Square lawn for an open spot.

It was an anniversary of sorts – their second Labor Day picnic together.

A kinship had formed between Evelyn and Art that day, one year ago. In the months that followed, they'd chatted over coffee after church and teamed up for bridge at the Millers' house. Art had helped Evelyn negotiate a lease for a bigger apartment. She'd helped him defrost his Frigidaire. They were not courting, not even after the requisite one year of mourning Frank's death had ended. They were friends. Now, here they were again at the Labor Day picnic.

"There!" Frankie pointed to a patch of green near the fountain. They zig-zagged around a potato-sack race and line of croquet wickets to claim their land. Evelyn shook open the blanket, high in the air, and let it drift down onto the grass.

Frankie ran off to join friends, leaving Art and Evelyn to settle on the blanket. Denny toddled around the fringed, tartan perimeter, dragging a sock monkey by the tail along behind him. Evelyn sat with one leg folded beneath her. She kept one eye trained on the baby, while she listened to Art regale the escapades of his recent business trip. There'd been deals negotiated in smoky offices and sticky-floored taverns in St. Cloud and Big Lake. There was a night slept in the car because the hotels in

Andover were filled to capacity for the annual Rum River Angler Classic.

Eventually, Art ran out of stories and Denny's little legs ran out of strength. The baby dropped to hands and knees and crawled to his mother. He sprawled onto his tummy, stuffed his fat thumb in his mouth, and rested his rosy cheek against Evelyn's thigh.

She ran her fingers through the boy's soft, sweaty curls, in quiet contemplation.

Her life was so different from the one Art enjoyed. Her days were spent alone with the boys, listening to the radio, scrubbing soiled diapers, baking bread loaves, stealing cat naps. Evenings, after the boys were tucked in bed, Evelyn sat at the kitchen table with pen and paper, reworking the budget, figuring how to make ends meet on the fifty-dollar military pension she received each month. It was never enough to fully pay the rent, the heating bill, the grocer's tab, the pediatrician's fee. She'd had to subtract a bit here and there, a little for this and that, from the $10,000 death gratuity she'd received after Frank was killed. The name of it always made her stomach seize. *Gratuity.* As if the United States government had tipped her in appreciation for giving up her husband.

Nights were a patchwork of sleep, feedings, pacing, worrying.

Art was stretched out on his back, hands folded beneath his head, watching the clouds waft on the currents overhead. *Relaxed,* Evelyn thought. *Successful. Steady.*

She tilted her head, studied him. Art was different from most of the men she'd known. His hands were smooth from working at a desk. He was slim, not beefy, narrow at the hips. She considered his straight nose, dark eyes, and dimpled chin. He was handsome in his own way.

"Why is it you've never married?" Evelyn asked.

Art rolled to his side to face her, bent his elbow, and propped his head in hand. His eyebrows drew together. The question lingered in the air with the sharp scent of cut grass and lighter fluid. The whole town wondered about him, that was no secret. Unmarried at forty-one. The eternal bachelor. Why? Few had been bold enough, like Evelyn, to ask outright.

"I suppose I've never been lucky enough to fall in love with the right person," he said finally.

Evelyn nodded slowly, digested his words. She'd been lucky in love once. Frank had been her Mr. Right. *Fat lot of good that did me.*

"There are plenty of reasons to get married besides love," she said.

Art sat up. "Are there?"

Evelyn shrugged her shoulders half-heartedly, as though the idea had just come to her. She didn't want Art to know it had been consuming her thoughts for months. Love was too fleeting. There was a lengthy list of other reasons to marry. Every night when she collapsed into bed alone and exhausted, when sleep somehow still eluded her, the list of reasons paraded through Evelyn's mind like a marching band of wailing trumpets, chirping piccolos, booming sousaphones, and thundering drums.

"For one thing, marriage is far more efficient than bachelorhood," Evelyn said. "With a wife to run the household, a man can focus on his career, enjoy his leisure time."

"Hiring a housekeeper and a cook would be efficient," Art interjected.

"Ah, but you have to pay a housekeeper and cook," Evelyn said with a grin. "A wife is free."

Art threw his head back and laughed. "I know quite a few fellas who'd debate that point with you."

The outburst made Denny jolt and whimper. Evelyn laughed silently at Art's retort, placed an index finger to her candy apple lips. *Shh.* She rubbed Denny's back, and the tot curled himself into a fiddlehead.

"When you're married, you always have a dinner date, a dance partner, a friend, a confidant," Evelyn continued delicately. *A provider. Someone steady to put food on the table.*

Art bobbled his head. Fair point.

"Parenthood, a legacy," she continued. *A father for my children.* "And getting married puts a stop to wagging tongues about why one never married."

A football flew between them, landing with a thud just beyond the edge of their picnic blanket. Young Billy Olson charged past them and scuttled to retrieve the ball.

"Sorry 'bout that, Mrs. Parson," Billy said enthusiastically. He glanced down at the blanket and its napping toddler, and in a hushed voice added, "Ope!"

The boy made an exaggerated tip-toe retreat, leaving the couple free to converse privately once again. But the interruption had broken Evelyn's stride. Her mind tumbled with thoughts on how to pick up where she'd left off.

Art took Evelyn's hand.

"Are you proposing, Evelyn?"

She turned and fixed her gaze on him for a moment. They searched each other's eyes for insight. Then Evelyn lowered her eyes, took in the sight of her sleeping babe.

"What would you say if I were?" she asked.

Art squeezed her hand, tilted his head to recapture her gaze.

"What we would have together," he paused, "it would never be love. You understand that?"

She nodded briskly, smiled. "What we'd have would be better than love. We'd have friendship."

TIME magazine, Monday, Sept. 7, 1970

Women on the March

"Don't iron while the strike is hot," advised the slogan of the Women's Strike for Equality.

No one knows how many shirts lay wrinkling in laundry baskets last week as thousands of women across the country turned out for the first big demonstration of the Women's Liberation movement. The strike, on the 50th anniversary of the proclamation of the women's suffrage amendment, drew small crowds by antiwar or civil rights standards. Yet, it was easily the largest women's rights rally since the suffrage protests.

The women had plenty of detractors, such as West Virginia Senator Jennings Randolph, who called the demonstrators "braless bubble-heads." The *San Francisco Chronicle*'s Columnist Count Marco urged his supporters to wear black armbands "mourning the death of femininity."

1990

Kearney, Nebraska

"Quit playing with your food and eat already," Gram tells April, shaking her head. "I want to go lie down."

The young woman continues twirling the spaghetti on her plate, lost in thought.

Frank spotted the Italian restaurant sign along the highway and decided it would be a good place to stop for dinner before checking into a hotel. The hostess sat them at a circular booth with a checkered tablecloth.

Red, white, and green décor. Twinkle-lights strung along the ceiling. It all reminds April of Christmas, which makes her think about her mom, which makes her sad. Most kids remember the year they found out gifts from Santa Claus were really from their parents. April remembers the year she found out gifts from her mom were really from her dad.

April was eleven years old, three years after her mom moved to California and her parents divorced. For three Christmases, April opened presents from Deborah that were perfect – a Smurfs lunch box, colorful My Little Pony figurines, and this particular year, a pudgy Cabbage Patch doll. The thoughtful gifts sustained April during all the days of the year when she missed and needed her mother the most.

That Christmas morning of her eleventh year, after all the gifts had been opened, the phone rang.

April knew it was her mom calling, but she stayed in the living room while dad went to the kitchen to answer. She knew the adults liked to talk first, that dad would call her in when it was her turn. She sat on the floor in a nest of ribbons and crumpled wrapping paper, cradling her new baby doll. She plucked a bow from the floor to put on her baby's head. That's when it dawned on her.

"The paper," she said. April stood and tiptoed toward the kitchen. She paused behind the door, held her breath, and listened.

"She loves it, Deb," Frank said. "She's playing with it now. I got the boy doll with curly red hair and freckles. His name is Alexei Jeremiah."

April let the doll fall from her hand onto the floor.

"I'm dead serious," he continued. "Alexei Jeremiah. It was on the little birth certificate that comes with it. That was the last one in the store. I was sweating bullets. I'd been to three other places that were already sold out."

April pushed open the swinging door and stepped into the kitchen.

"Oh, here she is now, Deb. Hang on..."

Frank handed the phone to his daughter.

"Hi, sweet girl," Deborah said. "Merry Christmas."

"Why is the wrapping on your presents the same as the ones I get from dad?"

"What?" Deborah asked.

April repeated the question.

"Is it? Oh, isn't that a funny coincidence." Deborah laughed nervously. "Great minds think alike, I guess."

Fat tears welled in April's eyes and rolled silently down her cheeks. She hung the phone back in its cradle on the wall and ran to her room.

Frank began to follow, but Gram grabbed his arm.

"Let me," she said.

He cursed under his breath, rubbed his forehead. Then he motioned with a palm of surrender to his mother.

April remembers every detail from that day, every word, every tear.

Gram came into her bedroom, told her it was true that Dad bought and wrapped the presents.

"She doesn't love me," April sobbed.

"Nonsense," Gram said. "She does so love you. She just has a different way of showing it than most other moms."

Gram told April that Mom always sent a check for Christmas, a big one, so Dad could buy the best gifts. It was the same on her birthday. Dad knew what April wanted, and that way Deborah didn't have to waste money on shipping, or risk things getting lost in the mail.

"She sends money for school supplies, too. Did you know that?" Gram asked. "You should be grateful she loves you enough to send her hard-earned money."

It was all perfectly practical.

So why don't I ever feel grateful? April has wondered a hundred times since.

She skewers a meatball with her fork, holds it up to her nose, and sniffs it. She sighs and sets it back down on the plate.

"You didn't like it?" The waitress frowns at the uneaten mound of spaghetti and meatballs on April's plate as she clears the empties from Frank and Evelyn.

"Huh?" April says. "Oh, no, it's fine. Really. It's good. I guess I just wasn't very hungry."

Frank asks if they should order some tiramisu. Gram smirks and folds her arms over her bosom. "The girl hasn't cleaned her plate, and you offer her dessert."

He blushes and hands the waitress his credit card. "We'll just take a doggie bag, please."

They walk through the parking lot, and Gram points at the container in April's hand. "Waste not, want not, young lady. You'll be eating that for breakfast."

April looks down at the box with *Grazie!* emblazoned on the side in bold green letters.

That's my Gram, she thinks as she fights the lump in her throat, *perfectly practical.*

* * * *

Frank and April park themselves outside the motel room door for their daily chat, while Gram relaxes in bed. The "official debriefing" of the day's intelligence, April jokes.

"So, where's your head at today, kiddo?" Frank asks.

She opens her eyes wide, squeezes the back of her neck, exhales noisily. "I dunno. All *over* the place."

"You and me both," he responds. He leans back in the lawn chair, props an ankle on his opposite knee. His hands rest on his thighs. *A lot of old wounds have been ripped open on this trip,* he thinks. *Some fresh wounds, too.*

The fall wind is crisp, earthy. It hasn't let up since they crossed the state line into Nebraska. It lifts a flurry of leaves from the ground, whisks them across the parking lot in a burst of red, gold, and russet crinkles. A bouquet of rosy finches twitter and chirp among the naked branches of the coffeetrees that line the walkway, like so many twinkle lights at Christmas. It's captivating, every part of it.

"I can't believe all the new things I'm seeing on this trip," April says, a little breathless. Frank smiles at his daughter. He watches as her expression turns meditative. Her eyes shimmer with reflection. *I can't believe all the old things I'm seeing in new ways,* she thinks.

"You know, since Mom left, I've always been a little jealous of how close you and Gram are," April says.

"Being in close proximity with someone isn't the same as being close," Franks says. His tone is flat.

"Yeah," April says, "I'm starting to see that now."

Growing up, April always considered Evelyn to be the ideal mom. Now, with everything she has been learning, April thinks maybe Evelyn has actually been the ideal grandmother, someone in whom April could always confide. It never occurred to her that Gram was not a person in whom Frank could ever confide. Who shares their deepest secrets and fears with their parent? April certainly never did. In hindsight, she realizes Frank and Gram hardly ever talked. Not about things that really mattered.

The new insight is making April think about her own mother more and more.

Deborah has been so far away, for so long now, it would sometimes be months before the woman popped into April's thoughts. Every now and then, April would consider calling. But what would she say? *I miss you, Mom.* It always felt too stupid. Too needy.

A shift in the wind sweeps April's long hair across her face. She pulls the tresses away, tucks them behind an ear. A shift in understanding sweeps a fresh idea across her mind. She pulls the thought forward, works it like a lump of clay. So much of April's perception about Deborah was formed after the woman left them. The memories from before, from when April was a little girl, are fuzzy, fading.

Was she ever a good mom? April wonders. *Did she ever love me?*

"Dad?"

"Yeah, kiddo?"

April hesitates, then presses forward.

"What it was like, before mom left? Were we ever, you know, like a family? Was Mom ever happy?"

Frank

When your mom and I got married, we both had full-time jobs. We'd each been living on our own, so we were used to doing all our own cooking and cleaning. We were newlyweds. All that stuff was like a game, something that brought us together. We did our grocery shopping together. We'd cook dinner together after work. Deb would wash the dishes, and I'd dry 'em. We'd spend Sunday mornings cleaning the apartment, and then haul our dirty clothes to the laundromat in the afternoon. We'd pack a lunch and have a picnic sitting cross-legged on the counter with a bottle of wine, watching the clothes tumble in the dryer. It was silly, and it was perfect.

After you came along, everything started to change. You became the center of our universe. Your mom made a scrapbook and kept track of all your milestones. The first time you rolled over on your own. Your first words. First steps. First tooth.

 Sometimes we'd just stand next to your crib and watch you sleep, mesmerized by the thick blonde lashes and the maroon of your lids while your eyes tracked your dreams. You had these long, delicate fingers, even as a tiny baby. We'd whisper, maybe she'll be a pianist, or a violinist. And when you started learning your numbers and letters and colors, we just knew you were the most brilliant child ever born. Maybe she'll become a lawyer or a judge, maybe a scientist or a doctor.

We'd lie in bed at night talking about what Santa should bring you at Christmas, whether we should sign you up for Girl Scouts, and where we should go for our first family vacation. A long weekend in Flagstaff to play in the snow? Or take a whole week, drive to California so you could see the ocean, build sandcastles?

But having a kid is a heck of a lot of work, too. And I guess that made marriage more work. Life wasn't all silly fun anymore. And I'm not just talking about all the diaper changes and late-night feedings. There was so much more to do. Always a mountain of laundry. More groceries to buy every week. More dishes to wash every night. Places like the laundromat and grocery store weren't nearly as much fun with a wiggly baby in tow, so we started splitting up for those things. There were doctor appointments. Little-tykes tumbling classes. Vacations we could never seem to find the time or money to take.

Daycare was expensive, and you were always picking up germs there, getting ear infections and such. Anytime you got sick, even if it was just a little cough, we were scared to death. That part was stressful enough, but then we'd argue about which one of us would miss work when you were sick. We debated whether it made sense to even send you to daycare. We finally agreed it would make more sense for only one of us to work and one of us to stay at home. That led to arguments about who should give up their career.

None of that was unique to us, I know. Every married couple goes through those gyrations when they start a family. The problem is, you never know how becoming a parent will change you. It's like the flip of a switch. One day you're just living your life, doing whatever the heck you want. The next day, you have this tiny, amazing human who depends on you for absolutely everything. It's an awesome responsibility.

For me, I was suddenly filled with this sense of pride, of having a bigger purpose in life. You know? Even when you were screeching at the top of your lungs at three in the morning, I didn't mind losing sleep, walking you through the house, patting your back, singing silly songs to try and comfort you. But for your mom, the change was different. She was suddenly filled with anxiety, this feeling of inadequacy. She fretted over every little thing, constantly worried she was doing everything wrong. Every time you cried, she was sure it was her fault, sure she was failing you.

I mean, everyone has their moments of self-doubt as a parent. You worry over whether you're saying and doing the right things. But for your mom, the doubt was always there. It was crippling.

Looking back, it would have made the best sense for me to quit my job and be a stay-at-home dad, let your mom "bring home the bacon." We'd both have been happier, more relaxed. But times were different then. Not as bad as the '50s, maybe, but still. Your mom wasn't making as much money as I was, even though she had a great career ahead of her. My job at Motorola was just a job. But I guess my self-worth was tied to it, to the idea that I was the man of the house. The idea of staying home while my wife worked and paid the bills embarrassed the heck out of me. I just couldn't bring myself to do it.

So, your mom took the bullet, so to speak. She quit her job at the interior design company and took over all the household responsibilities. My life got easier, and hers got harder. All I did was punch a clock for forty hours a week. She did everything else it took to care for our family, twenty-four/seven. The laundry, the cooking, the cleaning, the shopping, the errands, the childcare. She never got to punch out of work.

 It was only inevitable that she'd start to resent it. Resent me. It wouldn't have taken a rocket-scientist to figure that out. All I had to do was pay attention. But I didn't. I just didn't see it until it was too late to fix things.

LIFE IN THE 1940S

Feeding and Care of Baby

MacMillan and Company Ltd., Revised Edition, 1942

F. Truby King

CHAPTER XI – MANAGEMENT

Fond and foolish over-indulgence, mismanagement, and "spoiling" may be as harmful to an infant as callous neglect and intentional cruelty. Obedience in infancy is the foundation of all later powers of self-control; yet it is the one thing the young mother nowadays is most inclined to neglect. Instead of gently, wisely, and firmly regulating her baby's habits and conduct, she tends to allow him to have his own way and to rule her and the whole household. There are few sights more pathetic than that of the weak mother not daring to lay her child down because he will cry for the snuggling warmth of her arms.

1949

Bitter Rapids, Minnesota

"Say, kids! What time is it?" Buffalo Bob's voice rang out from the living room.

"It's Howdy Doody time!" Denny and Frankie shouted back.

The boys sat on the floor in front of the massive mahogany console with the porthole-sized television screen. Art was on the couch reading Winston Churchill's book of wartime speeches, *Blood, Sweat and Tears*. Evelyn listened to the boys giggle and cheer from the kitchen as she wiped dry the last of the dinner dishes. She held a drinking glass up to the light, swiveled it back and forth, smiled. *No water spots in this house.*

Four years since Frank's death, and Evelyn had pushed forward. With two young boys and a new husband, there simply wasn't time or excuse to wallow in emotion.

Evelyn carried the flatware to the kitchen table, retrieved the silver polish and a fresh cotton rag. Then she set about the task of cleaning and buffing each fork and serving utensil, spoon and butter knife.

"Kowabunga!" shouted Chief Thunderthud from the television.

Evelyn smiled. This new life wasn't what she'd dreamt of as a girl, but it was sufficient. It suited her.

She and Art had used the balance of her death gratuity to buy a house after they married. She managed the household, while Art's income was ample enough to provide for certain luxuries – a television, a car, a rose-cut engagement diamond set in a white-gold bow with matching wedding band. They'd settled easily into family life, playing canasta with the neighbors on Wednesday nights, hosting weekend barbecues in the summer.

The spray of Clarabell's seltzer-bottle blasting Chief Thunderthud led to laughter from Frankie and Denny and all the children in the Howdy Doody peanut gallery. It was followed by the honk-honk of the mute clown's horn and the show's ending music.

"All right, then," Art closed his book shut and stood. "Turn off the television set, boys. Get ready for bed."

Frankie jumped to his feet and turned the knob. Art told them to change into their pajamas, brush their teeth, and climb into bed. Then he'd come and tuck them in.

"I want Mama to brush my teeth," Denny said. He spoke with a lisp caused by the day-old gap of his first lost tooth.

Evelyn was working the pie server to a brilliant shine, and saw in it the reflection of her smile. She placed the utensil in its velvet slot of the flatware box and stood up from the kitchen table.

"You'll be five years old next month, Denny," Art said. "You're too old to have your mother brushing your teeth."

"But I'm afraid about brushin' the hole," Denny whined. He stuck his tongue in the gummy gap for emphasis.

Frankie put an arm around his little brother, "It's okay, Denny. I'll help you."

Art thumped the heavy, leather-bound book onto the coffee table. *Blood, Sweat and Tears.* He clamped his mouth closed, fought the words at the tip of his tongue. Grow up. Quit whining. His father's words.

"Good boy, Frankie," he said instead and smiled. "You help your brother tonight. Show him there's nothing to it. And tomorrow, Denny, you'll brush all on your own. Yes?"

"Yes, sir," the boys answered in unison and scuttled off.

Evelyn cleared the table and put the flatware box in the drawer, the polish can in the cupboard, the dirty rag in a basket beneath the sink. Everything in its proper place. Art moved into the kitchen, his slippers silent on the blue and white deco-patterned linoleum.

"Thank you for getting the boys off to bed," Evelyn said. She pulled a glass tumbler from the cupboard and three ice cubes from the freezer.

"It's no easy task undoing the work you did at spoiling those boys before we married," Art said, while overseeing Evelyn's work making his cocktail.

"Well, it was hard, with Frank gone off to war. I felt I needed to make up for it, by loving them twice as much."

"I don't mean to be critical, Evelyn. You did the best you could with the lousy hand you were dealt," he said. In a rare moment of affection, Art leaned in and kissed her cheek, soft and lingering, more than his usual peck. "You're a good mother and a good wife."

Later, after they'd retired to their room and twin beds, Evelyn lay awake, listening to the rumble of Art's breath rising and falling. The warmth of his lips on her cheek remained. She replayed his words in her head to the rhythm of his breathing. For the first time since she'd lost Frank, Evelyn considered the possibility of truly being a wife, of becoming a mother again.

1990

Kearney, Nebraska

Frank always told April that God gave her two ears and one mouth for a reason – so she could listen twice as much as she spoke. As a kid, she always figured it was just his polite way of telling her to shut-the-hell-up. Now, at the wise old age of nineteen years, she begins to understand the power of holding your tongue. For as long as she could remember, Gram and Dad were tight-lipped, saying only what needed to be said, never sharing too much. But on this trip, when April asks a well-timed, simple question and then closes her mouth, they miraculously open up.

April also notices for the first time the nuances of tone, the differences in their perspectives of events from long ago. She notices how much more each one shares when the other isn't around to hear it.

"Do you blame Dad for what happened to Denny?" April asks.

"What?" Gram recoils. "No! Of course not. How could you even ask me such a thing?"

April regrets her question. She does wish they could just get everything out in the open once and for all. But Gram's reaction gives her pause. The woman looks older with each passing day of this trip, older than even a moment ago. Tired. Fragile, somehow. But shouldn't Gram know the burden Frank has carried all these years? As much as April despises secrets and resents the insinuation that she too must preserve them, it still feels wrong to divulge one that isn't hers.

"I dunno, Gram. I guess it just seemed like it would make sense, if you did blame him. I mean, I would understand. Dad was the older brother, and it was his idea to take out the canoe."

Gram shakes her head.

"Frankie might have been older, but he was still just a boy," she says, closing her eyes. "What happened that day was an accident. I never blamed him. Not for one minute."

Another set of questions pop into April's mind. *What about Art? Did* he *blame her dad?* Listen twice as much as you speak, she remembers, and bites the inside of her cheek. *One-Mississippi, two-Mississippi,* she counts in her head.

It takes only four ticks of the Magnolia State for the silence to become intolerable.

"I *was* angry for a while," Gram continues reluctantly. "But that's a natural part of grief, or so they say. I was angry that Denny was gone. Angry at the doctors for not realizing right away how badly he'd been hurt. Angry at *myself* for missing the warning signs after I brought him home."

April takes hold of Gram's hand.

"I got past that pretty quick though," Gram says. She pauses to breathe deeply from the oxygen hose. "Moved right on to the bargaining, promising God I'd work harder at being a good mother and wife if He promised not to take anyone else away from me."

Gram pauses.

April can almost see the smog of anger and grief and fear hovering around her grandmother, shrouding the woman in shadow.

"Then depression joined the party," Gram continues, a tremor surging through her lungs. "I fought that darkness for a good long time."

"Oh, Gram." April's stomach contracts. She tries to breathe through it, tightens her grip on Evelyn's slender hand.

"Maybe I'm still fighting it," Gram admits to April, and to herself. "I suppose that's what this whole crazy trip is about – maybe finding the sun again before I die."

Evelyn

Maak was the one solid thing in my life back then, April.

I had to be strong for Frankie, you know, he was just a boy. And I had to keep up the house and such, for Art, like we'd agreed. Sure, I had my girlfriends, but we didn't air all our dirty laundry to each other or complain about our husbands the way women do nowadays. None of our lives were fairy tales, and we never expected otherwise. Whining about it didn't make things better. Dottie was the only one who had any inkling about how bad things had gotten for me, and even she didn't know the half of it.

But Maak…

He seemed to know everything, understand everything, even though I never came right out and told him any of it. It was like he could *feel* what I was feeling.

I know that sounds silly. But there really was something special about him. I don't think it's just a sad old lady looking back with rose-colored glasses. No, I really don't think that's it.

Once I had worked up the nerve to visit Maak a second time, and then a third, it became so easy.

Every few weeks meant a bus trip out to the prison with an armload of books. The gals just thought it was part of a Salvation Army volunteer program, teaching inmates to read. Of course, Art had no idea about it. Maak wasn't a strong reader, but he was more than literate and he delighted in having something to occupy his mind. That was our connection for a while, reading and discussing books.

In time, the conversation eased into something more like friends. Funny stories, memories from childhood, that sort of thing. Eventually, Maak started telling me more and more about his family, his life growing up. Ever since he'd talked about Denny going to *the Land of Souls*, I'd become terribly curious about the Ojibwe people and their beliefs. Their people lived all over the Great Lakes area and the southern part of Canada. Everybody knew about them. And yet we really knew *nothing* about them, their lives, their culture. It wasn't the sort of thing taught in schools or discussed in social circles. All we learned about Indians was that they were savages, and that the Europeans who came to North America gave them religion, taught them to be civilized. It wasn't until after Frankie and I moved to Phoenix that I started reading up on the real history and learning about The Trail of Tears and boarding schools and forced assimilation...

Oh, I'm getting off track now. I don't want to get into all that. I want to tell you about Maak.

He had this, I don't know, *connection* I guess you'd call it, to nature that gave him all he ever needed. It fed him and clothed him, sustained him. Brought him peace. He lived among wolves, if you can believe that. And he talked to trees! He talked to everything in the forest, from the snake slithering through the grass to the grass itself. It sounds ridiculous, maybe. But, Lord, how I envied him for having that connection, that understanding of what really matters in life.

The more I got to know him, the better I could see how being locked up in prison, away from nature, was draining the life right out of him.

One day, he told me he was up for early parole. There was a spark in his eyes I hadn't seen before. Like little rays of sunlight captured in black crystal. It was his jumping in the river to rescue the boys, you see, that gave him the chance at getting out early. It had been big news, featured in all the newspapers. He'd been a model prisoner from day one, but that act of heroism gave the parole board reason to give his record a closer look.

Maak asked if I would speak to the board on his behalf, and I told him nothing would make me happier. In truth, I was nervous as heck to speak to the board. I think Maak knew it, too. He told me I was brave. No one had ever told me that.

Anyway, he got his early release, in the winter of 1955.

Mr. Logdahl at the grocery had an open position for a clerk and a small room for rent at the back of the store. It took only a short conversation to secure that job and room for Maak in exchange for a small wage. Art and I owed him a huge debt for rescuing our boys. He'd paid his debt to society and proved himself a hero to boot. It would mean a great deal to us if Mr. Logdahl would take him on. That was my angle. It was a fairly easy sell. A sweet smile. A flutter of the eyelashes.

Those were different times, April, you have to understand. No one in that town would have approved of a white woman and a colored man being friendly. Not even my girlfriends. Sure as heck not my husband or his buddies. So, that part just didn't get mentioned.

That's how I was able to visit Maak at the prison all that time. I didn't lie to anyone about it. I just omitted a few things. That's what you tell yourself. That's how you rationalize your actions. Then all of a sudden you realize how easy it is to bury the truth. You go through the motions of life, and with a little time and practice, it gets easier and easier to just leave certain details out.

LIFE IN THE 1950S

Every Woman's Standard Medical Guide

The Graystone Press, 1948

CHAPTER 2 – PSYCHOLOGY OF THE WOMAN, BY MARYNIA F. FARNHAM, M.D.

Due to her biological inheritance, a woman's feelings tend to manifest themselves in their passive form. Girls are, from birth, more docile, conforming, and easier to train than are boys. This is the result of her sexual anatomy – she is the passive, receptive partner in the sexual act.

It must be understood that orgasm in the man represents the climax and end of his sexual cycle. The same cannot be said of women, however, where the end of the cycle is not achieved until the woman is impregnated, carries the fetus to term, goes into labor, delivers, and ultimately nurses the child. Orgasm for the woman is of far less importance than orgasm is for the man. Without it, the man is incapable of fulfilling his part in the reproductive cycle, while the woman is wholly independent of orgasm for the accomplishment of her reproductive goal. For the man, orgasm is all.

1953

Bitter Rapids, Minnesota

"Would you like more peas, darling?" Evelyn skittered around to Art's side of the kitchen table. She scooped a spoonful of bright green orbs from the bone china bowl. Frankie stared at his plate, stuffed a forkful of meat into his mouth.

Art had returned home that afternoon from two weeks on the road, and Evelyn had sprung into action. The beef rib roast was seasoned and tucked in the oven. The potatoes were peeled, boiled, buttered, mashed. The peas were shelled, cooked with baby onions. The good china, with the little pink roses and gold leaves around the edges, was set out. She'd even picked a few clusters of late-blooming White Asters and arranged them in a vase for a centerpiece.

"Isn't it nice to have your father home?" Evelyn asked, as she slid back into her chair.

He isn't my father, Frankie thought, gnawing on the too-large piece of meat. He pushed the lump to his cheek. "It's nice to have rib roast and mashed potatoes."

"Don't talk with your mouth full," Art said, pointing his fork at Frankie.

Evelyn scratched her cheek. She smiled faintly, took a sip of milk.

"Won't you tell us about your trip, Art? I'm sure it was quite an adventure. It always seems that way to me."

"I wasn't exploring the jungle," he snapped. "I was working my keister off."

Frankie breathed in and out through his nose. His mouthful of food had become unmanageable, an enormous beef-flavored wad of chewing gum. Impossible to break down. Too big to swallow.

"Even so," Evelyn said, looking at the flowers in the center of the table, with their sunny yellow faces and delicate white petals. "We'd love to hear about it. Wouldn't we, Frankie?"

She looked at her boy then. He opened his eyes wide and nodded enthusiastically. If Art started jabbering about the trip, Frankie knew he could discreetly liberate the meat into his napkin, slip it to Scout beneath the table.

"Drove more than 600 miles," Art said. "Down to St. Cloud, over to Duluth and back up through Grand Rapids on the way home."

"My goodness," Evelyn said, watching Art as he spoke. Her elbow rested on the table, her chin perched on her fingertips.

Frankie dabbed at his mouth with the napkin, discreetly spit the lump of meat into the fabric, placed the napkin back in his lap.

"Locked down seven new contracts along the way," Art said. "Signs for Synder's Drugs and Super Stores, J.C. Penney's, a few movie theaters. You saw the sketches before I left town."

"They were wonderful," his wife said.

Art had also sold an original creation to a gentleman's club in Bigfork on the trip. He kept that news and sketch to himself.

Scout gently extracted a glob of fatty meat from Frankie's fingertips beneath the table.

"I'll be going up to Ontario next month," Art prattled on with excruciating detail about his itinerary and customer list.

"May I be excused?" Frankie asked, during a rare pause in his stepfather's chronicle.

Art wiped his mouth and rose from the table.

"Wash the dishes and then go to bed," he said. "Your mother and I are going to relax in the living room."

Evelyn was pleased to be included in Art's after-dinner cocktails. He mixed two Black Russians, and then settled beside her on the love seat. She smiled and sipped her drink, while her husband's lecture on the art of bending neon tubing became more animated. Running water and the soft clink of flatware and china served as background music.

After a bit, Frankie emerged from the kitchen to announce he'd finished his chores. Evelyn stood to kiss him good night, but he deflected her as he hustled past. She watched Frankie disappear down the hall, heard his bedroom door click shut. The remaining ice cube in her glass popped. She picked up the glass and tipped the ice and last few drops of alcohol into her mouth. She crunched the cube and swallowed, felt the cold travel down her throat and into her chest.

"I'm off to get ready for bed myself," she whispered, tilting her head.

"Yeah, go 'head," Art replied, pouring himself a second drink. "I'll be there in a bit."

* * * *

White light from the bedside lamp glinted off the floor mirror in Evelyn's bedroom, casting a dark Picasso-like shadow of her naked figure onto the wall. She slipped into the ice-blue nightgown, guiding it past her full hips and round breasts, and smoothed the lace straps over the dip of her shoulders.

The Butterick pattern had caught her eye at the fabric store. A sheer chiffon she'd selected was the perfect complement. The hemline fell scandalously above the knees – the latest fashion, chic, risqué. It was a far cry from her typical flannel gowns. Evelyn's cheeks had burned when she purchased the pattern and fabric, and the clerk flashed a knowing grin.

Now she assessed her reflection in the nightie.

The fitted waist and shirred bra cups accentuated her curves. A dainty satin bow hung at her sternum, drawing the eye to her best assets. It was worth the earlier embarrassment.

Cherry-ice gloss on her lips and a sweet floral perfume dabbed behind her ears, both new samples from the Avon lady, punctuated the statement. A matching robe was the final touch – two floaty chiffon layers that swept the ankles and puffy three-quarter sleeves gathered with white lace. She swayed her hips to make the chiffon dance in the mirror, to boost her courage.

She jumped at the click of the bedroom doorknob turning. She regained her composure and struck an alluring pose as Art entered the room, hand on her hip, one knee bent. He paused to take in the sight, then cocked his head to the side and shook it.

"What on earth are you wearing?"

"It's called a *peignoir*," she said, twirling to flaunt the layers of chiffon. She eased the robe off her shoulders, let it flow down her arms to the floor where it became a gossamer puddle at her feet. "I made it while you were gone. I wanted to surprise you."

He took a step toward her, unbuckling his belt and slipping out of his loafers. The crests of her nipples couldn't have been more prominent through the sheer fabric. Evelyn drew her shoulders back, nevertheless. Her breath caught in her throat as Art unzipped his trousers and stepped out of his pants.

"I've missed you," she whispered.

"Yes. Me, too," Art acknowledged, even as he moved past her. He truthfully had missed her company in the comfortable home, the delicious meals she always prepared, even going out as a couple with their circle of friends. *But this?* "You'll freeze in that getup. What happened to the flannel nightgown I bought you at Christmas?"

"I love that gown. I'll change into it later," Evelyn pressed on, "when I'm ready to go to sleep."

"Suit yourself," Art said, plucking at invisible lint on his shirt sleeve. "I'm ready to go to sleep now."

Evelyn stood in her fashion magazine pose, frozen, as Art changed into his pajama shirt and pants. What remained of her confidence began to evaporate as he pulled back the blanket and climbed into his bed. She silently cursed the perspiration prickling her underarms, even as she moved across the cold floor in her bare feet.

She sat beside him on the mattress, leaned in and ran her fingers across his forehead, through his hair.

"My head is pounding, Evie, from all that driving. I need some sleep." Art's voice cracked, and he swallowed before he spoke again. "You said you understood, before we married, what it would be like. We had an agreement."

Evelyn nodded, blinked hard at the sting in her eyes. She traced the curve of his jaw with her finger, stopped to rest at the dimple in his chin.

"I don't need you to love me," she whispered. "I just need..."

Her courage fell away. Her unfinished sentence plummeted into the crevasse between them.

Art seized her wrist, thrusted her hand away. "I'm glad you had the sense to stop before completing that sentence, Evelyn."

She turned from him.

"It's unbecoming," he said. "What you were insinuating."

A new source of heat overtook her body. Humiliation. Shame.

He rolled onto his side, away from her, and clicked off the lamp.

"Good night, then," he snapped.

Ice-blue chiffon and soft lace. Cherry lips and smooth knees. Evelyn sat with her back to him, her hands in her lap, running the tally through her mind. Slowly, she rose and moved to her own bed. Tears pooled in her eyes, spilled onto the pillow as she lay back.

Yes, they'd had an agreement. The marriage would not be about love. But Evelyn thought they'd only been speaking about the emotions of love. Did he not have physical desires, needs, just as she did? Surely a man and woman could satisfy one another without being in love. Did he not desire her at all?

Art's rejection in the bedroom had whittled away at her. A sliver here, a flake there, for seven years, until the room was piled with shavings, remnants of her desirability and self-esteem. It seemed to exhaust them both. Already, Art's gentle breathing had progressed into the rumble of sleep. Evelyn lay deathly still, skin and bone, unable to move, unable to relax.

How I wish you hadn't left me, Frank.

Life with Frank had been exhilarating. Days packed with breathless laughter. Nights filled with breathless passion. It had been too short. No one ever looked at Evelyn the way he had – not before and not since. Perhaps it was selfish, too much to hope for, the notion that a woman could be desired by more than one man in a lifetime.

She willed herself to push the memories from her mind, to focus on her breathing.

With each deliberate breath in and out, an image materialized in the darkness of her mind. Sparkling obsidian eyes gazed upon her with desire, and respect. They admired all the things Art couldn't see, didn't want to see. The eyes became a face. The face became a man. He reclined down beside her, wiped away her tears.

Evelyn stroked the soft line of her collarbone with her middle finger. Her mind wandered further.

Muscular hands cupping tender flesh, limbs of dark walnut and milky white entwined. A bed of pine needles beneath bare bodies, a blanket of stars overhead. Full brown lips devouring her neck, a moist pink tongue teasing her curves.

Evelyn's hands wandered further, swept at the ice-blue hemline scandalously above her knees, chic, risqué. An intake of breath. An enraptured sigh.

LIFE IN THE 1950S

/National Newswire/ -- A House of Representatives committee learned today that 74 State Department employees have been discharged this year as a result of investigations concerning homosexuality. It brings the total number of U.S. federal employee dismissals for homosexuality to 381 since 1950.

The recent firings were part of an ongoing review of personnel files and subsequent interviews of suspected threats. The goal, according to Security Officer Scott McLain, is to "root out immoral, scandalous and dangerous government employees, whose personal conduct put the entire nation at risk."

1955

Bitter Rapids, Minnesota

The tang of wet wool and stale beer clung to the haze of cigarette smoke inside Wally's Tavern. As soon as the pungent odor hit his nostrils, Art knew he wouldn't be going home until morning. Evelyn would recognize the sour, wet-dog scent on him, like one knows the distinct smell of a grandparent's house. She would be upset that Wally's had been his first stop upon returning to Bitter Rapids. She'd want an apology. She'd have her feelings hurt again when he failed to give one.

Art hung his overcoat on one of the wall pegs at the entrance. The knee-length, double-breasted Chesterfield was a black sheep in the lineup of form-fitting, bright-plaid Mackinaw hunting jackets. His felt fedora, with its yellow silk band to match the handkerchief carefully folded into the breast pocket of blazer, also stood out among the assortment of wool caps.

"Well, well, is that Arthur Specht who just walked in the door, or Cary Grant?" the tavern's namesake belted out from his post behind the bar.

Art clicked a finger pistol at the man and winked. He strode up to his usual barstool beside his buddy, Ed. He gave his tweed pantlegs a tug at the knees, propped his black-and-white wing tips on the bar foot-rail beside Ed's red-russet leather boots.

The men gathered around the television waved and shouted hello without looking over. Middleweights Basilio and DeMarco were in round five of their bloody match, broadcast live from Syracuse. A young man nodded as he carried two martinis from the bar to a booth near the jukebox. His lady friend smiled at Art while she plucked an olive from its toothpick with her teeth.

Ed clapped Art on the back. "The man-about-town back to carouse with his lowbrow chums."

Wally pulled the tap on a lager with just the right amount of foam and placed the frosty glass in front of Art on a square paper napkin.

Art enjoyed the hero's welcome he received at Wally's after being on the road. His was a different life from his small-town peers. And while the other men of Bitter Rapids were mostly content with their existence, they also admired and envied Art's career, his freedom, his exposure to sights and places they only read about in the paper or talked about during pie-in-the-sky planning of trips that would never be taken.

Of course, being on the road wasn't nearly as glamorous as Art made it out to be. Sleeping in small, dingy hotel rooms on lumpy beds; conducting meetings in cramped, stale offices; and trying to persuade small-town companies that a neon sign would elevate their status on par with Vegas showrooms and Times Square department stores.

The real reward of being on the road, though Art never spoke of it, was the freedom to be invisible, out of the spotlight of hometown gossipmongers. He could make acquaintances in the kind of establishments Bitter Rapids did not have, would never have.

"Good trip for ya?" Ernest asked.

"Oh yeah, for sure," Art said and took a sip of his beer. "Pushed a lot of paper."

He rattled off the list of cities and companies he'd visited this go-around. Then he asked, "What have you all been up to the past couple weeks?"

A round of "nothing much" and "same old thing" made its way across the barstools. Ernest nodded along. He and his wife had six children under the age of fourteen. He escaped to Wally's every chance he got. Same old thing.

"Been spending all my free time on the water," piped up Bill from the end of the bar.

"Cooling off already," Art said. "The walleye still biting?"

"Sure," Bill replied. "Got the freezer in my garage packed full of them. Saving room for a few mallards and canvasbacks, though. And Jolene said she wanted a goose for Christmas this year. A group of us are heading to the boundary waters at the opening of the early season, if you want to come along."

"Hey, I appreciate that, but I'll be back on the road most of September," Art said. "Got a few more cities I need to call on before the holidays and heavy snow hits."

Cheers erupted from the group watching the boxing match, and the couple in the nearby booth laughed because the uproar made them jump. Then the place settled back down to its usual low drone. Art continued to watch the couple out of the corner of his eye, pretending to listen to Ed and Bill talk about ducks and grouse and pheasants. The woman tucked a strand of platinum hair behind her ear. A collection of empty martini glasses was smudged with the cherry red of her lipstick. Art took note of the shrinking distance between them in the booth, their exchange of glances. The man's hand moved discreetly beneath the table, made its way to the woman's hemline. She bit her lower lip.

A round of applause and an exchange of bills signaled the conclusion of the boxing match.

"Who won?" Art asked as the group dispersed.

"Basilio," one fellow said.

"Took twelve rounds to take DeMarco down, but he got the job done," another chimed in.

It was nearing ten o'clock, and the crowd began to grumble and thin. Alarm clocks needed to be set for the next day's work. Impatient wives waited at home. Wally filled the bar sink with soapy water.

"How 'bout you, Ed?" Art asked, as he motioned to Wally for another round. "Marjorie gonna chew your ear for staying out late?"

"Nah," Ed answered. "She took the kids down to St. Paul for the week to visit her mother before school starts back up."

"You don't say? So, you'll be living the bachelor's life for few days, eh."

"You betcha," Ed laughed and raised his glass. "Just like you, when you're on the road. You'll have to show me how it's done."

Art chuckled, drained his glass. He and Ed played a few rounds of nine-ball.

"Last call," Wally belted out to the stragglers a while later. He gathered the empty glasses from the bar.

The couple near the jukebox slid out of their booth. The woman stretched with her hands on the back of her neck beneath her hair, then extended her hands up to the ceiling, rocked her hips from side to side. She took a step toward the door, wobbling in her high heels, and the man placed a hand on her lower back to steady her. He helped her on with her coat, steered her out the exit.

Ed sucked his front teeth and tilted his head in a knowing way. Wally nodded slightly, eyebrows raised.

The bar was still, nearly empty. Ed threw back the last of his beer and stood up to pluck his wallet from his back pocket. He laid a bill on the counter, tapped it twice with his finger.

"Why don't you sleep at my place tonight," he said to Art. "Kid's rooms are empty. And you won't have to worry about waking Evie and Frankie coming through the door at this late hour."

Art glanced over at his friend. Their eyes connected for a heartbeat, and he looked back into his empty beer mug. Wally grabbed the bill and turned his back to the men to tuck it into the register till.

"We could play cards or something," Ed added. He brushed the small of Art's back with his fingertips as he stepped away from the bar.

"You betcha," Art said, tossing a bill onto the bar, taking a moment to relish the electric touch.

Wally dried a freshly-washed wine glass, hung it on the rack overhead. He watched the men head for the exit, put on their coats, exchange halting glances. The same inkling entering his mind as when he'd watched the man and woman from the jukebox leave a few minutes before. *They look like a couple.* Wally reached for another dripping glass, dried it with vigor, trying to rub the outrageous thought from his mind.

"Good night, then," Art said, angling his fedora just so.

"Yeah, good night fellas," Wally said.

Theirs were the only vehicles left in the parking lot. Still, Art strode past his car, flashed his companion a look of urgency, disappeared into the dark cover of foliage beyond. Ed glanced about nervously, then followed.

A blanket of stars overhead. A rustle of the wind. A stirring in the shadows, swaying branches, intertwined limbs. Scandalous, risqué. An intake of breath. An enraptured sigh.

1955

Bitter Rapids, Minnesota

*E*velyn's tools of the trade were sprawled across the kitchen table – cookbooks, recipe box, appointment book, pen and notepad. She jotted notes for the coming week, made a list of items she'd need from the market, the butcher, the liquor store. The activity took her back to her school days. She'd enjoyed most of her classes. But the lessons she'd learned in home economics were the ones she used as an adult. Knowing how to sew and mend clothes, create a meal plan, balance a checkbook.

The kitchen door flew open with a bang.

"Sorry, Mom!" Frankie sang, as he and Scout bounded into the house with a blast of frosty late-winter air.

"Mind the door, young man!" Art bellowed from the living room.

Evelyn shot her son a you-should-know-better look.

"Sorry," Frankie repeated. He pulled off his snow boots and set them on the mud porch, eased the door shut.

Scout trotted to the kitchen table and sat beside Evelyn. His tail swept the floor as he waited for her to notice. Evelyn glanced at him from the corner of her eye. She turned and took his massive head in her hands, rubbed the cold fur of his cheeks and ears. Scout stole a kiss on her wrist.

"There's a bologna sandwich for you in the Frigidaire," Evelyn told Frankie. "Wash up before you eat."

She reached for the bright red-and-white-checkered cover of her Betty Crocker recipe binder, flipped to the dinner tab. Evelyn wanted to make something special to boost Art's foul mood. Travel energized him, and when he was tied to Bitter Rapids because of heavy snow, Art turned morose, short-tempered. Evelyn understood. The four walls of home must feel like a prison if you were accustomed to the adventure of the open road. Being confined to home was easier for her, she told herself, since she'd never had that taste of freedom.

Evelyn turned the pages without reading them, stared unseeing at the cigarette burning down in the ashtray, a perfect crimson impression of her lips on the filter. She thought about freedom, and her mind drifted to Maak.

Today would be the first time she would see Maak since he'd been hired on at Logdahl's Market. She was giddy with the thought of catching a glimpse of him. Their visits had ended upon his release from prison, of course. She knew she wouldn't be able to have a decent conversation with him at the market. But seeing him, confirming that he was getting along well, just hearing his voice again. It would help appease her ache.

With fresh energy, she cleared the table, stuffed her shopping list into her purse. She moved into the living room.

"I'm off to the market." Evelyn leaned in to kiss Art's cheek, then extended her palm for the car keys.

The market was only a mile away, an easy walk in the summer with the wagon in tow. Evelyn usually went while Art was at work and Frankie was in school or off playing with friends. In the winter, she needed the car, which was only available to her when Art was home.

He set his book on the couch beside him and extracted the keys from his trouser pocket.

"Take Frankie with you," he said, dropping the keys into her outstretched hand.

Evelyn paused. With Frankie along, she'd have no chance to talk with Maak. And what if the boy remembered him from the river? She ran her thumb over the engraved crest of the metal Buick key chain.

"He just came in from walking Scout," Evelyn said. "Why make him go back out in the cold again so soon?"

"He's not a baby anymore, Evelyn. He's a teenager." Art gave her a hard look, and Evelyn dropped her eyes. "You want him sitting idle in his room just because it's cold out?"

"Of course, you're right," she said and called out to Frankie to get back into his coat and boots.

* * * *

"Get a basket, will you Frankie?" Evelyn said. "Meet me at the bakery counter."

She set off in the opposite direction, meandered up and down a few aisles. As she rounded a display of Coca-Cola bottles, Maak emerged from the other side, broom in hand. A spark of delight lit her eyes, though she managed to fight off the giant grin threatening to sweep her lips.

"Good afternoon," she said with a steady voice and polite nod.

Maak stepped aside to let her pass. "Good afternoon, ma'am."

Their eyes connected for a heartbeat as she walked by, and her breath caught in her throat.

Evelyn glanced back at him, pretending to deliberate over a can of peas. He resumed sweeping, and she tried to absorb as many details as possible without lingering too long. His nails were clean and trimmed. His shirt was white and neatly pressed. His shoes looked like he'd gotten them second-hand, but they were free of holes and freshly polished. *He looks well,* she told herself. She turned and approached the bakery.

Mr. Logdahl handed Frankie a chocolate chip cookie from behind the bakery counter.

"Oh, Urban," she feigned protest. "You'll spoil his dinner."

"He's a growing boy," the man said.

Frankie grinned as he stuffed the entire cookie into his mouth. Through chipmunk cheeks, the boy asked, "Who's the Colored fella? I never seen him before."

Evelyn blanched.

"You never *saw* him before," she corrected her son, hoping to steer the conversation away from *who*. She silently cursed Art for insisting she bring Frankie along, and herself for not standing her ground with him.

"Name's Maak," Mr. Logdahl answered Frankie. "I think he's half Indian, actually, one of those Ojibwe. An ex-con, too. Just paroled."

"No foolin'?" Frankie said under his breath and took a sidelong look at Maak.

"No foolin'," he confirmed, while handing Evelyn a box of *potica*. It was Art's favorite dessert, and she could never get the sweet and savory European pastry roll quite right herself.

"Figured everybody deserves a second chance," the grocer said with a wink at Evelyn, repeating the very words she'd used in persuading him to hire Maak. "Working out good so far. He doesn't talk much. He's respectful, works hard, keeps out of trouble."

Frankie stole another look. Maak kept his head down, swept his way up the aisle and toward the front of the store. If he knew they were talking about him, he didn't show it. The boy had a million questions, though he knew better than to ask anything else. His stepfather had told him many times that "children are to be seen and not heard." Even though Art wasn't there, the story of Frankie gossiping about the ex-con Indian at the market would likely get back to him, and Frankie's hide would get tanned for it.

Evelyn thanked Mr. Logdahl and moved away to fill her basket. She sent Frankie traipsing back and forth across the store to fetch items from the list and quash any further conversation. At the cash register, she gave him a penny for a Bazooka bubble gum, hoping it would keep his jaw busy on the car ride home.

A little way down the road, in between blowing giant pink bubbles, Frankie worked up the courage to broach the subject with his mom.

"You know," he began. He blew another bubble and sucked it back in his mouth with a pop. "That Indian had a familiar look, like I've met him before."

Evelyn chuckled lightheartedly. Inside, she cursed herself again for bringing her son on the excursion.

"Sometimes we just get funny feelings like that," she said. "Chalk it up to an overactive imagination."

She tousled his hair.

"Nah," Frankie shook her hand away. "I think it's more than that."

He blew a bubble the size of a baseball. It popped over his nose, and he carefully pulled the sticky film from his face, stuffed the pink wad back in his mouth.

Evelyn waved him off. "Well, I can't imagine where you would have met an Indian, much less an ex-convict."

Frankie shrugged his shoulders and blew another pink bubble. Evelyn breathed in relief as they turned the corner to their street, the perfect opportunity to change the subject.

"I'll be waking you a little early tomorrow," she began. "Your father wants you to shovel the drive before school."

"He's not my father."

"Oh, Frankie, don't start."

Evelyn feigned frustration, but it was guilt she felt. She knew bringing up Art, calling him Frankie's father, would poke a sore spot in her son. She'd done it anyway, knowing it would put an end to the conversation about Maak.

"Just make sure you get right up," she said.

"Yes, ma'am," Frankie responded, knowing the formal response would eat at her just as much as her calling Art his father ate at him.

1990

Des Moines, Iowa

Breakfast Served All Day.

The edges of the cardboard sign perched in the Country Kitchen window are wavy, browned. It's proof of the declaration, the effect of bacon grease in the steamy air twenty-four/seven. The restaurant is nestled in the Days Inn parking lot, a short walk from the hotel rooms. Frank and April take note of the sign. They order from the dinner menu, nevertheless.

"Boy, Gram seemed to fall asleep even before she was all the way in bed," April says after their food arrives.

Frank rubs his eyes with his meaty fingertips.

"She isn't the only one who's exhausted," he says. "How can a person get so tired just from driving all day? I feel like I've been hiking in the desert. Every muscle in my body aches."

April yawns her agreement.

"How much longer do you think it will take us to get there?" she asks.

He takes a bite of his grilled ham-and-Swiss on rye, mumbles "I don't know" with a full mouth.

The diner is reminiscent of their home kitchen. A sprinkle of blue flecks in the white linoleum helps disguise the scuffs and gouges created by the aluminum chairs and table legs. Meaningful conversation is easily avoided here. Its spareness encourages small talk.

April picks up a French fry, dunks it into the glob of ketchup on her plate. She flings the fry back down to the plate, a soggy gauntlet thrown to impel communication.

"Don't you think it's about time you tell me what this trip is all about? It's ridiculous for you and Gram to be so tight-lipped when the whole point is to finally set the record straight."

"Those were your grandmother's words, not mine."

Frank sucks droplets of soda through the straw in his ice-filled glass. The empty gurgle echoes off the tile floor and Formica tabletops. He picks up the glass and rattles the ice to catch the waitress' attention. She's reading a magazine at the end of the counter.

"I'm dying of thirst here," he mutters.

"You can't keep avoiding the subject, Dad."

April is motionless on her side of the booth. Frank feels her eyes bore holes in his forehead as he peers into the empty glass.

"There's not really much to tell, April. It's not like we plotted a murder or something. There was an accident. Somebody died. End of story."

Frank waves the glass in the air again. The ice jangles. The waitress sets down her magazine, slides from her seat, takes her time walking to their table. She snatches up the glass and disappears into the kitchen with it.

"Right," April says, drawing out the vowel. "Nothing to see here, folks. Somebody died. No big deal. Move along."

Frank huffs a frustrated grunt in her direction. This is a side of his daughter he dislikes. Smart-mouthed. Snide. Frank wonders if she inherited that attitude from her mother, or from his.

The waitress returns with a glass of soda. She gives Frank a saccharine smile as she sets it down, then walks away. Tiny bubbles fizz and pop. He reaches for the glass.

"Five bucks says she spit in that," April says.

Frank's hand pauses in midair.

"Dang it, April," he mutters. He grabs her glass instead, downs the last of her Diet Coke. The aftertaste of artificial sweetener lingers on his tongue. He grimaces.

"The accident," April says.

The subject is a jackhammer. It pounds relentlessly inside his skull.

Frank and Evelyn had never talked about that day. Not once in more than thirty years. Life had pressed on. Memories faded, blurred. There were even times when he wondered if any of it had actually happened. Maybe it was just part of a kid's overactive imagination. Maybe that's why his mother had never spoken of it. It never happened.

It was easy enough for him to believe. Until the long-forgotten quilt showed up in the newspaper.

"Sometimes bad things happen," Frank whispers, "and there's nothing you can do about it."

He clears his throat. April blinks. This trip has been a master class in the art of awkward silence. Endurance pays off.

"It's like when you're hiking in the mountains," he continues. "You're way out there, and maybe the trail is more rugged than you expected, or maybe the weather turns on you."

He's parched. Frank pulls the straw from his glass and gulps down the soda. The rush of carbonation makes his eyes water. He rubs at them again. April wasn't joking when she wagered on the probability of spit in his drink. They both knew that. His desperation softens her. She reaches for his hand.

"But once you've gone a certain distance around the loop, you run out of options," Frank continues. "It doesn't matter if you regret going on the hike, or if you're getting blisters on your feet, or you run out of water. It's too late to turn back. You have to just press on, push yourself until you make it out."

He pulls his hand away, squeezes the back of his neck.

"Okay. You pressed on," April cajoles. "By doing what, exactly?"

"We got the heck out of there," Frank says. "We left Bitter Rapids forever, never looked back, never spoke of it again."

Running away has a certain appeal, April admits to herself. Just leave. Put your mistakes behind you. Dodge accountability. Get a fresh start. Who hasn't entertained that thought at least once? But then, she thinks of her mother.

"You make it sound easy," April says.

"No," Frank's voice cracks, and he swallows. "Not at first, anyway. I suppose it got easier over time."

His response makes April wonder if it was hard for her own mother to run away. A vision of dresser drawers flashes through the young woman's mind. Drawers that looked like gaping mouths after Deborah had packed her belongings and left the empty receptacles hanging open. *Why?* they seemed to ask. Frank and April left those drawers untouched for days and days, as though waiting for an answer. All these years later, April still feels their emptiness, their lack of closure.

"Well, it doesn't get easier for the people you leave behind," she snaps, and stuffs a wad of fries into her mouth. The sweet tang of ketchup helps smother the bitter taste on her tongue.

Exhaustion soaks deeper into Frank's limbs. The ham-and-Swiss calls from the plate, an easy diversion from conversation. But he can't muster the energy to lift his leaden hands from the table. He knows the sensation of escaping in a speedboat on choppy waters, as well as how it feels to be left adrift at sea. Either way, the nausea is relentless.

"Heck, April, I don't know what to say." He bites at the inside of his cheek. "I was fifteen years old and scared to death. I lived in fear for years. I kept expecting the cops to come beating down our door at any minute."

April fiddles with the dagger-shaped charm dangling from her necklace, slides it back and forth along the chunky silver chain.

"By the time I finished college and got my own place, I started thinking about going back, setting the record straight."

"So, why didn't you?"

Because I fell in love with your mom, and then we had a beautiful baby, he thinks. *How could I possibly have said anything then? There was too much to lose.*

"I don't know," he says.

April shakes her head slowly from side to side. The new information doesn't quite gel. She slips the dagger into her mouth, sucks on it for a moment.

"I'm sorry, Dad, I just don't buy it," she says finally. Her tone has a rough edge. She stares at him with flinty eyes. "You say you were scared. But, you and Gram have always been so chill. You never seemed scared or, I don't know, burdened."

He takes a deep breath, releases it slowly. *Just because someone carries his burden well doesn't mean it isn't heavy.*

"I don't know what else to tell you," Frank says. He stands and pulls a few bills from his wallet, tosses them on the table. He heads toward the exit, leaving her alone with her fries. "Don't stay out too late."

Life through the Ages

"We are our memories,

we are that surreal museum of inconstant forms,

that pile of broken mirrors."

– Jorge Luis Borges, *In Praise of Darkness*

1990

Des Moines, Iowa

G ram and April wait on the sidewalk outside their hotel room as Frank moves their belongings from inside the car back to the roof. This daily routine in their trip seems a bigger torment than usual. Every minute or two, Frank takes in a labored breath, clears his throat, pinches the bridge of his nose between a thumb and forefinger.

"What crawled up his butt and died this morning?" Gram whispers.

April rolls her eyes. She's still frustrated with her dad, but her frustration with Gram is larger at the moment.

"Let's go," Frank grumbles.

They pile into the car.

The flat Midwestern landscape moves past the windows in a blur – emerald and gold cornfields awaiting harvest, striped patches of land stitched together by property lines of trees and fencing. The blanket of bounty spreads as far as the eye can see.

The local radio station fades to static, and Frank clicks it off.

April suggests they pop in a cassette tape. Frank says no with a quick shake of his head.

Words for small talk have all been exhausted. The whoosh of wind over the hood and roof taunts them. *Is there nothing left to say?*

Frank props an elbow on the window ledge, rests his ear in his palm. His other hand keeps the wheel steady. Dutifully, after an hour on the road, he pulls into a rest stop. The women head to the restroom. Frank waits in the car, head tilted back, eyes closed.

He'd chalked up his lingering headache to stress. But now, pressure fills his skull, his eyes water and throb. A fire burns in the back of his throat. He curses himself for getting sick.

"Your dad's always been oversensitive," Gram declares from behind the stall door. "Gets in these 'woe is me' moods. 'Life isn't fair. Boo hoo hoo.'"

April refuses to respond when Gram talks while she tinkles.

"Maybe I coddled him too much as a baby. I tried to toughen him up later," Gram continues. "I guess I failed."

April washes her hands with the powdery pink soap from the dispenser. She splashes cold water on her face. The towel contraption is jammed. She lifts the front of her sweatshirt to dry herself.

"Life is hard, April." Gram emerges from the stall. "The sooner a person learns to accept that, the easier it is to get on with it."

Outside, they walk the length of sidewalk lining the parking lot.

Gram stops and extracts her cigarette case from the pocket of her quilted jacket. She snaps open the coin-purse style top, taps out a cigarette, and places it between her lips. She removes the lighter from its custom side pocket, takes a deep drag as she lights up. The smoke billows from her nostrils as she exhales around the oxygen tube. The pressure of April's continued silence builds inside her like steam in a teakettle.

"No use crying over spilled milk," Gram snaps at her silent granddaughter, jabbing the cigarette in the air to punctuate the point. "You've heard that before, haven't you?"

April watches the tip of the cigarette burn fire red as Gram takes another fierce drag. She turns and heads back down the sidewalk toward the car.

"Yes, Gram, I've heard it before." *From you, about a billion times.*

She takes a few more steps, then stops and turns to face Gram.

"Maybe this trip just has him thinking about what happened in Bitter Rapids," April says. "Maybe he misses old friends, the life you guys ran away from."

Gram crinkles her nose in disagreement.

"There wasn't much to miss, April. So-called friends, who cared more about appearances than whether either one of us was happy. I felt no great loss for the people we left behind, and I doubt any of them missed us."

"But you and Dad never talked about it," April presses. "How can you know he didn't have friends, people he missed and who missed him when he disappeared?"

Gram pauses, drops her cigarette to the pavement, and stamps it out with the toe of her sneaker.

"I know," she says, "because Frankie had run away again. He'd already put everything in his life behind him at that point, even me, until that final horrible day at the river. And then he was stuck with me."

* * * *

The family inches their way farther east and farther north. The days have gotten shorter, the nights darker. On this day, they grab an early dinner, decide to drive a couple more hours before stopping for the night.

Their compact car is alone on the highway for miles in either direction. Its headlights cast a wide radiance on the asphalt ahead. Beyond the arch of light, black emptiness.

Every few minutes, the car speeds beneath a lone set of highway lights. The cab is set ablaze with a flash of light, then goes dark again.

Frank fights the urge to give into the darkness and closes his eyes for a moment. He turns the dial on the radio, past crackles and dead air, until he lands on a Southern rock station and a familiar guitar riff.

For the next few minutes, he and April sing along.

"I get that same old bad feelin', baby," they croon, "every time you come 'round."

Frank pantomimes the drum solo, holding the steering wheel steady with his knees. Aprils bobs her chin up and down to the beat.

"Every time you come 'round. Every time you come 'round."

The song fades and the smooth-talking deejay says, "And that was 'Old Bad Feelin' by Whiskey Winter. The album of the same title went platinum in '75, just two months after five of the six band members and their manager died in a plane crash."

Frank shakes his head, remembering exactly where he was and what he was doing when news of the band's demise broke on the radio.

"Returning from a show in Texas, the band's chartered plane ran out of fuel and crashed in the mountains. Only drummer Billy Barnes and the copilot survived. Ten years later, Barnes revived the band playing old favorites and new material that gave Whiskey Winter a second life. The original band's founder and lead songwriter Samuel Winter never lived to see the impact his music made on the world."

"That's awful," April says. "I never knew that. How come I've never heard that before?"

In middle school, April hung a poster of Whiskey Winter's lead singer Eddy Keys on the wall beside her bed. She studied the album cover and memorized the song lyrics printed in the glossy foldout from the cassette case. She knew the band had been around since the 1960s, yet she never made the connection that Keys would have only been a child then.

April's heart shrinks a little. The singer on her wall, with his messy long hair and piercing brown eyes, was an imposter. He wasn't the poet who'd poured his soul into the lyrics she'd committed to heart. The betrayal stings.

"I'll never be able to enjoy their songs now," she says.

Frank glances at his daughter in the review mirror, bemusement in his raised brow. "Why not?"

"Because now I know there was an actual man named Winter, and he died tragically, and these other dudes are singing his songs and taking all the credit for something he created."

The new information makes April wince.

"It's just wrong," she adds. "He deserves to be remembered, and acknowledged."

Frank's eyebrows draw together, a hard line that darkens his eyes.

"Nobody gets what they deserve, April."

The young woman tilts her head. "What the heck is that supposed to mean?"

"It means plenty of criminals who deserve to be locked up are walking free. And plenty of decent people who deserve to live a good life end up miserable. People live and die every day. And only a small handful of them get to be acknowledged or remembered," he says. "All the rest of us are destined to be forgotten."

These don't sound like her dad's words. They're too heavy. April crumbles a little under their weight.

"That's a horrible thing to say," she scolds. Then, more gently, she adds, "You don't really believe that."

Frank scrunches his shoulders to his ears; his way of avoiding debate. He says nothing, but his silence shouts, *Maybe, I do.*

Gram waggles a finger in the air.

"Your father's right," she says.

It's a rare declaration of agreement, and April is knocked down even further. The elder woman senses weakness, goes in for the kill.

"Someday, you'll have kids, and then they'll have kids, and I'll have kicked the bucket long before," Gram says. "Oh, they may hear mention of their Great-Great-Grandma once or twice, but that'll be it. They won't know a darn thing about me, and they won't care. And I won't care either, 'cause I'll be dead. Ashes to ashes, dust to dust."

Frank's head bobs slightly in agreement, his eyes steady on the dark road ahead.

April puffs her cheeks, tries to exhale the heaviness from her gut. She rattles her head to cast out their cynicism. The upcoming highway light beams through the car's interior, illuminates the hard lines in Gram's expression, the tightness of Frank's jaw. They fly past the light, descend back into shadow.

"That is one piss-poor perspective on life," April says finally.

"Maybe," Gram concedes from the darkness, her voice a mere whisper now. "But that doesn't make it any less true."

1935

Duluth, Minnesota

"I never seen shoes like those before." The woman tilted her head as she spoke, then slid onto the barstool beside Maak. She motioned to the bartender as though he would know her drink. Her plump lips and tapered nails were firetruck red. Her bare shoulders were radiant umber.

"They're funny looking," she added, eyeing his feet again.

Maak wore the moccasins his mother had fashioned from moose hide just months before, a gift to celebrate his return home from boarding school. It was her last accomplishment before going to the Land of Souls. Maak had aged ten years while he was away. His mother, it seemed, had aged thirty. He'd come home a man. She'd died an old woman.

He glanced sideways at the young woman beside him. She smiled and took in his gaze.

"You are bold," he said and drank down his beer, tapped the bar twice to signal he wanted another.

The woman laughed. Her eyes glinted at the unusual compliment.

"You talk funny, too," she said. "I like it."

They exchanged names. Hers floated on the air like a song. Perlie. And then Maak. Her lips formed a pleasing O as she said his name slowly, deliberately. The night edged on. Pleasantries, small talk, a fire-tipped finger dancing along his forearm, sending heat through his body.

"You're not from around here," she said.

"No," Maak responded. "I am not."

He was new to town, he told her. Looking for work, a place to set roots.

"Work's hard to come by these days," she said. "The mine is the only place that'll hire Colored men. I do washing and ironing at General Hospital. It ain't a bad job, but it's hard on my hands. All that water and lye and heat and steam."

Perlie set her hands on the bar to examine them, tilted her head and pouted. Maak inserted his hands beneath hers, palms to palms. He studied the delicate wrists, the slender curve of her fingers.

"You have lovely hands," he said.

She tucked chin in toward her shoulder, smiled at him through thick lashes. "My, my. I do like the way you talk."

Electric heat pulsed through him. He retracted his hands and threw back the remainder of his beer. He motioned to the bartender, in the way Perlie had, for another round of drinks.

The bartender set the glasses down harder than before and gave Perlie a long, stern look. She flashed an insolent smile, then turned her attention back to the unusual stranger beside her.

"So, where'd you grow up?" Perlie asked.

In the river, and the trees, and the marsh, and the sandy banks of my ancestors, Maak thought. *And in the concrete, and the steel, and scratchy wool of the Indian school.*

"Many places," he said.

The bar door swung open. Cold air gusted through, along with a boisterous group of laborers after their shift at the mine. They called out to Perlie to join them.

"No thanks, fellas," she said with a flip of her hand. "I'm otherwise occupied."

The bartender snorted loudly, crossed his arms across his chest. He exchanged looks with the men – his jaw hard, his eyes cold. One of the men broke from the group, approached the bar, and positioned himself between Perlie and Maak.

"Don't be that way, baby doll," he said. "Come on over and sit with me and the boys."

The man bobbed his chin in the direction of his table.

"I said, no thanks, Elias." Perlie turned her attention back toward Maak and smiled. Elias slid in further between their stools.

"What are you doing playing with this Injun fool?"

Perlie blinked as understanding set in – the funny shoes, the funny way of talking. Maak had the thick hair and coffee skin of a black man, but she now saw the other, more subtle qualities that hinted at his Indian roots – the almond shape of his eyes, the slender nose, the sharp angle of his high cheekbones.

"What I'm doing ain't your concern," she said. "Now move along."

"You don't know what you're doing." His voice was hard, as he took hold of her wrist in one hand, her drink in the other. "Come sit with us."

Perlie twisted and jerked her arm free.

"You don't own me," she snapped. "I'll do as I please."

Maak stood, took a step back from his stool. "The lady asked you to move along."

She grinned wide. *Bold. The lady.* Yes, she liked the way this man spoke of her.

"Look around, Red," Elias said. "You don't belong here."

The muscles in Maak's jaw tightened. His aunt's voice sounded in his ears. *You're only half Indian. If you bled, it would run black.* The nuns' scolding flooded his mind. *We're doing God's work, you little heathen.* The boarding school's directive pulsed through his veins. *Kill the Indian, save the man.* All his years, all the voices, always telling him the reasons he did not belong where he was. Maak's eyes locked on Elias'.

"Perlie, do I belong here?"

Fear crept up the hairs at the base of Perlie's neck, worked its way into her throat, extinguished her voice. *Be bold,* she told herself. Yet, she couldn't speak. Her stomach turned hard.

Elias laughed at her silence, gave Maak's chest a shove. "There's your answer. Move along, Injun."

Maak barely registered the impact. He was hard and steady, like an oak standing strong against a winter gale. The men at the distant table took to their feet.

"Take yourselves outside," the bartender spoke up, a wood club gripped tight in his fists. "I won't have you bustin' up my joint."

Maak nodded solemnly, pulled a crumpled bill from his pocket and dropped it on the bar. He turned and walked toward the exit, followed by the man and his crew and Perlie. Maak wasn't more than two steps out the door when Elias punched him in the kidney from behind. Maak fell to his knees, and the crew roared with laughter.

"You bastard!" Perlie shouted. She pounded on Elias' back with her fists. "That was a cheap shot!"

He turned and struck her cheek with the back of his hand. She staggered into the other men, just as Maak regained his bearings. Now it was Elias' turn to be caught off guard, as Maak charged him from behind, slammed him to the ground.

The two men tussled and rolled in the hardpacked dirt of the parking lot. Maak remained on top, held Elias down with his left arm, punched with his right. Once, twice, three times in rapid succession to the side of the head.

Elias threw a fistful of gravel into Maak's face and rolled free as his opponent recoiled. He pulled a switchblade from his pants pocket and slashed wildly while scrambling to his feet.

A fiery sensation sped across Maak's torso. He clutched his gut and felt the wet of a hot gash. He looked down at his hand. *Ninoshenh was wrong*, he thought, *my blood runs red.*

Perlie pushed through the men and ran back into the bar. "Call the cops!"

Outside, Elias swaggered, and the other men cheered his certain victory too soon.

Maak was on him again. A twist of the arm, a crack, a cry of pain, and the knife fell to the ground. Maak kicked it away, out of sight, out of reach, and hoisted the man off his feet, thrust him back to the ground.

The mob stood watching, shocked, frozen in place as time seemed to stop. Both men were covered in blood. It was difficult to tell who held the advantage.

Maak struck his opponent's head, again and again in rapid-fire succession. He felt a cheekbone crack beneath his fist. He did not stop. Another blow, and another. Elias' face became a crumpled mass, unrecognizable. An eye dislodged from the socket, fell to the dirt, still tethered by its optic nerve.

Finally, the others sprang into the fray. They pulled Maak from the motionless form in the dirt. His adrenaline evaporated, his body went limp, and he sank to the ground. Steel toes pounded his back and ribs, stomped the limbs of his crumpled body, until the flashing lights of the police car appeared in the distance. The mob quickly scattered. Only two bodies remained.

LIFE IN THE 1950S

The Strange Career of Jim Crow

Oxford University Press, 1955

C. Vann Woodward

INTRODUCTION – OF OLD REGIMES AND RECONSTRUCTION

One of the strangest things about Jim Crow is it was born in the North.

By 1830, slavery was virtually abolished by one means or another throughout the North. The Northern free Negro enjoyed obvious advantages over the Southern slave. He could not be bought or sold, or separated from his family, or legally made to work without compensation.

For all that, the North political leaders and their constituents made sure in numerous ways that the Negro understood his "place" and that he was severely confined to it. One of these ways was segregation, and with the backing of legal codes, the system permeated all aspects of Negro life in the free states by 1860.

Negroes found themselves systematically separated from whites. They were either excluded from railway cars, omnibuses, stagecoaches, and steamboats or assigned to special "Jim Crow" sections; they sat, when permitted, in secluded and remote corners of theaters; they could not enter most hotels, restaurants, and resorts, except as servants. Moreover, they were educated in segregated schools, punished in segregated prisons, nursed in segregated hospitals, and buried in segregated cemeteries.

1955

Bitter Rapids, Minnesota

"Six ball, corner pocket."

Art shook his head no. "Your angle's off."

The crack of Ed's stick sent the cue ball back-spinning across the felt. Thwack, click, clack reverberated through Wally's Tavern, as the six banked off the cushion, ricocheted into its colorful compatriots, and propelled the eight ball straight into the side pocket.

Art laughed out loud, clapped his friend on the back.

"Aw, heck," Ed grumbled, even as he secretly relished the brief touch.

"I got winner," said Urban Logdahl.

The grocer had been watching from a high-top table nearby, enjoying a pint. He circled the table, plucking balls from the pockets and rolling them to the center of the table.

"How about we play teams," suggested Ernest.

The men agreed and paired off, and a friendly wager followed. Ed racked up the balls. Weeknights at Wally's were for the bachelors, and the husbands who yearned for old times.

Art leaned in to break. The balls exploded across the emerald table, a detonation of frenetic sound and color. Three balls dropped in the pockets.

"Solids," Art announced as he surveyed the field, walked to the opposite end of the table. He pointed with the cue. "Two, side pocket."

The tap of the stick left a moon-shaped imprint of chalk on the blue orb, sent it flying into the side pocket. And the cue ball followed behind.

"Scratch," Ernest snickered. He retrieved the cue ball, placed it on the felt, called his shot.

"Say, how's that Colored working out for you down at the store?" he asked as he sunk his target.

Urban was mid-swig in his beer. He nodded a couple times while he swallowed.

"Better'n expected," he said. "Don't mind saying, I was a little uneasy taking on a mixed-breed fella. An ex-con to boot. But it's working out okay. He gets the job done. Keeps his nose clean."

Art held his pool cue like a scepter, cocked his head in Urban's direction. "What's this now? You hired yourself a Negro ex-con?"

A hush fell on the nearby chatter. Color drained from Urban's face. He took a long, slow drink of his beer. Art glanced about the room. All eyes and ears were trained on their conversation. Heat in the room seemed to tick up five or ten degrees. Urban cleared his throat, took another swig.

"What's this, now?" Art said again.

"I thought you knew," the grocer finally spoke.

The tilt of Art's head, the pierce of his stare, asked without words. *Thought I knew what?*

Feet shuffled here and there. Someone coughed. Ed picked up his mug now, downed the last of his drink in a long series of gulps. He stifled a deep belch.

"I gave the fella a shot, on account of him plucking your boys out of the river," Urban said. "Your missus, she said how grateful y'all were. It takes a good heart to risk your own life for a child, she said, and that, well, you know, he'd paid his debt to society and all. Everyone deserves a second chance, she said. Couldn't argue with that, now could I?"

Ed gave Urban an elbow nudge to stop his rambling.

Art tilted his head the other way, struggled to make sense of it. His eyes gave him away – unfocused, windows to the gears turning in his mind. The bar was frozen in speechless tension, like fishing on late-spring ice. Ernest was the first to shatter the silence and risk the icy plunge.

"We all thought you knew," he mumbled.

Art smashed the cue stick down on the table in a shocking blow. Urban took a leap back.

"Hey now!" Wally shouted from behind the bar.

A raised palm from Art let the group know he needed a bit more time, more of the unbearable silence. His eyes were trained on the scattering of balls. He picked one up, rolled it in his palm, tightened his fingers around the cold, hard sphere. Comprehension wormed through the crevices of his brain. Comprehension, and humiliation, and anger. And finally a queasy feeling deep in his gut, the realization he'd been the last to know.

Art pulled his billfold from his back pocket, extracted a few bucks, and dropped them on the felt. He walked to the exit, retrieved his coat and hat from the pegs, and slipped out the door before putting them on.

A collective breath broke free. Someone whistled. Two fellows sitting at the bar exchanged whispers and chuckled nervously. Ed placed his hand on the grocer's back.

"Thinking, you best fire the Colored," he said.

Urban loosened his tie to gather more air. "Oh, yah."

* * * *

Scout lay on the small deck outside the kitchen door. At midmorning, sunbeams crested the treetops and warmed his fur. The smell of bacon seeped through the cracks and crevices of the house, wafting out to the yard. Scout sniffed the air in short, quick breaths, eyes closed to the sun.

Inside, Evelyn sat at the table, coffee in hand. A ribbon of smoke rose from the Lucky Strike resting in the ashtray. The Sunday newspaper lay on the table at Art's spot, still neatly folded. Heaven forbid she embezzle his birthright and be first in the household to read the day's news. A pan of biscuits and a skillet of bacon waited for the man of the house, as well, tucked under a towel inside the oven to keep warm. Evelyn waited right along with them, though not as peacefully tucked in warmth.

She trained her eyes on the upper half of the kitchen door. Through the window, she watched platinum clouds glide across the pale blue sky. Her stomach gurgled with hunger. Or was it a rumble of resentment? How she envied those swift-moving clouds for their lightness, their freedom.

A scuffle of slippers along the carpet interrupted her pensive daydream. Art entered the kitchen, slouched into his spot, opened the paper. Evelyn rose to pour him a cup of coffee.

"Where's Frankie?" he asked.

"Still in bed," Evelyn said.

"We're letting him sleep in 'till all hours, then?" Art snapped.

Evelyn froze midway retrieving the pans from the oven. The air between them was thick with the bouquet of pork fat and menthol. She deposited the skillet onto the stove top harder than she intended. The clatter brought Scout to his feet outside.

"That's mighty righteous talk from a man who stumbled home in the wee hours, and just rolled out of bed at nine o'clock himself."

Art leaned back in his chair and sipped his coffee. His eyes narrowed as he watched her assemble a plate of food. She kept her back to him. After a moment, he said, "*Man* is the key word in that statement."

Evelyn pressed her tongue into her cheek, bit down. She set two fluffy biscuits and three slices of thick bacon on a plate. With a deep breath, she turned and walked the breakfast to him. Their eyes locked as she placed the food on the table.

An eternity passed before she finally cracked, lowered her eyes and took a seat. She had already spat her dose of sass at him. She swallowed down the bitter pill of additional back talk forming in her mouth. Her cigarette had burned down nearly to its filter, tucked in its ring of brown glass. A long snake of ash stretched the length of the ashtray. Evelyn tapped it free, took one last drag and smashed out the stub.

The man of the house pursed his lips as he chewed a mouthful of biscuit, washed it down with a swig of coffee. Evelyn lit another cigarette. Art planted his elbows on either side of the plate, forming a teepee with his crossed fingers.

"Heard the most interesting thing last night over at Wally's," he said.

The tone of voice was precise, the subsequent pause strategic. Evelyn was no stranger to Art's "salesman" intonation, his practiced way of leading a one-sided conversation the direction of his choosing. She took a small drag from her menthol and savored a large slice of pride in knowing the tactic no longer worked on her. She raised her eyebrows and tilted her head, silently dared him to dangle bait she refused to bite.

He snatched a piece of bacon from his plate, stabbed it toward her like a weapon.

"It was about you," he said, and took a bite. He chewed slowly, made a show of swallowing with difficulty. The remaining bacon strip dropped to the plate. "It's dry."

"It was perfect at *breakfast* time." She lifted her coffee cup to her lips, realizing too late it was empty. She pretended to drink.

Art nodded. His eyes never strayed from her. Tiny fissures began to form in her confidence. She stood to prevent herself from crumbling.

"More coffee?" she asked, retrieving the pot from the stove. She filled her own cup, then held the pot toward Art in a question. He nodded again.

They watched the black liquid swirl into the white mug.

"The guys were yammering about this mixed-breed fella working at Logdahl's," Art said, his head continued to nod like the smiling Bob's Big Boy figurine planted on the car dashboard. "Negro-Indian, to be more precise, they said. Ex-con, too. A friend of my wife's. That's what I learned."

Another strategic pause.

"Imagine my surprise," Art concluded.

Evelyn shrugged her shoulders almost imperceptibly, leaned her backside against the counter. She cradled the coffee mug between her hands. The cigarette protruded from between her index and middle fingers.

"You wouldn't have been even the smallest bit surprised if you ever listened when I talk," she said. "I've been telling you about my literacy work out at the prison for years."

Art pushed the table away and stood. He wasn't physically imposing. Yet, he held all the power. The kitchen walls closed in on her.

"So, you make a habit of fraternizing with men who flaunt the law." His words had gotten louder, sharper. "It should come as no surprise to me. That's what you're saying, then?"

Scout's paws thumped against the glass of the kitchen door. The couple turned and saw the dog standing on his hind legs, peering in at them. Air blasted from his snout, fogging the window.

"Get down!" Art yelled.

The dog's ears went flat. One paw eased off the window. Art thrust his shoulders in the dog's direction, shouted his command again. Scout shifted his eyes to Evelyn. She motioned to the dog with her chin. *It's okay, boy.* Scout dropped to all fours.

Only Scout's ears were still visible in the window, standing at attention just outside the door. The dog's deference to Evelyn ratcheted up Art's anger. He closed the remaining space between them.

"Well?" Art demanded a response.

"Fine, you caught me," she exclaimed, throwing her hands in the air. "I throw big tawdry parties every time you leave town, with dozens of men, criminals one and all. Yes sir, the cat's out of the bag now."

Sarcasm was the wrong approach. Experience told her that. Yet, she couldn't hold her tongue.

"Making light of it, are ya? My wife sneaking around behind my back, asking favors of my friends, making me look the fool for not knowing she's been keeping company with undesirables."

The tendon in his jaw bulged as he spoke through clenched teeth. "Has he been in your bed, this mixed-breed of yours?"

"How dare you," she fired back. "I've been teaching inmates to read at the prison. That's all. And you should think twice about disparaging a man who risked his life to save our boys from drowning."

"Which he wouldn't have had to do if you were a capable mother!" Art reached for the cupboard door beside her head, opened and slammed it shut, twice. She flinched and stepped to the side.

Two deep barks and a forceful scratch of claws made the kitchen door quake.

"Art, please," Evelyn whispered. "You're worrying Scout."

"You're the one who should be worried," Art bellowed, seizing her upper arms.

The coffee mug jolted from her grasp, crashed to the floor, shattered. The cigarette shook loose from her fingers, searing her ankle as it tumbled to the ground and drowned in a pool of hot coffee.

Scout's rapid-fire bark thundered outside. Mighty paws, backed by a hundred pounds of muscle, pounded the glass. Cracks shot up the windowpane like lightning bolts followed by a thunderous explosion, shards crashing to the floor. In another flash, Scout flew through the gaping window. The dog thrust his body between Art and Evelyn. Tail erect, ears forward, fur bristled along his spine. Art staggered back.

The sounds of war shook Frankie from the warmth and comfort of bed. He rushed bare foot to the kitchen and froze in the open doorway. Scout stood sentry in a rubble of broken glass and porcelain, weight shifted forward, teeth exposed. Centuries of canine instinct seethed from deep within, erupted in a prolonged, threatening growl.

Art jerked a kitchen chair between himself and the dog. He was a lion tamer who'd lost control of the performance, cowering behind wooden legs and spindles as the beast roared and snapped powerful jaws.

"Scout, no!" Frankie shouted.

The dog quieted, though he held his ground, muzzle tensed.

"Get that dog out of here," Art ordered.

Frankie called out, and Scout obeyed, followed his boy through the living room, out to the yard toward the garage.

Time stood still, and Evelyn experienced a flash of enlightenment that made her shudder. She could have called off the dog, but a small black corner of her heart had stopped her. Evelyn felt something shift in her chest. The darkness expanded.

* * * *

"I don't like what I've become," Evelyn said, staring in the inky black hole of the coffee mug cupped between her hands.

Dottie sat beside her friend on the couch. Wheels in her mind had been spinning since she'd heard Evelyn's shaky voice on the phone asking her to come over, right away. It was the same voice she'd heard ten years before, when the Western Union telegraph man had knocked on Evelyn's door with a message from the Secretary of War. A voice steeped in loss and fear.

Art had stormed out after the altercation and sped off in the car. Frankie and Scout rushed back into the house, and Evelyn insisted all was well. Just a misunderstanding. No need to worry. She told Frankie to take Scout for a long walk in the nearby woods to settle the dog's nerves. And then she called Dottie. And then she crumbled.

Dottie had hurried over to find Evelyn sitting on the kitchen floor amidst the rubble. A gusty chill swept through the gaping window frame. She quickly performed triage to confirm Evelyn's well-being, the whereabouts of Art and Frankie. Then she sent Evelyn out of the room to change into clean, warm clothes while she took a broom to the floor and taped cardboard over the empty window.

A fresh pot of coffee percolated on the stove. Crackling logs in the fireplace had pulled the chill from the air.

Now it was time for answers.

"And what exactly have you become?" Dottie asked.

"Cold," Evelyn said.

Dottie shook her head no, cupped her hands around Evelyn's. "What the heck happened, Evie?"

"The men down at Wally's were talking about some hogwash," Evelyn said. "Art came home all worked up about it."

"About the Colored working at Logdahl's," Dottie said.

A prickly tone soaked her statement. It fell on Evelyn like a wool blanket. Heavy. Dank. Irritating. The women studied one another. Evelyn remained mute. A log in the fire popped and drew their eyes to the dancing flames.

"The men aren't the only ones talking," Dottie said.

Evelyn's reticence continued to fill the room. Dottie stood and retrieved a decanter from the liquor cabinet. She added a splash of whiskey to each of their coffees. They drank.

"Who else is talking?" Evelyn asked, staring into the fire.

"Mrs. Logdahl has been complaining about that man working at the market," Dottie revealed. "She says Urban didn't like the idea at first either. He only did it as a favor to you."

Flickering flames reflected in Evelyn's eyes. "He's actually only half-colored. His mother was Ojibwe."

"Oh, for Pete's sake, Evie. Are you messing around with this man?"

"No!" Evelyn set her cup down hard on the coffee table, turned to face her friend. She slowed herself by taking a deep breath, and said more steadily, "No. And I'm hurt you'd even ask such a thing."

"So you *haven't* been seeing him?" Dottie didn't back down.

Evelyn bought a moment with another sip of her Irish coffee.

Dottie's eyebrows and shoulders rose in tandem. The question thundered from her once more, in the jut of her chin, the flare of her nostrils, the tightness of her lips. It wasn't curiosity that propelled the question. Nor was it empathy. It was injury. Perhaps even disgust.

A single tear rolled down Evelyn's cheek. Regret. A second tear followed. Fear.

"Not in the way you're implying," she whispered.

Dottie's indignation fell away. She took Evelyn's face gently in her hands, brushed the tears aside with her thumbs. She sighed, "Talk to me, doll."

LIFE THROUGH THE AGES

The Problem of Pain

MacMillan, New York, 1944

By C.S. Lewis

Appendix by R. Havard, M.D.

Mental pain is less dramatic than physical pain, but it is more common and also more hard to bear. The frequent attempt to conceal mental pain increases the burden: it is easier to say "My tooth is aching" than it is to say "My heart is broken."

Sometimes the pain persists and the effect is devastating. Yet, if the cause is accepted and faced, the conflict will strengthen and purify the character and in time the pain will usually pass. Some, by heroism, overcome even chronic mental pain. They often produce brilliant work and strengthen, harden, and sharpen their characters till they become like tempered steel.

Pain provides an opportunity for heroism; the opportunity is seized with surprising frequency.

1990

Central Iowa

Motel 6 is their lodging choice tonight.

The *Atlas* coupons for nicer places have all been used. Plus, they've decided to rent a couple of rooms after a two-to-one vote. Frank's scratchy throat and dull aches progressed into a full-blown cold, and April insisted he have his own room, so he could rest and recuperate undisturbed. Gram agreed, so he couldn't cough and sneeze his germs all over the two of them.

April made a quick run to the store for essential supplies: herbal teabags and honey, mentholated cough-drops and aspirin, liquid nighttime medicine and lip balm, crossword-puzzle book and pencils. Last but not least, the most vital item her dad always purchased whenever April was sick – chocolate bars.

Gram rolled her eyes when April stopped in the management office to get an extra blanket.

"In case you get the chills," April says, setting the folded blanket on the foot of Frank's bed. She pours hot water from the coffee maker into a paper cup and dunks the teabag a few times. The bear-shaped honey container smiles.

"Thank you, sweetheart." Frank kicks off his shoes, slides under the covers still fully-clothed. He swigs the green nighttime medicine straight from the bottle. "I'll be good as new in the morning."

"Call our room if you need anything during the night," April says. "Or just bang on the wall."

"Enough, already," Gram bellows from the walkway outside. "He's a grown man. Leave him in peace."

April quickly plants a kiss on his forehead, to say good night and double-check for a fever. Frank's mind flashes with an image of his wife doing the same when their baby girl had the croup. The memory causes a sharpness in his eyes, makes them water. He squeezes his lids shut to prevent the image from leaping to his daughter's mind.

Outside, April and Gram begin their nightly stroll. The exercise increases blood flow. It loosens stiff muscles. It eases conversation.

"Dad and I were talking the other night, about mom," April says after they turn the first corner of their lap around the motel. "He's got me thinking."

Gram had always been her confidant, had always been a source of wisdom and insight. With all that had happened on the road so far, April was beginning to notice hairline fractures in the woman's outer walls. She worried further prodding could shatter it. The idea of what might lie beneath was a little terrifying. Yet, April still needed that wisdom, that insight.

"Do you think I've been too hard on her?" she asks.

"On Deborah?" Gram says, dropping her cigarette butt on the sidewalk, snuffing it out with the toe of her white sneaker. "Heck no."

April cringes at the words, at the action. She crouches to retrieve the lipstick-stained butt as Gram shuffles onward, oxygen wheelie in tow.

"Dad said she left because she thought I'd be better off without her," April presses on.

"Well, there's one thing she and I agree about," Gram hisses the same sharp words April used the other night. The young woman feels their edge now, in the same way her dad must have.

They pass the designated smoking patio. April drops the butt into the sand-filled ashtray.

"Do you remember the party you had when you turned five?" Gram asks.

April smiles. Warmth fills her chest.

Gram's eyes are trained on the sidewalk ahead. "What a disaster."

The young woman's lungs deflate.

"Deborah would never have survived being a wife or mother in the fifties," Gram says. "She couldn't even cut it in the seventies or eighties, for goodness' sake."

It's not something April could dispute. Her mom never made cookies for school bake sales, was never a homeroom mom or field-trip chaperone. April's kindergarten birthday party was an anomaly, a glimmer of light in a dark tunnel of memories.

"I begged her to let me help plan the party. I gave her my sherbet punch recipe, and got her a book from the library on how to make party favors," Gram continues.

"You know what she said to me? 'Chill out.' A party should be 'spontaneous.' Can you imagine? When all I wanted to do was help?" Gram waves her hand in the air. "She ended up buying a giant sub sandwich and putting an ice chest on the patio filled with juice boxes and cans of beer. Didn't plan any games. Just played her ridiculous hippie music on the tape deck."

"We played freeze tag in the backyard," April interjects. All these years later, she still gets a little giddy whenever Steppenwolf comes on the radio. Zipping through the yard, and dodging around trees, on a magic carpet ride. Feeling the breeze rustle sweaty hair; built-in evaporative cooling.

No, Gram exerts with a dramatic shake of her head.

"Pin the tail on the donkey. Musical chairs. Bobbing for apples. Those are appropriate games for a children's party," she says. "Not running all over the place like maniacs, while parents drink beer."

They walk a few more steps in silence, then Gram adds, "And I'll never forget that ridiculous blue cake she made!"

"Cookie Monster," April says smiling. She could still see her friends laughing, showing off blue-stained tongues and teeth.

Gram snorts with contempt at the same vision. "I told her not to use so much food coloring. Your mother never listened to my advice."

April remembers Gram sending her to the bathroom to brush her teeth a second time, and then a third, before Dad finally tucked her into bed. The sound of hard whispers made its way through the walls.

"Your mother cried and cried the rest of the night," Gram says. "But it was her own darn fault, for refusing any help. I told her she needed to quit feeling sorry for herself, learn from her mistakes, and the next birthday party would be better."

A burning sensation flares in the back of April's throat, makes her eyes tingle. She picks up the pace of their walk. The urge to full-out run — to escape her grandmother and this new insight — is overwhelming.

There never was a next party.

1955

Bitter Rapids

The banishments came soon after the battle.

First, Scout was evicted from the house.

What had once been a peace offering from Art – a gift to his stepson – had since become a threat. Tearing his slippers to shreds had been one thing. The idea of the animal tearing flesh from bone terrified Art. The man had to re-establish himself as the alpha of the household.

The decree came down. Scout was to be tethered to the old white cedar in the yard. Frankie would walk the dog, on a leash from now on, twice a day for exercise. When the weather turned bitter, the animal could have a kennel in the garage. The house and free range were forbidden.

It was, in fact, a compromise. Art's original verdict had been to put the dog down. Evelyn knew that would devastate Frankie. The boy had been slipping from her, little by little, for years. Losing Scout would be the final push, and he'd pull away from her completely. Evelyn begged Art to allow the dog to live. It was her fault Scout didn't behave, she insisted. Discipline would resolve it. Her argument touched home. Art softened. An accord was struck.

Frankie was devastated nonetheless. He had no knowledge of his mother's negotiations. Scout's banishment fueled his smoldering hatred for Art and the blame he placed on Evelyn for bringing the man into their lives. He retrieved his parents' wedding quilt from the trunk of the car. For weeks, Frankie and

Scout slept in the yard together, in the small den the dog had created beside the towering tree.

Second, Maak was evicted from town.

Mr. Logdahl had promptly fired him, told him to vacate his bedroom at the back of the store. There were no other establishments in Bitter Rapids that would hire a Colored, or an Indian, or rent either a room. Maak had a small amount of cash saved from his employment at the store, some of which he applied toward a backpack, blanket, knife, and mess kit at the Army surplus store. The remaining funds went for supplies – salt, flour, raisins, coffee, tobacco.

Maak loaded the pack, hauled it onto his back, and walked the main road from town. Disappeared into the forest.

1955

Koochiching State Forest, Minnesota

S moke curled around Maak's head as he exhaled in rhythmic breaths. He had carved the tobacco pipe from a fist-sized chunk of soft red stone, just as his grandfather had, and his grandfather before him. Pipestone was sacred to the Anishinaabe, forged from the flesh and blood of ancestors who'd died in the Great Flood. Maak sat on the earth outside his freshly-constructed wigwam, a domed dwelling of willow branches and birch bark. Eyes closed, he smoked and called upon Kitche Manitou.

Today, I will hunt. I hope the bear will give his life, so that I can live.

Maak felt like a young man again. Alive. Free. One with creation. The musk and mildew of his room at the grocery had cleared from his sinuses. The rough cold brick of his prison cell had faded from his memory. The darkness of his boarding school room had lifted from his eyes. He was finally home. The cushion of rich soil beneath his feet. The embrace of open blue sky overhead. The tingle of pine-scented air in his lungs.

When the pipe was empty, Maak tucked it in its leather pouch, stowed it inside the hut. He gathered his hunting supplies – black ash dug from the fire pit, rope snares woven from bottlebrush grass, wild raspberries harvested for the offering, tobacco leaves bundled to give thanks. He set out to the river.

A bear trail meandered on the opposite side of the river. It edged the shallow wetlands of the lake, just inside the first row of trees. The trail curved through the underbrush of goldthread, veered around and into a small sunny opening in the boreal forest, rich with nuts and insects. Maak stopped on the opposite side of the narrow bay to prepare. He extracted a handful of ash from its pouch, patted it up and down his arms and neck and face, spread it along the snares. The bear would give its life willingly. That was its purpose. But Maak must not cause the animal undue fear. That was his purpose.

Trudging through the shallow passage of water further removed his scent. At the small clearing in the trail, Maak set two snares, ten feet apart, and left a scattering of berries within the circle of rope closest to the water. He trailed the ropes to his lair in the underbrush, covering them with shrubbery and dirt and ash as he worked his way backward. He crouched in the bushes, motionless, a rope in each hand. He waited.

A light breeze rustled the aspen leaves overhead, and the sun peeked through the gaps. Shards of light danced on the carpet of pine needles amongst the long morning shadows. A deer mouse crept across the snare, snatched a fragrant berry, and scuttled into the brush.

Sparrows and insects twittered and buzzed in the boughs overhead. The sun trekked across the sky. Maak remained crouched in the bushes, motionless. He waited.

The shadows had nearly disappeared when the bear emerged from the trees like an apparition. It lumbered along the trail, stopping several feet from the raspberry snare. It stopped and rose to full height on its hind legs. Head angled upward, the bear sniffed the air, its tawny snout twitching and tapered ears lying flat. It dropped back onto all fours, eyeing the berries, and took a step. It stopped and sniffed the air again.

Maak waited, every muscle in his bent legs and hunched back burning. He must not move, must not breathe, or the alert bear would sense danger and bolt back into the brush.

Do not be afraid, Maak spoke to the animal through prayer. *It will be swift. Because of your gift, others will live and be strong.*

The deer mouse skittered back into the snare, as if to also encourage the bear. Take the berries. Help the man. The rodent plucked a second berry from the pile, gazed up at the giant animal with miniature obsidian eyes. It blinked once, twice, and darted away.

With a flick of its ear, the bear moved toward the offering, lowered its head to eat. Maak waited still, allowed it to savor the sweet flesh of the berries. Allowed it to swallow and drop its head for another taste.

In one swift motion, Maak jumped to his feet and pulled the snare in his right hand. The rope cinched tight around the bear's muscular neck. The animal reared. Maak braced himself against the trunk of a giant pine, drawing strength from its deep roots. As the animal lurched back toward the second trap, Maak pulled the snare tight on its rear paws.

The man worked quickly to secure the ropes low to the tree, drawing the animal tight to the ground from head to toe. This allowed him to approach from the back and the side, without the danger of curved claws piercing his flesh or muscular limbs shattering his bones.

Maak rushed the animal, plunged his long blade between its ribs, puncturing both lungs.

In the split second the bear lay paralyzed from the strike, Maak thrust his arm under its head, pulled up its chin, and drew his weapon across its neck. The bear went limp. Its blood emptied onto the spongy forest floor, as Maak lay sprawled along its back. Their hearts pounded in concert, until there was one.

Maak closed the bear's eyes. He stroked the gray hairs on the animal's snout. It had lived a full life. Maak rose and removed a bundle of dried tobacco leaves from his hunting pouch, laid the bundle on the ground nearby.

"Thank you, Kind Spirit."

With speed and precision, the ropes were adjusted, and the bear was hoisted into the air by its neck. The metal pot was filled with cold marsh water. The tip of the blade was inserted below the sternum. Heart and kidneys were placed into the water. Deep cuts came next, at the joints of the paws, the base of the skull, along the underbelly.

Maak grabbed hold of the skin at the neck, pulled down. His weight did most of the work. Hide peeled away from muscle. Maak folded the hide in half, rolled and tied it, set it aside. He lowered the majestic bear to the ground, cradled its head as he removed the rope. He used his axe to remove the animal's toes. The sharp, curved claws would be fashioned into tools. Finally, Maak gathered his belongings and hauled them to the river to wash.

Back at camp, the fire popped and snapped while the sun slipped behind the granite cliffs in the distance. The pelt was strung to dry, high in the trees. Into a boiling pot of fresh water, Maak stirred the chopped heart and kidneys, diced turnip and ramps, wild rice and mushrooms. All gifts of Creation that sustained him.

Over the ridge and across the narrow bay, a pack of wolves feasted on flesh and bone of the animal Maak had left behind. His gift to sustain them. When their bellies were full, their snouts stained red, they spread themselves along the ridge and the river's edge, and joined in a soulful chorus of thanks to their Spirit Brother.

LIFE IN THE 1990S

WASHINGTON, D.C., Sept. 16, 1990

FOR IMMEDIATE RELEASE

/National Newswire/ -- Nearly half of Americans now favor marriage between blacks and whites, according to a recent Gallup Poll on Minority Rights and Relations. Those polled were asked, "Do you approve or disapprove of marriage between whites and blacks?" Approximately 48 percent said they approved. By comparison, only 4 percent said they approved when the poll was first conducted in 1958.

At that time, laws prohibiting interracial marriage and sexual relations (also known as miscegenation laws) were passed by all but nine states in the country. They primarily banned relations between blacks and whites, but often also included interracial marriages involving Native Americans, Asians and other ethnic groups. In 1967, the U.S. Supreme Court ruled in *Loving v. Virginia* that such laws were unconstitutional.

(Source: Gallup Organization)

1955

Koochiching State Forest, Minnesota

Evelyn steered off the highway and onto the dirt of the old logging road. She maneuvered the Buick along the bumpy, rutted thruway until it became too narrow to navigate by car. It looked just as Maak had described it when he told her stories of setting up camp there long ago.

"This is it, Scout," she said to the dog in the back seat. "The end of the road."

She turned off the engine and placed both hands back on the steering wheel. She stared into the shadows between and beyond the trees at the forest's edge. Scout paced the back seat, from one door to the other.

The end of the road.

Evelyn contemplated both the figurative and literal meanings of the statement. Maybe being here was all wrong. She longed to see him, to wrap her arms around him, to tell him he haunted her dreams. Maybe she should turn around. Go home. Forget about Maak. But what if he was sick, or injured? What if he was starving, and cold? She just needed to see him, just one more time, to make sure he was safe. That was all. Evelyn tilted her head, loosened her grip on the wheel. How could that be wrong?

"Okay, let's go."

Evelyn gathered herself and stepped out of the car. Scout bounded over the front seat and out the driver's side door. He shook from head to tail, then scuttled to a stand of maple saplings, nose close to the ground, sniffing as he went. Evelyn watched him as she buttoned her coat and slung the strap of her bag over her head, onto her shoulder. She'd packed apples, salt, flour, coffee, sugar, boiled eggs, chocolate bars.

"Here, boy!"

Scout turned an immediate one-eighty and bolted to her. Evelyn smiled, marveling at the dog's intelligence, his obedience, his loyalty. She removed a beige kidskin glove from her pocket, from the set she'd worn on her last visit to the prison, when she'd taken Maak's hand to congratulate him on his early parole. Their only touch. Evelyn had kept the gloves in her bureau drawer since that day, to preserve the moment.

She crouched down in front of the dog and held out the glove.

"There you are," she said as Scout inspected the offering. "You're going to help me find Maak. Have a good sniff. Attaboy, Scout. Good dog. Now let's go find him."

Evelyn set off in the woods, down the narrow logging road. Scout pranced beside her. He looked ahead, then up at the woman, then back toward the trail. She stopped a short way in, at a fork where the dirt split into two equally overgrown trails. Scout stopped and sat at her side, waiting.

"You'll have to lead the way from here, boy." She held the glove to Scout's nose again. "Go, Scout!"

With that, the dog leapt up onto all four paws. He stood at attention, tail straight. The nostrils of his shiny black nose vibrated, searching the air for the scent. He bolted up the path on the left and disappeared into the brush.

Evelyn had been mesmerized by Scout's focus and remained frozen for a second as the dog vanished.

"Oh, shoot!" she shouted. "Wait, Scout. Wait for me."

She charged into the woods, ducking to avoid a low-hanging tamarack bough. And there was Scout, waiting for her to catch up.

They made their way along the makings of a trail, Scout's nose close to the ground, then held high, leading them deeper into the wilderness. The muscles in Evelyn's thighs began to burn as she clamored over rocks soft with gray-green lichen and deadwood alive with shimmering beetles. The earthy-sweet fragrance of decaying leaves and the incessant buzz of wood wasps made her head feel light.

The trail ended without warning. Evelyn bent forward in frustration, hands on her knees, heaving to catch her breath. Scout whimpered and leapt through a dense wall of leaves and brush. Evelyn gasped, unsure how to follow – whether to follow. *You've come this far*, she told herself, and pushed into the brush with her arms extended in front of her. She parted the leafy limbs and emerged into a clearing flooded with golden light.

At the center was a domed structure layered with bark, nearly invisible against the backdrop of trees. A ring of jagged, charred rocks circled a pit of damp wood ash. Beside it, a black pelt lay in a heap.

Evelyn remained at the edge of the clearing, wisps of steam escaping her parted lips as she steadied her breath. Scout charged ahead, exploring the new smells and wonders of camp. Maak's camp.

Scout darted inside the hut, disappearing from Evelyn's sight for a moment. She stopped breathing, listened, waited for evidence of Maak. The dog emerged again, as quickly as it had vanished, still alone, ears erect, tail sweeping the air. Dread crept up from her gut and into her chest.

She took a cautious step forward, closer to camp, to where Maak cooked and ate and slept. She looked up at the sky, imagined the window of stars it provided in the black of night. She closed her eyes for a heartbeat or two, trying to settle her nerves. She opened them and Maak was standing before her like a mirage.

Evelyn's hands flew up to her mouth. She yelped like a frightened pup. Scout spun and charged toward them, firing two deep warning barks like bullets from his muzzle. His teeth flashed against the pink flesh of his gums and his ears lay flat. A wave of heat rose inside Evelyn as the scene clicked into slow motion.

Maak didn't flinch, or run, or shout. He stood tall, shoulders back, and raised his hand gently toward the dog, palm out.

"She is safe," he said, his voice soft and steady, confident and firm.

Scout slowed his approach. His mouth closed and his tail relaxed. He lowered his head and ambled over to Maak, sinking to the ground at the man's feet. Scout rolled into Maak's shins, exposing his underbelly. Maak laughed and stooped to scratch the dog's chest.

Evelyn shook her head in disbelief.

"My God, I thought he was going to kill you," she faltered. "How? How did you do that?"

Maak tilted his head to look up at her. "He is good. He will not let harm come to you."

"Yes, I know!" she yowled. "So why weren't you afraid of him?"

Maak stood and took a step closer to her. The corners of his mouth turned up slightly. "He is my Brother."

"You're brother?" Evelyn crinkled her brow.

"I am sorry I frightened you, Evelyn."

"No," she said. "I wasn't frightened. Just startled, that's all."

Maak nodded once.

"Why are you here?" he asked. There was no tension in his voice, no hint of anger or distrust. It was a question. That was all.

"I was worried about you. I wanted to make sure you're safe. That you had food and a warm place to sleep."

"There is no need to worry." He extended his arms like a massive bird, angled his head back and spun slowly to draw attention to their surroundings. "I am home, Evelyn. *Kitche Manitou* provides all that I need. You see?"

His words warmed her, like a goose-feather quilt on a frozen night. It was how she always felt with Maak. Warm. Safe.

"Look," he said, extending a palm toward the tumbling river in the distance.

The river provides water for the soul, he explained, food for the body. For shelter, birch saplings are bent and tied with twine, covered with bark to keep out the rain. Inside, a heap of birch branches makes a bed, soft and warm. Sweet balsam fir at the head.

"You will have good dreams if you use the balsam fir as your pillow," he said with a single nod.

Her eyes fell on the fur pelt beside the fire pit.

"And the black bear?" she asked.

"He gives warmth," he said, "and strength."

"Did you kill it?"

"Yes."

"All by yourself?"

"*Kitche Manitou* was with me. The bear died willingly. It knew I would need his coat to survive the winter."

Evelyn shook her head again. So often, Maak's words made her pause, question, disbelieve.

"You're saying it was easy?"

"No," Maak said. "It was not easy. My heart is still broken."

"Your heart?" Evelyn felt her throat tighten. She labored to swallow.

Maak looked toward the thick of trees. "I buried his bones at the base of the black spruce. He will return in spring. It is the way of the Great Creation. There is a time to take and a time to give. It must be done to keep balance in the world."

A single tear rolled down Evelyn's cheek. Maak extended his hand, caught the drop as it fell from her jaw. He closed his fingers around it, pressed his fist to his chest. He remembered the last time she wept in his presence.

Then he dropped his hand to his side, unfurled his fingers. Scout licked the salty moisture from his palm. *Purity. Renewal.*

"Seeing you again has brought me great happiness, Evelyn. But you must not come back."

But I never want to leave. Evelyn smiled, and he watched her eyes dance.

"I can bring you food and supplies," she said.

"The earth provides what I need."

"I'll bring books." She took a step closer.

"I will get my wisdom from the trees now."

"You'll be lonely." Another step closer.

He wavered.

Evelyn placed her hand on his chest.

"Don't you want to see me again?"

Maak took her small hand, pressed it between his.

"What I want and what I can have are different things, Evelyn. They always have been. They always will be."

He opened his hands and lowered them to his sides. Evelyn's hand remained where he left it, suspended in midair. She stared at it, could almost see it pulsate with the energy of his touch.

"You want me here with you," she said. "I can feel it."

"How could I not?"

Their voices fell to whispers. Evelyn lowered her head, moved in closer. She looked up, blinked slowly. "You want to kiss me."

"What I want does not matter."

"It matters to me," she said.

Maak closed his eyes, filled his lungs until he felt they might burst. He exhaled slowly.

"I murdered a man, and I paid the price with twenty years in prison," he said.

"That doesn't matter to me," Evelyn shook her head. "I know that's not who you are. You're a good man."

The remaining distance between them evaporated. She pressed both hands to his chest, tilted her head back and rested her chin on his sternum. Maak cradled her face in his hands, lost himself for a moment in the water of her eyes.

"If I kiss a white woman," he paused. "A beautiful, married, white woman..."

Her lips parted.

"The price to be paid...," his words trailed away as he spoke them.

Thoughts of Evelyn's moist, petal-soft lips had diminished the hard walls of his prison cell more times than he could remember. Just as often, thoughts of her other moist, petal-soft places had made his life confined by those walls unbearable. In this moment, he envied Scout for having tasted the salt of her tears.

It could never happen. It would be a death sentence.

It would be worth it, Maak heard the words in his head.

"The risk for you would be too great," he said. They would call her a whore, an unfit mother. They would take her son away. He knew this. She knew this.

Evelyn could not stop the flood of tears.

"It's not fair," she whispered.

"It is not," Maak said.

The energy drained from her limbs. She began to crumble. Maak pulled her close, his strong arms holding her gently, firmly to his chest. She nestled her cheek into the opening of his shirt, skin on skin, and wept. He felt the water, and salt, and essence of her tears absorb into his pores, into his soul.

1955

Bitter Rapids, Minnesota

*E*velyn watched a sheet of fall rain pour from the steel gray sky. Through the front window, she eyed the edge of the yard, where bulky, emerald cedars quivered behind a veil of misty fog. Along the house, leafless, slender-branched azaleas wept. Evelyn pulled the curtain closed.

She lay down in the center of the living room, neatly crossed her ankles, folded her hands on her stomach. The swirling deco pattern of the plaster ceiling resembled drifting clouds. They were mesmerizing. Evelyn imagined herself lying in cool moist grass, bright blue heavens above. Wispy trundles rolling across the sky. Her soul ached from withdrawal. It yearned for the tonic of summer days.

Scout wandered in from the kitchen and nestled in beside her, rested his head upon her chest. Evelyn had been allowing the dog into the house again when Art was on the road. She stroked Scout's face, ran her thumb gently over his closed eyes. Within minutes, he was lulled to sleep. The steady rhythm of his breath eased back the shroud in her chest, allowed in a small shaft of light. It helped her to breathe.

A crush of gravel in the driveway roused the dog. He lifted his head, mountain-peak ears on alert.

"It's okay, boy," Evelyn whispered. "Go back to sleep."

She felt the muscles along his torso relax as he laid his head back down. A knock at the door made them both tense, but Evelyn did not rise and Scout followed her cue.

They lay motionless, in a hush. Then, another knock.

"I know you're home, Evie," Dottie asserted. "I'm not leaving."

Evelyn sighed. "Come in, then."

A shower of droplets sprinkled the foyer as Dottie entered and removed her rubber-ducky-colored raincoat and hat. She placed them on the wall pegs and turned to find her friend stretched out on the floor. Scout's tail thumped the carpet.

"How long have you been lying there?" Dottie asked. She stood with her shiny black pumps together, her hands clasped at the buckle of her matching belt.

Evelyn rolled her head to view her friend. "Is that a new dress?"

Dottie smiled and ran her palms along her rib cage. The scooped neckline and darts along the bodice accentuated her figure. The soft pink of her pearl choker matched the tiny polka dots in the sage-colored fabric.

"Yes," she said. "But you're changing the subject."

Dottie walked into the room and reached down to grasp Evelyn's hands. She hoisted the woman to her feet. "Come on, then. Behave like a proper hostess."

Scout shook the sleep from his body and followed the women into the kitchen. When Evelyn slumped into a chair at the table, he laid down at her feet. Dottie moved through the kitchen with ease, filling a pot at the sink, retrieving the coffee can from the cupboard. The stove was lit. Cups and sugar and cream were set out. She tapped two cigarettes from the pack, placed them between her lips. She lit both at once and handed one off to Evelyn.

Percolator music and a nutty aroma replaced the musty stillness in the house. Scout's paws twitched on the linoleum as he chased raccoons in his sleep. Evelyn pushed off her rabbit-lined slippers and buried her toes into the dog's thick belly-fur. Dottie poured the coffee.

The drum of rain on the roof replaced the percolator as background music, shifting the ambiance back to somber.

"You can't go on like this, Evie."

Evelyn blinked. "I'm fine."

The Specht household had been strained for several weeks after the confrontation over Maak. In time, conversations around town shifted to other tittle-tattle. Life at home returned to uneventful. Even Scout seemed to be more at ease.

Dottie fiddled with the pearl strand at her neck, pressed her lips into a thin line.

"We've missed you and Art at pinochle," she continued. "And you've stopped volunteering down at the Salvation Army."

Evelyn lifted her shoulders and let them fall again with an exaggerated breath. "There's so much to do around the house. I just haven't had the time to get out."

Dottie snorted, angled her head toward the living room. "Oh, for sure. You looked positively overrun with chores when I came in."

"I don't know what else to tell you, Dot." Evelyn's eyes darted to the ceiling, the dog, the imaginary hangnail that suddenly plagued her – anywhere but Dottie's face. She sprang from her seat and hustled to the sink piled with crusty dishware. The faucet squeaked as she turned the hot water to full blast.

Suds filled the basin, forming in frothy mounds between yolk-crusted plates, coffee-stained cups, and grease-smeared pans.

Dottie retrieved a towel from the drawer. Evelyn worked at the yoke with a soapy steel-wool pad, rinsed and handed items off for drying. The women made their way through the stack. Evelyn dried her hands, returned to the table, and laid her head down on folded arms.

There was nothing Dottie could say that her friend's exhaustion didn't already shout. She wiped down the sink and counter, stovetop and table. She squeezed water from the scrubber pad, hung the towel on the edge of the sink to dry. She sat at the table and stroked Evelyn's hair.

"You can't go on like this," Dottie repeated. "People are back to talking."

Evelyn expelled a gust of air, sat up, and swept her hair from her face.

"What are they saying now?"

Dottie studied the pattern of the tablecloth. The rumors were humiliating. She'd debated with herself on whether to even bring them up. But now she had, and the words were difficult to muster.

"They're saying you and that Colored man were lovers," Dottie whispered, even though the women were alone in the house. "And that now you're behaving this way because you're heartbroken he's gone."

Evelyn let those final words hover over her. They'd been living in her subconscious for weeks. She hadn't known they were out in the world, too – drifting on the air, circulating around the small town, being stirred into coffee, teasing the tongues of gossipmongers.

She stood from the table to retrieve the coffee pot, refilled their cups. As Evelyn sat back down, she said, "Maybe I *am* heartbroken."

Dottie studied her friend for a moment. The idea was absurd. She backed her chair from the table a few inches. Some distance was necessary. She drummed her fingers on the table.

"For the life of me, Evie, I do not understand your fascination with that man," she said. "Nor do I understand why you'd be willing to risk what you've got for some disgusting fantasy."

Evelyn's head jerked as the words struck her. A fetid brew churned in her stomach – shock, offense, anger – threatened to heave up. Other ingredients – grief, despair, hopelessness – were more potent in the mix. They were the sedative against all other emotion, against any movement or action.

"What exactly have I got?" she asked.

The flat tone of Evelyn's question was more than Dottie could stand.

"Oh, honestly," Dottie huffed. "Look around you. You're married to a man who provides for you and your son. You have food on the table, a beautiful home."

Evelyn closed her eyes. A tear rolled down her cheek, and she didn't have the strength to brush it away. Dottie softened.

"I know Art isn't a perfect husband," Dottie said, "but no man is."

"Frank was," Evelyn said, her eyes and chin tilted skyward.

"You have no idea what kind of husband Frank would have been," Dottie countered. "I adored Frank, don't get me wrong. But you were high school sweethearts, Evie. Your life together had barely even begun when you lost him."

Dottie lit a cigarette and blew the smoke toward the gray window.

"Men change," she said.

Life through the Ages

"In our bones we need the natural curves of hills,
the scent of chapparal, the whisper of pines, the possibility of
wildness. We require these patches of nature for our mental
health and our spiritual resilience."

— Richard Louv, *Last Child in the Woods*

1955

Bitter Rapids, Minnesota

Wooded islands and mossy ponds. Granite cliffs and indigo lakes. Basalt peninsulas and burbling rivers. The rugged wilderness of northern Minnesota was a vast patchwork of land and water. It blanketed hundreds of square miles, stitched together with glittering strands – creeks, tributaries, brooks, channels.

For the school-aged children of Bitter Rapids, it was heaven on earth. From the moment they escaped the confines of the classroom in June to the final, shortest day of summer, they took to the outdoors.

They gobbled down breakfasts and darted from houses to gather at nearby clearings and sandy beaches, their arms laden with lunch boxes and fishing rods, ball bats and leather mitts. Teenage girls huddled together on blankets, applied bubblegum lip gloss, and shook Magic 8 balls to predict what boy might steal a kiss that day. Boys launched into cannonballs from rope swings, baited hooks, and dared one another to steal second base.

All returned to their homes in time for dinner, smelling of pine and lake water, sweat and ryegrass.

Frankie had been right there in the mix, until the year Denny died. Like the pop of a light bulb filament, the brightness of his childhood had gone out with the flick of a switch. It became impossible to goof around with the other kids if they were within sight of a lake or pond, river or creek. He'd spent two summers in his backyard reading Edgar Rice Burroughs novels about jungle adventures and outer space escapades, tossing sticks for Scout to fetch.

The dog's sentence to remain tied while in the yard was the impetus Frankie needed to once again venture beyond the confines of home. He and Scout took to the woods each morning. Frankie imagined he was one of the early voyageurs to the area, living off the land, trading for fur with the Dakota and Ojibwe.

When the nearby woods became too familiar, Frankie took the highway bus out of town. He always brought a chocolate bar or fresh-baked cinnamon roll to bribe the driver into looking the other way as Scout bounded up the vehicle steps and down the aisle. Ten or fifteen miles later, the boy and his dog disembarked at one of the old logging roads and hiked into the forest.

It was freedom. It was adventure. It was a secret mission.

The gossip about Maak's employment hadn't been limited to the adults in Bitter Rapids. By the time the man was fired, word had made its way through the halls of Marshall Junior High. Everyone knew he was the prisoner who'd plunged into the river to rescue Frankie and Denny. Many suspected improper relations between the dark man and Mrs. Specht. After he disappeared into the woods, the school was abuzz with theories as to what became of him.

Then the final bell rang, summer adventures began, and interest in the ex-con mixed-breed evaporated.

Only Frankie remained immersed in the mystery.

Each day, he and Scout ventured deeper into the wilds, exploring new territory, getting to know it like a friend. They traipsed through thick underbrush, verdant and damp, and past vine-covered trees vibrating with life. Searching, always. At every turn, there was the rush and ripple of water. Frankie learned to navigate the terrain without entering the threat – scuttling fallen trunks, hopscotching river stones, traversing beaver dams.

While making their way along a deer trail one crisp morning, Scout halted and lifted his head. His powerful nose, moist with exhilaration, bobbed upward.

"What is it boy?" Frankie asked, reaching into the pocket that contained his folded knife.

Scout's mouth relaxed. His ears folded back. He took flight down the trail. Frankie followed, and they soon emerged from the brambles onto the rocky beach of a lazy river. Standing waist deep in the flowing water, fishing spear poised ready to strike, was Maak. Scout charged to water's edge, tail sweeping back and forth, and emitted a high-pitched hello yap.

Maak smiled. He strode to the beach, laid his spear on the rocks, and stooped to scratch Scout's jowls as though the two were long-lost friends reunited.

"Hi," Frankie shouted from the edge of the wood.

"Hello," Maak said. He rose and walked toward Frankie, while Scout scampered and danced in circles between them.

Frankie swallowed and took a step back. Not because of the man, but to add more distance between himself and the flowing river. Maak maintained a relaxed approach, stopped at a respectable distance.

"I don't know," Frankie said, and after a pause, "if you remember me."

"I remember you," Maak said.

They studied one another.

"You have grown," Maak added.

Frankie stood a little taller. Scout nudged his snout under the boy's hand, prompting Frankie to scratch the dog's head.

"My brother died," he said.

Maak looked into his eyes. "I am sorry."

Scout trotted back to the man, sat tall facing him, extended a paw to tap at his thigh.

Frankie's mind raced in search of words. All the scripts he'd rehearsed for this anticipated first meeting seemed childish to him now. He opened his mouth to speak, and clamped it shut again.

"Are you hungry?" Maak asked.

Frankie bobbed his head.

Maak retrieved the fishing spear and eased back into the water. He said, "I am hungry."

Frankie sat down on the smooth rocks, locked his arms around his bent knees. Scout lay at his side. The sun rose above the pine tops, moved to the center of the teal sky. A yellow warbler flitted overhead coming to rest in a nearby birch. Maak stood straight in the water, swaying slightly with the flow, like a willow. His spear mirrored him. From time to time, he thrust the weapon into the depth beside him.

Fish were tossed to shore. One. Two. It was all that was needed. Maak returned to his belongings on shore, retrieved a handful of tobacco from a hide pouch, and sprinkled it along the bank. Frankie observed every action, every movement with curiosity.

Squatting with his catch over a rivulet, Maak gripped a fish by the head, ran a knife along its abdomen from tail to gills, not too deep. He scooped the entrails from the opening in one smooth motion, scraped away the scales, rinsed it all clean in the cold, flowing water. An otter on the far shore bounded from a hollowed log, hopscotched across smooth stone, and dived into the stream for the easy meal. As Maak began work on the second fish, he looked over at Frankie and jutted his chin toward the brush.

The boy jumped to his feet to collect dry twigs and kindling. Together, they built and lit a fire. Maak withdrew a handful of aromatic sage and cedar bark from a hide pouch and tossed it into the flames to help repel the prehistoric-size mosquitoes that inhabited the wild.

They roasted the plump fish like marshmallows over the fire. They tore the hot flaky meat from the skin with their teeth, tossed the heads to Scout.

With full bellies, they laid back on soft clumps of creeping, flat-leaf grass, eyes to the pale sky. The wind stirred and shaped cotton-puff clouds. The afternoon pulsed around them, alive with the shudder and click and hum of creatures big and small, seen and unseen.

"You should go now," Maak offered the first words they'd spoken in hours. He sat up, collected his belongings.

"Why?" Frankie asked.

"The moon sleeps tonight," Maak said. "You should be out of the forest before nightfall."

"Oh," Frankie said and rose to his feet, brushed the dirt from his backside.

"You know the way?" Maak asked with piercing eyes.

Frankie nodded, *yes.*

Maak turned and strode through the river to the opposite shore.

"Can I come back?" Frankie shouted. His voice pitched higher than he wanted. "Tomorrow?"

Maak paused, glanced back over his shoulder, and nodded. *Yes.*

1990

Interstate 35, Northern Iowa

The yellow Corolla makes its way north along the gently rolling highway, past golden fields and cow-dotted pastures. The dusky sky is aglow with watercolor shades of orange and violet as the sun eases below the horizon. Black silhouettes punctuate the landscape – barns, farmhouses, silos. The goal was to reach Minnesota before nightfall. The pace of their trip seems to lag a bit more each day.

"Look," Gram points to a large plywood sign propped against a sawhorse up ahead.

Hand-painted black and gold letters announce the event: *Northlake High School Homecoming Bonfire.* The time and date are painted in smaller print below.

"It's tonight," April says. Her voice lifts an octave. "We should go."

School bonfires are the stuff of Midwest small-town mythology and Hollywood movies. In Phoenix, where it was still ninety degrees on a fall evening, high schools didn't celebrate homecoming with bonfires. They celebrated with dances in air-conditioned gyms.

Frank exits at the lone Northlake turnoff. They check into a small motel, unload their belongings, and freshen up in the room's pastel-tiled bathroom with tiny pink bar soaps. The hotel clerk tells them the high school is a few blocks away on the main road. They decide to walk.

"Just follow the crowd," the clerk says.

They offer a friendly laugh at the clerk's joke. As they head toward the road, there is, in fact, a crowd moving toward the school. Kids schlep aluminum lawn chairs with bright nylon webbing. Men pull wagons loaded with ice chests and blankets. Women push strollers, tote bags slung over their shoulders.

"Just follow the crowd," Frank repeats with a grand motion of his arm.

They move en masse, enticed by the perfume of wood smoke and the melody of excited chatter.

Little plots of land have already been claimed by families and groups of teenagers, spread out in all directions around an immense teepee-stack of logs. Frank stops at a card table sporting a fundraising sign for the student council and drops a few bucks in the donation jar.

"Thank you, sir," chirps the fair-skinned girl stationed there. Her braces flash in the firelight. "Help yourselves to some food. We've plenty of pop and coat hangers for roasting."

They move deeper into the festivities, and Gram becomes animated. Several small fire-pits are already burning. The aroma of charred sugar and hotdog fat wafts on the breeze.

"Grab a wire, Frank," Gram says, "and cook us some wieners."

April laughs. "Wieners?"

Although Gram slipped comfortably back to Midwestern vernacular, the Parsons stand out in the crowd. A young man offers folding chairs for Gram and April. Another directs Frank to the ice-filled buckets of soda cans. A little girl with curls the color of buttermilk appears out of nowhere with a bag of marshmallows.

The *rat-a-tat-tat* of snare drums draws eyes and ears toward the gymnasium. The tenor joins in, and a trio of drummers march to the wood stack. The bonfire is lit. It takes only a moment for the giant teepee of two-by-fours to burst into a tower of flames. The crowd erupts in cheers and applause. The remainder of the small band – trumpets and trombones, clarinets and piccolos, saxophones and cymbals – is led by a lone bass drum across the football field. Cheerleaders in black and gold uniforms and flesh-colored tights bound alongside. They skip and kick and leap and flip in rhythm to the school fight song. The crowd claps in time and sings.

"On, dear Northlake!

"Fight on for your fame.

"Take the ball right down the field,

"For a victory sure this game."

A gangly, shirtless student clad in fringed pants and feathered headdress leaps and dances through the gathering. He wields an oversized foam hatchet, slicing the air.

Boom, boom, boom, boom, goes the bass drum.

"Let's go, Thunderhawks!"

Boom, boom, boom, boom.

"Let's go, Thunderhawks!"

April stands by a small fire pit, a misshapen coat hanger jutting from her fist. Her eyes are drawn to the larger flames of the bonfire. Its enormity is mesmerizing, its heat astounding. A collective energy pulses through the gathering, vibrates in her bones. The marshmallow at the end of the wire ignites in a flash of orange flame.

Frank chuckles and eases his daughter away from the fire. The glob of charred sugar sags and falls into the dirt. He stabs a fresh white lump onto the blackened wire tip. April laughs.

"Thanks, Dad."

Spirited youngsters lead the group in a few more cheers.

The flaming teepee collapses on itself, signaling a shift in the festivities. Families and cliques of teenagers splinter off here and there to sprawl on blankets and fill their bellies with campfire fare. Soft laughter and easy conversations flow like a gurgling creek. April and Gram settle into their borrowed chairs. Frank sits on the ground between them, legs outstretched, palms planted in the dirt behind him. The fire continues to shrink. Small flames dance and snap. Logs glow hot from within.

The Thunderhawk boy has changed out of the fringed getup into a pair of baggy jeans and sweatshirt and joined his friends. Only the red and white face paint remains on his cheeks.

Frank watches the youngsters with a tinge of melancholy. The mascot is identical to the wild Indians in the Old Western movies he enjoyed watching as a little boy. And it's the antithesis to the man he'd gotten to know in Maak.

"You know, Mom, I recognized Maak when I saw him working at the grocery store," Frank says. "Not right at first, but soon after. I'm sorry I never told you."

It wasn't something he planned to say. The suddenness of the words startles him, more than it does Gram. She smiles at him and nods, but his eyes are trained on the glowing embers.

"Then he got fired, and all the kids were talking about it at school," he continues. "It became like a ghost story, almost, the way he packed up and walked into the woods, disappeared in the mist."

In fact, it hadn't been just the kids who breathed life into lore. The men and women of Bitter Rapids had their fun with it, too, Gram knows.

"I took off into the woods that summer, determined to find him," Frank says.

"And you did find him," Gram steals the dramatic twist of his story. "And you kept going back to see him all summer long."

"You knew?" Frank is incredulous.

"How could I not?" she asks. "You were out there in the woods from morning to night, practically every day. You came home smelling of wood smoke. I knew you'd been with Maak. I could see the difference in you, in the way you carried yourself, in your demeanor. You seemed, I don't know, more confident, I guess. More mature. I knew it was Maak's influence."

Frank stands up and claps the dirt from his hands with more force than is needed.

"You're full of bull crap!"

"Dad!" April glances around, embarrassed by her easygoing dad's rare outburst. "Keep your voice down."

"There's no way you could have known." Frank lowers his volume, but the hardness in his voice remains. "You never paid enough attention to me to notice anything different in my *demeanor.*"

The dying bonfire glows in the lenses of Gram's glasses, hiding her eyes.

"You're only saying that now, because of all the other memories you've dredged up on this trip," he says. "To deal with your guilt and regrets."

Logs shift in the fire, break open and send a rush of sparks into the night sky. April flinches, but Frank and Gram are unmoved.

"I knew," Gram says. Her voice is steady. "Guilt and regret aside, I knew you. And I knew Maak."

Frank studies his mother, her expression and her posture, in the increasing dark. It's the truth, he realizes. She had known, after all. Anger wells up from deep in his gut. He imagines himself striking her with the back of his hand. The wind shifts direction. A funnel cloud of smoke swirls and stings his eyes.

"Take your Gram back to the motel," Franks says. "I need to be alone."

He turns and strides off across the field, past the gymnasium, into the black.

April stands and faces her grandmother. She shakes her head, "You're unbelievable."

"What did I do?" Gram asks.

"You really don't know?" April asks. Helpless frustration floods her voice. "He was just a kid. Can you even imagine how hard it must have been for him to keep all your secrets? You were the adult. You should have talked to him and helped him. You shouldn't have lied to him."

Gram flips her hand through the air, as if shooing a pesky fly.

"I didn't lie," she says. "I just didn't tell him everything."

April scoffs at the absurdity of her grandmother's excuse. Lies or omissions of truth? What's the difference?

The young woman gathers their paper plates and empty cans, thrusts the heap into a nearby trash can. She folds the chairs and leans them against the card table. Gram adjusts her oxygen tubing and angles the wheelie for her granddaughter to pull it. They begin walking in the direction of the motel.

"You're right, April, I was the adult then," Gram says after a minute or two passed. "But he's an adult now, and he should act like it instead of storming off like a spoiled kid who didn't get his way."

"Seriously?" April protests. "He stormed off like a grown man who was betrayed by a mother he loves and trusts."

"Don't you speak to me that way," Gram shoots back. She reaches for her cigarette case, places a smoke between her lips.

"You think you're so smart?" Gram pauses, cups her hand around the lighter flame, takes several quick drags of a fresh cigarette. "You have a lot of growing up to do, little girl. You have no idea what it's like to be responsible for someone else. What it's like to sacrifice everything for somebody you love."

You're full of bull crap, Frank's words repeat in April's head. She chews on the inside of her cheek. She stops walking. The women face each other, standing on a sidewalk in the middle of small-town Iowa, 1,200 miles from home. April flings her arms up and around in big swooping circles.

"Look around you, Gram! Look at where we are!"

April wants to shout all the things she gave up to embark on this crazy trip – her classes, her job, her privacy, maybe even her sanity. She remembers all the phone calls from the nursing home, all the little gifts she'd bought the staff to ameliorate Gram's abrasive behavior. Her mind flashes to all the times on this trip she helped Gram in and out the shower, even on and off the toilet.

Then she looks at Gram, sees stubborn strength in the crinkles around soft blue eyes.

"Never mind."

April takes hold of the oxygen wheelie, and they resume their trek to the motel in silence.

✳ ✳ ✳ ✳

Frank sits on the cement curb of the motel lot, facing out to a dark empty field. A six-pack of Rolling Rock is at his feet, minus one. There are only two cars in the lot now – theirs and the primer-painted '69 Camaro belonging to the motel's night clerk. Frank is easy to spot when April steps outside in search of him.

"Hey," she says as she walks up. "Can I join you?"

"Pull up a curb." He tips his head back and drains the remainder of the green bottle.

She squats down beside him. A nighthawk passes overhead, calling out to anyone willing to listen.

April angles her head to the sky, but the bird is invisible.

"How's Gram doing?" Frank asks.

"Oh, she's fine," April says. "Oblivious as ever. Seems to have no idea why we're both pissed at her."

April adds that Gram said she wanted to "retire early." The young woman uses air quotes to mock her grandmother's formal behavior.

"Funny how Gram gets more old-fashioned when she's acting indignant," April says. "I guess the formality does sting more than her usual 'bite me.'"

Frank smiles knowingly and twists the cap off a second beer. He takes a long drink, then looks at his daughter. He'd been worried that April was mad at him for losing his temper at the bonfire. Knowing she's on his side is an unexpected comfort, despite the embarrassment he still feels.

"Want one?" Frank motions toward the six-pack with his chin.

April blinks at him. "Yeah, right."

"No, I mean it," he says. "You can have one if you want."

She looks at the bottles. She mulls the idea.

"I'm not naive enough to think you've never had any," Frank adds.

"Oh," she says, thankful for the pale parking lot lights, knowing the color just drained from her face.

"It's okay. I trust you to be responsible. You're a great kid, April. I'm sorry I don't say it more often. You've always been so responsible and hardworking, so much older than your age."

He takes another drink, and adds, "Sometimes I wonder if you weren't the one taking care of me all these years, instead of the other way around."

April plucks a bottle from the cardboard carrier.

"I guess I'd better have one, then," she says. "Only to make sure you don't drink them all yourself and end up puking all night."

"Right," he says, and pats his protruding belly. "We all know what a lightweight I am."

They laugh, and April rests her head on his shoulder for a moment.

"I love you, Dad."

"I never had any doubt, kiddo."

A crisp breeze causes the crimson leaves of a nearby sugar maple to let go and take flight. They flutter along with the nighthawks' calls and crickets' chirps. The air smells earthy. April breathes it in with gusto. *This is why people say they love fall*, she thinks.

"So, how are *you* doing?" April asks her dad. She takes a sip, gives him time to answer.

"Oh, I'm doing okay," he says. "A little tired, I guess."

April takes another sip.

"Tired of being on the road? Or tired of all the secrets?"

Frank exhales wearily, chuffs like a horse. *Both.*

"I spent a lot of time with Maak that summer, my last summer in Bitter Rapids," he says. "The things I learned from him have stayed with me my whole life, guided me, in a way. I know it sounds hokey."

"No, it doesn't." April places her hand between his shoulder blades.

He gulps a giant breath of air through his mouth and exhales the same way. His sinuses are still too swollen to take in sufficient air; he feels as if he's drowning. April rubs his back.

"It felt good to finally be able to talk about it. That's probably why I got so mad at your Gram tonight," he continues. "I always felt I'd betrayed her, somehow, by being friends with Maak. It weighed on me, and I guess I was hoping for some relief in shoving off that weight. Then wham, it turns out she betrayed me, too."

She knew all along.

He wobbles his head, tries to make sense of it.

"Why didn't she just tell me?" he says. "Why didn't she encourage me to talk about it?"

Frank blinks back the tears welling in his eyes.

The sight of it makes April's throat constrict.

She swallows hard, and whispers, "Talk to *me* about it."

Frank

Maak wasn't big on conversation. Sometimes we'd go an entire day without saying a word to each other. Yet, in his quiet way, he taught me things. At first, it was just practical stuff, like how to build a snare and trap a rabbit. He showed me how to smoke fish, and find strawberries, and harvest wild rice.

When he did talk, it was mostly stories about his mother's people and their beliefs. He never told me what happened to his dad, only that the man was black and that he died when Maak was just a baby.

One morning, we were sitting in camp, working over a deer hide with a smooth rock. I was pretty focused on the work, which is part of what I loved about being out there with him. A single sense of purpose. You know? No distractions. No demands other than doing what was necessary to survive.

Anyway, after a while, I looked up. And there in the shadows of the trees, not twenty feet away, was a wolf. Just standing there, watching me with these giant amber eyes. I nearly wet my pants. Scout was a pretty big dog, but this animal made him look like a pup.

I sort of gasped and looked over to Maak, to warn him, and that's when I saw the rest of them. We were surrounded by wolves, April. A couple of them were sniffing around the fire pit. A few others were lying in the dirt nearby. A couple were sprawled out, sound asleep. There had to be a dozen of them. I swear to God. And there was Scout, resting beside Maak, completely at ease.

Maak just kept working the hide, but he smiled when he heard me sputtering.

"The *ma'iingan* are my brothers and sisters."

That's what he said. That was his people's word for wolf. My-een-gun.

He told me the Ojibwe believe wolves are family and guardians of their community. After the Creation, they traveled together, all part of the same pack, the same tribe. What happened to the wolf also happened to them. In the beginning, wolves were as plentiful as the stars in the sky. They protected and guided the Ojibwe. Then the white man came along. He hunted the wolf, killing hundreds, thousands. And he took over the land from the native people.

Maak told me all this. He said he was alone when he lived among the whites, and the *ma'iingan* were also alone. Once he was back, at the river, living among the trees and stones and birds and insects, he was not alone, and the wolf was not alone.

Wolves are free spirits, even though they live and travel in packs. They're strong hunters. They survive with what the earth provides. They each know their places in the pack, understand they must work together, and all do their individual share. Without working together, not only would he die, but the pack would also die. Together, they remain strong. Maak said man and wolf are the same. I've come to believe he was right.

I think about you, April. You're a free spirit. That was clear from the day you were born. But you're also part of a pack. You know? You and me, and your mom, and Gram. We all need each other to survive. I've tried to teach you that, what Maak taught me, even though I never really explained it quite that way.

There were a lot more days after that, when the wolves were at Maak's camp. We ate together, slept together, even played together. Scout would romp and run with them. After a while, I'd tussle and play with them the same way I did with Scout. They were my brothers and sisters, too.

It sounds ridiculous. Right? Totally bananas.

I've thought about it probably a thousand times over the years. But I never talked about it with anyone. Now that I've said it out loud, I feel a little foolish. It can't possibly be true. Can it?

Have you ever reminisced with a friend about something you did together, years ago, and your friend looks at you like you're crazy? "What the heck are you talking about?" he says. "We never did that." And you stare at each other and shake your heads. Could it be that your friend completely forgot? Or maybe it never actually happened? You imagined the whole darn thing.

Maybe Gram is making the whole thing up, about knowing I was spending time with Maak, about even knowing Maak.

Maybe none of it even happened. My memories of Maak are just a trick of the brain, a defense mechanism to erase the bad stuff and replace it with something wonderful and amazing, something that would help me become strong and survive, instead of wither and die.

After all these years, after all the silence, how can I know for sure?

1990

Northlake, Northern Iowa

"Next stop, Minnesota," Frank declares and piles the last of their bags onto the Corolla roof. April notices his hands are shaking a little as he secures the bungee cords. They're all a little nervous, she thinks, that the trip is nearing its end.

Evelyn does a final sweep of the motel room, to make sure nothing is left behind. She's still kicking herself that they forgot the no-slip bathtub mat at the last place. April bought the mat and a shower chair after that first precarious shower on the road. Remembering the thoughtful gesture makes Evelyn smile. *Darn it,* she thinks.

"All set to go, Gram?" April asks as Evelyn exits the room and approaches the car.

"Not just yet," Gram says. "I've got something I want to say first, to both of you."

Frank and April exchange a quick glance. They wait for Gram to speak. It takes a bit of time for her to muster the words. April helps fill the void by twisting her hair back and up into a bun high on her head, secures it with a black scrunchie.

"I'm sorry," Gram finally says. "For the stuff I said last night. For a lot of stuff."

"It's okay, Mom," Franks says, and April concurs.

"No. It's not." Gram emphasizes the point with a raised palm. "You deserve better than that. Both of you. You've sacrificed a lot for me. And I know I can be a royal pain in the behind."

It's a rare moment of contrition, and Frank can't help but step toward her with open arms.

"Don't go all squishy on me," Gram says. She tries to dodge his hug, which only makes things worse.

"Awww," April says, moving in, too. "Group hug!"

Father and daughter sandwich Gram between them, laugh and press their cheeks against hers.

"Squishy, squishy," they tease.

Gram squirms and protests, groans and rolls her eyes. They don't stop until she cracks and laughs along with them.

"All right now, that's enough you blockheads," Gram says. "Let's get rolling."

"Next stop, Minnesota," Frank announces again with more vigor.

LIFE IN THE 1950s

ST. PAUL, Minn., Jan. 15, 1955

FOR IMMEDIATE RELEASE

/National Newswire/ -- Minnesota game officials increased the wolf bounty payment to $25 per wolf. The bounty program is administered by the state and overseen by the U.S. Fish and Wildlife Service. It has a record of success dating back more than 100 years. Professional and civilian wolf hunters began receiving a bounty of $3 per animal when the program was established in 1849. Between 50,000 and 100,000 of the predators were eradicated annually in Minnesota until the turn of the century. Now that the wolf population is controlled, approximately 250 animals are taken annually under the state's bounty system.

(Source: U.S. Fish and Wildlife Service)

1955

Koochiching State Forest, Minnesota

Midsummer was a good time to harvest mullein leaves, a key ingredient in Maak's traditional tobacco mixture. By July, its club-shaped spikes of densely-packed yellow flowers rose nearly two feet, like beacons identifying where to locate the long, flat leaves spreading from its base.

"*Nimaamaa* taught me to make *asemaa,*" Maak told Frankie, as they combed the sunny, sandy banks where mullein could be found. His mother taught him many things. Mullein, mint, red willow bark, sage. Tobacco to please the spirits. To begin a journey, to hunt. To ask, to give thanks.

Frankie walked beside him, listening. Scout scuttled through the underbrush.

"I don't think I could smoke that much," Frankie said. "I swiped my mom's cigarettes once, for me and the guys at school. We smoked 'em behind the gym. I almost puked."

Maak smiled. *There,* he pointed. A cluster of bright, yellow-fringed spikes peeked out from between wispy clumps of sand bar lovegrass.

"It is not only for smoking." Maak crouched beside the mullein. He plucked an oval leaf from the stem and handed it to Frankie. "Sprinkle a handful of *asemaa* at the trailhead, beside the river, after the rain. For many reasons. Many handfuls."

Frankie turned the leaf over. It was the length of his forearm. It felt like the soft flannel his mom bought to make pajamas.

A loud snap and a hair-raising cry came from the wooded brush across the stream. Scout launched into the water, crossing quickly, and disappeared into the brush on the opposite side. He let out three thunderous barks in rapid succession. *Come quickly, help,* he seemed to be saying.

Maak heeded the alarm without hesitation. He strode into the stream. At its deepest point, the water reached Maak's waist. He soon emerged on the opposite side and turned back toward Frankie.

The boy was tethered in place. The hammer of his heartbeat pounded in his ears. He saw Denny, pale and lifeless in a cold hospital bed, in cold dark water. Frankie's diaphragm constricted. His lungs refused to take in oxygen. Hot panic flared deep in his gut, traveled like wildfire through organs and limbs, muscle and bone. Sweat prickled his underarms.

Maak did not call out. He lowered his eyes. He waited. Wind whispered through the aspen leaves overhead. It breathed in hushed agreement with the gentle lap of the water, tranquil chatter of birds, and the steady patience of the man on the shore.

All at once, Frankie understood. So many condolences had been offered, so much advice given, in the wake of Denny's death. Yet, this moment spoke the loudest and held the most wisdom. Three years without his brother, and it finally made sense to him. *Grief feels exactly like fear.*

It wasn't actually the water that terrified him. It was the emptiness of grief. It was loneliness, a void he hadn't been able to fill – might never be able to fill.

Frankie took a deep breath and balled his hands into fists. He strode boldly into the water. He emerged on the opposite shore, dripping wet, trembling. Maak placed a hand on his shoulder. *Well done. Water is life.*

Scout sounded the alarm again.

Maak and Frankie pushed their way through the brush. A black wolf thrashed and snarled at them, its hind leg oozing blood, caught in the teeth of a steel trap.

"Shh, brother," Maak said, palm raised. "We will help."

He prayed to the spirits – for strength, for wisdom, for guidance. Scout lay down in the scrub grass. The wolf settled somewhat, though it continued to whimper, reflexively jerking its leg to break free.

Maak handed his walking stick to Frankie, dropped his bags to the ground, removed his shirt. Bare-chested, he approached the wounded animal like a breeze, speaking with soft words Frankie did not understand.

Then, to Frankie, he said, "You must open the trap. You will know when."

Maak draped the shirt over the wolf's muzzle, head, and shoulders. He grasped the animal firmly under its rib cage and around its front legs. He pinned the animal to the ground with the full strength of his broad torso. It was a fluid succession, a swift dance. All the while, Maak spoke ancient words of comfort to his Spirit Brother.

Frankie was subdued by Maak's movements almost as completely as the wolf. Then his eyes met Maak's, and he realized now was the time for him to act. Frankie stepped closer and inserted the stick into the thin gap of the steel jaws. He anchored the end of the stick into the earth, braced himself and the trap with his boots, and leaned in to trigger the release lever.

With a metallic snap, the jaws broke open and Frankie fell backward to the ground.

Maak rose to his feet, the wolf limp in his arms, and charged back across the stream toward camp.

Scout sprang up and waited for Frankie, as he gathered Maak's belongings. Boy and dog ran toward the stream together, but Frankie paused before entering the water. He turned back. Near the trap, Frankie pulled a handful of tobacco from Maak's leather pouch and scattered it over the bloody dirt.

* * * *

Swollen pewter clouds brought the chill and mood of night, though it was still early afternoon. Frankie stoked the fire to dry their clothing and fur, to warm their bones. Even still, he couldn't stop trembling. The young wolf was stretched out on the ground beside him, also trembling.

Maak boiled a strong broth of venison jerky and valerian root for *maakade-ma'iingan*, the black wolf. He cooled it with river water, and set a bowl beside the wolf. The animal lifted its head briefly, and then refused the malodorous brew. Without the relaxing effect of the valerian, it would be impossible for Maak to tend the animal's injury.

"Here, Scout, you drink it," Frankie said.

If the dog would drink, he reasoned, the wolf might follow suit.

Scout approached the bowl, sniffed it warily. He sneezed and retreated. Frankie called him back to the bowl, coaxed him to give it a try. Scout complied. He dipped his giant pink tongue for a taste, and sneezed again. This time, he did not retreat. With more encouragement from Frankie, and a hint of venison on his tongue, Scout obediently took several laps.

The young wolf raised its head again. It watched Scout with intent amber eyes. Then it lowered its head and drank.

An hour passed.

Scout and the wolf were laid out beside the fire, snoring gently. Maak rinsed the animal's wounds with clean water and applied a poultice of herbs to ease pain and fight infection. He fashioned a makeshift muzzle by cutting the toe-seam of his moccasin and slipped it over the wolf's snout. Finally, he wrapped its head and shoulders in his shirt like he had at the trap.

"You will hold him down," Maak said. "I will straighten the bone."

"Me?" Frankie gasped. "I can't."

"You will hold him down," Maak repeated. His voice was gentle, composed; his instruction firm, direct.

Frankie had held Scout when the veterinarian administered a rabies vaccine. The general idea of what must be done was understood. Yet, this would be more than a needle prick. He looked at the wolf, shook his head.

Thunder rumbled in the distance. *Baashkikwa'am.*

"We must be quick," Maak said. "The spirits beat their wings."

The fresh intensity of Maak's instruction brought Frankie an unexpected calm. The boy lay down beside the animal. He wrapped his arms around its head and neck, eased his body weight over its shoulders and torso.

Maak placed his hands on the wolf's mangled leg, gently probed muscle and bone with his fingers. The animal whimpered. Frankie strengthened his hold. Maak nodded his head once, grasped either side of the broken bone, and thrust the ends back in alignment with one swift snap.

The wolf yelped from within the muzzle. Its body convulsed. It tried to rear its head, but Frankie held firm. Just as quickly, the animal went limp, passed out from the pain. Maak wrapped the leg with soft birch bark, secured it with sticks and twine. Thunder rumbled overhead. Lightning crackled, illuminating the camp. Plump rain drops began to fall.

"You must stay here tonight," Maak spoke as he worked. He unwrapped the shirt, removed the muzzle.

Maak carried the wolf into the wigwam. Frankie roused Scout, and the groggy dog staggered in behind. Hot stones from the fire warmed the shelter beneath a carpet of birch bark. A feather above the door told the *baashkikwa'am* this place was home to Ojibwe. It would keep the storm from entering.

Frankie was conflicted. He sometimes camped out with Scout and loved the idea of staying with Maak. But he always told his mom his plans. Would she worry if he didn't come home for dinner? Would she even notice?

Suddenly, the skies opened. The decision was made for him.

Sheets of rain gusted across the clearing, dousing the fire. Inside the wigwam, the ragtag pack of brothers was warm and dry. The canines slept peacefully.

"Why do they kill wolves?" Frankie sat with crossed legs, stroking the wolf's lush black fur from head to rump.

Maak watched the boy. After a moment or so, he answered, "Men fear what they do not understand."

1955

Bitter Rapids, Minnesota

The kitchen window would tell Art how the rest of his night would go. He clicked off the headlights, killed the engine, coasted up the driveway to park beside the garage. A soft glow in the window would mean Evelyn had left on the small light above the stove for him and gone to bed. A bright radiance would mean she was sitting at the kitchen table, waiting up. She'd be facing the door, thumbing through a cookbook or lady's magazine, as though her presence then and there had nothing to do with him.

From the dark drive, Art could see the brilliant ray of light cast from the kitchen out to the lawn. He leaned over to examine himself in the rearview mirror, touched the bloody split in his lip. Evelyn would have a look at him eventually. What difference did it make if it was now or in the morning? At least now, she could tend to his wounds.

Evelyn kept her eyes trained on the colorful pages of *Modern Homemaker's Cookbook* as Art entered the house and eased the door shut behind him. She'd wait for him to speak first, to acknowledge the late hour, to offer up his excuse.

"Could use a little help, Evie."

Panic scurried up the back of her neck like a beetle. The last time he'd called her Evie was at Denny's funeral. She looked up, took stock of him – the bulging lip, cherry red jaw, scraped and swollen knuckles.

"Let's get you out of that coat, then."

Art grimaced as she pulled up and back on his overcoat, eased it down his arms.

"Easy," he whimpered. "The ribs."

She hung the coat, motioned for him to take a seat. She pulled two bags of frozen peas from the icebox, grabbed the small metal first aid box from the kitchen drawer, pulled a chair around the table to sit down facing him.

Learning how to tend injuries of husband or child is something a proper wife mastered early in a marriage – a dab of iodine for cuts and scrapes, a cold compress for bumps and bruises. If nothing else, Evelyn took pride in being a proper wife. Art held the peas to his face with his left hand, while Evelyn silently swabbed the knuckles of his right with the copper-colored antiseptic. Next, a thin paste of baking soda and water was mixed, applied to the split lip.

"Thanks, Evie."

She nodded you're welcome, placed the second icy bag of peas on his swollen knuckles with care. She scooted back in her chair, spine ramrod straight, hands neatly folded in her lap. Art closed his eyes, focused on his breathing under the glare of the kitchen spotlight. Evelyn tilted her head, watched him. The tick-tock of the grandfather clock in the living room ricocheted through the otherwise still house.

After a few minutes had passed, she said, "Let's have a look at the rest of ya, then."

They stood. Evelyn loosened and removed his necktie, set it neatly folded on the table. She tugged his shirttails up from his pants' waist, undid the buttons, eased the garment open and off his shoulders, exposing Art's bare chest and back. It was a rare sight, and that alone would have made her pause, take in a quick breath. But this. The bruises along his ribs, at his kidneys, on his shoulder were already deep purple. The delineation of knuckles and steel-toe boots unmistakable.

"Sit," she told him.

Evelyn retrieved a glass from the cupboard, filled it with cold water from the tap, and set it on the table in front of Art. The aspirin bottle rattled as she tapped two tablets into her hand. The brush of his fingertips against her palm further softened her austerity as he plucked up the pills.

The bulb in the overhead light buzzed as Art gulped down the aspirin and cold water. A plate of pork chops and roasted potatoes she'd served up for his dinner was still on the counter, neatly covered with a flour-sack towel. Its bouquet of meat and grease and rosemary mingled with the sharp smell of iodine.

"What was it this time?" Evelyn finally asked.

"Aw, you know. Just the usual nonsense."

She drew in a long deliberate breath, exhaled slowly. It had been a while since Art had gotten in a tussle, and she couldn't help but wonder if this latest one had something to do with the gossip about her and Maak. A stab of shame – for hoping she was the reason for the fight – pierced high in her gut.

"Was it all this nonsense about the man who rescued the boys?"

That was how she referred to Maak now. Always. *The man who rescued the boys.* It helped keep a conversation from degenerating into something bitter or tawdry.

"No," Art said.

Silence slipped back into the air.

And then he said, "Probably didn't help matters, though."

Art couldn't resist throwing one more punch that night, even if the recipient of the figurative blow was an innocent bystander.

She accepted the strike without protest; the penance for sweet, satisfying guilt.

＊＊＊＊

Evelyn moved briskly along the sidewalk, shopping list in hand, on a mission. Gossip about town was subdued. The atmosphere at home had returned to normal – quiet, boring, acceptable. Even Art's scuffle at Wally's the other night was a sign of life returning to normal. Tonight, there would be fried chicken and buttered corn for dinner. Evelyn completed her final errand – a stop at the liquor store for a six-pack of Ballantine, Art's beer of choice.

"Good afternoon, Mrs. Specht!"

A small gathering of men across the street waved and laughed. Evelyn politely waved hello in return, though their glee was baffling to her. They weren't even looking in her direction. Evelyn followed their gaze further up the block. Ed Miller was headed her way on the sidewalk. He kept his head down, took long, swift strides. His hands were plunged deeply in his pants pockets. He nearly collided with her, and the chatter from across the street died.

The laughter had been at his expense, of that Evelyn was sure. The joke, however, was lost on her.

"Hello, Ed." Their eyes connected for two seconds. Evelyn fought the urge to glance sideways to the men across the street.

"Hiya, Evie," he said, tipping his hat.

A yellowish-green mark on his left cheekbone gave away a half-healed bruise.

"Goodness," Evelyn said. She reached up to touch his face, then thought better of it, placed her fingertips to her ear instead. "Am I to assume you were part of the same scuffle that brought Art home with bloodied fists the other night?"

"You should see the other guys." Ed chuckled nervously, toggled his hat back in place.

Evelyn tugged at her faux pearl earring. She was deciphering clues, assembling facts. He could see it in her eyes.

"Well, I best be off," Ed said urgently, to thwart any conclusions from settling in Evelyn's mind. "If I don't get this milk and bread home to the missus, she'll give me a new shiner to match the old one."

They shared a forced laugh and parted ways. After a couple of steps, Evelyn glanced back over her shoulder to watch Ed walk away. Her eyes narrowed in thought as the distance between them grew.

LIFE IN THE 1990S

FOR IMMEDIATE RELEASE

/National Newswire/ -- Three years after winning their first World Series title, the Minnesota Twins have closed their Major League Baseball season dead last in the American League West division. Despite the abysmal showing, Twins outfielder Dan Gladden made a bold prediction today, during Fan Appreciation Day festivities at the Metrodome.

"We're looking forward. We're going to improve next season," he said. "And we're going to bring another World Series championship to Minnesota."

Only time will tell if Gladden's strident belief in his team's ability to recreate itself proves to be astute or naïve.

(Source: Sports News Today)

September 30, 1990

Minneapolis, Minnesota

The trio rolls into Minneapolis in late afternoon and finds a nice hotel with two room vacancies. They discuss dinner options. The litany of gravy-doused food in greasy diners and handmade bologna sandwiches in motel rooms is wearing on them all. By unanimous vote, they decide it's time to splurge on a restaurant with chef's specials and linen napkins.

They order the house merlot and Caesar salads, rib eye steaks and au gratin potatoes. During dessert, Frank announces they'll spend an extra day in Minneapolis before continuing north.

"I have a surprise planned for tomorrow night," he says, jiggling his bushy eyebrows. He refuses to provide hints.

Frank drops April and Gram off at the hotel and sets off on a secret mission. The digital marquee on the bank building downtown says the current temperature is sixty-three degrees.

"I still can't get over that," April says. "It's probably twenty degrees warmer in Phoenix right now."

"At least," Gram agrees.

They decide to change into sweatpants for their nightly walk. Because of the nip in the air, they say, not because they're bursting at the seams from dinner. A chilly wind blusters in from the north, makes their faces tingle. Gram smiles at the long-forgotten feel of wind-kissed cheeks.

Evelyn

These walks have been good. Haven't they, April? I'm feeling stronger. Not so wobbly on my feet. Could be my imagination, but I might even be breathing better. I'm gonna keep up the habit when we get back home. You hold me to that.

I might even try tossing the cigarettes. Maybe. Don't hold me to that one.

The change of scenery has helped, too, I think. Clears the mind. I'm thinking about things and remembering things I haven't thought about in thirty, forty years.

I've been thinking a lot about Art.

He used to get into fisticuffs every so often. It's part of what attracted me to him, if I'm being honest. He wasn't brawny by any measure. But he was scrappy. He'd come home with bruised knuckles, or a black eye, and I'd play nursemaid. He never told me exactly what the fights were about, and I never pressed him. I used to imagine he was defending my honor in some way, or maybe standing up for someone getting bullied.

Art was a good man, a good provider, and I do believe he cared about me and the boys.

But, well, he never pined for me. It wasn't that kind of relationship.

I beat myself up over that for a long time. I wasn't pretty enough or sexy enough. That's what I told myself. Or, I didn't do enough for him to earn his love. It even made me start to question my relationship with Frank Sr. We were just kids, me and Frank. High school sweethearts. A teenage boy will sleep with any girl who'll let him. Right? It's possible Frank never really loved me. That's what I started to believe.

Looking back, years later, that's when I finally started piecing things together about Art. He waited so long to get married. And it wasn't because he was too focused on his business and career. It wasn't that he just hadn't met the right woman yet. It was because no woman was right for him, if you get my meaning.

Oh, it's different now. People can talk about it. People can live their lives. That's not how things were back then. A person could lose a job for being *that way*. Get beat up. Get arrested, even.

You probably learned about the "Red Scare" when you were in school. Right? The McCarthy hearings in Congress, trying to root out communists after the war? Well, I bet they never taught you about the "Lavender Scare." It was all going on around the same time. McCarthy and his goons were so afraid of the gays, went to great lengths to expose them, too. Claimed they were a threat to national security, just like the commies. People's careers were destroyed. Their lives destroyed.

Looking back, I wish Art would have just told me. I would have supported him. I really think I would have. We both said "I do" knowing we weren't in love. But I always felt guilty about it, tried my darnedest to fall in love with him, to get him to fall in love with me. Who knows, maybe he felt guilty, too. It's a helluva way to live. Trying to be something or someone you're not. Keeping the truth hidden away from people you care about the most.

October 1, 1990

Minneapolis, Minnesota

"**T**har she blows!" Frank says in his best sailor voice.

The Corolla speeds south along Highway 35. From the bridge crossing the mighty Mississippi, the view of their destination is unobstructed. The enormous white blob dominates the skyline.

"What the heck is that?" April asks.

"The Dome!" Gram claps her hands.

"I got us tickets to the Twins/Mariners game, kiddo," Frank says.

"Oh," April says. She opens her eyes wide, offers a toothless smile. *Great.* The voice in her head speaks with drawn-out disdain. *Four hours of baseball.*

When they reach the stadium parking lot and the "Welcome to Hubert H. Humphrey Metrodome" sign, Frank proudly hands over the parking pass he procured the day before. Attendants motion their car forward with orange wands, direct Frank to an open spot.

April eyes the enormous rectangular structure – beige, windowless, crowned by a white puffy rooftop. She thinks, *It's Paul Bunyan's inflatable mattress.*

"So, who's poor Hubert?" April asks. "And why do the people who named this place hate him?"

"Okay, it's not the most regal ballpark in America," Frank laughs. "I'll give you that. But just wait 'til we get inside."

A line of people snakes halfway around the building, clad in Twins red-white-and-blue jerseys, ball caps, T-shirts, and foam fingers. As the Parsons join the end of the line, Gram takes the opportunity to get in one last cigarette before they enter the stadium.

"Hubert Humphrey was the vice president under Lyndon Johnson, by the way," Gram says, while exhaling a lungful of smoke. "Didn't they teach you anything at that high school of yours?"

A young woman balancing a toddler on her hip waves her free hand in the air around them, discharges an exaggerated cough.

"My goodness, what a sweet baby," Gram offers up a saccharin smile, takes another deep drag on the cigarette and exhales.

April feels heat flash in her cheeks. *Sorry,* she mouths to the woman.

The group moves forward a bit and stops. They wait beside a bronze plaque mounted to the stadium wall. Gram reads it aloud.

Hubert H. Humphrey (1911 – 1978) was a pharmacist, politician, and ardent sports fan. He served as the Mayor of Minneapolis, a U.S. Senator for Minnesota, and U.S. Vice President under Lyndon B. Johnson. A staunch champion of civil rights, Humphrey fought against discrimination of Jews and African-Americans, and he urged the Democratic Party to repudiate segregation.

"He sounds like a good guy," April admits. "But his stadium is still horrifically ugly. Wait. Is the roof moving?"

"Yeah, isn't that cool?" Frank says. "It's inflated with air pressure. That's why there aren't any windows."

April revives her polite smile and wide-eyed expression. *So, it really IS a giant air mattress.*

They reach the entrance and its expansive revolving doors. Frank slips into an opening, offers a hand to help Gram hustle in beside him. April quickly takes up the rear with the oxygen wheelie. A powerful gust of air whips their hair in all directions as they proceed through the revolving wind tunnel.

"Waahoo-hoooo!" Gram hollers, and Frank joins in with a "yeehaw!" They emerge on the other side, and April works to detangle her long hair. Gram's hair-sprayed coif is standing on end, and April's is wrapped around her head. *The Bride of Frankenstein and the Mummy*, April thinks. She can't help but laugh out loud.

"This is the weirdest place I've ever been," she says.

They make their way to the left-field stands, stopping at concessions to buy hot dogs, a couple of beers, and a diet cola. Before the game begins, they stand and place their hands over their hearts, sing the national anthem. The Twins rack up five runs in the second inning. The crowd goes bananas. By the seventh inning stretch, the Mariners have answered back with four runs, and the crowd is grumbling. They stand and belt out "Take Me Out to the Ball Game" nevertheless.

Gram heckles the umpires. Frank fist pumps the air when the Twins score on a wild pitch, and the next batter singles to bring another home in the bottom of the seventh.

Fans lunge and scramble to recover foul balls. Everyone stands to dance and sing along to "Y.M.C.A." and "Eye of the Tiger" between innings. April asks approximately 300 stupid questions. They eat peanuts and drop the shells at their feet. They laugh – loud and often and freely.

A young man seated in front of April turns around and flashes a picture-perfect smile.

"This your first baseball game?" he asks.

His ice-blue eyes and flaxen hair peek out from beneath his cap. April answers with a giddy nod of the head. Gram snorts and pokes an elbow into her ribs. April feels a little drunk – on diet cola and salty peanuts and unexpected fun. Introductions are made. They all shake hands with their new friend, Travis. He holds on to April's hand just a little longer than necessary, spends the next inning trying to impress her with his baseball knowledge.

The batter pops the ball high to left field. April tracks it as it soars up and up in their direction. She loses it in the vast expanse of the white fabric ceiling.

"Where did it go?" April shouts.

Someone nearby yells, "Heads up!"

Gram shrieks and ducks for cover. Everyone else takes to their feet. Travis extends his arm and makes a barehanded catch over April's head. He topples off balance a bit, and she touches his rib cage to steady him.

The crowd goes wild. Frank and Gram give him high fives.

"That was amazing!" April says. "Didn't that hurt?"

"Nah," he lies. He tosses the ball up and catches it again, then hands it to April. "Here, you take it. A souvenir of your first ball game."

＊＊＊＊

In the morning, Frank and April take advantage of the hotel's complimentary breakfast. He dives into a plate of scrambled eggs, sausage links, and hash browns. She nibbles on a muffin.

"Gram's pretty tuckered out from all the excitement yesterday, huh?" Frank asks, cutting a link in half with his fork.

April swallows before answering. "Yeah, she's pretty much out cold. I left a note saying we'd bring coffee and a Danish up for her, just in case she wakes up."

Subdued chatter circulates through the makeshift cafeteria. A mother shows her son how to operate the waffle maker. A line forms at the juice dispensers. Families plan for the day's activities. A man wearing a tie sits alone with coffee and newspaper.

April holds the foul ball from yesterday, runs her thumb over the laces, inspects the smudge from the strike of the bat. Frank watches her. He smiles.

"I haven't seen you have that much fun in a long time," he says.

"Right back at you, mister."

He plucks the ball from her hand, presses and twists it between his palms.

"We should take in some Spring Training games back home," Frank says.

The smell of fresh-cut grass. Blue sky and bright sun. A warm spring breeze. Hot dogs and cold beer. Not a care in the world. It doesn't even matter who wins the game.

"I think you'd like it even more," he adds.

April studies him – the slackened jaw and smooth forehead, the twinkling eyes and relaxed shoulders.

"You look like a new man," she marvels.

"I kind of feel like a new man," he says. "Or, maybe like a younger man. Like the kid I used to be."

Frank

Man, April, I was a different kid after that summer with Maak. That's clear to me now, when I look back. It was seeing how he lived, on his own terms. You know? Realizing it was possible to be completely on your own, even with the whole world against you, and still be fine. More than fine. Happy, even.

Getting back into the routine of school that fall was brutal. Following someone else's schedule. Doing math equations and memorizing the periodic table. All that had nothing to do with living a good life in my view. Being fifteen years old didn't help matters. At that age, there's no pressure of having a mortgage, putting food on the table, paying medical bills.

Sleeping under the stars, and fishing in the river. Chopping wood, and cooking over a fire. Living off the land. That was all I wanted, all I needed.

School and homework? It was stupid and pointless. I remember saying that to myself. Before long I said it out loud, to my teachers. Shouted it at my mom. One day, it was late September, I said that to Art. That's when the turds really hit the fan. It was just a matter of time. All those teenage hormones. The pent-up resentment for Art. I was like one of those teakettles boiling on the stove. The ones that shriek like a banshee when the steam finally blows.

So, I throw a fit, refuse to do my homework. Art's whole face turned red. He told me to go to the garage, which I did.

Or, I started to anyway.

Halfway across the yard, I stopped.

Art went nuts. He was shouting, "Quit stalling! Go to the [bleeping] garage!" But I just stood there and shook my head no. He totally lost it. He grabbed me by the arm and tried to pull me to the garage. When he realized he wasn't strong enough to move me, he shouted, "Fine, then! We'll do this right here!"

He took off his belt and swung it at me. It was like slow motion. I grabbed the belt with one hand, took a swing at him with the other. I only grazed him, but we were eye to eye. I'd grown taller that summer. Stronger, too. And in that split second, we both knew. The days of him "disciplining" me were over.

The whole thing probably would have ended then and there, except that your Gram saw it all happening from the kitchen window. She flung open the door and ran across the yard screaming at us to stop. I guess neither of us wanted her calling the shots, and so the fists started flying.

I don't quite know what happened in the melee, but somehow your Gram took a hit to the face trying to break up the fight. She yipped and threw her hands up for cover. That ended things pretty fast.

Can you imagine what we must have looked like to the neighbors?

That was the beginning of the end of our time in Minnesota, I think, even though we never talked about it.

I started sleeping out in the yard with Scout. By September, the nights were freezing, the morning ground was covered in frost. Mom begged Art to let the dog sleep in the house again. I guess she knew I was too stubborn to give in, and she was afraid I'd freeze to death out there. After some heated debate, Art agreed to put a kennel in the garage. I should have taken the victory and gone back to sleeping in my room. Instead, I marched out to the garage at bedtime and crawled right into the kennel with Scout.

That was too much for Art to take. He announced that he'd registered me at Riverside Military Academy, a boarding school in St. Paul for troubled youth. I was to start school there after Christmas break.

October 1955

Bitter Rapids, Minnesota

*M*iss Wallace wrote instructions for the next day's classes on the chalkboard at the front of the room. Students had gone home for the day, and she was expecting Frankie Specht's parents for a conference.

Evelyn stood in the doorway a moment, watching the young teacher with a combination of admiration and envy. Miss Wallace looked stylish and modern in her navy pencil skirt and crisp pink blouse, her sophisticated French twist and practical kitten heels. She had a career, a purpose outside the home. Evelyn cleared her throat.

"Mrs. Specht, I'm sorry I didn't hear you come in," Miss Wallace turned and extended her hand. "Please, have a seat."

They shook hands and settled into chairs on either side of the teacher's desk.

"I was hoping to speak with both you and your husband," the young woman said.

Evelyn crossed her ankles, set her clutch purse on her lap. Her posture was perfect.

"Matters of the household are my responsibility," she said.

"Oh," Miss Wallace said. "Yes, of course."

The young woman studied Evelyn's expression – proud, polite, and something more that Miss Wallace couldn't interpret. The mother's perfect curls peeked out of a silk scarf draped loosely over her hair and tied around her neck.

Miss Wallace folded her hands neatly on her desk. *Best to get right to it,* she told herself.

"Mrs. Specht, Frankie has bruises on his face and knuckles. He's clearly been fighting. His grades are suffering. I'm concerned."

"I appreciate your concern," Evelyn said. "Boys scuffle. It's just a phase. It will pass."

Evelyn uncrossed her ankles, as if to stand. "Was there anything else you wanted to discuss?"

Miss Wallace persisted. Frankie was also struggling socially. A creative outlet like the theater club or young men's choir, she said, could be quite beneficial. Both groups met for one hour after school, three days a week.

"No, Mr. Specht would never condone such a diversion from homework and household chores," Evelyn answered without giving the suggestion any thought. "Certainly not if Frankie's grades are suffering."

"But household matters are your responsibility." The young teacher looked Evelyn square in the eyes. Neither one blinked.

"That's correct, Miss Wallace, which is why I really should be getting back to them now."

Evelyn's words were measured, her rise from the chair unhurried. It allowed time for an apology from the young woman. Evelyn's feelings of admiration and envy had evaporated, replaced by indignation and umbrage.

Miss Wallace's exuberant youth and passion caused her to misstep. Her astute observation and wit helped her to redirect.

"I don't presume to know what a difficult job you have, Mrs. Specht, as a wife and mother. I only wish to offer you my support. We both have Frankie's best interest in mind. That much I do know."

There was a visible softening in Evelyn's posture, in the tilt of her head. It was in that moment Miss Wallace first noticed the greenish discoloration on Evelyn's jaw, the over-application of powder and rouge.

"My goodness, Mrs. Specht, how did you get that nasty bruise?"

Evelyn feigned ignorance. She extracted her compact from her purse, snapped open the mirror to examine her face.

"Oh that," Evelyn forced a laugh. "I'd already forgotten about it. Bumped my cheek into the car door a few days ago, unloading bags from the market. I'm a clumsy fool."

She laughed again.

Miss Wallace pressed her lips together, bobbed her head a little.

"Yes," she said. "My mother was often clumsy that way, too."

* * * *

Feeling his fate was already cast, Frankie ventured out to the woods again on the weekends. Boarding school was already set. What more could Art do to punish him?

Frost covered the mossy forest floor, shielded from the midday sun by the thick foliage overhead. It crunched beneath Frankie's boots as he and Scout made their way along the familiar path to Maak's camp. The dog panted with anticipation as he trotted alongside his boy. Wisps of steam puffed from their mouths.

They were greeted at the edge of the clearing by the black wolf.

"He's getting stronger," Frankie said.

Maak smiled from his position beside the fire. *Yes.* The boy approached him, flanked by canines. A mild limp was the only evidence of the wolf's injury. Flesh had healed. Bone had mended. Thickened winter fur concealed the scars.

Seeing the black wolf always led Frankie's mind back to that day, to the trap, to the water, to memories of Denny, to his newfound understanding of fear and grief and regret. There was so much more he wanted to understand.

The four brothers settled around the fire. Frankie took up a fist-sized stone and portion of elk hide to assist Maak in his winter preparations. They worked silently, running the smooth stones over the leather to soften it. Scout and the wolf slept, their feet twitching in dreams of the hunt.

"What happened with the man?" Frankie could no longer be silent. "The one you killed?"

Maak looked up from his work, studied the boy. He added a piece of wood to the fire.

"We argued," he said at last. "We fought with our fists. He drew a knife and cut me. I beat him until he no longer fought. I survived."

He left much unsaid. He always left much unsaid.

Frankie resisted the impulse to fire off a barrage of questions. *Who was the man? What was the argument about? Where did it happen?* With Maak, one must whittle away small pieces to reveal what lies beneath.

"Do you feel bad that he died?" Frankie asked.

Maak watched the flames shift and flicker. He placed his hand on the black wolf's neck, worked his fingers down to the soft undercoat of fur.

Frankie carved a little deeper. "I mean, if you could go back in time and have a do-over, would you try not to kill him?"

Maak returned to smoothing his portion of leather. Time passed as it often did when they were together, without words. Then, Maak set down the stone, tilted his head to the sky, began to speak.

"If I set out to hunt the bear, if I am overpowered and killed, I do not blame the bear," he spoke with relaxed simplicity. "For one to live, another must die. It is the way of the earth. That is all."

Frankie leaned closer, his lips parted slightly.

"Sure," he said. "I mean, it was self-defense, right?"

"It was survival," Maak said. He retrieved the stone, returned to his work, and Frankie knew that was all he would say.

Self-defense had not been argued at trial. There was no trial. No lawyer. Not really. The public defender told Maak his only hope was to explain what happened, to apologize before the judge, and ask for leniency in sentencing. Maak told the judge the story of the bear and the way of the earth. The judge laughed.

"The earth doesn't make laws or govern society," the man had said from behind his tall desk. "Civilized men do that. Even savages need to abide those laws or pay the price."

The strike of the gavel had sounded like a gunshot.

The clang of the cell door had been a steel trap.

If I could do-over, Maak thought, *I would not get caught.*

1990

Minneapolis, Minnesota

April's note about breakfast is propped against the digital alarm clock on the nightstand. Evelyn reads it for the umpteenth time, tells herself to get out of bed for the umpteenth time. She finally hoists her aching bones and pounding skull from the mattress and shuffles into the bathroom. Cool water from the sink provides momentary relief from the heat in her cheeks.

"You shouldn't have had that second beer," she scolds her reflection with a crackling voice. Oh, but how that cold foam had soothed the fire in the back of her throat.

Dark circles beneath watery eyes provide the best comeback from the reflection. *You shouldn't have gone to the baseball game with a fever.*

The smart thing to do now would be to tell Frank and April she has a cold. A day or two of rest at the hotel will knock it out. Evelyn laughs at her own irony. *Because you have such a great track record of doing the smart thing.* They'll be in Duluth by midday, in Bitter Rapids tomorrow. The idea of delaying that for even a couple of days is intolerable.

"You can rest in the car," Evelyn tells the haggard reflection.

* * * *

The Corolla is packed. Evelyn splashes cool water on her face one last time before leaving the hotel room and climbing into the back seat. The coffee and Danish sit untouched on the nightstand.

Frank turns off the radio. They drive north on Interstate 35 to the music of Gram's raspy snore. The tiny town of Sturgeon Lake is the best place to stop for gas and Gram's exercise. She and April set off along a pebble-paved walk.

April is giddy from the fragrant shock of foliage. She inhales its earthy aroma, its autumn hues. The lake is still. It casts a mirror image of the sky and landscape – a gemstone kaleidoscope of amber, citrine, lapis, and garnet. The air has a brisk edge. She thinks about Phoenix, where it's still warm enough to swim in the backyard pool today.

"I just cannot get enough of this weather," April says with an exalting sigh. "This scenery!"

Gram shuffles with leaden feet a few steps behind.

"You'd get sick of it soon enough," she mutters.

"Geeze, Gram. You can be a real buzzkill sometimes. You know that?"

They all pile back in the car. Gram is asleep again in the back seat before they reach the highway entrance ramp. April cranks up Metallica in her Walkman headphones to drown out the old woman's snores. ... *"off to never-never land."*

*** * * ***

DULUTH - 5 MILES.

The green highway signs lead the way to gas, food, and lodging ahead.

"Time to wake up sleepyhead," Frank says. He cranes his neck to view his mother through the rearview mirror. His voice raises an octave. "Mom?"

April removes her headphones.

"What is it?" she asks.

"Gram isn't waking up."

April reaches back, shakes Gram's shoulder, puts her hand to the woman's cheek.

"Oh, shit. Dad, she's burning up."

The car speeds along the highway. Frank's mind is racing, and yet it's blank. His knuckles turn white on the steering wheel.

"Dad!" April points to the highway sign.

Hospital Next Exit.

"Dad, turn off here."

Frank lurches the wheel toward the off-ramp. The car rumbles over the gore, narrowly cutting off an exiting minivan. He's deaf to the squealing brakes and blasting horn behind them. He's lost.

April searches for the rectangular blue signs with the giant white "H" and calls out directions. Frank follows them blindly. Make a left up ahead. Turn right into the parking lot there. Park by those double-doors. That's the emergency room entrance. She flings open the car door and leaps from the vehicle as it rolls to a stop. She turns sideways to hurry between the sluggish sliding doors.

"We need help."

There's authority in her voice. A brawny paramedic taking a coffee break in the waiting area chucks the disposable cup into the trash, follows the young woman out to the car. Frank remains frozen in the driver's seat as a team extracts Gram from the car and onto a gurney. They run alongside, a blur of hands and shiny instruments, as they wheel her inside.

Temp, one-o-two.

Pulse is thready.

Pupils nonresponsive.

April opens Frank's door, grabs hold of his shoulders, eases him from the seat.

"You have to go with them, Dad. Gram needs you. I'll park the car and meet you inside."

* * * *

April studies the vending machine, decides on cheese and peanut butter sandwich crackers. The metal coil turns and the crackers drop from the shelf into the basin. Lunch. Frank hasn't moved from his seat in the ER lobby. His gaze is fixed on the parking lot outside the glass doors. April returns to the seat beside him.

"Hungry?" She angles the open package in his direction.

"Thanks," he says.

Frank extracts an orange-colored cracker sandwich from the cellophane. He rests his hands on his thighs, turns his attention back to the glass doors. An ambulance pulls into the circle drive. A patient is wheeled past the waiting area and through the swinging doors marked "Medical Personnel Only."

April tilts her head up to watch Phil Donahue on the television mounted to the wall. The spry, white-haired host zigzags among his studio audience, handing off the microphone here and there, so ordinary folks can ask today's celebrity guest a question. Eventually, Donahue gives way to Sally Jesse Raphael, who steps aside for Gilligan's Island and Brady Bunch reruns. A handsome, local news anchor follows with the day's top headlines.

"Evelyn Parson?" A young doctor in green scrubs and white coat scans the waiting area.

"Yes." Frank jumps to his feet. "That's my mom."

"She's a firecracker," the doctor says smiling, extending a hand for introduction. Frank blinks. The orange cracker sandwich is still pinched between his thumb and index finger. April steps in to shake the doctor's hand.

"Tell us something we don't know," she says.

"She's doing well," the doctor says. "We gave her IV fluids and a little something for pain."

"Can we see her?" Frank asks. He sets the crackers down, wipes his fingers on the front of his Grateful Dead T-shirt. A smear of orange crumbs looks right at home with the neon-colored dancing bears.

"In a little bit," the doctor pauses to read something in Evelyn's chart. "I spoke with her doctor in Phoenix, got up to speed on your mother's medical history. Bronchitis, emphysema. Still smoking. I want to keep her here a day or two, to run a few tests, and make sure she takes it easy. She's not too happy with me about that."

The doctor smiles, an easygoing flash of brilliant white.

"They're moving her to a room right now," he adds. "Assuming she doesn't sucker punch the orderly and make a run for it, someone will take you up to see her. You might want to get her some dinner from the cafeteria. It'll be faster than putting in an order with the nurses."

They give the doctor their thanks and wait to be escorted upstairs.

* * * *

"You gave us quite a scare, old lady," April says after their long day in the ER. She plants a kiss on Gram's paper-like cheek.

"A bunch of whoop-de-do over nothing," Gram says. "Just a little head cold."

Frank takes his mother's hand in his, kisses her knuckles. He pulls up a chair and parks beside the bed. He clears his throat as if to speak, but says nothing. He hasn't said ten words all day, April realizes. *That's Dad. A deer in the headlights whenever there's a crisis.*

"You hungry?" April turns her attention back to Gram.

"Starved!" she says. "Guess that big-shot doctor never learned you're supposed to *feed* a cold."

The young woman laughs and sets off to find the cafeteria.

Frank and Evelyn are alone with the rhythmic operation of the oxygen machine. *Hiss, click, shoop. Hiss, click, shoop.* She asks him what he and April were up to all afternoon while the doctors and nurses were poking and prodding her. Frank shrugs, *nothing.* He squeezes his eyes shut, but he can't hold back the wave of tears that roll down his cheeks.

"Oh," Evelyn says. "What's all this?"

Frank sniffs and smashes the tears from his eyes with the heel of his hand.

"I'm not ready to lose you, Mom," he says and clears his throat again.

Evelyn pats his hand.

"You're not going to lose me, Frankie."

1955

Bitter Rapids, Minnesota

Dear Mom,

By the time you read this, me and Scout will be far away. Don't try to find us.

I hope you have a happy life with Art. I'm not mad at you. It's just time for me to be my own man.

Please don't worry. I'll write to you when I find a job and place to live.

Love,

Frankie

* * * *

Six fat strips of bacon sizzled and popped in the cast-iron skillet. Coffee percolated in the pot beside it. Evelyn gave a sideward glance to both as she cracked an egg with the edge of a fork and emptied the shell into a Pyrex mixing bowl.

"Good morning," Art sang as he walked into the kitchen. He kissed Evelyn's cheek, giving her a jolt of surprise.

"Oh, now look what you've done, you chipper fool," she teased, and fished an errant piece of eggshell from the bowl.

Art chuckled and sat down at the table, unfolded the morning paper. "I like my eggs with a bit of crunch, dontcha know."

Evelyn smiled. It occurred to her the household had been quieter since Art's declaration that Frankie would attend boarding school in the new year. The boy had settled down, focused on schoolwork and chores, and finally quit sleeping in the garage. Art had relaxed, pleased with his decision and with Frankie's response to it. At first, Evelyn had been distraught by the idea of Frankie leaving home. Yet, it was inevitable. Wasn't it? For a boy to leave his home and his mother?

She cracked another egg. The yolk plopped into the gelatinous pool and sank. Evelyn stared at the sunny orbs at the bottom of the blue-sky bowl.

Certainly, Frankie and Art would be happier with the separation from one another. Perhaps, she would be happier, too. There would be less food to shop for and prepare, fewer loads of laundry to wash and hang and iron.

"But what else would I do?" Evelyn muttered.

"Hmm?" Art asked. His eyes remained on the newspaper. "Did you say something, Evelyn?"

"Just talking to myself." She whisked the eggs into a foamy frenzy.

"Frankie out walking the dog?" he asked.

"No, he's still in bed," Evelyn said.

"What?" Art folded the paper, set it on the table, directed his full attention to his wife. "It's nearly seven o'clock."

"It's Sunday," she said.

"And yet, you and I are up," he said.

Evelyn walked to the table with the coffee pot, filled Art's cup.

"I don't see the harm of sleeping in a bit," she said softly, and set the pot on a trivet.

Art took her hand, sandwiched it between his.

"It's about discipline, establishing a routine. The boy needs structure." He patted her hand then discharged it, picked up the newspaper again. "You understand."

"Yes, of course," she said. "I'll go wake him."

She walked down the hall and tapped lightly on Frankie's closed door.

"Frankie? Time to wake up, sweetheart," she said, and waited for a response.

Silence.

She knocked a bit harder, called out his name. The quiet roared in her ears. Heat rose in her body. Evelyn flung open the door to see Frankie's neatly-made bed. A letter in his handwriting rested on the pillow.

Art heard the scream from down the hall. He bolted from his seat and ran to Frankie's room. "What's wrong?"

Evelyn pressed the letter to his chest, as she ran past him, through the house and out the back door, across the yard into the garage. Scout's kennel was empty. Frankie's camping gear was gone. Tremors overtook her limbs, and she crumbled to the wood floor. Her lungs refused to inflate. The garage dimmed.

Then Art was there, easing Evelyn to her feet, ushering her back to the kitchen. He pressed a cup of coffee into her hands. He added a splash of rum.

"Drink this," he said. "It'll settle you. I'm calling Don."

Evelyn sipped from the cup, while Art called the sheriff. Her mind flashed through a dozen scenarios, each more perilous than the last. Art's voice drifted to her, questions, curses, none of it comprehensible. Her mind was too muddled.

"Do you have any idea where the boy might have run off to?" Sheriff Carrigan asked her.

"Oh! Don," Evelyn responded, "when did you get here? Where are my manners? Would you like some coffee?"

Evelyn began to rise from her seat at the kitchen table. The sheriff placed his hands on her shoulders, gave her a shake, repeated his question. He eased her back into the chair, slid a pen and notepad across the table to her. Write down names, places, anything that comes to mind, he repeated the command.

"I'll cancel my appointments for the week," Art said. "Don and I will gather the men. We'll form a search."

The mention of a search party was a bucket of ice water on Evelyn's bewilderment. Her thoughts jolted into sharp focus. In her bones, she knew Frankie must be with Maak. If the men took to the woods and found the boy with him, Maak would be hauled into the sheriff's office for questioning, likely sent back to prison. Or worse.

"My sister-in-law," Evelyn blurted. "Frank's sister, that is. He must be at her place down to Aurora."

Sheriff nodded, yes, good Evie. "Call her."

Evelyn's fingers shuffled through her address book. She picked up the handset on her phone, asked the operator to place a long-distance call to Garfield 6295.

The line rang three times before a woman answered.

"Hello, Doris? It's Evelyn."

The line was quiet. The women had rarely exchanged letters in the past ten years, much less spoken on the phone. Doris had made it no secret she didn't approve of Art as her brother's replacement.

"Doris?" Evelyn asked again.

"What do you want, Evelyn?"

"Sorry to bother you. I'm calling to see if perhaps Frankie is there with you. He's run away."

"Why on earth would he come here?" Doris asked.

It was Evelyn's turn to be quiet.

"At any rate, he's not here," Doris said. "I haven't seen him since Frank's funeral."

Evelyn looked to Art and the sheriff. Their eyebrows were raised. *Well?* Evelyn smiled, placed her hand to her heart.

"Oh, thank goodness," she said into the phone, while nodding to the men to confirm Frankie was with his aunt. "May I speak to him?"

"Have you lost your mind?" Doris snapped. "I told you the boy isn't here."

"Sleeping? No, don't wake him," Evelyn responded. "He must be exhausted."

Silence shouted from the other end of the phone line. Evelyn nodded slowly up and down, tilted her head, as though listening intently to details of Frankie's condition.

"Yes," Evelyn said in response to nothing. "Okay."

More silence. Then Doris finally spoke, her voice leaden and cold. "I don't know what kind of trouble you and your boy are in, Evelyn. But I'll thank you to leave me out of it."

Evelyn heard a click, and the line went silent for good.

"Thank you, Doris," she said. "I will. You're a dear. Good-bye."

Art rubbed Evelyn's shoulder as she placed the receiver back in the cradle.

"Okay then," the sheriff said. "You two get your coats. I'll drive you down there. We'll get your boy and have you all back home in time for dinner."

"No," Evelyn said.

"No?" the men asked in unison.

Evelyn's mind scrambled for an idea.

"No," she repeated, to buy time. She massaged her temples. Then continued, "Doris said they can keep him a few days, put him to work around the house, while we decide what we want to do.

Art nodded his approval of the idea. Yes. Put the boy to work.

"I don't want to let him off the hook too soon," Evelyn added for good measure. "Not after making me worry so. You always say I'm too soft with him, Art, and you're right."

Her husband pulled her into an embrace. She allowed herself to melt into it. How she craved that warmth, the comfort of human contact. Then she withdrew from him. *Too little, too late.*

She gulped down the remainder of her rum and coffee, allowed her plan to finish noodling through her mind. For a moment, she marveled at how easily the lies came to her now, how smoothly they rolled off her tongue.

Go to work tomorrow, she said to Art. There's no reason our livelihood should suffer because of Frankie's impertinence. Let the boy work and sweat for a couple days. Yes, Art agreed, let him sweat.

"We'll head out tomorrow evening to get him," she concluded.

Art hugged her again. An embrace of approval, of conquest.

* * * *

Monday morning Art sat in the car at the end of the street, the engine idling. He was nearly to work. A tall stack of paperwork awaited him. He glanced left, then right. The sun was still low on the horizon. The road was clear, yet his foot remained on the brake.

Evelyn hadn't slept a wink, he knew. She'd sat in a chair by the front window all night, looking out into the black. She'd been calm this morning, as she'd sent him off with a kiss on the cheek, a thermos of black coffee, and a sack lunch. Too calm. The whole thing just didn't sit well with him.

Art recalled the darkness that had descended upon her after Denny had died. It made him shudder. Would she get dressed? Would she remember to fix herself a meal? He worried about leaving her alone, for even just the day. He moved his foot to the gas pedal, turned the car in a U to head back toward home.

As he rounded the curve, a block or so from the house, he turned his head to the right and saw Evelyn sitting on the bus stop bench.

No, that couldn't be her.

He pulled to the side of the road and stopped. He stared at the woman on the bench dressed in a faded pair of blue jeans, boots, and plaid jacket. Evelyn wouldn't take the bus into town dressed like that. Art squinted to get a better look. The woman sat ramrod straight, her ankles crossed, hands neatly folded in her lap. There was no mistaking Evelyn's posture. A small suitcase rested on the ground at her feet.

"What on earth is she doing?" he muttered.

Confusion rapidly ceded to suspicion.

Is she going to Aurora to fetch Frankie without me?

She looks more like a child running away from home herself.

With a squeal and a hiss, the bus stopped at the bench, and the door swung open. Evelyn boarded, and the door swished closed behind her. When the bus pulled away, reflex caused Art to follow. He grew more baffled by the minute as the bus turned north onto the highway, away from Bitter Rapids, the opposite direction of Aurora. His grip on the steering wheel tightened. Anger took control of his mind.

What is she up to?

Maybe Frankie didn't really run away.

Maybe it was all part of a plan Evelyn concocted to humiliate me, to leave me.

The bus continued up the highway, ten minutes, twenty minutes. Art followed at a distance. He breathed noisily, flexed his grip on the wheel.

I never should have married a widow, a woman with ideas of what marriage should be already engraved in her mind. And so young, too. Impetuous. Disrespectful. She's as undisciplined as the boy.

1955

Bitter Rapids, Minnesota

The slender heels of Dottie's pumps sank into the soft, black dirt outside Evelyn's bedroom window. She shifted her weight to her toes, cupped her hands to block the sun's glare as she peeked through the glass. The closet door was ajar. Dresser drawers were open to varying degrees. The beds were unmade.

Dottie moved around the perimeter of the house, peering into the living room, the kitchen, any window she could reach where the curtains had not been drawn. She tried the doorbell one last time before getting back in her car and driving to the Sheriff's office.

"I've been calling the house for two days," she told Carrigan. "There's been no answer, no matter the time of day or night."

Carrigan ran his fingers back through his thinning hair.

"I'm sure everything is fine," he said. "Art and Evelyn were going down to her sister-in-law's place in Aurora on Monday night to get Frankie. They probably just stayed over."

Dottie shook her head. "That doesn't make any sense. Evie and Doris had a big falling out after she married Art. They haven't spoken since. I doubt Frankie even knows he *has* an aunt in Aurora."

Carrigan's eyebrows drew together, his eyes squinted. That piece of information was unexpected. Dottie could see it in his eyes. She pushed forward.

"Something is wrong, Don. I just know it. Evie and I rarely go a day without talking to each other," Dottie said. "Go see for yourself, and then tell me I'm being foolish if that's still what you think."

His chin dropped to his chest. "I never said you were being foolish, Dot."

Carrigan rose from his desk and plucked his hat and coat from the rack.

"Let's go have a look," he said.

At the house, Carrigan followed the path Dottie had earlier. He rang the bell and knocked on the front door. He walked the perimeter, peered in the windows. He stood on the screened porch, angled his head back, and scratched the stubble under his chin. Finally, he searched for the spare key, which he found under a flowerpot, unlocked the door, and stepped into the foyer. He told Dottie to wait outside.

"Evie? Art?" he called out. "Anybody home? Frankie?"

Dottie whisked through the open doorway and past Carrigan. He let out an overly-loud sigh to show his displeasure, which she discounted with a swish of her hand. The two made a quick sweep of the house and concluded it was, in fact, empty and in disarray.

"The place is a mess," Carrigan said. "I'll grant you that. But there's no sign of a struggle or robbery. The only things missing seem to be clothes, personal things from the bath."

They made their way into the kitchen and paused. The sour smell of unwashed dishes made their noses twitch. Dottie moved instinctively to whisk the butter dish from the table to inside the Frigidaire.

Carrigan noticed a piece of crumbled paper on the floor between the trash can and the cupboard. He stooped to pick it up, carefully smoothed it open and read.

Dear Arthur,

I'm grateful for all you've provided for me and my boys, but I think we both know our lives have changed and not for the better. I can no longer turn a blind eye to the tension between you and Frankie. My sister-in-law has a large home and said both he and I are welcome to live there. I have accepted her offer. Please do not try to contact me or ask me to change my mind. I have told no one else of my plans. You may tell people what you wish, so as not to tarnish your standing. I wish you the best.

Evelyn

The lawman contemplated the crumpled note. Had Evelyn lost her nerve and thrown it away? Or had Art come home to find it, crushed it in anger, and set off after her?

"Did you find a note?" Dottie asked. A ray of hope lit her expression.

"Uh, no," Carrigan said, crumpling the paper back into a ball. "I thought, maybe. But it's just, you know, a list for the market. Eggs, butter, whatnot."

Dottie's shoulders sank. Her face began to contort, and tears welled in her eyes. She shook her head in frustration. Carrigan stuffed the paper into his coat pocket and put a hand on her elbow.

"Don't you fret, Dottie," he said, guiding her toward the door. "There's no sign of mischief here. I'll make a few calls and see if I can't find something out. Why, I'll bet Evie and Doris patched things up on account of Frankie running away. Things like that have a way of bringing family together."

"Do you really think so?" she asked.

"Oh, you betcha," Carrigan said. "They're all having a nice visit and working things out. That's where my money's at."

February 1956

Bitter Rapids, Minnesota

Ed stood on the walkway in front of Art and Evie's place, watching snow fall on the empty yard, empty driveway, empty house.

The sheriff finally had to board up the doors and windows a few weeks before to keep teenagers out. The youngsters had taken to sneaking in at night to drink beer and tell ghost stories. If you were quiet, they'd say, you'd see the shadowy apparition of the boy who'd died in the river walking the empty rooms.

"Where the heck are ya, Art?" Ed muttered into the wind.

The falling snow turned to sleet, firing at an angle from the pewter sky. Ed adjusted his scarf tighter around his neck, cinched up his coat. He didn't walk away. He couldn't walk away. He thought about the last time he'd seen his friend. Art had met him at Wally's the night Frankie ran away and they'd learned the boy was in Aurora.

"Evie and I are heading down there tomorrow night to fetch him," Art had said. His speech was rushed. His index finger tapped the bar in machinegun fashion. Then, softer, more relaxed, "You and I'll have a beer when I get back."

That was nearly four months ago.

Art had been out of sorts for a while before that. Distracted. Suspicious of Evelyn's whereabouts. Quick to anger.

"I know she's up to something," he'd said one evening, sprawled out on his back, staring at the ceiling, after he and Ed had "had a beer" together. "I need to put an end to it."

"What does it matter?" Ed had asked and ran his thumb along Art's bare shoulder. "If it makes her happy, if she's discreet."

"It matters because she's my wife," Art had snapped. He pulled on his pants, snatched his shirt from the chair. "I have a business to run, a reputation to uphold. If she's so discreet, why are people talking?"

Ed had sat up then, watched Art tie the laces on his wingtips.

"People in this town talk about a lot of things," Ed had said, regretting the words even before they finished leaving his lips.

Art had turned to him with a cold stare. "Maybe it's time I put an end to that, too."

He hadn't meant it. Ed knew that much. And when he'd come to the bar that day to say goodbye, just like always, Ed's heart had swelled.

Then the family vanished.

Nearly four months ago.

And Ed's heart was gripped by a dull ache that wouldn't go away, still.

July 1956

Koochiching State Forest, Minnesota

S heriff Carrigan slapped the back of his neck as he followed Deputy Eriksen along the overgrown deer trail toward the river. He inspected the smear of blood and broken mosquito wings on his fingers before wiping them on his pants.

"It's just a bit farther," Eriksen shouted back over his shoulder. "Couple of teenagers stumbled on it over the weekend."

The men emerged from the brush and into a sandy clearing. Carrigan walked toward the crumpled ruins of a wigwam. He paused to kick at a half-circle of jagged rock, likely the remains of a fire pit. The muscles in his jaw bulged as he ground his teeth together.

"The body is over here, then," Eriksen said. He pointed as he walked, drawing Carrigan's eye to a scattering of bones and heap of muddy fabric. "I've got the coroner coming out, but I figured you'd want to take a look before he got here."

"Oh, fer sure," Carrigan confirmed. He removed a small notepad and pencil from his shirt pocket, jotted a few notes. Human remains. Likely adult, based on size of skull. Advanced decomposition. Probably buried beneath snow for some time, unearthed by carnivores during the spring melt.

"I already took a roll of photos," Eriksen said.

"You get some of the quilt here?" Carrigan asked.

"Oh yeah. Didn't disturb the scene, though. Just took shots as I found it. Got ones of the camp, too."

"Good," Carrigan nodded. "Let's get a closer look at the quilt. Help me spread it out."

The men carefully unfurled the blanket, revealing an assortment of smaller bones on top of the bright patchwork on the inside. Eriksen pointed to the missing corner, snapped a few more pictures. The pop of the flashbulbs sent a flutter of sparrows squawking from the nearby brush and high up into the trees.

Carrigan jotted more notes. *Corner of quilt cut away. No jewelry or signs of clothing.* He recognized the interlocking circles of blue and yellow – the wedding quilt Frank Parson's ma had sewn as a gift when her boy got married. Carrigan's pencil hovered over the notepad. He decided not to write that just yet.

"It's only speculation," he muttered.

"What's that, then?" Eriksen asked.

Carrigan shook his head. *Nothing.* He turned back toward the camp ruins. With the toe of his boot, he shifted a sheet of birch bark. A small bowl and pestle, crafted from skullcap and femur bone, shone white among the black dirt and debris. *Indian tools.* Carrigan tucked away his notes.

"I've seen enough," he said.

"What do you think?" Eriksen asked. "Some out-a-towner come up north to camp last fall? Got in over his head?"

"Yeah, probably so," Carrigan agreed. He stamped his heavy boots, as if to shake loose some mud, and crushed the weather-worn tools of bone to shards. "City folk don't understand how it gets up here. Wake up half-froze in September, under a cover of snow."

He didn't say the shelter looked like it had been well-built. He didn't say this was likely an Indian camp. He didn't say half the adults in town would know the owner of that quilt if they saw it.

"You stay here and wait for the coroner," he said. "Give me the film. I'll head back and write up the report, drop the film off at the lab."

As he marched back down the trail, Carrigan's mind marched back in time. Six months before, he'd boarded up Arthur

Specht's house. The family had vanished without a trace. The town had been abuzz with speculation – about Art's secret life, and what had become of the mysterious Indian-Negro, about where Frankie had run to, and what Evelyn might have done to cause their model family to unravel.

Only Carrigan knew of the crumpled letter Evelyn left. He had followed up at the time. Traveled down to talk to Doris and learned that Evelyn lied about Frankie ever being there. Called Evelyn's mother and assorted cousins. None had corresponded with her for many months or new anything of the rumors. Likewise, Art had missed meetings with clients, had never returned to home or office. Carrigan had fought off his worst fears. Hoped the family had gone off together, for a fresh start.

This new discovery – the human remains, the quilt, the Indian camp – sent his mind back down a sinister path. He knew Art was prone to handling problems with his fists. What if the man had finally gone too far? Carrigan wondered how far he himself might go, if he were to discover his wife run off with an Indian, a Colored. The thought made him shudder.

* * * *

Carrigan wrote "John Doe. Koochiching State Forest. July 1956" in black marker on the side of the box and taped the lid shut. The quilt was neatly folded and stowed inside, along with the sparse case notes, skeletal remains, two rolls of undeveloped film. He placed the box on the metal shelves in the evidence storage room and shut the door.

LIFE IN THE 1990s

"What Makes Us Human:
Exploring the Truth of False Memories"

Total Health Magazine, October 1990

By Hilde Radulovic, Ph.D.

Humans do not corner the market on memory or emotion. Dolphins can remember the distinct whistles of their friends after 20 years of separation. Ravens not only remember individual human faces, they also remember who treated them unfairly and will avoid those people in the future.

Yet, humans possess the unique ability to dream. We remember events from our past; we process those memories and emotions; and, we construct a vision for our future.

How does it work? The hippocampus stores short-term memories, organizes and prioritizes them, and later sends them to other parts of the brain for long-term storage. In the future, to remember, the hippocampus pulls those stored bits and pieces from the archives and reassembles them like a jigsaw puzzle.

Forgetting is just as important as remembering. It occurs not only because of cognitive decline, but also out of emotional necessity. Forgetting helps us manage painful events and trauma. It helps us see what's important, to enjoy life in the moment.

Each time we remember or share a story, the hippocampus reconstructs the memory using our collective experience. It takes details from a specific event, adds in knowledge gained after the event, and omits components that cause excessive pain. More often than not, that combination of puzzle pieces creates a whole new picture, a new memory which we use to craft our future.

Altogether, our memories – whether accurate or distorted, forgotten or false – are what make us human.

October 1990

Duluth, Minnesota

Hospital visiting hours are over. Frank and April sit on a cement bench outside. Neither wants to head to a hotel just yet. After so many days together in tight quarters, it feels strange leaving Gram all alone in an unfamiliar place. They need to stick together. Don't they?

This feels like the tipping point for all the ambiguity of the road trip. Both are feeling it. They're so close to Bitter Rapids, so close to putting all the silence and secrets to rest. Yet, this delay could just as easily set them back to where they began.

April decides she won't allow a backslide. "Gram told me that a few years after Denny died you ran away again."

"Did she?" Frank senses the muscles in his jaw tighten. Soon, his teeth begin to ache.

There have been times when Frank regretted throwing away the mouth guard his dentist insisted on years ago. Other times, he welcomed the self-inflicted throb of ground molars and cracked enamel. *Which is it now?* Frank wonders. *Regret or justice?*

"What else did she tell you?"

"Something like, 'Quit giving me the third degree and go ask your dad.'"

Frank rolls his eyes. "Sounds about right."

The fluorescent bulbs hum overhead. Moths flutter and dart around the beams of light. Their shadow dance creates a blue-gray kaleidoscope on the paved walkway. Is it possible all creatures carry secrets with them? Perhaps that's what draws them to the light.

Frank senses his daughter watching him. He turns his head, and their eyes meet. The copper and emerald flecks of her hazel eyes sparkle in the fluorescent glow. A flame of encouragement flickers from deep within her wide pupils.

"I was fifteen," he says, moving toward the light.

Frank closes his eyes. He draws in a lungful of oxygen, for strength, and releases it slowly. "I did run away again, but not far enough. What happened that last day at the river, it was all my fault."

Frank

I already told you about that summer I spent with Maak in the woods, fishing, cooking over an open fire, talking about life. That was the summer before my tenth grade, and going back to school, back to my old life, well, it was rough. I felt claustrophobic. The desks were too close. The halls were too narrow. I was surrounded by kids, and yet I never felt more alone. My classes bored me to tears. The teachers were completely oblivious to the things I was desperate to know and understand, important things, the things Maak taught me.

My grades were suffering.

Art was on my case all the time.

Then Art said I had to go away to boarding school.

I just couldn't stand any of it any longer.

One night, in October, I loaded up my backpack with everything I thought I'd need to survive in the wild. It was one of those big camping packs, with all sorts of pockets on the outside and a frame with leather straps to hold a bedroll and tent. I snuck out the window in the middle of the night, got Scout and his quilt — *the quilt* — from the garage. Then we headed off into the woods.

My plan was to stay with Maak for a little while and then head up north, cross the border into Canada. I figured I could get a job at one of the tourist spots up there. Maybe an old fishing lodge that had fallen into disrepair because the proprietors were a little old couple whose children had moved on and they had no one to help keep the place up. I'd perform odd jobs and repairs in exchange for room and board. They'd grow to love me like a son and leave me the place in their will when they died.

It sounds silly, I know. But I was fifteen. I had it all figured out. That's what I thought, anyway. I suppose that's what every fifteen-year-old kid thinks.

So, I hiked out to Maak's camp and told him my plan. He didn't say a word. He just nodded. I remember that so clearly. He was the only adult in my life who didn't tell me what to do, or tell me why I was wrong or naïve.

We fished all day. That night, at camp, we smoked tobacco from Maak's little stone pipe and slept on a bed of balsam fir under the stars with Scout lying across our feet.

That was the best moment of my life up to that point. I felt free and safe and in complete control of my own destiny for the first time. I never wanted that feeling to end. I thought maybe I could stay with Maak forever.

But the next morning, your Gram comes into camp. I was so shocked. Couldn't process how on earth she'd found me so fast. Of course, now I know she knew about my spending time with Maak all along. But there she was, so suddenly, saying I needed to come with her.

And then, just a few minutes later, Art came charging through the brush like a rabid animal. He was spitting mad.

It all happened so fast. I don't even remember what any of us said, honestly. Art was so angry, his face fire red. That, I remember. That, and his shotgun.

The next thing I know, Scout was flying at him, teeth flashing.

He knocked Art to the ground. They were thrashing all over. Art was screaming in pain.

I just stood there.

Scout would have obeyed me, if I had just called out for him to stop. I'm sure of it. But I didn't do anything, or say anything. I just stood there, watching.

Maak ran over, and all three of them got tangled up, rolling around on the riverbank. Next thing I know, they were *in* the water, tumbling downstream.

It was just like in the movies. Everything moving in slow motion.

Scout emerged from the foam first. He swam hard against the current, and for a split second, I swear to God I saw my brother in the water, too. Scout pulled himself from the river a little ways down, and shook the water from his coat. I ran to him, dropped to my knees and buried my face in his thick, wet fur.

I was so scared. I couldn't breathe. To this day, the smell of a wet dog knocks the wind right out of me.

Mom ran downstream.

I don't know how much time passed.

The next thing I remember was Mom stumbling back to camp, telling me to gather up wood and kindling to build a fire. Maak was behind her, carrying Art slung over his shoulder.

Thick, black clouds had moved in. It gets bitter cold and dark up there, in the snap of a finger. We needed to get dry and warm, Mom said, then we'd get Art to the car, and the hospital.

She removed Art's wet clothes and wrapped him in the quilt. I got the fire going. And then Mom was crying. Her hand was on Art's chest. All the color had drained from his face. He was dead.

My heart was beating so fast, pounding in my ears.

"No one can ever know," Mom said.

Her voice was faint, like she was a hundred miles away.

It started to snow.

She said it again. Louder. "No one can ever know."

Part of me couldn't believe what she was saying. It was crazy to even suggest it. Yet, I knew. She was right.

We knew what people would think, what they would say. Maak would've been blamed. He would've ended up back in prison. Or worse.

So, it was agreed. No one would ever know.

We hid the body in the bushes.

We gathered our belongings.

We hiked to the car and drove away.

We never looked back.

October 1990

Duluth, Minnesota

T he hotel walls are ablaze in the crimson light of the digital clock. Frank and April finally checked in at around ten o'clock, shut off the lights about eleven. It's five past midnight now.

Frank lies on his back, tries to focus on the pattern of the ceiling tiles. After what seems like an hour has passed, he glances at the clock again. Twelve-sixteen. His mind is racing through myriad thoughts, leaping from events in his childhood to his mother's current hospital stay, tumbling back to April's childhood and staggering forward to the day that damned article appeared in *USA Today*. The zigging and zagging of his thoughts makes his heart hammer, his lungs seize.

April lies in the second bed. Her back is turned to him, and her dark silhouette reminds Frank of Camelback Mountain back home in Phoenix. Solid, still, steadfast.

"You asleep?" His whisper is barely audible, even to himself.

"No," April says, at full volume, and it startles him.

Frank asks if she's having trouble sleeping because she's worried about Gram. She rolls onto her back, says no, and volleys the question back to him. No, it isn't that, he says.

It's, well, it's *everything*, they agree.

A few more minutes pass as they inspect the ceiling tiles.

"So, what did you guys do?" April asks. "You know, after?"

"After we left Art hidden at the river?"

"Yeah."

Frank concentrates on inhaling and exhaling. He marvels at how aware he has become of his breathing on this trip, how something that should come easily and naturally has become ridiculously hard.

"We took turns driving...."

Frank

Mom drove during the day. Maak drove at night. I drove in the early morning and at dusk. We drove and slept in shifts that way for days. I'd never even driven before, and neither had Maak. But it wasn't too hard to figure out, once you got used to the clutch. Plus, there wasn't much traffic back then.

We didn't really know where we were headed. West. That was all we knew.

Mom said she had some money, that she'd been scrimping at the market and socking a little away here and there. We also had whatever was in Art's wallet, and even found a few bills folded into the road map in the car's glove box. We hoped it would be enough to get by.

It was scary, traveling in our little group. Not because of what we were running from, though, not really. In those days, people didn't like seeing a fair-skinned, blonde woman and kid keeping company with a dark-skinned man. We hoped that the further west we got, the better things would get.

Somewhere not too far along the way, we stopped in an alley and Mom had us toss Art' s suitcase and all his work stuff into a dumpster. We stopped at a thrift store and got Maak some jeans and sneakers, put his deer-skin pants and moccasins into the trunk with his other things. Mom bought scissors at the drug store to cut his hair and a box of do-it-yourself hair dye to turn herself and me into brunettes. That helped, I think.

We still avoided people as much as we could. Drove west. Ate in the car. Peed in the bushes along the back roads. I think Maak knew we would be safer if we split up. One morning we woke up and he was gone. It was awful. I never felt so lost.

Mom and I kept heading west. What choice did we have?

We landed in Vegas. Mom got a job as a cocktail waitress at one of the casinos, and we lived in the hotel upstairs. After a few months, we packed up and drove to Phoenix. She never said why she chose Phoenix, but it ended up being a good fit, I guess.

I've always wondered what became of him.

I can sort of see him in my head, but I couldn't really describe to you what he looked like. All my memories of him have this sort of misty quality, surreal almost.

The only thing I know for sure is that Art died that day in Bitter Rapids. And Mom said we must never, ever talk about it, any of it. So, I didn't. Not with her, not with anybody.

It's a helluva way to live, with something like that, buried deep, and yet always threatening to come to the surface.

I probably should have talked to someone I could trust, like a therapist, or at least your mom. Especially your mom. But you just don't feel like you can trust anyone when you're living with something like that.

Maybe *that's* why your mom left. It's gotta be hard to live with someone when you know they don't fully trust you. Right? I mean, she must have known, intuitively, that I was never completely honest with her about my past. Heck, I don't know.

I told you that some people just aren't cut out to be parents. And I do believe that.

But, the more I think back on things, the more I wonder if maybe the reason your mom had such a hard time being a mom was because I wasn't exactly the greatest husband. I was always guarded. I never really opened up to her. I acted as though it was her problem, not mine.

My God, I was such a jerk.

Deb told me more than once that she felt like I was holding back. She worried it was because I didn't love her as deeply as she loved me. Or that she was falling short of what I wanted in a wife or a mother to my child. How could I tell her it was my fault? That I had such horrible, dark secrets? I was convinced she'd take you and leave me if she knew.

So, I brushed off her attempts at communication. I denied holding anything back, told her she was imagining things. I was on the defensive, always.

I never told her that I loved her with all my heart, that I was proud of how hard she worked at her career and at being a mom. I'd change the subject, or just walk away. A person can't keep getting shut down like that. It was only a matter of time before she shut down herself.

Your mom left because she couldn't deal with *me* anymore, not because she couldn't deal with being a mom. My God, April, I'm so sorry. I wish I'd figured all this out a long time ago.

I guess I'm glad Gram pushed all this on us, finally. I don't know if it's the right thing or not, but it's a relief to finally spill my guts. It really is. It's like I'm starting to breathe again for the first time in almost forty years.

October 1990

Duluth, Minnesota

"It was a long night," the doctor tells Frank and April when they arrive back at the hospital in the morning. April grabs hold of her dad's hand.

The doctor lifts the papers of Gram's medical chart one by one, carefully scanning the notes and vitals on each page. Then he tucks the chart under one arm and says, "Your mother gave the night nurse holy heck every time she came in to take check her vitals."

Frank squeezes his daughter's clammy hand, and they laugh.

"That means she's feeling better," April says.

The doctor confirms Gram's fever is down, and her blood-oxygen is up. He still wants to keep her at the hospital another day or two, for rest and observation. He's not as easygoing as he was the day before. He suggests they buy the night nurse some chocolates.

Frank apologizes for his mother's behavior. Then he and April head toward Gram's room.

"Well, Mom," Frank says, sandwiching her hand between his. "I've been informed yet again by a doctor that you are not exactly a model patient."

"He can bite me, along with all the others," Gram says. She jerks her hand away. "And that darned nurse, too, coming in here to poke and prod me every hour on the hour. Honestly. Was that really necessary?"

Frank lets the rhetorical question linger.

"You *were* in pretty bad shape when you got here," April points out. "You looked like hell."

"Well, I can't imagine I look any better now," Gram says, "after Nurse Ratched tortured me all night long."

April laughs. *There's the Gram I know and love.*

They make small talk. Gram complains that the doctor won't let her smoke, gave her some "stupid gum" instead. Then she moans about being half-starved, still waiting for someone to bring her breakfast. *Don't they feed patients in this dismal place?*

"I'll go talk to the nurses," Frank says. "If they don't have you on any diet restrictions, I'll go to the cafeteria and get you a pastry or something."

April opens the blinds and sunlight pours into the drab room. She pulls a chair next to the bed and plops down. She considers telling Gram that she's also exhausted and half-starved. Instead, she charges headlong into taboo conversation.

"Dad and I were talking last night," she begins. "He told me about what happened to Art."

Gram lowers her chin, rubs her thumb over the liver spots on the back of her hand. "He remembers?"

My God, how could he not?

"Some parts are fuzzy," she says. "But, yeah, he remembers."

Tears flood Gram's eyes, overflow down her cheeks.

"So now you know," she whispers. "You know it was me who killed him."

"What? No. No, Gram," April stammers. "Dad said it was an accident."

Gram shakes her head slowly from side to side. *No. Frankie was just a boy. Maybe he didn't see. Maybe he doesn't really remember.*

The tears continue to cascade down Gram's cheeks.

A knot forms in April's throat. Comforting words fail her, so she settles for offering Gram a tissue. The old woman dabs bloodshot eyes, breathes heavily, coughs.

"Did your dad tell you we stayed at camp after Maak pulled Art from the river?"

Yes, April nods.

"I knew Art had a head injury, because of what happened to Denny. You see? I knew the signs. I knew it was bad and that we needed to get him to the hospital right away."

The old woman dabs at her eyes again, pulls down the oxygen tube, blows her nose. April hands her a dry tissue, strokes her hair. Gram repositions the tubing in her nostrils, breathes in deeply. She stares straight ahead and resumes speaking. Each sentence unfolds smoothly, one after the other. Rehearsed precision.

"Art and I had been arguing a lot. He suspected there was something going on between me and Maak, just like everyone else in that blasted town. I should have known he would follow me if I went to the woods. I should have been more careful. I knew people would blame Maak for everything. But it wasn't Maak's fault. He was a hero. He'd saved all of us in one way or another."

Gram turns her head. Her eyes lock on April's.

"So, I told Frankie to build a fire, and I waited. Instead of getting Art to the hospital, I just waited for him to die. I killed him just as surely as if I'd bashed his head with a rock myself."

The hair on the back of April's neck prickles. The hospital room shrinks. She glances over her shoulder at the open door, imagines the nurse poised just outside, eavesdropping on Gram's confession. A tightness in her lungs won't allow her to stand and close the door, prevents her from telling Gram to speak softly.

"It was me," Gram continues. "Everything that happened before, and everything that's happened since. It's no wonder your dad blames me for his screwed-up life."

"No." April seizes the old woman's hand as her voice returns. "Dad doesn't blame you for anything, Gram. He blames himself, for running away, for not calling off Scout."

Frank's muffled voice comes to them from somewhere down the hall. He's delivering pastries to the nurses' station.

"You guys *have* to talk about this," April says. "You have to tell him what you just told me."

Gram waves off her granddaughter's entreaty.

"Not until we get to Bitter Rapids. I have it all planned out. Of course, I didn't exactly plan to be here," Gram says. She pauses, glances around the hospital room, and adds, "Maybe I need a backup plan. After breakfast, would you go back to the hotel and get me my box?"

LIFE IN THE 1950S

Ádahooníłigíí (Current Events)

Navajo Language Monthly, Editorial Page

"Fight to Restore Our History"

By Suzie Yazzie

When I was born, my mother buried my birth cord in the sheep corral so the animals would think well of me, and so my heart would always return home to the herd. When I was small, my aunt carried me on her back after the sheep. Later we walked with them, hand in hand. During lambing in the snow and cold and fog, we stayed with them and built fires to keep the newborns warm. We knew each animal, each personality, which ones were quiet, or cranky, or likely to wander. They were our family.

It was our way of life, from the beginning of time. And then it was taken from us.

U.S. President Franklin D. Roosevelt created the Indian New Deal in 1934 to solve the problems of the Great Depression and Dust Bowl. The intent, the Bureau of Indian Affairs said, was to terminate federal control over tribes and allow us to create our own governments.

But they were more concerned about drought, grass, and soil erosion than tribal self-governance. Their scientists said Navajo herds caused the problem. They ordered a reduction of our animals. Goats were the first to be selected, gathered, and slaughtered. More than 145,000. Next, 50,000 sheep were killed. Cattle and wild mustangs were massacred.

The white man gave our families "allotments," pieces of land they said would support one cow, one horse or five goats. But how many people would that support? There was not enough milk, meat, or wool to sustain us. And what of the emotional connection to our herds? Just imagine taking the animals away from the children that tended them, and slitting their throats before the very eyes of those children? Many of our people died before their time because of the great sadness this caused.

We suffered a great loss, the most devastating since our Long Walk to Fort Sumner. By 1950, the same scientists determined the livestock reduction did not fix the soil erosion problem. Yet, it *did* erode Navajo life. The children no longer understand our history.

We must fight for our land, our history, our way of life. We must not let it die with our elders.

1955

Tse 'Bii 'Ndzisgaii (Valley of the Rocks)
Navajo Reservation

*D*riving the Buick bestowed Maak with unexpected gifts. Control. Speed. Freedom. Everywhere he'd traveled in his life had been either on foot, or in a back seat to a destination not of his choosing. Behind the wheel, he could put greater distance between himself and those who wanted to confine him. Behind the wheel, he could view more of the Great Creation.

Sometime past midnight, Maak cruised the black roadway that lay across the wide, flat expanse of southern Utah. It was a ribbon of a road, pulling Maak through a mystical place.

Frankie and Scout slumbered in the back seat, their lungs expanding and contracting in unison. Evelyn slept up front. Her temple rested against the passenger window, breath fogging the glass. She had slipped off her shoes and tucked her knees up sideways on the bench seat. The soles of her slender feet pressed against Maak's thigh. Her warmth radiated through his body.

The night sky was clear and sharp, flush with stars. The low moon accented the landscape, elegant formations of layered sandstone eons old. In one shape, Maak saw a rabbit, sitting tall on its haunches, ears alert. Another was a giant bear dipping its head to drink. Three silhouetted columns of rock stood off to the side, close together, like sisters. They were *omaamaayan* and *onoshenya,* his mother and aunts, watching over him.

In the distance, miles of buttes and mesas surrounded the remote paradise like fortress walls. Maak's eyes roamed the tranquil vastness and thought, *nothing bad could happen here.*

A flash of light in the black overhead caught his eye. High above the pinnacles of rock, a meteor left a silver trail as it shot across the sky and vanished. Another followed, and another.

Maak steered the car onto the sandy shoulder and turned off the engine.

The absence of movement jolted Evelyn awake. She moved her feet to the floor, rubbed the sleep from her eyes.

"What is it, Maak?" she whispered.

He angled his chin to the windshield, to the light show beyond.

"Oh!" Evelyn took in a quick breath, huffed it out with wonder. She slipped on her shoes, clicked open her door.

The air outside the car was cold and fresh, hollow with the stillness of the low desert. It flooded the car and shook Frankie from his deep sleep. Within minutes, man, woman, boy, and dog stood beside the car, heads tilted to the heavens. Silhouetted columns layered of blood, flesh, and bone, soft spires of consciousness melding with the hard landscape.

Frankie clambered onto the Buick hood, leaned back against the windshield to watch.

A chill ran along Evelyn's arms, beneath the flannel lining of her coat sleeves. She ducked into the car to retrieve a blanket. Maak helped Evelyn climb onto the hood next to Frankie, then stretched out beside her. Beneath the blanket, warmed by the engine below, they watched the meteor shower as one.

"Make a wish, Frankie," Evelyn whispered.

"I'm gonna make a hundred wishes," he said. "One for each shooting star."

Evelyn leaned her head against his.

"What does it mean," Maak asked, "to make a wish?"

A wish is a hope, Evelyn said.

Or a dream, Frankie added.

"When you see a shooting star, you close your eyes and make a wish for something you want," the boy continued. "But you can't say it out loud, or else it won't come true."

"I was taught stars that move through the sky are spirit stars," Maak said. "They are on an important journey."

"Like us," Frankie replied.

"Yes," Maak said.

Like us, Evelyn thought. She reached for Maak's hand beneath the blanket.

And then, as if by an unspoken command from the stars, they were silent.

They kept their faces to the night sky and watched, and wished, and drifted off to dream.

On the ground beside the car, Scout kept vigil over his pack.

* * * *

The sun broke on the horizon, flooding the expanse of red, sandy plains and scrub brush with golden light. The travelers opened their eyes to the soft blue sky. A red-tailed hawk glided on the current high above them. The dawn was draped in frost.

They slid off their cold steel mattress, planted their feet on the hardpacked ground. Stiffness seized the muscles in their necks and backs. Dull aches bound the joints in their hips and shoulders. Breath puffed from their mouths in misty, bulbous clouds as they walked off in different directions. They walked to loosen their rigid bodies and to relieve themselves in private.

Evelyn squatted behind a clump of brittlebush the size of her oven back home. The mass of fuzzy gray-green leaves at its base provided plenty of cover. Its umbrella of tiny yellow flowers smiled down at her from their long, naked stems. A car's length away, a leopard-spotted lizard sprawled on a low, flat slab of granite. Its tail was missing, only a fat stump of it hung over the edge. The creature blinked lazily, watching Evelyn with almond-shaped obsidian eyes while it warmed in the morning sun.

Only days before, she had peed outdoors for the very first time.

The act had set Evelyn off balance, literally and figuratively. Her stomach had tumbled with fear of being seen, or heard, as the stream of pungent urine soaked the dirt and splattered her shoes. Her face had burned with embarrassment.

And now?

Crouching behind a bush, feeling the open air on her exposed bottom, knowing the correct position and angle to protect her shoes – it felt more natural and right than anything she'd done in her careful, calculated life.

Back at the car, Frankie assembled their breakfast, peanut butter and jelly on white bread. Maak had a road map spread open on the hood.

"We are not far from Arizona," Maak said. Evelyn positioned herself at an appropriate distance beside him. She studied the map. Maak placed his finger on their approximate location.

"We're on the Navajo Indian reservation," she observed.

Maak nodded, yes.

"The state route ends at the border," he continued and traced a blue line with his finger, south through Monument Valley to the small Navajo town of Kayenta. "This road is not paved."

Evelyn considered this new information. Dirt roads would likely double the travel time. Even more if they weren't graded. In her mind, the journey was a high-stakes game of chess. She strategized three steps ahead, always.

"We'll fill up the car and the gas cans there," she said. "Check the tires and refill the canteens before heading to Kayenta."

Evelyn pointed to the map. Her hand touched Maak's as she did, and she let the connection linger a moment. Maak closed his eyes to shut out all other sensation. He etched the all-too-brief feel of her flesh in his memory.

* * * *

The Buick rolled into town late afternoon, cloaked in a camouflage of red dust and bug splatters. Evelyn parked in a rough-paved lot outside the Kayenta Lodge and Café. A couple of equally-dusty pickup trucks were the only other vehicles there.

"Pretty quiet here," Evelyn said, glancing through the rearview mirror to the back seat. Maak remained low, as he did whenever they drove through populated areas in broad daylight. Their eyes met in the reflection.

A petite, ancient woman wearing a substantial necklace of silver and turquoise sat in a folding chair under the lodge awning. Beside her, a card table was neatly stacked with woven blankets for sale. Her white hair was parted in the middle and drawn into a thick braid that hung down the full length of her back. She waved at the dusty travelers still sitting in their car. Deep creases accentuated her dark eyes and gummy smile.

"I'll take Scout out," Frankie spoke up.

It had quickly become their litmus test on the road. If Scout was at ease, they would stay. If his posture was stiff and alert, they would move on.

Frankie got out and called Scout to follow. The dog bounded into the parking lot, shook the confinement of the car from his body. The old woman patted her leg. Scout went to her, placed his giant head on her small lap.

"Good morning, ma'am," Frankie said. "I wonder if there might be a spigot around back, somewhere we could wash up?"

"Restrooms inside," the woman said. She gazed into Scout's amber eyes, smoothed his face with her weathered hands. "*Łééchąą'í* can stay with me."

Maak sat up straight, drawn to the light by her soft voice and dulcet diction. He didn't know the Diné word for dog, but his heart leapt to hear the woman speak her native language in the presence of a white person with no hesitation or fear.

They all looked to the café. Its ornate wooden door was propped open by a hunk of granite that glittered in the sunlight.

A paper sign tucked in the window read, WELCOME!, not WHITES ONLY.

Evelyn and Maak emerged from the car cautiously, even so, ever wary of the risks posed by traveling together. A middle-aged Navajo man exited the café. He tipped his wide-brimmed hat to them as he passed. Still, Evelyn could not quite reconcile the signals. Could it really be that, in this tiny, isolated town in Navajoland, the different colors of their skin were not noticed or spurned?

Scout sprawled out at the old woman's feet.

Inside the café, the trio washed their hands and faces in the restrooms, then sat at a table. Together. A young woman brought bowls of mutton stew with corn and potatoes, plates of fry bread, glasses of iced tea. A feast.

After, they visited with the old woman, Chooli, and bought a blanket woven of brightly-dyed wool – teal, magenta, yellow, and black. The wool had come from Chooli's sheep, raised on Chooli's land, handed down from her mother, and her mother's mother, she said. The woman swept her hand toward the distant mesas of layered siltstone, uranium, and shale, the windswept plains of sand, sage, and creosote.

"Soon it will belong to my daughter," the woman continued. "And one day, my daughter's daughter."

Evelyn felt a stab deep in her gut. A pang of disbelief, perhaps. Or envy. She wondered how it must feel, as a woman, to own something of value, something as vital as sheep and land. She bought a second blanket despite their limited funds.

* * * *

Leaving Kayenta was difficult.

It was a dream. Beautiful. Welcoming. Safe.

Yet, for Evelyn, those very qualities also made it feel like a hoax. Perhaps she was never meant to feel safe.

They piled back into the Buick and headed south in the waning sunlight. They had the road to themselves. Maak drove, mesmerized by the cinnamon landscape awash with brilliant gold light. About ten miles out, he spotted a sandy clearing bordered by a small stand of juniper. Still hesitant to venture too far from this mystical place, they all agreed to make camp for the night.

Blankets and belongings were rearranged, so Evelyn and Frankie would have room to sleep in the car. Maak would sleep out under the stars, where he was most comfortable. The sound of bleating sheep carried faintly on the night breeze.

"This is where I would like to stay," he said. "Tonight, and for all nights."

Evelyn shook the idea away with a twitch of her chin.

"It's lovely here," she said. "But it's so remote."

"You and the boy should continue on," Maak insisted. "This is where paths must part."

"No!" Frankie argued. "I want to be with you, Maak."

They stood facing one another, the three unlikely companions. Maak placed his hand firmly on Frankie's shoulder.

"Your mother needs you," he said. "It will be safer for us all, if we separate."

"No," the boy repeated, a whimper this time.

Evelyn nodded silently. Like her son, she wanted to argue, to shout. But she could not. Maak was right. She reached out and took his hand in hers.

"Now is not a time for sadness," Maak said. "We must rest. I will leave in the morning."

"Come, Frankie," Evelyn finally spoke. "Let's get some sleep."

She put her arm around the boy, opened the car door and guided him into the back seat. She squeezed her eyes shut to expel the tears that had pooled in her lashes. Before turning toward Maak, she quickly swept the tears away with her fingertips.

"Good night," she whispered.

Maak closed his eyes, nodded, in his steadfast way. Evelyn climbed into the car and closed the door behind her.

He slept on the bear pelt beneath the Navajo blanket, beneath the same stars of his youth. Early in the morning, he awoke to the raucous howling of coyotes in the distance, different than the call of his Wolf Brothers. It sounded like laughter. And that made him laugh.

Maak rose and rolled his bedding, stowed away his belongings. He peeled the foil band and cellophane from a fresh pack of Lucky Strikes – Evelyn's brand – and tapped out two cigarettes. Maak plucked off the filters, shook the tobacco loose into his hand. He walked the perimeter of the Buick, sprinkled a blessing.

The car windows were fogged when the sun finally broke. Frankie jolted awake in the hazy wash of light.

"Mom!"

His voice cracked, and she bolted upright. The night had gone so quickly. Neither was ready for the reality of morning. They hurried from the car, surveying the frost-covered landscape. Maak was already gone.

Frankie shouted into the emptiness, ran to the road, fell to his knees, and sobbed.

On the hood of the Buick lay a pack of Lucky Strikes.

Evelyn snatched it up and pressed it to her heart.

1955

Bitter Rapids, Minnesota

There was a pause in the rain, so Dottie slipped on her galoshes and made a run for the mailbox. She pulled down the flap and waited a moment to let the water drip from the opening before retrieving the stack.

The air had been washed clean and felt fresh in her lungs. The sun peeked through a sliver in the dark clouds, casting a heavenly ray onto the neighborhood. It did little to lift her spirits. Four weeks. That's how long it had been since the Specht family had vanished. Rumors continued to swirl, though it felt little was being done to find them.

Dottie had called every friend and relative in the address book she'd found at Evie's house, to no avail. Ed Miller took to running the sign shop. Sheriff Carrigan kept an eye on the empty house. In every other way, life in the small town had rumbled on as usual.

She took her time, standing out by the street, to sort through the day's post. A bill from the gas company. Another from the department of water and sanitation. The hefty *Sear's Christmas Book* catalog. The kids would be thrilled to see that.

The final item in the stack made her stomach seize.

A hand-addressed envelope with a Nevada postmark. No return address. Dottie had no relations in Nevada, but she recognized the penmanship as sure as she recognized the sun that rose every morning. It was Evie's flawless cursive, right down to the perfectly parallel slant of the ts in Dottie.

She tore open the envelope with shaking hands, unfolded the pink stationery adorned with cheerful daisies in the corners.

October 24, 1955

Dear Dottie,

We two have known each other since we were knee-high to a mosquito, and I suspect my absence has made you worry to no end. Please forgive me, dear Dot. You can put your mind at ease. Frankie and I are well.

You know I've been socking away some of my household allowance for emergencies. Well, it seemed to me that Art threatening to send Frankie to military school and Frankie running off was nothing if not an emergency. I found my boy, and we took a Greyhound bus out west. There's a place in Las Vegas, I've learned, where you can get a divorce without your husband present. You can even get a whole new name, for a certain price. We shall see how much my savings can purchase.

Please don't tell anyone you've heard from me. Especially not Art. He'd come after me, I'm sure of it, and I don't want to spend the rest of my days looking over my shoulder.

I'll miss you terribly, my dear friend. I wish you a happy life.

Love,

Evie

LIFE IN THE 1990s

"Natural Regeneration and the
Study of Regenerative Medicine"

JOURNAL OF GENERAL MEDICINE AND SCIENCES; 1990

All living organisms must regenerate as part of natural processes to maintain tissues and organs.

Some animals have extensive regenerative abilities. The tiny freshwater animal called Hydra can form two whole bodies after being cut in half. The Mexican salamander can regenerate limbs, organs, and other body parts. More complex animals, such as mammals, have limited regenerative capacities. These include knitting together fractured bones and forming thick scars in tissues to promote the healing of injured body parts.

The history of "regenerative medicine" extends to the days before modern pharmaceuticals and scientific processes. The ancient civilizations of Egypt, China, India, and South America all pioneered medical discoveries that still impact the field today. In the centuries since, generations of doctors and scientists have taken up the challenge of restoring damaged tissues.

While extraordinary progress has been made, the full potential of human regenerative powers is still not fully understood.

1990

Duluth, Minnesota

April schleps the now-familiar maze of hospital hallways to the cafeteria, while her mind navigates the labyrinth of conflicting details from Dad and Gram about that fateful day at the river. It's like walking through a carnival house of mirrors. She feels disoriented, misled at every turn. Whose memory is more reliable? What details are distorted by the passage of time? Was Art's death an accident or not?

Rounding the corner of the hospital gift shop, she sees her reflection in the window, moving like a ghost past the flower vases and teddy bears that fill the shelves and cubicles. She pauses, places her hand on the glass. Perhaps the truth of what happened all those years ago still hovers in the mist of the river, lingers in the cracks and crevices of their minds.

Their conflicting accounts do share things in common, April admits. Both made mistakes, and both blame themselves. They each made sacrifices, and they each doubted their ability to protect the people they love. Each loved the other, fiercely, without pause.

Flashes of April's mother tumble through her mind with these fresh thoughts – mistakes, blame, sacrifice, self-doubt. Love.

She postpones the purchase of the coffees and Snickers bars that are the purpose of her trek, slips into a padded chair at a bay of pay phones in the hall. *Maybe forgetting is just as important as remembering,* she thinks. *It helps you see what's important.*

April peels back the paper on a roll of quarters she got at the gas station the day before; she inserts twelve coins into the payphone slot.

Her finger circles the rotary dial. Around and back, around and back, through each of the eleven digits, she holds her breath. The phone on the other end of the line rings. April holds the handset with both hands, hunches her body close to the breadbox-sized wall phone.

"Hello?" a woman answers.

"Hi, Mom."

"April?"

"Yes, it's April," the young woman says. "Do you have other people who call you mom?"

"No," the woman responds. "It's just, well, you usually call me Deborah."

The line is quiet, and April regrets her immediate slip back to snide teenager.

"April, what is it?" her mom recovers quickly. "Are you okay? Has something happened?"

"Everything's okay. I just wanted to say hi."

Dead air, again.

"It's good to hear your voice," Deborah says.

"Yeah. It's good to hear yours, too."

April can't find her words. She covers the mouthpiece of the phone and exhales. Her eyes scan the cafeteria. An old man sits at a table in the corner, staring into a foam coffee cup. He's alone. Two young women sit by the window, sisters perhaps, eating white-bread sandwiches and pale macaroni salad. They avoid making eye contact with one another, do not speak. They're alone, too.

"So, um, is Evelyn still in the hospital?" Deborah asks, partly to make sure her daughter is still on the other end.

"Yeah," April says. "I guess Dad called you, huh?"

"He did."

A beep sounds in their ears, and the operator enters the line. The woman instructs the caller to insert more coins to continue the call. April fumbles with the quarter roll and plunks in three more dollars. She needs to say what she called to say before she goes broke.

"So," April says, "I've been doing a lot of thinking on this trip."

"Oh?" Deborah leads her.

"About people, you know, and relationships," April says. She pauses to breathe again. *Why is it I have to remind myself to breathe?* she thinks, then presses forward. "About how sometimes people hurt the people they love and let them down, even when they don't mean to. Especially when they don't mean to."

Another pause.

"Uh-huh," Deborah says.

"I guess what I'm trying to say is, I'm starting to figure things out."

April pauses again. Then, her words breach the dam. "Look, I get how hard it is to live your life and choose happiness and, somehow, still be there for the people you love. Everybody makes mistakes. Everybody doubts their decisions. Nobody really knows what the hell they're doing. The only thing that matters is that we keep trying, keep doing the best we can."

A tear rolls down April's cheek. She sweeps it away with her fingertips.

"I understand now that you did the best you could for me, that you wanted to be a good mom. You made mistakes. But being a parent is hard and, well, I know there have been times when I made it even harder."

"No," Deborah interrupts. "Oh honey, you've never done anything wrong. Nothing to deserve..."

"Mom, wait. Please. Just let me finish. Okay?"

"Okay."

The operator interrupts again.

"Dammit," April says and fires more coins into the slot.

"I've been hurt and angry for a long time, Mom. I don't want to feel that way anymore. I'm letting go of it. You're a good person, and I know you love me, that you've always loved me the best way you know how. I know you never wanted to hurt me. And I forgive you for leaving. I really do. And I hope you can forgive me, for taking so long to finally get it.”

April’s breath comes naturally again. She feels lighter, somehow, unconstrained.

“I love you, Mom.”

The silence on the other end roars in April’s ear.

“Mom? You still there?”

Deborah releases a short burst of air.

“Yes,” she says. She clears her throat. “I’m here.”

April can hear the woman’s muffled sobs now. Her own eyes burn. She squeezes them shut. Tears flows down her face, drip from her chin. “I didn’t mean to make you cry, Mom.”

“No, honey. These are good tears.” Her mom’s words surge between stuttering breaths. “I love you, too. So much.”

Mother and daughter weep together a moment more. Then, the blasted operator chimes in again.

“Mom, I’m almost out of change. I’ll call you again when we get back to Phoenix. Okay?”

“Okay,” Deborah says. “I’d like that.”

They say goodbye, and April places the handset back on the receiver. Her hand continues to grip it for a moment. Her knuckles turn white. Then she buries her face in both hands and sobs. Good tears.

* * * *

April balances a cardboard tray with two large coffees in one hand and a box of donuts in the other. She thumps the outside of the motel door with her foot.

“It’s me, Dad. I’ve got breakfast.”

They settle at the small table and chairs to eat. April notices the beds are both made. It makes her smile. *Even at a hotel, Dad always makes the bed in the morning.* He’d taught her to do the same. That way, no matter how your day ends up, you will have begun with one accomplishment, one job well done.

They dive into the donuts. She pops the plastic lid off her coffee, sips the hot milky brew.

"Your Gram and I talked yesterday," Frank says, "while you were at the cafeteria."

April pauses mid-sip. She swallows. "About the river?"

Frank looks up at the ceiling, wobbles his head, expels a gust of air.

"No. I don't think either of us is ready for that just yet," he says.

He takes a bite of an apple fritter. Chews a few times.

"We talked about after we get back home," he says and then swallows. "She said the gum the doctor gave her isn't *that* bad, and maybe she'll stick with it, give up the cigarettes for good."

"No kidding?" April sucks powdered sugar from her fingertips.

"No kidding," Frank says.

They ponder it for a while. April tries to remember if she has ever spent time with Gram without the reek of Lucky Strikes clinging to the woman's hair and clothing. She did at the hospital, the past few days. Beyond that, no.

"Helluva trip," Frank mumbles through another mouthful of apple fritter. His gaze is unfocused, aimed at the hotel window.

"For sure," April says, though she suspects he isn't seeking agreement. Maybe he isn't even addressing her, but the window. Maybe he isn't even speaking of the road trip, but of life.

"Do you regret it?" she asks.

"The trip?" Frank asks.

Yes, she nods. *Or life, the choices you've made.*

"Yeah, maybe a little," he says. And then, "No. Heck, I don't know."

She smiles at him.

"What about you?" Frank asks. "How are you holding up?"

April pouts her bottom lip, tilts her head with a little shake, a shrug of her shoulder. Her mind races through the events of their road trip, the arguments and the revelations, the fears and the freedom.

"Remember that time we had those guys come to the house and shampoo the carpet?" she asks. "What was it, five, six years ago?"

Frank tilts his head, blinks at her.

"Um, yes," he says slowly. "That was random."

"No," she says, "I'm going somewhere with this. Stay with me. What do you remember about it?"

Frank stares at the donuts for a moment. He plucks a second fritter from the box.

"I remember it took all day and was a royal pain in the behind," he says. "And they moved the couches and credenza and revealed years' worth of dust bunnies and crumbs. Man, I was so embarrassed. Perfect strangers seeing all that. I was kicking myself for not just doing it myself."

"*You* were embarrassed?" April squeals. "What about my wadded-up pair of underpants under the couch? I could have died!"

"I don't remember that!" Frank's head falls back in laughter.

"That's probably because you were rushing off to get the vacuum cleaner, and I was diving onto the floor to snatch them up before anybody saw. It. Was. Horrifying," she says, laughing, too. "But then, while I was down there in the dust and popcorn kernels and God-knows-what-else, I also found my necklace with the snowflake charm I thought I'd lost."

They found other things under the furniture that day, too, she reminds him – an orphaned jigsaw-puzzle piece, a petrified apple core, about five bucks in loose change. After the floor was dry and the furniture was back where it belonged, the house smelled so fresh. The carpet was bright and soft, like new again. They sprawled on the floor to eat pizza and complete the long-neglected jigsaw puzzle, saving the newfound piece for last.

"That was a good night," Frank says.

"Yeah, it was," April agrees. "And that's kind of how I feel right now, after everything on this trip. I mean, we definitely uncovered a lot of stuff and some of it was hard to look at. But some of it was pretty great, too. Either way, it was long overdue. You know?"

Frank wipes his mouth with a paper napkin, fixes his eyes on his daughter.

"How did you get so smart?" he asks.

"It's in my genes," she answers.

His eyes gleam, and he winks at her.

The ring of the hotel-room telephone shatters the moment. The fritter sits like a brick in the pit of Frank's stomach as he reaches to answer. There's only one person who'd have any reason to call them this early in the morning. It's the nurse.

LIFE THROUGH THE AGES

The Gulag Archipelago

By Aleksandr Solzhenitsyn

Harper & Row, 1973

... the line separating good and evil passes not through states, nor between classes, nor between political parties either—but right through every human heart—and through all human hearts. This line shifts. Inside us, it oscillates with the years. And even within hearts overwhelmed by evil, one small bridgehead of good is retained. And even in the best of all hearts, there remains... an unuprooted small corner of evil.

1955

Koochiching State Forest, Minnesota

A crisp fall wind swept through camp, carrying the smell of wood smoke and grilled fish into the thick underbrush and towering stands of aspen, pine, and spruce. Frankie crouched beside the fire, keeping an eye on the meal. Not far off, Maak sat in the dirt, carving a buckhorn. Scout lay between them, chin set on the ground, eyes trained on his boy.

Chopped, wild ramps sizzled in the cast-iron fry pan. The rich aroma of charred onions wafted into the air.

A deer mouse skittered into the clearing, made brave by the pungent smells. It paused and rose on its hind legs, pink nose and long whiskers twitching. Then it dropped to all four paws and darted back into the nearby brambles.

Scout lifted his head, looked away toward the forest, ears on alert. He stood.

"What is it, boy?" Frankie asked.

The dog trotted in the direction his ears and nose instructed, vanished into the underbrush. A moment later, he emerged, mouth gaping in a relaxed grin, a skip to his gait. Evelyn came into view behind him, pushing through the scrub with a leather case. Scout spun in a circle, pranced about the woman, and spun again before trotting back to his place beside the fire.

"How'd you find me?" Frankie huffed. His frustrated breath escaped in white puffs of mist on the brisk air.

Evelyn offered a patronizing smile, the kind that says, *a mother knows.* She set down her luggage and stuffed her frozen hands deep into her coat pockets.

They were mute for a moment, their minds wrestling with silent deliberations. Should introductions be made? Should past meetings be divulged? Maak rose to his feet. Only Scout was at ease, content to lie back down beside the fire now that all the members of his pack were finally in one place.

"You need to come with me, sweetheart." Evelyn was the first to abandon the rules of etiquette, to get right into the meat of the matter.

Frankie shook his head no, tended to the fish in the pan.

"The boy is safe," Maak said.

Evelyn held out her palm to him. *Quiet.* Safety wasn't the issue. A fifteen-year-old boy belonged with his mother. After all she'd lost, she was owed that, at least.

"I know things between you and Art are," Evelyn paused, "not good. But you have some more growing up to do before you're ready to be on your own."

"I know what I'm doing," Frankie shot back. He held his chin high, pulled his shoulders back. "I can take care of myself."

Evelyn nodded. She let her silence buzz around him, sting him here and there, until he wore down and took another swat at her.

"I'm going to hike north, get a job in Canada," he said.

Amusement and pride tangoed inside of her, though her expression remained hard. Frankie was still her idealistic, hopeful child, despite it all. She envied that. Or, did she resent it? A mixture, perhaps.

"I know what I'm doing, too, you know," she responded, and then pursed her lips. *You sound like a child yourself, Evelyn,* she silently scolded herself.

"I've been socking away money from my allowance every month, built up quite a nice little sum." She began again and motioned to the luggage. "I've got my things. I'm not saying we have to go home. I'm only asking you to come with me. We'll take a bus somewhere, anywhere you want, get a fresh start."

Frankie's posture softened. This new piece of information found a gap in his armor.

"What about Scout?" he asked.

Evelyn hesitated.

Scout sprang to his feet, ears erect, facing Evelyn. She wavered for a half-second before realizing his intent eyes were looking past her, to the clearing's edge. A rustle made them all turn, just as Art charged from the brush.

"What about Scout?" Art said, striding toward the group, a downturned shotgun at his side. "That hellhound is going to the pound, that's what."

Frankie's hands tightened into fists. Evelyn's breath caught in her throat.

"And what about the rest of you?" Art asked unhurriedly. The question drifted toward them on the breeze, sharp, with the tang of fish and onion.

"I can explain," Evelyn offered.

It was said to buy a little time – a moment to think. There was no good way to explain.

"Be quiet, Evelyn," Art halted his approach. "Not a word. You hear me?"

He began to pace from where he stood, twenty, perhaps thirty feet from the fire and the others.

"It's my fault, I suppose," he said, more to himself than anyone else. "All this nonsense has to stop."

Art ceased pacing, rested the shotgun across his stomach. The stock rested in his right elbow. The barrel was held tight in his left fist. Then he spoke, his voice steady, his tone resolute.

"You agreed to be my wife, Evelyn. Heck, you're the one who suggested it. You're a good woman, and it's high time you came to your senses and honored that commitment." Art paused, turned his gaze toward Frankie and Maak. "The boy is going to Riverside Academy, so he can finally learn some discipline. It's for his own good. And that damned Colored, or Indian, or whatever he is will go back to prison, where he belongs."

"No," Frankie whispered, a single word steeped in dread. His legs were suddenly shaky and weak, like he'd been treading water for too long. He felt himself sinking.

Scout crept to the front of his pack, head held low. A rumble welled from deep within his chest.

The animal's expression was one only Maak had ever seen, in his Wolf Brother when a bear had lumbered near its den of pups. Ears flat. Hair bristled along its spine, from neck to tail tip. Lips drawn tight. Teeth bared. A glint in the eye that revealed something instinctive, primal.

Art took a step back.

"That dog's a menace," he said, raising his rifle. "It needs to be put down."

"You can't!" Frankie screamed.

Scout sprang forward in two long strides and leapt at Art. Powerful jaws clamped onto the man's forearm, and the shotgun fell to the dirt. Man and beast crashed to the ground. Art punched and kicked to break free, as Scout's teeth tore through tender flesh and into muscle. Art cried out, fought to reach the gun.

Frankie and Evelyn stood frozen in shock and terror.

Maak charged into the bloody fray. Entangled, the threesome thrashed and rolled. They tumbled down the bank as one, plunged over the rocky edge and into the river.

Primal instinct and frigid water told Scout to abandon his enemy and swim to land.

Primal fear and searing pain triggered Art to panic. He flailed in the swift current, careened toward the rapids, disappeared in the foam.

Strength, clarity, understanding born from millennia. That's what the glacial melt of the river provided Maak. He swam downstream. When he reached the rapids, Maak clasped his arms around his head, relaxed his body, and allowed the current to sweep him over the rocks, pull him to inky depths, and thrust him back to the surface on the other side.

Art had been pulled to an eddy at the river's edge, where he whirled helplessly in the vortex. Maak swam to him, railed against the water's pull, and heaved Art to the sandy bank.

Prone on hands and knees, Art coughed and convulsed, sputtered for air. Maak sat beside him, half frozen, laboring to slow his breath and his heartbeat.

An unnatural hush fell upon the forest. Only the tumult of the river spoke. Art sat back on his heels, torn and bloodied hands on his thighs to prop his torso. Icy water had numbed all physical pain. Fresh adrenaline provided a surge of strength to the psychological ache.

"You'll hang for this," Art said.

In a flash, he was on his back. Maak reigned over him, strong fingers squeezing his throat. Maak raised Art's upper body and pounded him back to the unforgiving ground. Reverberations from the impact of skull striking earth traveled up Maak's arms, like a surge of electricity, fuel for the attack.

Evelyn heard the struggle as she pushed her way through the thicket. She paused in the cover of brush when she saw the men entangled. Art flailed helplessly, his arms rendered useless by Scout's attack. Maak pounded him to the ground, again and again. Evelyn watched, motionless. She felt a darkness swell in her chest. It wasn't caused by a fear that Art might be killed. No. The shroud was caused by the hope that he would be, by the appreciation she felt toward Maak for doing it.

Art's body went limp. His mouth gaped, and his eyes bulged, as Maak squeezed his neck.

Self-preservation coursed through Maak's veins. Evelyn could almost see it. Yet, in her eyes it was self-sacrifice. In that fresh light, she couldn't allow it.

"Maak!" Evelyn's voice called to him from the thicket.

Art's eyelids fell shut, as Maak's grip eased. His breath came in shallow rasps.

"Here!" Maak shouted. "I am here, Evelyn."

Maak stood and called to her again. She rushed out between the trees, toward the beach, and into his arms. They embraced fiercely.

"Are you all right?" Evelyn asked. She pulled away, looked him over from head to toe.

Maak nodded, *yes.*

"You're sure?" she demanded. "You're not hurt? Nothing is broken?"

"I am not hurt," he said.

Maak cradled her face in his hands for a moment. He searched the pools of her eyes, trying to see what she might have seen a moment ago. Then he looked to Art.

"He is hurt badly," Maak said. "But he is alive."

"We have to get him back to camp," she said. "Can you manage it?"

Maak hoisted Art over his shoulders like a fallen doe and turned upstream.

1990

Duluth, Minnesota

"Evelyn had an undiagnosed brain aneurysm," the doctor says. "It ruptured last night."

He's looking down at a clipboard, writing notes with a blue and silver pen. He'd led Frank and April into an empty corner of the hospital wing to talk. Or, rather, for them to listen.

"It's not uncommon in smokers and women of her age," he continues.

Frank purses his lips, nods slightly in acknowledgment, though his gaze is fixed on something beyond the doctor, something indiscernible. April places her palm on Frank's shoulder blade. He still doesn't speak.

"What does that mean?" she asks the doctor.

An aneurysm is a balloon that forms in the wall of a blood vessel, he explains. Often, they don't present any symptoms or health problems. But they can rupture at any time and cause internal bleeding. In Evelyn's case, the rupture caused a hemorrhagic stroke.

"If this had happened outside the hospital, it would have been fatal." The doctor looks up, clicks the ballpoint and tucks it in the breast pocket of his white coat. "We were able to stem the bleeding and save her life, but not before it caused severe neurological damage."

The doctor's words come rapid-fire. They ricochet off the hospital walls, hiss past Frank's head. April feels his body sway, and she grips his bicep with her other hand to steady him.

"How long will it take," she asks, "for Gram to recover?"

The doctor's eyebrows draw together as he hugs the clipboard to his chest, tilts his head.

Frank stiffens, emerges from his trance. "She's not going to recover. Is she?"

"I'm afraid not." The doctor drops his focus to the gray rainbow-speckled linoleum. "The damage is too extensive."

A white-haired man in neon green socks comes at them from down the hall. He shuffles along, tethered to a rolling IV pole. His pale buttocks peek out from the opening in his sky-colored gown after he passes.

They watch silently, until the old fellow rounds the corner and disappears.

"We have her on a ventilator and IV fluids," the doctor returns to the matter at hand. "You should go in, spend time with her, talk to her. I'll come back in a little while to discuss end-of-life care with you."

* * * *

Evelyn looks tiny in the hospital bed, and Frank's mind flashes to the last time he saw his little brother. He strokes Evelyn's hair.

"Hi, Mom."

Frank studies his mother's face. For the first time, he sees Denny's nose, the delicate curve of the boy's cheeks. Denny had been the spitting image of his mother. Frank wonders if Evelyn saw the boy every time she looked in the mirror. He wonders if she'll see him again soon.

April crawls onto the bed beside Gram, drapes an arm across her body, nestles into the soft curve of her neck and shoulder. Hot tears burn down her cheeks. She whimpers. "Oh, Gram."

The sight of it drains the little remaining strength from Frank's limbs. He slumps into the chair beside the bed.

* * * *

The doctor comes and goes. The hospice nurse comes and goes. The hospital attorney comes and goes. Options are discussed. Papers are signed. Hours pass.

April and Frank sit side by side, holding hands, willing time to stop.

The chaplain comes and goes. The social worker comes and goes. The hospice nurse comes and goes. Tubes are removed. Machines are shut off. Minutes pass.

April and Frank sit side by side, holding hands, holding Gram's hands. They weep.

★ ★ ★ ★

It's late.

And Evelyn is gone.

The hush of the hotel room is unnerving. April lies in bed, her back propped up against the pillows. Her eyes are closed. Frank can hear her breathing, in and out. He wonders if she's asleep. He hears the thump-dump, thump-dump of a beating heart. He wonders if it's his own, or April's. It must be hers, he decides. His is shattered.

Gram's wooden box sits on the bedside table. Frank picks it up. The heft of it surprises him. He sits cross-legged on his bed, sets the box in front of him, opens it.

There's an envelope with his name written in his mother's hand. Another envelope is addressed *Bitter Rapids Sheriff.* Frank sets them aside. He finds life insurance papers, a thick stack fastened with industrial-strength staples.

He finds a bundle of letters addressed to Evelyn Parson, dozens of them, tied with red yarn. The return address reads only Kayenta, Arizona. It lacks a name. Frank thumbs through the envelopes without disturbing the bow. The first postmark date is 1956. The last, 1984.

Frank pushes his fingers through a jumble of loose photographs in the box. Some black and white, some color. Spanning decades.

Beneath it all lies a simple bronze box, engraved MAAKADE.

A tightness seizes Frank's gut. The heat of queasiness rises. Sweat breaks above his brow. His tongue pulls to the back of his throat, and he gags.

Frank fights against the onslaught of feelings. He squeezes his eyes shut, presses the cold metal box to his forehead, exhales.

Evelyn

My dear Frankie,

If you're reading this letter, it means I've kicked the bucket before I got the chance to say things to you that I've been wanting to say. Gosh darn it. I really wanted to stand on the bank of Rainy River with you by my side and clear my conscience before my time came.

But better late than never, I figure, so here it goes in a letter instead.

First off, I know I wasn't the warm and fuzzy mother you deserved. I'm sorry for that. But I loved you fiercely, and I always believed you knew that. It wasn't until we got halfway through this trip that I began to wonder if you didn't know after all. So, I'll write it again now, to set the record straight, no question. I love you, Frankie, with all I've got.

Second, everything we've been through, it was all my doing. Don't you blame yourself for one bit of it. You were a good boy, and you grew into a good man and an even better father. I'm proud of you.

Third, I'm so sorry I never told you that I kept in touch with Maak over the years. I've been thinking about that a lot lately, trying to figure out why I kept it from you. Maybe he was the one thing in my life that was just for me. The letters he and I exchanged over the years were my lifeline. It's not a good excuse. I realize now maybe you needed that lifeline, too. Denying you that is my biggest regret as your mom.

Read the letters. Or tear them up. Doesn't matter to me. I have no use for them now. Do whatever helps you feel better about things and live a good life.

Deliver my letter to the sheriff in Bitter Rapids. It contains the truth of what happened that day. You should read it first.

I'd like to be cremated. You've already seen the box, we've got Maak's ashes. I think you'll know what to do with them.

If there's an afterlife, a Land of Souls as Maak called it, I'll miss you terribly while I'm there. You were the one steady thing in my life, Frankie. I'm so grateful for that.

Love,

Mom

LIFE IN THE 1990s

ST. PAUL, Minn., Sept. 25, 1990

For Immediate Release

/National Newswire/ -- The Minnesota Department of Natural Resources (DNR) announced a long-range plan that calls for maintaining wolves in the wild and expanding an understanding of wolves.

Minnesota ended its wolf bounty program in 1965, though private and state lands were still open to wolf harvest. Superior National Forest was closed to the taking of wolves in 1970. At that time, only about 750 wolves remained in the state.

In 1973, the Endangered Species Act (ESA) was enacted into law by the U.S. Congress, and public harvest of wolves ended in the lower 48 states. By 1988, Minnesota's wolf population had doubled to approximately 1,500 wolves.

(Source: U.S. Fish and Wildlife Service)

1990

Duluth, Minnesota

F rank and April sit on the hotel bed, and he opens the box. First, he hands April the bundle of letters addressed to Gram from Maak. She fans through the stack, shakes her head slowly in shock.

"There are so many," she whispers. Frank only nods.

Next, he lets her read the letter Gram wrote him, and April cries.

Then Frank shows her the other contents of the box – his dad's military dog tags, the fateful Western Union telegram, his parents' marriage certificate, Evelyn's first simple gold wedding band. April slips the ring on her right ring finger. A perfect fit.

"It's yours now," Frank says.

She smiles and extends her arm for a full view of her hand. The glint of sunlight of the precious metal matches the gold flecks in her eyes, and it makes Frank smile.

April lifts a yellowed newspaper clipping from the box. She handles it carefully, to avoid breaking off tiny fragments of the brittle paper, as she reads.

Maakade Carpenter and another prisoner receive credit for pulling two youngsters out of the water. However, most of the praise is heaped on the quick action of Foreman Ogren and his prison guards, who "orchestrated the rescue efforts and called for help." April notices the article appeared on page three, even though it was the talk of the town at the time. She thinks, *if the white men had truly been the heroes, the article would have appeared on the front page.*

She reaches out and squeezes her father's hand. "I'm so thankful Maak was there when you needed him."

They sit in silence for several long minutes. The housekeeping lady rolls her cart past their window. She's humming a familiar tune. Finally, Frank returns to fumbling with the box, pauses again, and looks up at his daughter.

"These are pictures of my little brother," he cradles the stack of small Polaroid's in his meaty hands before handing them over.

April is careful to hold the photos by the white-edged borders as she flips through them. One of Denny as a baby, another as a toddler dressed in a little jacket and tie like he was going to church. Denny blowing out the candles on a birthday cake. Finally, an image of her dad and Denny in their Cub Scout uniforms, standing at attention side by side, giving the Scout salute.

"I wish there were more pictures of us together," Frank looks away, his eyes moist with tears.

April stares at the young smiling faces full of innocence and wonder. Before the accident that changed everything. She has never seen her dad quite like that. April plucks a tissue from the box on the nightstand and dabs her eyes.

"Hey, here's something you might find interesting," Frank says, smiling again, as he hands her another picture. It's of Evelyn as a Las Vegas cocktail waitress.

"No way!" April exclaims, and they both laugh.

"Yeah, I'm a little surprised she saved that one," Frank says.

"Are you kidding me? Gram was *hot*," April laughs again. "Why wouldn't she save it? The real question is why didn't she get it blown up and framed?"

"That does sound more like something she would do," Frank chuckles.

He rummages through the box again. Legal paperwork, a couple of postcards, a few more photos. He scatters the rest of the contents across the bed.

"That's it," he says with a solemn finality.

A lump forms in the back of April's throat. No letter from Gram to her? No last words of advice, no final expressions of love? She scrambles from the bed and into the bathroom, closes the door, buries her face in a towel, and sobs.

* * * *

It takes a few days to settle things with the hospital, make cremation arrangements with the mortuary. Frank does all this alone. April stays in her hotel bed, bunched up under the covers with a pillow over her head, all cried out, numb.

"Hey, sweetheart," Franks says, entering the hotel room with a long, thin bag of sandwiches. "I picked up some subs for dinner. Time for you to get out of bed. You need to eat."

April stirs, rolls onto her side, pulls the blanket up under her chin. "Not hungry."

Frank sits beside her on the bed. "Will you at least eat the chocolate chip cookie?"

She looks at him from the corner of her eye and sighs.

"Give it," she says, folding back the covers and sitting up.

Frank hands over the cookie.

"You might want to think about a shower, too," he says. "You're getting a little ripe."

"Not funny, Dad."

"It wasn't meant to be a joke."

He moves to the small, upholstered chair by the window, opens the waxy paper surrounding his meatball sub, takes a giant bite.

The sight of it makes April queasy. She turns her head away, and her eyes fall on Gram's box, lying open on Frank's bed. She notices the stack of Maak's letters still neatly tied with Evelyn's signature yarn bow. The envelope addressed to the sheriff also appears unaltered.

"Did you read any of the other letters?" she asks.

"No," he says, and takes a long gurgling sip through the soda straw.

"Are you going to?" she presses, looking at him now.

He shrugs.

April wants desperately to read the letters from Maak. Isn't that what Gram wanted? Wasn't the whole point of the trip to let go of secrets, set the record straight, share lessons learned? Then again, maybe it was more about figuring out what to share, what to hold on to, what to bury once and for all.

The young woman hoists herself from the bed, pulls clean clothes from her duffle bag, moves toward the bathroom.

"We'll head out in the morning," Frank says without looking up. "To Bitter Rapids."

April pauses with her back to him, exhales heavily. She turns her head toward him just a bit, bobs her chin. *Okay.* She shuts the bathroom door behind her, runs the hot water.

Life through the Ages

"I know now, after fifty years, that the finding/losing, forgetting/remembering, leaving/returning, never stops. The whole of life is about another chance, and while we are alive, till the very end, there is always another chance."

– Jeanette Winterson,
Why be Happy When You Can be Normal?

1990

Bitter Rapids, Minnesota

I t's good to be back on the road, April tells herself as they enter the highway on-ramp in the morning.

Still, being in the car without Gram feels wrong somehow. April can't shake the sensation they've left something important behind – like a journal left in a hotel drawer, or a gold ring forgotten on the bedside table. Something that would be sorely missed, after it's too late to go back for it.

"Only a couple hours' drive to Bitter Rapids," Frank says. "Maybe less."

"Mm-hmm," April responds absently. She leans her head against the cold glass of the passenger window, closes her eyes.

They left Gram's oxygen tanks and wheelie at the hospital, her shower seat and nonslip mat at the hotel. Instead of piling their suitcases and bags on the roof, they laid the rear seatbacks flat and stuffed the back half of the Corolla to the ceiling. And yet, emptiness fills the car.

Frank keeps the radio off, lets his daughter sleep. He envies her. All April seems to do since Evelyn died is sleep. Frank's exhausted, and he can't slumber for more than a few hours before his mind starts cranking, jolts him awake, makes his heart flutter offbeat. *You're an orphan now*, reminds the voice in his head.

Driving helps.

He heads north on Highway 53, past Central Lakes and through Mesabi Iron Range, beyond Littlefork and into Koochiching State Forest. The byway is cast in shadow, even at midday. Aspen and birch loom tall along the roadway, while a kaleidoscope of green mosses, ferns, and ivies crawl among the silty deposits and bedrock at their exposed roots. A fine mist rises from the wide stream that runs parallel to the road. Not far ahead, a young moose emerges from the foliage, tall and thin, all nose and ears and knobby knees.

Frank slows to a stop. "April, wake up."

The young woman lifts her head, massages her stiff neck. "Are we there?"

"Not yet," Frank says. "But look."

She rubs the crust from the corner of her eye and peers through the mist.

"Oh, wow," she gasps, and Frank giggles at her awe.

The calf ambles across the road, down the bank, and into the stream. Only its head is visible as it swims out to deep water. Then it squeezes its nostrils shut, like a hippopotamus, and submerges itself completely.

"What!" April exclaims and laughs. "Did you know they could swim underwater like that?"

Franks laughs. "Pretty cool, huh?"

The moose emerges on the far bank and disappears into the woods.

Frank puts the car in drive and continues along the winding ribbon of road.

"So where are we?" April asks, more alive now than she has been in days.

"About fifteen miles outside of Bitter Rapids," Frank says. "We'll be there in maybe twenty minutes."

The familiar sting returns to April's eyes.

"It totally sucks that Gram didn't get to see it," she says.

"Yeah," Frank says. "Sure does, kiddo."

When they reach town, Frank drives down Main Street, past Central Square, over to the lane where he grew up. The old house is gone, along with all the old houses and spacious yards that once filled the block, replaced by tight, neat rows of condominiums, freshly-painted in trendy colors – faded denim, rosy taupe, creamy beige. Up the road, he idles in front of Marshall Junior

High and examines the red-brick building, smaller than he remembers, but otherwise the same.

They stop for gas.

Frank wonders if he'll see anyone he recognizes, anyone who would remember him. It's a terrifying thought. Questions would be asked. What on earth could he say after all these years? He pulls up the hood of his jacket and asks April to pay the attendant inside.

It's early afternoon when they park in the dirt lot at the trailhead. In his backpack, Frank carries the food, water, and sleeping bags, the letters, tarp, and cremation ashes. April hauls the lighter items, their long underwear and rain ponchos. Frank picks the forest service trail he thinks will get them closest to Maak's old camp, and they set out on their trek.

The landscape patchwork has shifted over the decades, new paths carved by flowing water and roaming wildlife, old trails hidden under thick foliage and fallen trees. It's rugged terrain. They clamor over bedrock outcroppings, and skate down mossy gullies. They traverse narrow suspension bridges over foamy rapids, and cross muddy beaver dams past glassy lakes. The air is damp and cold. It raises the hair on their arms. When the shady trail leads them onto a sunny beach beside a gurgling river, Frank halts and lowers his pack to the ground. He surveys the clearing. It's all too easy to get mixed up and turned around in the boreal forest. There's no way to know for certain whether this was Maak's camp location. Still, something about it feels right.

"Here?" April asks, looking around.

"Here," Frank says.

They set up camp. Frank builds a fire. The crackle of the flames and hum of the forest soothe their weary nerves. They devour one of two foot-long sub sandwiches they packed. Night falls gently around them.

Finally, Frank digs into his pack, removes the two boxes of ash, the stack of letters, arranges them in a row between their unrolled sleeping bags. He kneels down beside her, holds the sheriff's letter in his lap. The seal remains unbroken. April watches her dad and waits.

Frank turns the envelope over in his hands once, twice, then stretches forward and drops it into the flames. April yelps.

"Didn't you at least want to read it first?" She's incredulous. "So you'd know the truth about what happened?"

Frank watches the envelope curl and burn.

"I believe it happened exactly the way I remember it," he says. "And that's the truth."

He picks up the stack of Maak's letters next.

"Dad, no."

April stops herself from saying more. She knows it's his right to decide the letters' fate. She holds her tongue, and her breath.

"As a parent, you have so few things that are yours alone," Frank tells her. "And that's okay. It's the unspoken agreement you accept when you have a child."

He pulls back the corners of envelopes with his thumb, riffles through the stack like a flip-book.

"These letters from Maak were the only thing that kept my mom tethered to the life she dreamed of having but never could. I just wouldn't feel right spying on those dreams now that she's gone, even if she said I could. You know?"

Frank looks at his daughter, eyes pleading for understanding, for permission.

April smiles, nods. *I know.*

He tosses the stack onto the flames.

The fire spits. A bright blue flare rises as the postage stamp on the top envelope ignites. Another flash follows, green this time, and then another blue. The brilliant, beautiful interment of tender secrets. They watch until the last remnants of paper crumble into ash among the glowing embers at the heart of the fire.

"And now," Frank says.

He takes off his shoes and socks, sets them at the edge of the tarp, rolls his pant legs up to his knees. Then he stands and reaches out to April, hoists her to her feet. They walk to the river's edge, hesitate.

April gives her dad's hand a squeeze and then releases it.

Frank pulls a tin of chewing tobacco from his pocket, sprinkles half the loose leaves along the bank. He hands it to April, and she empties the tin. He steps into the water, gasps at the icy shock to his bare skin.

Maak is first. The bronze box opens. The ashes tumble out, carried away by wind and water. Tiny fragments of bone sink to the river bottom. Evelyn is next. Body and spirit poured out. The last vestiges of their two bodies comingle, become one with the Creation. Tears drop into the water.

Across the river, hidden in shadow atop a jagged outcropping of rock, beside trembling aspen, a lone black wolf stands watch over the ceremony.

Father and daughter return to the campfire, change into long underwear, hoist the bear bags of food and dirty clothes high into the trees. They tuck themselves into the sleeping bags, lie on their backs, gaze up at the abundance of stars.

A single bright light shoots across the dark sky, leaving a tail of silver glitter in its wake.

"A shooting star," April says. *Maybe it's Gram.*

"Did you see it, Dad?"

"I saw," Frank says. *Goodbye, Mom.*

Not far off, a soulful choir of wolves sing to the heavens.

Life in the Beginning

The Vision of Kitche Manitou

Out of nothing, He made rock, water, fire, wind.

From these, He created the physical world of sun, stars, moon, earth.

    To the sun, Kitche Manitou gave the powers of light and heat;

    To the earth, He gave growth and healing;

    To the waters, purity, and renewal; and

    To the wind, music, and the breath of life.

He formed plains, mountains, valleys, lakes, islands, rivers. He made

    Plants of leaf, bark, fruit, and grass.

    Creatures of scale, feather, fur, and flesh.

The Great Laws of Nature established order, harmony, and the rhythm of life.

Finally, Kitche Manitou created man – the most dependent, weakest in physical power, yet bestowed with the greatest gift.

    The power to dream.

Author's Note and Acknowledgements

Readers often ask where, precisely, the line between fact and fiction is drawn in historical fiction. There is no true line. It's a thin, often frayed and tangled thread that weaves through a story. The same is often true of nonfiction works. That said, the following contains details of my research and highlights areas where I unraveled strands of information to craft more engaging fiction. It's not all-encompassing, but it is a deeper dive into history and my sources of inspiration for those who are curious.

This is a work of fiction about the stuff of real life. The characters who inhabit this story represent a wide swath of ages, ethnicities, beliefs, social classes, races, upbringing, and sexual identities. As I do in real life, I worked hard to understand and respect the unique and complex ethos of each. My goals as a novelist are to entertain, enlighten, and inspire; to create an authentic sense of time and place; and to be as historically accurate as possible, within the constructs of fiction.

So, how did this story develop?

I keep a file in my office of random news articles and other snippets that catch my eye from one day to the next – things torn from magazines, quotes copied from books, pieces printed from the Internet. Every so often I rifle through the file and see how these fragments of inspiration may fit together. It sometimes takes years for an idea to form.

In 2013, I came across a news article about members of a prison work crew who dove into a cold, fast-moving river to rescue three young brothers whose canoe had capsized. When asked by the reporter why they'd risked their lives to save the boys, one inmate, Jon Fowler said, "You see three helpless kids in a river, you help. Just because we're incarcerated, doesn't mean we're bad people." That brief news piece – and Fowler's quote in particular – grabbed me. I wanted to know more. What crimes had those men committed? Why was it the inmates who jumped in to rescue the boys, and not the correctional officers on the scene? I printed the article and tucked it into my idea folder.

About a year later, I read a news piece about authorities in California hoping to solve a 25-year-old murder. They shared a photo of the quilt found with the body of a mother of two who had been strangled. The hope was that someone might be able to identify the owner or maker of the quilt after all that time.

Then, in 2017, I read an article by *National Geographic* about the five coldest rivers on earth. Among them was the Rainy River, which runs through the rugged wilderness along the Canadian and U.S. border in Minnesota.

My mind clicked: on the ability of people to keep secrets for decades, the love represented by a handmade quilt, the primal instinct of a convicted criminal to risk his life to save a child, the way lives often intersect in unexpected ways, and the untold stories behind them all. In a matter of minutes – after years of thinking – the characters, setting, and hook to my story snapped together.

Bitter Rapids is a fictional town I placed near the real-life Koochiching State Park near the Rainy River. I chose the year 1990 for the Parson family to make their cross-country journey because, while it's in the modern era, it was still a time before online maps, GPS, and smartphones became the norm. With 1990 as my starting point, I used my remedial math skills to move backward, calculating the ages of my characters and factoring in key historical events that would add context to their stories.

The novel's epistolary elements were included to frame historical context and tie together multiple themes. The book excerpts are from published works, though some were edited slightly for space and impact. On a personal note, I found the 1948 edition of *Every Woman's Standard Medical Guide* to be particularly interesting and, frankly, shocking. It's a striking example of how dramatically women's lives have changed for the better in the United States.

The other nonfiction elements – news items, press releases, and so on – are pieces I wrote based on research from multiple sources, though the publications or organizations cited are fictional names in most cases. The exceptions being:

- "Women on the March," was an actual excerpt from Time magazine in the 1970s. (http://content.time.com/time/subscriber/article/0,33009,902 696,00.html)

- The editorial about the Indian New Deal is a compilation of interviews and testimonials from multiple Navajo elders spanning the 1950s to 1990s. The publication, Ádahooníłígí (Current Events), was a newspaper published in Diné (Navajo) language and translated to English by William Morgan, a member of the Navajo tribe. The paper was written in Window Rock, Arizona, and printed at the Indian School in Phoenix. A slogan in the masthead read, "Ihoo'aah biniighé, t'áá hó honitsékees bik'ehgo na'adá biniighé, dóó náás 'adooldah biniighé." "For Education, For Liberty, and For Progress." It ceased publication in 1957. (https://chroniclingamerica.loc.gov/lccn/sn92024097/)

- The Gallup Poll on interracial marriage has been conducted since 1958. While issues of race in the United States remain imperfect, this poll shows how incredibly far we've come as a nation. In 1958, only 4 percent of Americans approved of marriage between African Americans and whites; in 1990, approximately 48 percent; and by 2013, the number had risen to 87 percent. Now, the gap has nearly closed – 94 percent of Americans said they approve of interracial marriage in the 2021 poll. What's more, regional differences in opinion are now gone. In decades past, those living in the South were generally more disapproving than those living in the East,

West, and Midwest. Today, the percentage is almost universal across all four regions.
https://news.gallup.com/poll/354638/approval-interracial-marriage-new-high.aspx)

For the Native American cultural and historical elements of the novel, I scoured many helpful websites and books. Among the most useful were:

- *Ojibway Heritage* (University of Nevada Press) and *Anishinaubae Thesaurus* (Michigan State University Press), both works by Basil Johnston
- *Dibaajimowinan (Anishinaabe Stories of Culture and Respect)* and *Mino Wiisinidaa! (Let's Eat Good!)* (Great Lakes Indian Fish & Wildlife Commission Press)
- *Books & Islands in Ojibwe Country* (Harper Perennial), by Louise Erdrich
- *Sister Nations: Native American Women Writers on Community* (Minnesota Historical Society Press), co-edited by Laura Tohe and Heid Erdrich

Much credit also goes to Laura Tohe, whom I had the privilege to interview for an article many years ago. Tohe is Diné. She is Tsénahabiłnii, Sleepy Rock People clan, and born for the Tódich'inii, Bitter Water clan. I've attended her poetry and story readings, and have heard her speak on Navajo history several times through the years. She is Professor with Exemplar Distinction in the English Department at Arizona State University, and also was honored as the Navajo Nation Poet Laureate. Tohe is warm and wise, and she taught me a great deal. (https://www.lauratohe.com/)

The Ojibwe People's Dictionary (https://ojibwe.lib.umn.edu/) was an invaluable online source that includes the Minnesota Historical Society's Ojibwe collection of photos and historical documents. Most importantly, it features the voices of Ojibwe speakers and detailed language entries. The language is complex and contains many dialects. During my research, I found words as elemental as Ojibwe and Anishinaabe spelled many ways. It was worrisome. I wanted very much to get everything right, though it felt impossible.

I found great comfort in a statement by Larry Smallwood (Amik O'Gaabaw), one of the speakers recorded for the Ojibwe People's Dictionary and a contributor to several of the books referenced previously. Smallwood said, "Namanj igo ge-inwegwen a'aw waa-nitaa-ojibwemod, booch igo da-nisidotaagod iniw manidoon." "Whatever dialect you learn or however you learn to speak Ojibwe, the Creator will always understand you, no matter how you sound."

That wisdom gave me the courage to press on with telling the story in the best way I knew how, even knowing there would likely be those who would find fault with it. If there are any errors or oversights within these pages, they are due to my own inadequacies and not that of the many books, archives, and people I consulted. I can only hope that the spirit of my intentions compensates for the inevitable flaws.

The brief mention about President Roosevelt's Indian New Deal remains in my idea folder. I did a great deal of research about the Great Depression era, the Dust Bowl, soil erosion, overgrazing of livestock, and conservation farming for an earlier novel. What I learned about the Bureau of Indian Affairs and the Roosevelt administration was intriguing, though it did not seem to fit neatly into either that novel or this one. It may be something I revisit in the future.

In their zeal to reverse damage done to the Great Plains, the U.S. government put many experimental programs into place. These included halting plowing of remaining grasslands, reseeding vast stretches of farmland with native grasses, and altering livestock grazing practices. Their efforts impacted Native American land, as well. On the Navajo reservation specifically, it included the removal and slaughter of wild mustangs, and mass reduction of Navajo livestock.

As someone who places great value on conservation, I know overgrazing hurts the land and disrupts the balance of natural ecosystems. As a person who advocates and respects Native sovereignty, the actions taken by the U.S. government in the name of conservation breaks my heart. My beliefs often conflict, and I won't pretend to know the most appropriate or equitable solution. Our world consists of so much gray area; this piece of history is more evidence of that. On this matter, I'll defer to the wisdom of Carl Sagan referenced on page 49. Life is rare and precious, and all life on our blue planet deserves protecting.

Wolves play a large part in this story. For research, I spent a great deal of time on the websites of the International Wolf Center, based in Ely, Minnesota, and the Voyagers Wolf Project, based at the University of Minnesota. In addition to the conservation and behavioral information they provided, both sites have several cameras and live streams set up in the region. Watching their videos provided much inspiration for *Bitter Thaw* and further fueled my lifelong fascination with wolves. I'm thrilled to report that in 2012, the gray wolf was removed as a listed species of the federal Endangered Species Act. In 2020, a Minnesota Department of Natural Resources study estimated the state's wolf population to be 2,700. Nationwide, their numbers are estimated at roughly 6,000. You can learn more about these organizations and support their efforts by visiting https://wolf.org and https://www.voyageurswolfproject.org.

The article about memory on page 317 is a fictional citation, though it is in essence a nonfiction article based on research I conducted on cognitive behavioral science and the plasticity of memory. It is also the underpinning to one of the novel's primary themes. How much of what we remember from our past is accurate? How much have we altered, either intentionally or subconsciously? What is forgotten, and why?

In his book *Proust Was a Neuroscientist*, author Jonah Lehrer wrote, "Our memories are not like fiction. They are fiction." In the journal *Psychology of Learning and Motivation*, Alan D. Baddeley and Graham Hitch asserted,

"Forgetting is an important aspect of memory; it helps us see what's important."

These assertions fascinate me on multiple levels. At the beginning of my professional writing career, many of my first significant article assignments were for Barrow Neurological Institute at St. Joseph's Hospital and Medical Center in Phoenix. That introduced me to both the physiological and psychological wonders of the human brain. I've written on a wide range of topics in the field – from traumatic brain injury and learning disabilities, to cognitive degeneration and mental illness.

Regarding the mysteries of memory, I know very little about my family history. My older brother and I often have extremely different recollections of events from our childhood together. My parents rarely discuss their pasts with me; whether that has been by choice or because they don't remember, I'll never know for sure. I do know they each experienced traumatic events when they were young, and those events informed their decision-making the rest of their lives.

Perhaps writing a novel about family secrets and past trauma was a way for me to mine my own psyche, to make amends with what I know and don't know about my own past. I'm not implying this book is biographical in any way. It is not. But I do believe certain elements of life – love and loss, fear and hope, regret and redemption – are universal.

For those interested in delving deeper into the study of the human mind, I strongly recommend the book *Adventures in Memory: The Science and Secrets of Remembering and Forgetting,* by Norwegian sisters Hilde and Ylva Østby. Hilde is a novelist and Ylva is a clinical neuropsychologist. Together, they crafted a book that is both easy to read and packed with data and scientific research. It was a great resource for me as I crafted this novel.

A few minor notes about areas where I exercised literary license with historical events:

- Metallica's song "Enter Sandman" was released in 1991, not 1990. Still, it felt like a good fit with April's mood.
- The story about rock band Whiskey Winter's plane crash was fictional, though I drew inspiration from the real-life tragedy of Lynryd Skynryd. A quote from one of the surviving band members about honoring those we've lost and continuing on struck me as powerful and wise. (https://lynyrdskynyrd.com/band).
- The chapter in which Frank shares his memories of marriage and early parenthood with April was inspired by the controversial essay "A Marriage Agreement" by novelist Alix Kates Shulman. In it, she proposed that spouses share childcare and housework equally. According to Shulman's website, "This idea was so explosive in 1970 that the 'Agreement' was reprinted as a *Life Magazine* cover story (1972) and was attacked by the likes of Norman Mailer and Russell Baker." (https://jwa.org/media/marriage-agreement-by-alix-kates-shulman)
- I highlighted the Minnesota Twins because they did, in fact, win the World Series in 1991 after an abysmal 1990 season. It was serendipitous to both the time and setting of the story, and it fit perfectly with the novel's themes regarding perseverance and regeneration. Plus, baseball.

Now, a final parting thought. Our world today is far from perfect. As long as it is inhabited by humans, as Aleksandr Solzhenitsyn stated in *The Gulag Archipelago*, both good and evil will always exist. Yet, that reality mustn't stop us from dreaming of a perfect world and striving toward something better, while also seeing the beauty and goodness in what we have now.

Gratitude

In addition to those previously mentioned, there are several people who were instrumental in the writing and revising of this work.

Melissa Crytzer Fry, a fellow writer and reader with a passion for historical fiction, has been a long-time friend and sounding board for my novel ideas. Developmental editors Cherri Randall and Annie Mydla helped me fine-tune the story's thematic and literary elements; they also made helpful observations and recommendations to strengthen cultural sensitivity. Nancy Prenzno provided meticulous copyediting and factchecking services, as she did for my previous novel.

Finally, my husband Mike has done so much in our nearly thirty-five years together to encourage and support my writing career. His love and wisdom live and breathe in every word I set to the page.

Thank you, one and all.

Discussion and Self-Reflection Questions

1. What do you think were the central themes of *Bitter Thaw*? How well do you think the author explored them?

2. How thought-provoking did you find the book? Did reading it change your opinion about anything? Did you learn something new? If so, what?

3. You may have noticed several events in which Frank and Evelyn gave different accounts from one another or from the actual event. Do you think they were being dishonest, or were they misremembering?

4. Think about your favorite character(s). What were some of his or her flaws? Conversely, what were some redeeming qualities of character(s) you disliked?

5. April is often shocked by how many secrets her family has kept from her and from one another. Have you ever learned a secret about your own family? Was it shared with you, or did you discover it on your own?

6. Connection to nature as a balm and source of inner strength is a recurring idea in the story. Does nature have this significance for you? Where do you find comfort and strength?

7. Compare *Bitter Thaw* to other books you've read by Jessica McCann, or other books you've read with similar themes. How are they the same or different?

8. Would you recommend this book to a friend? Why or why not ? Would there be any caveats?

About the Author

Jessica McCann is a historical novelist and has worked for thirty-five years as a professional writer for magazines, universities, corporations, and other organizations. The Freedom in Fiction Prize, Arizona Book of the Year Award, and international Rubery Book Award shortlist are among the recognition she has received for her novels. McCann is the proud mother of an adult daughter and son; she lives with her husband, son, and two dogs in Phoenix, Arizona.

Connect with her online at www.JessicaMcCann.com

www.ingramcontent.com/pod-product-compliance
Lightning Source LLC
Chambersburg PA
CBHW030922120726

47906CB00002B/450